KYIV

BY THE SAME AUTHOR

DI Joe Faraday Investigations

Turnstone
The Take
Angels Passing
Deadlight
Cut to Black
Blood and Honey
One Under
The Price of Darkness
No Lovelier Death
Beyond Reach
Borrowed Light
Happy Days

DS Jimmy Suttle Investigations

Western Approaches
Touching Distance
Sins of the Father
The Order of Things

Spoils of War

Finisterre
Aurore
Estocada
Raid 42
Last Flight to Stalingrad
Kyiv

FICTION

Rules of Engagement
Reaper
The Devil's Breath
Thunder in the Blood
Sabbathman
The Perfect Soldier
Heaven's Light
Nocturne
Permissible Limits
The Chop
The Ghosts of 2012
Strictly No Flowers

NON-FICTION

Lucky Break
Airshow
Estuary
Backstory

Enora Andressen

Curtain Call
Sight Unseen
Off Script
Limelight

KYIV

GRAHAM HURLEY

HEAD
of ZEUS

ISBN (HB) 9781838938321
ISBN (XTPB) 9781838938338
ISBN (E) 9781838938352

MIX
Paper from
responsible sources
FSC
www.fsc.org   FSC® C020471

Printed and bound by CPI Group (UK) Ltd,
Croydon, CR0 4YY

Head of Zeus Ltd
First Floor East
5–8 Hardwick Street
London EC1R 4RG

WWW.HEADOFZEUS.COM

For Yuri
with thanks

'Nothing works until it does'

– Russian proverb

1

SUNDAY 22 JUNE 1941

They called him The Pianist, and for a while no one knew why because his real name was Ilya Glivenko. He looked old. Fifty-five? Older? Again, no one knew. Most of the time he kept himself to himself. He appeared to have no friends, and no need for friends. He was small, rotund, and people who'd seen him with his shirt off, down by the river in the blazing heat of mid-June, thought he might once have been a weightlifter. He had the shoulders for it, the once-firm ledges of muscle around the base of the neck, the deep chest, thighs like tree trunks, and when he splashed waist-deep into the Dnieper some of the older women on the riverbank paused to take a look. He swam, murmured one of them, like a bear. And she meant it as a compliment.

Then came the Sunday evening, that same Sunday the Germans invaded, and a handful of the NKVD guys from the Big House in Kyiv found themselves in a nightclub in the bowels of one of the hotels on Khreshchatyk. They'd got drunk the way Russians get drunk when the news is especially bad, abandoned and morose by turns, tossing down vodka, plum brandy, anything to stop the Germans in their tracks and turn the clock back. There was a small stage in the nightclub, partly occupied by a battered piano, badly out of tune. The guys from the Big House were on their feet, looking for a fight with a neighbouring table of Ukrainian locals, when a little old man, broad in the beam, appeared from nowhere and settled himself at the piano. He had a drinker's face, scarlet with blotches, and he wore a full moustache, a relic from the last war, the grey threaded with yellow nicotine stains. He had glasses, too, slightly crooked on his bulb of a nose, and when he was in a good mood – which was often – there was a hint of gold in one corner of his crooked smile.

The Ukrainians were on their feet now. They hated the Russians and, thanks to the vodka, whatever fear they had for the Big House had gone. No one remembered who threw the first punch, but it didn't matter. Within seconds, the nightclub was a battlefield, the militia men swinging wildly at any available target, the Ukrainians forming a tight little circle, moving slowly outwards, glasses smashing, women screaming, anyone still sober making for the door. Then came chords from the piano, a jazz version of a waltz, upbeat, slightly out of tune, a glorious cascade of music that briefly stilled the violence.

The NKVD men looked round, as if a fugitive was loose in the room, a hint of anarchy, definitely a threat. One of the Ukrainians wiped the blood from his face and beckoned a comrade closer and began to waltz. Others kicked chairs and tables aside and cleared a space on the floor. Then the pianist changed key and quickened the tempo before reining back again and roaring an invitation for everyone to dance. Remarkably, it worked, and it was at least five minutes before the militiamen slipped their jackets off, rolled up their sleeves and set to again.

*

Nearly a month later, German armies were deep into Russia, and Ilya Glivenko, the little man at the piano, found himself in the deepest of the two basements at the Museum of Vladimir Lenin off Khreshchatyk. A dim light came from a smoky kerosene lamp and shadows danced on the bare stone walls, glistening with the moisture that infested this tomb. Glivenko was squatting beside an apparatus the size of a small cabin trunk. Cables and what looked like valves were encased in metal. When Glivenko tried to move it, the effort made him grunt. Beside the apparatus was a big battery, the kind you'd find in a truck. Two wires ran from the battery to the apparatus, but what drew Glivenko's attention was a light bulb held by another man he addressed as Osip. A single wire trailed from the apparatus to the light bulb.

Glivenko asked for the light bulb, and then gestured vaguely towards the door.

'You want me to do it now?' Osip was already on his feet.

'Yes. Quick as you like.'

'Just the one transmission?'

'Yes. The red button. Press it down and hold it on a count of five.'

Osip nodded. He'd been coughing from the kerosene fumes. He was glad to get out. Two NKVD guards watched him leave.

One of them turned back to Glivenko.

'This is OK?' he said. 'Safe?'

'Sure,' Glivenko was looking at the light bulb.

Nothing happened. Within a minute Osip was back again. 'Well?'

'It didn't work.'

'Again?'

'Yes.'

Osip disappeared. Glivenko took off his glasses and gave them a polish. The guard watched him for a moment or two. This time he was bolder.

'You're the specialist, the one who blows everything up. Am I right?'

Glivenko had put his glasses back on. Still squatting beside the apparatus, he didn't move, didn't answer. All that mattered was the light bulb. Then came the clump-clump of Osip's heavy footsteps on the wooden stairs outside, and the familiar white face at the door.

'Five seconds,' he said. 'I counted.'

Glivenko was still gazing at the light bulb. At length, he got to his feet, put the light bulb carefully to one side, wiped his face with the back of his hand, and produced a packet of cigarettes. Ignoring the guards, he tossed one to Osip and lit his own.

'This stuff is shit,' he said at length, stirring the apparatus with his boot. 'We'll need to start again.'

2

TUESDAY 9 SEPTEMBER, 1941

Scotland. Isobel Menzies was upstairs at the Glebe House, asleep in the big enamel bath, when Kim Philby appeared at the open door. A moment of contemplation, then a cough, politely muffled. Bella opened one eye. Startled, she reached for a towel. She'd been helping Tam saw timber all day but now Moncrieff had gone, summoned to Aberdeen by a surprise phone call.

'You,' she said.

'Me.'

'How did you get in?'

'The front door was open. I took the liberty of coming in. I called,' he nodded down at the bath. 'You must have been having a doze in there.'

'So, what is it? You're supposed to be in St Albans with all those chums of yours. What on earth are you doing here?'

Philby shook his head, wouldn't answer. Unusually, he was wearing a suit and tie. He'd be outside in the sunshine, he said. He had a plane on standby at Dyce. The airfield was an hour or so away. The pilot needed to be in the air by seven at the latest.

'Why?'

'We need to get you down to London. You'll be briefed at Northolt. You'll need clothes for at least a month. We're thinking Kyiv by the end of the week. Back to the homestead after that.'

The homestead was an apartment in a grey government block overlooking the Moscow River, three cluttered rooms that already belonged to another life.

'This is official? Not some kind of joke? You know I'm on leave up here? Six whole days, so far? Nearly a fortnight to come?' Bella was on her feet now, ankle-deep in the bath, drying herself off with the towel. 'So, what's so important it can't wait?'

'A war? *Barbarossa?* How does that sound? Hitler is pushing south-west as fast as he can. He wants the Ukraine bound hand and foot by the end of the month.'

'And I'm supposed to stop him? Little me?'

'Northolt,' Philby repeated. 'I'm simply here to deliver you in one piece.'

'You're telling me I don't have a choice?'

'I'm telling you we're wasting precious time. And the answer is no.'

Bella hated the word, always had done, but three years in Moscow had made her even more aware of how helpless you could be when your masters called.

She carefully folded the towel and stepped out of the bath. Philby's eyes never left her face.

'Is the prisoner allowed to leave a note?' she enquired. 'For Tam?'

'As you wish, my dear. We leave in five minutes.'

'That sounds like a diktat.'

'I'm afraid it is.'

'No room for negotiation?'

'None.'

Bella nodded, holding his gaze.

'This is very NKVD,' she said. 'But I'm guessing you might know that already.'

Philby stared at her for a long moment. There was little warmth in his smile.

'Five minutes,' he repeated. 'I'll be waiting outside.'

*

Barbarossa was the German code name for the invasion of Russia. Back in June, more than three million *Wehrmacht* troops had plunged into the vastness of the Soviet Union, supported by thousands of aircraft and tanks. After roasting Poland, France and the Low Countries on the spit of blitzkrieg, Hitler now needed to fire up the barbecue pit again, and torch Leningrad and Moscow by the onset of winter. Both Russian cities reduced to ashes was the Christmas present he'd promised the German *Volk*, but the real prize lay in the rich grain basin of Ukraine, and the priceless oil fields of the Caucasus beyond.

Bella Menzies had first heard the news in a phone call from an NKVD colonel named Shebalin. It was a Sunday morning, and she'd been invited to a picnic at a dacha in the woods north of Moscow.

'Don't bother,' Shebalin had growled on the phone. 'The *Vodzh* can't believe it, and neither can anyone else. War feeds on rumours but never anything like this. Thieves in the fucking night. Millions of them.'

The *Vodzh* was Stalin, the Great Leader, and lately Adolf Hitler's key ally. The last time Bella had seen him in the flesh was the evening earlier in the year when he'd addressed senior members of Molotov's Foreign Ministry at a Kremlin reception. As a valued defector, with inside knowledge of the workings of British intelligence, Bella had won herself an invitation. She'd always thought that Stalin was hopeless on his feet, or even on the radio. The man was a mumbler, stolid, flat as a pancake, full of menace, yes, but no fire, no imagination, none of Lenin's magic. This was an opinion you'd be wise to keep to yourself, but that evening the *Vodzh* had surprised her. He was playful. He was light on his feet. He radiated confidence. The class enemies, he'd said, were tearing each other to pieces while the Soviet Union lay in wait, readying herself for the moment when the global Proletariat would be ripe for the many blessings of Marxism-Leninism.

Now, barely months later, this.

*

The twin-engined aircraft, an Avro Anson, was small, slow, cold and very noisy. The airfield outside Aberdeen was an hour behind them. Bella and Philby were seated side by side in the narrow cabin behind the pilot and only by shouting was any conversation possible. Bella was huddled in a full-length fur coat that had once belonged to Tam's mother. Bringing it along for the ride had been Philby's idea.

Now, as the aircraft hit yet another pocket of turbulence, she leaned across the aisle and gestured Philby closer. She wanted to know the latest from the Eastern Front.

'How bad?'

'Very. The northern thrust is closing on Leningrad. In the centre, Panzers are within sight of the October Railway.'

Bella nodded. The October Railway tied Leningrad to Moscow. She'd ridden it herself on a number of occasions, taking advantage of the modest luxuries offered to those favoured by the Party, and spending most of the journey beside the window, marvelling at the sheer size of the country, but she knew only too well that western Russia would be only a nibble for someone with Hitler's gargantuan appetite. Further east, beyond Moscow, lay thousands of miles of barren nowhere. This is Napoleon, she thought, with thousands of tanks.

'And the south? He's still pushing hard?'

'He is. He wants Kyiv in the bag first. I gather *le mot juste* is encirclement.'

'Meaning?'

'He's throwing a noose around the place. Tighten the rope, and the Ukrainians will be learning German in no time.'

'That bad?'

'Probably worse.'

'So why am I going there?'

Philby studied her for a moment. The pilot had frowned on cigarettes but he'd been smoking non-stop since take-off. Close to, she could smell the tobacco on his breath, on the folds of his jacket. She'd also noticed a slight tremor in his right hand, and a rather endearing stammer that surfaced from time to time. This man had immense charm – she'd thought so from the moment she'd first met him – but there was a hint of vulnerability as well. Maybe his age, she thought. Twenty-nine was young for someone who was already a high-flyer in the Secret Intelligence Service.

'You mean Kyiv?' he said at last, in answer to her question.

'Yes.'

'Wait until we land. This bloody war is no friend of the obvious.'

*

It was dark and wet by the time they arrived at Northolt aerodrome, the sprawl of north London invisible under the blackout. The pilot nursed the aircraft to a bumpy landing, the runway marked by a line of burning kerosene flares, and after the Anson had rolled to a halt Philby waited at the foot of the aluminium ladder before leading Bella to the low outline of the building that served as a reception centre.

Bella had never met Colonel Stewart Menzies before. 'C', the Chief of MI6, was wearing a light tweed overcoat and was carrying a black homburg pebbled with raindrops. Bella noticed his ears, unusually large, his carefully clipped moustache and the attention he'd obviously paid to his immaculately polished shoes. According to the NKVD file she'd read back in Moscow, 'C' was immensely wealthy, a rumour confirmed from what she'd heard from other sources. He'd attended Eton, fought a gallant war on the Western Front, rode to hounds and never missed a day of Royal Ascot. He was also, said the file, the rumoured love child of Edward VII and drank a great deal.

When Philby offered a deferential handshake, the Chief shook it warmly. Then he turned to Bella. Pre-war, with a desk in the British Embassy in Berlin, and the ear of key journalists and diplomats in the capital, Bella had been sending back intelligence to this man's organisation for nearly a year, but the fact that she'd later betrayed it, disappearing one dank Berlin afternoon only to surface three days later in Moscow, seemed of no importance. On the contrary, 'C' was extremely civil. He apologised for the abrupt flight south, and then introduced her to the two colleagues who were to serve as a briefing team. Maybe it was the fact that they shared a surname. Maybe.

The bar was still open, a scattering of uniforms in the battered wicker armchairs. Philby signalled to the lone waiter for a round of drinks. One of the Chief's two colleagues turned out to be Russian. The other turned out to be Russian. He was small and squat, with greying curly hair and dirt under his fingernails. The glasses perched on the end of his button of a nose gave him a slightly comical look, but he had a sudden smile that would melt any woman's heart and Bella liked him on sight.

'My name is Glivenko.' He spoke with a thick Leningrad accent. 'Please call me Ilya.'

The other man was English, uniformed, a Major in the Royal Engineers. At a nod from 'C', he explained that Bella was to accompany a consignment of equipment already loaded into the belly of a Halifax bomber on the apron outside. The aircraft would be leaving for Gibraltar at first light. After refuelling, it would be tracking east, making a long detour over the North African desert that would bring it to Cairo. From there, it would route north to Simferopol in the Crimea.

'And then?'

'And then, Miss Menzies, another aircraft will be waiting, Russian, smaller, more agile. The equipment will be transferred for the last leg of the journey. Under the care of our Russian friend here.'

'Going where?'

'Kyiv. The Germans nearly have the place surrounded but not quite. We can still get aircraft in and out.'

'*Da,*' Glivenko nodded. '*Da.*'

'And this equipment?' Bella was still looking at the Major. 'Am I allowed to ask what it might be?'

The Major exchanged looks with Menzies. The drinks had arrived.

'No need,' 'C' reached briskly for his whisky. 'Normal rules, I'm afraid. Less said, the better.'

'But I'm in the plane, too? Off to Kyiv?'

'Good Lord, no, perish the thought. I'm sure they'll need you back in Moscow, my dear.'

'They?'

'Your new friends. And ours, too. Am I right, Kim? An ear to the ground? A seat at the right tables? An occasional invitation to the Kremlin? Are we not lucky to have Miss Menzies' services again?'

*

Tam Moncrieff was back at the Glebe House shortly before midnight. The note on the kitchen table was brief, a Bella scrawl that barely occupied a couple of lines. *Duty calls, my darling. Have been Philbied back to London and God knows wherever next. Rumours of Kyiv. I love you.*

Kyiv? Philbied? Moncrieff blinked, poured himself a whisky, read the note a second time and then stepped out into the semi-darkness of a summer night. A nearby stand of conifers were etched black against the last of the daylight and he lifted his face to the warm kiss of the wind. These last few weeks, after an exhausting operation that had taken him in and out of Portugal, his father's house had worked its usual magic, slowing his pulse, stilling the thunder in his head, reminding him that there was still the possibility of a real life out among the bareness of his precious Cairngorms.

He'd first met Bella Menzies in Berlin. War was still a year away and she, with a guile he'd yet to fully understand, had taken charge of him. They'd begun an affair. He'd killed a man, an American, in a park in the suburbs of Berlin, and it was Bella who managed to cover his tracks. The weeks to come were freighted with surprises, none of them pleasant, and he'd ended up in one of the basement rooms on Prinz-Albrecht-Strasse that the Gestapo reserved for difficult conversations. What followed would stay with Moncrieff for the rest of his life but expulsion from Berlin had been a blessing and, as it turned out, yet another debt he owed Bella Menzies.

Shortly afterwards, for reasons that made little sense at the time, she'd defected to the Soviet Union, and Moncrieff, like everyone else, had accepted that Comrade Bella had disappeared for good. Wrong. With his duties in Lisbon nearly discharged, she'd turned up on a flight from Moscow, official Politburo business, with time in hand to renew an acquaintance that seemed to matter to her. And so, for a second time, they'd ended up in bed together, both bruised by the last three years, both harder, more wary, yet both – in their separate ways – still curious about the other. In essence, to Moncrieff's delight, not a great deal had changed except the raw fact of Bella's defection to the enemy, a problem Hitler obligingly solved by invading the Soviet Union. As Bella herself had been the first to point out, they could officially be friends again.

Kyiv. Philby.

Moncrieff swallowed the last of the malt. Working for MI5, fighting the counter-espionage war, had changed his life, sometimes for the better, sometimes not, but one of the blessings of the job had been a growing instinct for the presence of danger. The latter came from a variety of sources, by no means all of them German. The sprawling intelligence empires on both sides of the front line bred a series of turf wars, and one of them pitched MI5 against the Secret Intelligence Service. The SIS had regarded Moncrieff's presence in Lisbon as nothing short of an act of trespass, a land-grab, and it had fallen to Kim Philby – as the new Head of the Iberian Station – to gently warn him off. MI5, the grammar-school boys, took care of upsets at home. While SIS, the toffs, trailed their capes abroad.

So far, so good, but what took bureaucratic prickliness to another dimension was a suspicion that there might be more to Mr Philby and his employers than met the eye. Moncrieff had spent the last few months unpicking a tangled plot to lure Hitler's Deputy Führer, Rudolf Hess, to fly to Scotland. Hess had arrived with peace proposals that were music to the ears of powerful figures in the upper reaches of the Establishment. Whether or not these might have Hitler's backing had never been clear but the threat to Churchill's conduct of the war was only too obvious, and the PM had readily agreed that Herr Hess was mentally unbalanced, a judgement that brought the whole episode to an end. Hess was now safely tucked up in an institution in Wales, but what had lingered in the corridors of Downing Street and the Security Service was a suspicion that the SIS – MI6 – were somehow co-conspirators in this piece of comic opera.

True? Moncrieff didn't know, couldn't be sure, but he had a gamekeeper's nose for tell-tale scents, an instinct bred in these mountains, and he didn't altogether trust Philby and the rest of the young Turks from the SIS. They were in the nation's service to plot, to lay traps, to wrong-foot the enemy, and Moncrieff knew from experience that this kind of duplicity could have consequences rather closer to home.

The moment he stepped back into the Glebe House, the phone in the hall began to ring. Moncrieff glanced at his watch and frowned. Half past midnight. Who'd want to phone at this hour?

'It's me. Comrade B.'

'Bella?'

'The same. Picture me in a little room of my own at Northolt. I'm lying in bed and there are pictures of aeroplanes everywhere. Treats for the boys, darling. You'd love it. Such a shame you're not here. But guess who I met tonight? You're allowed one guess, just one.'

'Tell me.'

'"C". The real thing.'

'You mean Menzies?'

'I do, you clever, clever man. And there's something else you ought to know. He loves Kim. Adores the man. You can see it in his face. Strange, *n'est-ce pas?*'

'Is this a secure line?'

'I've no idea.'

'Are you drunk?'

'A little. Six have deeper pockets than your lot. Talisker Single Malt? I told them they should have bought the whole bottle. It would have been cheaper.'

Moncrieff was smiling. He'd no idea whether this was tradecraft, a beautiful woman pretending to be loose-lipped, but it didn't really matter. She'd always had a talent for making him laugh and now was no different.

'Kyiv?' he asked. 'They're serious?'

'Tomorrow at dawn. But not me, alas. I get to go on to Moscow. I gather I'm an asset now.'

'They've signed you up again?'

'They think they have, or at least that's the impression I get. Live and let live? Eternal forgiveness? These people are either deaf or deeply cynical. I keep telling them I'm a true believer, that the comrades matter to me, but that's something they don't want to hear. And so, with the help of a little malt, I become the sum of all their precious assumptions. I'm white. I speak the King's English. I'm moderately well behaved. If you ask the right questions, I might even have the right connections. And so, I must be one of theirs. Case closed.'

'Theirs?'

'Yours,' she laughed. 'But that's because you don't listen either, which is why a girl has to put it on paper sometimes. The bit at the end, Mr M. Take a leaf out of my book. All you have to do is believe it.'

'Believe what?'

'That I love you. Off now. Some other time, eh?'

Moncrieff was staring at the phone. The precious connection had yet to break which meant that she was still listening.

'A word in your ear,' he said slowly. 'Are you still there?'

'Yes.'

'Don't go to Moscow.'

'Why not?'

'Just don't. I know how these things work, and I'm guessing you do, too. We all have a role to play and then the day comes when the show moves on and you find yourself in one of those basement rooms on the wrong side of the desk. You understand what I'm saying?'

'Of course. And you know what they call people like that in my country? In Russia?'

'Tell me.'

'Camp dust.'

3

WEDNESDAY 10 SEPTEMBER 1941

Camp dust.

The two words, so graphic, so simple, so horrifying, stayed with Moncrieff for most of the night. He tossed and turned in the suddenly empty bed, trying to rid himself of the image of Bella in some penal colony deep in Siberia, but next morning her voice – lightly drunk on the phone – was still there.

Camp dust.

He rubbed his eyes and checked his watch. He knew the time had come to return to London but it was barely dawn and so he lay back for a moment or two, still bewildered by this latest turn of events. He thought he knew this woman, and one of the many things he admired was her candour. In conversation after conversation, in answer to his many questions, she'd been happy to describe her new life in Soviet Russia and the pictures she'd painted defied belief.

So was Moscow really where her heart belonged? Trying to reconcile that luminous moment of conversion – to Marx, to equality, to the glorious victory of the Proletariat – with the realities of daily life under a tyrant like Stalin? Was she really prepared to lie awake at night, forever waiting for the footsteps outside her apartment in the dead of night? Replaying every chance conversation she might have had? Every reckless confidence she might have shared? Wondering about the friends or enemies who might have betrayed her? Not because she didn't believe hard enough, but because even true believers could never be immune from the knock at the door and the madness that had kidnapped Mother Russia and carried her away?

The latter phrase had come from the transcript of a screening interview with a Soviet exile Moncrieff had remembered during his pre-war months with MI5. The man was an academic from Leningrad, an astrophysicist of international repute. The fact that he'd spent years behind a high-powered telescope peering into deepest space was, to the NKVD, evidence of consorting with the enemy. At first, he'd dismissed the accusation as ridiculous. He'd tried to point out that distant nebulae didn't have a counter-revolutionary thought in their heavenly bodies, but the dead-eyed interrogators at the Big House mistrusted jokes, and when they offered him the opportunity to flee he knew he had no choice but to accept. The decision to leave still rankled, but he'd decided that the much-loved country of his birth had fallen into the laps of the insane.

When Moncrieff had shared his wry remark about the abduction of Mother Russia with Bella she'd chuckled.

'It's true,' she'd admitted. 'So does that make me crazy, too?'

*

Next morning, the train south to London was, as ever, packed. Moncrieff, who had boarded at Laurencekirk, found a compartment with an empty seat and settled his long frame into the sagging upholstery. There were seven fellow passengers. All but one were in uniform, mostly Army, and all of them were trying to sleep. The lone civilian was reading a copy of the *Aberdeen Press and Journal*, his face hidden behind the newspaper. The war in the East, according to the front page, was not going well. The *Wehrmacht* were swarming south towards the Caucasus, while the northern thrust had encircled Leningrad. Children under twelve, meanwhile, were being evacuated from Moscow.

Moncrieff settled back, uncomfortably warm in the tobacco fug of the compartment, trying to brace himself against the sway and rumble of the train. The war, he decided, was an easy read compared to Isobel Menzies. He thought about the times they'd shared in Berlin, back in '38; about her abrupt defection to the Soviet Union after he'd been expelled from the Reich; and about the widespread astonishment among her family and colleagues that she could ever have made such a move. Operation Barbarossa, the German invasion of the Soviet Union, had brought her back to Britain – quite how and why she wouldn't say – but he'd been deeply grateful for the days they'd just spent together. They'd had very few visitors, and none for more than an hour or so. They'd talked incessantly, heading out into the Cairngorms and following Moncrieff's favourite trails. In the evenings, he'd insisted on doing the cooking and they'd eaten late, poached salmon off trays in front of a small fire, before stepping outside at the approach of midnight to savour the very last of the daylight.

Over that snatched interlude, barely a week, there'd been much laughter, and much else. Work for MI5, and you learn never to trust anyone, but every conversation, every glance, every touch, told him that she was real, and when she'd confessed again – only yesterday – that she loved him, and that she needed him – he swore she meant it. And yet there still remained a locked door deep inside her, beyond which lay – he assumed – the explanation for her betrayal.

He knew from MI5 sources that she'd been delivering top-secret material from the Berlin Embassy to a Soviet agent for more than a year. Moscow – once she'd defected – had treated her well, rolled out the red carpet, extended privileges to their newly arrived comrade. All love affairs, in the end, are tarnished by routine and the irritations of daily life, but she'd weathered Moscow's many disappointments and showed absolutely no signs of regretting the decision she'd taken. On the contrary, she made light of the often surreal excesses of the regime. She'd experienced a kind of rebirth, she'd told Moncrieff only days ago. And that, she insisted, made her lucky.

Really? He didn't believe her, not for a second, and he knew the moment had arrived to find out more.

*

MI5, the Security Service, was headquartered in a handsome building in St James's Street that had once belonged to MGM. There was a To Let sign attached to the railings and callers with no official business were speedily sent on their way. Ursula Barton occupied a second-floor office next to that of Guy Liddell. The Head of 'B' Section trusted her implicitly, offering access to material way above Moncrieff's pay grade. It was early evening before the train had delivered Moncrieff to King's Cross station, but Barton was still at her desk.

Moncrieff knocked lightly on her door and stepped into the office. Studying a fan of papers on her desk, Barton looked up, not bothering to mask her surprise. She rarely started a conversation without a precautionary glance at her calendar.

'It's still September. You're supposed to be convalescing.'

The mention of convalescence drew a smile from Moncrieff. His time off, he reminded her, had been a thank you for the Hess operation. He'd never felt better in his life.

'A settling of accounts, then?' Barton was watching him carefully. 'Our hero gets the reward he deserves?'

'Indeed. And we enjoyed every moment.'

'So I gather. She left this morning, if you're interested. Early flight from Northolt.' Barton checked her watch. 'She should be in place by now.'

'Place?'

Barton held Moncrieff's gaze. She was fond of the ex-Royal Marine and it showed.

'You're telling me she never shared the glad news?'

'I'm telling you we had better things to talk about. She mentioned Kyiv, but only as a possibility.'

'So, what are you doing here?'

'I need to find out more.'

'Why?' Barton was frowning. 'Am I allowed to ask?'

It was a question Moncrieff had anticipated. Barton was German by birth, English by marriage. She'd left her husband years ago, and she'd also parted company with MI6 after serving in the Hague out-station. Barely months after the start of the war, two of her colleagues had been lured into an artful trap and kidnapped at Venlo on the German border, a schoolboy error that had blown entire networks of agents across Europe. She'd resigned in anger, and in shame, and MI5 had been only too grateful to acquire her many talents. Now, to Moncrieff's best knowledge, she led a solitary life in a slightly neglected West London semi with her cats and, she'd once told him, an extensive collection of Rossini LPs.

'Bella and I are close.' Moncrieff hated conversations like these. 'And I like to think we've been honest with each other.'

'But?'

'There are still things she won't tell me.'

'Do you blame her for that?'

'Not at all. Normally we leave our baggage at the bedroom door.'

'And now?'

'Now's different.'

'Why?'

Moncrieff shook his head, wouldn't say. In the sudden silence, he caught the scrape of a chair from the office next door. Barton had heard it, too. She began to tap her fingers on the top of the desk.

'She matters?'

'She does.'

'So what do you need from me?'

'I need to know what she's doing here. I need to know why she was sent, why she was allowed in, why she hasn't been arrested. In May, she'd have been the enemy. Pre-Barbarossa, we'd have taken her down to 020 and set the dogs on her. If she was very lucky, she might have survived. Otherwise, we'd have strung her up.'

Camp 020 was MI5 parlance for Latchmere House, MI5's interrogation centre out in the wilds of Richmond. While it was true that some double agents could face the death penalty, Barton was looking – if anything – amused.

'That was almost a speech,' she said. 'Do I hear a thank-you?'

'For what?'

'For Miss Menzies,' her smile widened. 'Bella.'

Moncrieff studied her for a moment, not quite believing what he'd just heard.

'You're telling me she was some kind of *present*?'

'I'm suggesting we take your welfare seriously. And hers, too. She did a wonderful job in the Wilhelmstrasse, before she decided to push off. Everyone says so. The fact that she'd made friends in the wrong quarters and swallowed all the Soviet claptrap was unfortunate, but at the time we assumed she was barely old enough to know better.' 70 Wilhelmstrasse was home to the British Embassy in Berlin.

'That sounds like forgiveness,' Moncrieff said. 'Have we all kissed and made up? Or is it just me?'

'Under any other circumstances, Tam, that might be funny. The sad truth is that the Russians have been lucky. For whatever reason, they've acquired a prime asset. She appears to be a real convert and that, to be frank, comes as a surprise. We need to test that faith of hers and we're rather hoping you might shed a little light on why on earth she ever went there in the first place.' The smile again, colder. 'Is there anything you might like to share with us?'

'Sadly not.'

'She wouldn't tell you?'

'No.'

'But you asked?'

'Of course.'

'And?'

'She told me about a boyfriend, a man she met at Oxford. Love of her life. Committed Communist. Made no secret of it.'

'We understand he wanted to join your lot, the Marines.'

'Indeed. And when they wouldn't have him, he went to Spain and died in some Republican trench.'

'For the cause.'

'Yes.'

'Anything else? Anything we didn't know already?'

Moncrieff shook his head. He still wanted to know how Bella, a self-declared defector, had managed to arrive in Britain just a week ago and avoid arrest.

'Our MI6 friends brought her back. They had the conversations in the Big House in Moscow and cobbled together some kind of démarche. One of them in London counter-signed the laissez-passer and guaranteed to look after her.'

'Would this be Mr Philby?'

'It would, Tam, and when the time came Broadway guaranteed that she'd be returned to Moscow intact.' Broadway housed the London headquarters of MI6.

'But what was the point?' Moncrieff asked. 'Why did she want to come home?'

'To see you, Tam. For whatever reason, she missed your company.'

'Sweet.'

'You don't believe me?'

'Of course I don't. Since when have MI6 been paying so much attention to my welfare? There has to be another reason.'

'You're right.'

'So, what is it? Am I allowed to ask?'

Barton wouldn't answer. Instead, she scribbled herself a note and then checked her watch again.

'I suggest you pay MI6 a visit. Their Section Five, to be precise.' She ducked her head and began to write again. 'They're camping out in St Albans. The MI6 central registry is nearby. A place called Prae Wood. Miss Menzies will doubtless have a file of her own. That might be a useful place to start.'

Moncrieff nodded. Section Five acted as a bridge between MI6 and MI5, analysing intelligence reports from foreign out-stations and passing on relevant items to the home Security Service. In theory, this created neutral ground between the two organisations, but MI6 kept their secrets close to their chests and were scrupulous in defending their territory.

'So why am I there? What do I tell them? What's the cover story?'

'You're tidying up after the Hess operation. Take something they might like to add to their own operational file. Go in the spirit of peace and goodwill. The officer in charge at the Registry drinks like a fish, which may or may not be an advantage.' She looked up at last. 'Be honest, Tam. Are you having difficulties with this proposition?'

'Not at all.'

'Then do I hear a yes?'

Moncrieff nodded. As ever, Ursula Barton appeared to have conjured a plan from the merest handful of clues, but Moncrieff knew that nothing this woman did ever happened by accident. He was about to push her harder about Bella but the door to the adjoining office opened and he found himself looking up at the rumpled figure of Guy Liddell.

Moncrieff got to his feet. The proffered handshake was the MI5 equivalent of a salute.

'Sir...' he muttered.

Liddell gazed at him for a moment. At first glance, he looked like a country solicitor – benign, well fed, slightly vague – but Moncrieff understood only too well the perils of underestimating this man. The sleepy eyes missed nothing.

'Tam,' he murmured peaceably. 'Good to have you back.'

4

THURSDAY 11 SEPTEMBER 1941

War, as Ilya Glivenko gently pointed out, is no friend of the clock. He and Bella had been waiting in the grey dust at the airfield outside Kharkov for nearly a day, sprawled on a threadbare Army blanket just metres away from the aircraft that was to take Glivenko and his precious wooden crates to the beleaguered city of Kyiv. The crates had already been transferred from the Halifax bomber that had brought them from Cairo, but a couple of engineers were still kneeling on the wing of the Soviet Il-2, working on the starboard engine.

Stripped to the waist in the late-summer heat, they paused from time to time to wipe the sweat from their faces and then shake their heads. According to Glivenko, there was a leak in the oil system they couldn't locate, and the more of the engine they dismantled the worse the prognosis became. Maybe tonight. Maybe tomorrow morning. A spare aircraft? With things as bad as they are? Forget it.

Bella had never been in a war zone before and found the changes of tempo fascinating. Gibraltar, in the early afternoon after leaving Northolt, had been bathed in sunshine. The landing strip lay at the foot of the looming Rock. She and Glivenko, plus a handful of other passengers, stayed aboard to save time while ground crew pumped fuel into the wing tanks. Watching them through the open door, Bella was grateful for the silence and the warmth after the deafening hours at altitude en route south.

The Halifax had never been designed to carry passengers and the conversion offered few comforts: a handful of canvas seats, earplugs fashioned from twists of cotton waste, plus a couple of blankets each to fend off the intense chill. For hour after hour, flying a huge loop over the Bay of Biscay to stay clear of Luftwaffe fighters, she'd done her best to relax but the thunder of the engines made sleep impossible. Now, back on the ground with the sudden heat seeping into her bones, she felt herself dropping off. Glivenko, sitting beside her, tapped his own shoulder. I'm a pillow, he murmured. Don't be shy.

They were on the move again within the hour, the engines roaring as they climbed away from the curl of Algeciras Bay and left Europe behind them. In Cairo, eleven hours later, it was five in the morning, the rising sun casting long shadows from the pyramids beside the Nile. This time they were allowed to clamber down from the aircraft and stretch their legs. A khaki marquee, open-sided, offered tea and a selection of fruit, and Bella was grateful for a latrine with a door after squatting unsteadily over a bucket at the back of the aircraft. When she'd soothed the Despatch Officer's worries about the cargo they were carrying, and returned to the marquee, she found Glivenko nursing a kitten.

'Meet Mitya,' he was eyeing the nearby table of food. 'Here, take her.'

Bella reached for the tiny bundle, feeling the sharpness of her bones through the thin veil of flesh. One of the kitten's eyes was gummy with an infection, and when Bella held her close she felt the needle prick of her claws as she sought for something to eat. Then Glivenko was back with a bowl of goat's milk. He dipped a finger and offered it to the kitten. The sudden pinkness of Mitya's lapping tongue made Bella laugh.

'More,' she told Glivenko. 'The poor scrap's starving.'

In the end, with the Despatch Officer trying to hurry them back to the waiting bomber, Mitya had drunk the lot. Bella held the kitten close while Glivenko returned the empty bowl. A single exchange of glances, a tiny nod from Glivenko, and Bella slipped the tiny bundle inside her blouse. Moments later, with a helping hand from Glivenko, she was climbing the aluminium ladder into the belly of the Halifax. Days later, in very different circumstances, she knew she owed a great deal to this moment of complicity.

*

Now, still marooned at Kharkov, still nursing Mitya, she was getting to know the little Russian sapper. He'd been lucky enough to be born in St Petersburg, he told her, and luckier still to have had access to a piano in his grandparents' apartment. His grandmother had taught him to play and his infant talents had caught the attention of the music teacher at his school. At the age of fifteen, he won himself a place at the Conservatoire. The city of his birth had now been renamed Petrograd and by the time the Bolsheviks seized power he was in his final year.

Lenin's mob, he said, had raided the city's richer districts in search of booty, and as winter settled on Petrograd the young Ilya found himself in a borrowed greatcoat and a pair of his sister's woollen gloves playing a liberated grand piano beside the big tram intersection round the corner from the Hermitage.

'Rachmaninoff and Bach and lots of folksongs,' he said, 'at minus nine degrees. Frost in your nostrils and the audience stamping their feet to keep warm.'

'Lots of people?'

'Hundreds. I knew I'd never be good enough to play at concert level but in a way this was better. Those October days had taken people out of themselves. Play the right tunes and everyone would sing. You'd see the same faces day after day. We called ourselves the Kerbside Choir.'

'And you? What did they call you?'

'The Pianist. And people who really know me still do. There was another Pianist in the city called Zhdanov. He became the party boss after Kirov was killed in '34, but that's another story. You should come to Kyiv with me. Bring little Mitya.'

'I'd love to.'

'So why not? We get along fine. You've been a great help. Anything's possible in this bloody war. Just do it.'

Anything's possible in this bloody war. Bella smiled, watching the battle-scarred Soviet aircraft come and go, trailing clouds of dust across the busy chaos of the airfield, and lying on the grass she held the little kitten even closer, aware of its soft mewing. En route to Kharkov, especially with the Despatch Officer in Cairo, she'd done Philby's bidding and smoothed Glivenko's path through the usual tangle of self-important military busybodies. She was still clueless about the contents of the wooden boxes, but nobody seemed to care. Now, again according to Philby, she was due for a rendezvous with a senior NKVD officer called Bezkrovny with whom she'd return to Moscow. She knew this man by reputation and didn't much like what she'd heard. He was Jewish, and clever, and ambitious, and was rumoured to have the ear of Lavrentiy Beria, a career sadist who specialised in breaking the toughest men in the name, as ever, of the Proletariat.

So far there'd been no sign of Bezkrovny, and for that she was glad. She needed, above all, time. Time to take stock. Time to fathom exactly what kind of catastrophe was threatening to overwhelm her. Her years at the heart of the pitiless Soviet machine had sharpened both her instinct for danger and the survival skills that went with it. Tam had been right. Best, at all costs, to avoid Moscow.

Glivenko, as calm as ever, was still waiting for some kind of decision. His offer of a ride appeared to be genuine.

'I speak German,' Bella said lightly, 'as well as Russian and English. Might that be useful in Kyiv?'

Glivenko's derisive bark of laughter made the kitten jump. Bella gentled it as best she could. Nearby, two young soldiers had started trading blows over a can of gasoline. Glivenko was on his feet at once. Older, and much smaller, he chose the bigger of the two men to attack. A flurry of blows, and the man was on the ground, holding his face while blood pumped from his shattered nose. The other soldier stared at Glivenko for a moment while the little man delivered a volley of abuse, and then turned and ran, leaving the gasoline behind.

Glivenko seized the can and carried it across towards the aircraft. Like Bella, the engineers on the wing had been watching the brief fight. The gasoline, one of them said, would be more than welcome. The engine was back in one piece, the oil leak rectified, and – yes – the plane should be ready as soon as they woke the pilot up. He called Glivenko *Otets*, Father, and Bella recognised the respect in his voice.

'Miss Menzies?'

Bella looked round. Bezkrovny, she thought. He was wearing a belted brown jacket. His blue jodhpurs were tucked into knee-length leather boots, and his shoulder boards told Bella everything she wanted to know.

'Senior Major of State Security?' she feigned approval. 'I'm flattered.'

'I'm down here on other business,' Bezkrovny pocketed his purple NKVD card. 'It will be a pleasure to escort you back home.'

'When?'

'Our plane has yet to arrive. It will be two hours, at least. Have you eaten?'

'No. But everything is taken care of.' It was Glivenko. He was standing in the sunshine, rubbing his knuckles. The sight of senior NKVD officers disturbed most serving soldiers but Glivenko seemed untroubled. When Bezkrovny asked for his papers, he produced his Army ID. Bezkrovny inspected it carefully, turning the worn pages one by one.

'And you are going where?'

'Kyiv.' Glivenko nodded towards the nearby Il-2.

'Kyiv is under siege. The city's fucked. You have to be crazy to go to Kyiv.'

'I know. That's the point.'

'Being crazy?'

'Making sure the city's fucked.'

'I don't understand.'

Glivenko shrugged, then gestured at Bella.

'You're taking her to Moscow?' he asked Bezkrovny.

'Yes.'

'And you're over there? With your comrades?'

'I am.'

'Then it will be my pleasure to bring Miss Menzies over when we've finished our conversation. Might that be in order?'

Bezkrovny looked uncertain for a moment, then nodded, tapped his watch, muttered something about 'soon', and turned on his heel. Bella watched him striding across to a group of fellow NKVD officers, deep in conversation. He's as impressed by The Pianist as I am, she thought. Anyone heading for Kyiv obviously deserves a degree of respect.

'You work for these people?' Glivenko asked.

'*With* them, yes.'

'And you sleep at night?'

'Sometimes.'

'You're on some kind of assignment? From the British?'

'In a way, yes.' It seemed a small lie.

Glivenko nodded. He was still watching the tight little circle of NKVD officers and he was looking thoughtful. Then his brown eyes found Bella again.

'You still want to go to Kyiv? With me?'

'I do, yes.'

'Might I ask why?'

'Not here. Not now.' Bella smiled. 'Maybe later.'

'But you realise how dangerous this might be? The flight in? What has to happen afterwards?'

'Yes. Trust me, please. I don't know what you're up to but the answer's yes.'

'It's really that important? That you don't go on to Moscow?'

'I'm afraid it is, yes.' She heard the nearby cough of the engines starting, one after the other, but her eyes were still on

Bezkrovny. The way he commanded attention among his fellow officers told her a great deal. 'If I get on that plane it might not go well with you, either,' she murmured. 'Isn't that a concern?' Glivenko laughed softly.

'From where we're going,' he said, 'there'll be no coming back.'

*

They began to taxi out towards the take-off point minutes later. Watching through the quaintly curtained window, Bella had the satisfaction of watching Bezkrovny throw an inquisitive glance over his shoulder, then frown and stiffen and reach for the pistol hanging from his belt. Bella alerted Glivenko, who was sitting in the seat behind. He took a look for himself, and then laughed. This aircraft, he said, was the Soviet copy of the American DC-3. It could soak up endless punishment and it would take more than a gramme or two of NKVD lead to bring it to a halt. Let the man shoot all he likes. We're still going to Kyiv.

Anything's possible in this bloody war.

Bella smiled, the kitten curled peaceably in her lap, stretches of the airfield bumping past the window. For the first time since the day the Germans crossed the border and fell on Mother Russia, she felt truly at peace. What might happen next was totally beyond her control, but she trusted this man. He had the dignity and the brave fatalism she'd met so often in Moscow – in the street, on the new Metro, in countless chance encounters – and she sensed that in his company it would be a privilege, as well as a pleasure, to confront whatever Kyiv might have in store.

The flight was brief compared to the interminable haul from Northolt. The pilot flew very low, dragging the shadow of the aircraft over the endless steppe as the sun began to set in the west, and when Glivenko appeared at her elbow and shouted that the pilot was trying to avoid German fighters she said she understood. It turned out that he'd paid the cockpit a visit. The NKVD bastard, according to the pilot, had loosed off a couple of rounds, aiming for the aircraft's undercarriage, but only when they landed would anyone know whether the tyres were still intact.

'And if they aren't?'

'We slow down quicker,' Glivenko was looking at the kitten. 'That's the pilot talking, not me.'

Moments later, without warning, the aircraft lurched to the left and the kitten began to struggle in Bella's lap, alarmed by the howl of the engines as the pilot fought for altitude. Glivenko, thrown off his feet, was lying in the narrow aisle, face up, and Bella caught a shrug of resignation as the pilot banked sharply, this time to the right. Then they were straight and level again, the danger evidently over, and when Bella checked through the window she could see the broadness of a river disappearing into the haze, and the endless sprawl of a city beyond.

The aircraft was dropping now, a descent that seemed to steepen and steepen until the pilot abruptly hauled back on the controls and settled the aircraft onto what looked like wet sand. Mercifully, there was no damage to the undercarriage and Bella, still at the window, watched a quartet of figures striding towards the aircraft as it slowed to a halt. The uniforms were all too familiar. NKVD, she thought. For a moment, her blood icing, she knew she'd fallen into a trap baited by Bezkrovny.

But then, as the pilot throttled back and the engines died, she felt a gentle pressure on her arm.

'I know these people,' Glivenko, back on his feet, was smiling. 'Everything's different here.'

5

FRIDAY 12 SEPTEMBER 1941

It took Tam Moncrieff a day at his desk in St James's Street to prepare for his visit to Section Five. He spent the morning and half the afternoon preparing a comprehensive report of his dealings with Rudolf Hess. Reading between the lines, he knew it was impossible to miss the thrust of his conclusions – that MI6 may have been complicit in the Deputy Führer's flight to Scotland, and in the subsequent disappearance of a set of peace proposals authorised at the highest level of the Reich – but Moncrieff suspected that Broadway had marked his card already. Moncrieff? A troublemaker, they'd murmur. An ex-bootneck, far too chippy for his own good. And, just in case any of this Hess nonsense ever merited serious attention, a bit of a fantasist as well.

He finished the report in time to snatch a late lunch, leaving the typed copy for Ursula Barton's attention. By the time he returned to his office, a note had appeared on his desk. Barton, he thought.

'Nice work,' she'd written. 'We need to talk about Krivitsky.'

Krivitsky? The name seemed familiar, but Moncrieff couldn't remember why. Hundreds of names, possibly more, had come across his desk in the last three years. Moments later, he was back in Barton's office. Walter Krivitsky? Chasing biscuit crumbs across her plate with a moistened finger, she was happy to explain.

'During the thirties he was working for the NKVD, based in The Hague, running Soviet agents all over Europe. I met him a couple of times. He was an intense little man, hard to like, married to a blonde called Tonia. They had a rather nice townhouse in the Celebesstraat. Krivitsky awarded himself a doctorate and took another name and pretended to sell art books. His real job was to make things tough for us if it ever came to war with the Soviets, and there were some in the office who thought he was rather effective. I'm afraid I was never one of them. The man had survivor written all over him.'

Moncrieff nodded. Walter Krivitsky, he thought. The man from the heart of Soviet intelligence who'd fled to the West.

'This is the defector who took a boat to America and wrote a book about what Stalin was really up to,' Moncrieff raised an eyebrow. '1938? 1939? Am I right?'

'Thirty-eight,' Barton nodded. 'Until then he'd kept his doubts about the *Vodzh* largely to himself, but then the show trials got under way and it became obvious that his Leader's wrath would spare no one. Fellow agents in the West, friends of his, solid Communists, were being hauled back to Moscow and stuffed into the mincing machine. There was no logic, no discernible plan, only blood. To no one's surprise, Krivitsky decided to make his excuses and leave. Next thing we know, he's living in an apartment in New York and writing articles for the *Saturday Evening Post*. Hoover was livid, by the way. Krivitsky insisted America was wide open to penetration and it turned out he was right.'

MI5, she said, asked him to come to London and share what he knew about Soviet agents. Krivitsky agreed.

'He gave us a couple of names in the first interview, Foreign Office people, both of whom we knew about already, so we turned him over to Jane Archer who took him to St Ermin's for a proper chat. She did a wonderful job, by the way. An absolutely textbook piece of work.'

Moncrieff nodded. St Ermin's Hotel, a favoured haunt of MI5 interrogators, was a couple of minutes' walk away.

'I thought Archer was sacked?'

'You're right, she was. In my book, she never overstepped the mark, but she had decided views on the management and didn't bother to hide them. OH was both incompetent and a fool. Someone had to make the point, and Jane paid the price.'

OH – Oswald Harker – had briefly held the post of MI5 Director. Looking back, Moncrieff remembered muted applause from offices on the upper floors when he, too, was given his marching orders.

'So, what else did Archer get out of Krivitsky?'

'A lot. The key was the investment the Soviets were making trying to recruit agents-in-place. These were people whom they'd identified as future high-flyers. They tended to be young, and clever, and happy to work for the cause. Most of them, in Jane's lovely phrase, were cursed by idealism. Our Soviet friends think long-term. Most of these prospects were still at university but in fifteen or twenty years' time they might find themselves with access to all kinds of information. Money, incidentally, rarely came into it. It's always the power of the *idea*, Tam. Krivitsky's word, not Jane's.'

'And?'

'And what?'

'What else did the man have to say?'

Barton shot him a look, and then shook her head.

'I suggest you ask for his Registry file when you're up in St Albans,' she said.

'You don't know what he told her?'

'Of course I do. But what I've never seen is their version of events. You're paying them a visit to put fresh meat on the bones of poor old Hess. A peek or two at other files won't hurt.'

'Files? Plural?'

'Of course. Krivitsky is one of them. Your lovely Bella will obviously be the other. The power of the idea, Tam.' The smile was icy. 'Do I sense a yes?'

*

Next morning, Moncrieff took an early train to St Albans. Section Five was based in a rambling Edwardian villa on the outskirts of the town. The heavens opened the moment Moncrieff stepped out of the station and he buttoned his trench coat while waiting for a taxi. When one finally arrived, the driver turned out to be an oldish man with thick pebble glasses and a comical Bairnsfather Old Bill moustache. Sensing something military in Moncrieff's bearing, he was quick to point out that he'd fought – and been gassed – at the second Battle of Ypres.

'Ever happen to you, sir?'

'Happily, not. I was still in nappies at the time.'

'Best out of it, then. The chlorine stuff they were using was vile. Where to?'

'Glenalmond. You know it?'

'Me?' The cabbie wheezed with laughter. 'You're one of them, sir?'

'One of what?'

'Them spies? They'll tell you that place is full of archaeological wallahs busy on the dig but most blokes in my trade know better. I'm taking people up there all the time, and you know the clue that gives you lot away? Crisp new fivers. Which means you're either on the Black or in the Funnies. Begging your pardon, sir, but you don't look like a criminal so I'm guessing you must be a spy. Take it as a compliment, sir. It sounds more fun than driving a bloody taxi.'

Still chuckling, the driver joined the trickle of mid-morning traffic, and Moncrieff sat back against the scuffed leather as street after street of neat little semi-detached houses slipped by. The driver, he knew, was right about the cover story MI6 had concocted for Glenalmond. The finds at a nearby Roman site had attracted international attention and headquartering the Verulamium dig at somewhere like Glenalmond would be entirely plausible.

The villa lay at the end of a gravel drive. Water was dripping from a huge elm tree as Moncrieff bent to pay the driver. To his slight irritation, he only had a couple of five pound notes and they were both brand new.

'You've got change?' he asked.

The driver nodded, opening his wallet and counting out four one-pound notes and a handful of coins.

'Sorry they're so grubby, sir,' he handed over the notes. 'Good luck with the dig, eh?'

Moncrieff stood in the rain, watching the taxi depart, then glanced round at Glenalmond. In his many trips out of London over the last couple of years, he must have seen dozens of properties like this – tall sash windows on the ground floor, a steepish pitch to the tiled roof, hints of Home Counties mock-Tudor in the timberwork – but he didn't doubt for a moment that it perfectly served Section Five's purposes. A modest flight of stone steps led up to the front door. Inside, he found a well-spoken young woman behind a desk, deep in an old copy of the *Illustrated London News*.

Moncrieff unbuttoned his trench coat, waiting for some kind of acknowledgement. Eventually her head came up. She was very pretty.

'Major Moncrieff?' She had a dazzling smile. 'We've been expecting you. I'm sorry about the rain but Kim insisted that nothing would put you off. Upstairs, Major Moncrieff, second door on the right. I'd offer you coffee but the stuff we're getting just now is undrinkable. Can you bear to make do with tea?'

Moncrieff said yes, but her finger was still anchored in the text of the article she'd been reading, and the moment he turned away her head went down again.

The door to the office upstairs was already ajar. Moncrieff knocked twice and stepped inside. The room was bigger than he'd expected, six desks, all occupied. There was a powerful smell of pencil shavings, pipe tobacco and wet dog. The latter, a black and white spaniel, was curled in a Pending tray on the floor beside the fireplace. The tray was lined with a sodden copy of that morning's *Times*. Moncrieff recognised the headline from the newsstand at St Pancras station. After brave resistance by Norwegian trades unions, the Nazis had declared martial law in Oslo.

'His name's Sammy. You'll be glad to know he only bites the enemy.' A hand briefly descended on Moncrieff's arm. 'Welcome to our little nest, Tam. We're here to make life sweet for you.'

Moncrieff, already wrong-footed, had last met Kim Philby on a flight home from Lisbon earlier in the year, and it wasn't until the end of the journey that Philby had mentioned his role in MI6. He was responsible, he'd said, for the welfare of the Iberian out-station, impressive for someone still in his late twenties. Over the intervening months, he'd put on a little weight, but the stammer was still there, lurking at the edges of every sentence, and so was the effortless charm. Philby appeared to have dressed for the pub, and Moncrieff, bending to stroke the dog, was curious about the Army blouse he was wearing, unbuttoned.

'Belonged to my pa,' Philby smiled. 'In the rain, when it gets wet, I can still smell him.'

A tray of tea arrived in the hands of a young man Philby introduced as Tim. The men behind the desks were broadly the same age and most of them were busy annotating mountains of typed sheets. The atmosphere, like the dress code, was relaxed to the point of informality. No one appeared to use surnames and as pencils sped over lines of text there was much comparing of notes. This material, Moncrieff suspected, had probably arrived in diplomatic bags from distant corners of unoccupied Europe, and the frequent laughter that greeted yet another gem felt totally unforced. Deeply collegiate, Moncrieff thought. A bunch of young friends, undoubtedly clever, trying to make sense of other people's wars.

*

Philby insisted on taking Moncrieff to lunch. The dog accompanied them, bounding ahead, nose to the ground, leading the way to a nearby pub called the White Hart. The landlord had a bag of bones readied for the dog and pulled a couple of pints without Philby saying a word.

'There's a brewery he uses in Letchworth,' Philby was organising a couple of bar stools. 'We trust this lovely man with our lives and he never lets us down. *Salud.*'

They touched glasses and Moncrieff sensed already that he'd have to make the running if this conversation was to lead anywhere worthwhile. Philby, he'd decided, had a talent for masking an undoubted intelligence. On one level he got close to you, sometimes uncomfortably so, while on another he appeared to step back, keeping his distance, watching, listening, cracking a joke, benign, unruffled, smiling his quiet smile. In a certain light, like now, his eyes were an intense blue.

'Souk?' Moncrieff asked. 'Any news?'

Philby studied his glass for a long moment and then shook his head, a gesture laden – it seemed to Moncrieff – with something less than regret.

'I'm afraid not. The bloody man's disappeared. No one's had sight nor sound of him. The temptation is to put it down to the monkeys in the PVDE but that might be asking a little too much of them. Those people can do the business when they really try but Souk had the measure of them. He was also putting serious money in the right pockets.'

'You know that?'

'I do, Tam. It was my job.'

Moncrieff held his gaze. The PVDE were the Portuguese secret police. Agent Souk, in real life, was an English-born chancer called Gordon Hesketh who had tested their patience to its limits. Hesketh, who excelled in playing rival clients off against each other, had briefly been on MI5's payroll, much to Philby's irritation.

'He conned you, Tam. Just like he conned every other bugger. All he ever sold was gammon. Take it from me. The man was peddling lies.'

'You really think so?'

'I know so. Swelp me, I mean it. I know what you're going to say. You're going to tell me that the real trick is sieving all that dross and picking out the bits you think might have some value. Only one problem, my friend. It was *all* porkies.'

Moncrieff shook his head. In his own mind, he knew that Hesketh had – intentionally or otherwise – flagged the path to Rudolf Hess. Thanks to Souk, Moncrieff had come close to the truth about the Deputy Führer's dramatic descent on Scotland, an operational coup that had sorely embarrassed the spymasters in Broadway. Hess had arrived on British soil to make a peace to which Churchill would never agree, a proposition that had earlier won quiet support from Philby's bosses.

'You may be right about Souk,' Moncrieff murmured. 'The rest of it? I'm not so sure.'

'You'd like to help us further?'

'That's why I'm here. We conducted a post-mortem afterwards. We thought you might be interested.'

'Someone died? I didn't know.'

A smile played on Philby's lips. Moncrieff ignored it. He had yesterday's typed report on the Hess operation in an envelope in his pocket. He put it carefully on the bar. Philby gazed at it. He looked, if anything, even more amused.

'Golly,' he said.

'Take it.'

'Must I?'

'This is inter-operational. At least, that's what my masters tell me. Sunlight is the best antiseptic. Did anyone ever tell you that?'

'Often. Which is why we all fall in love with Lisbon. Did you succumb as well, Tam? The temptations of the place? All those wonderful meals? All that wickedness? Visits to the casino at Estoril? Little crooks like Souk pissing your money – *our* money – away? Is this what I'll find in there?' He gazed at the envelope a moment, then slipped it into the pocket of his Army blouse. Moments later, he drained his glass and nodded at a table at the other end of the bar. 'Enough. We must eat.' A sudden grin, seemingly artless. 'Never mix business with pleasure, Tam. My pa taught me that. It was a lesson he learned from the Arabs and I've every reason to believe they were right.'

*

Lunch was liver and a curl or two of bacon swimming in cabbage leaves, overboiled potatoes and a thin gravy. Offal, as Philby remarked, was one of the war's great blessings. Keen to avoid the contested turf that was Agent Souk, and aware from Barton that Philby had been a journalist before the war, Moncrieff asked about his brief posting to the BEF. The British Expeditionary Force had crossed the Channel some months after Hitler invaded Poland, and the government was keen to wave the flag.

'It was a joke, Tam. A calling card. Our German friends had the best army in Europe and everyone knew it. They were also doing alarming things in the air. I'd seen their pilots in Spain and believe me they understood the dark arts. Flying against them was a death sentence. Crouching in some miserable bloody trench was no better. Once the weather cheered up after the winter, Europe was in for *die Behandlung.*

'The treatment?'

'Indeed. You speak German?'

'I do.'

This news appeared to come as a surprise. Philby bent a little closer over the table.

'Amiens, Tam. You know it?'

'Picardy,' Moncrieff nodded. 'A fine cathedral.'

'We were there in May, a whole bunch of us scribblers. The bid was to conjure good news out of disaster but there was no lie big enough to disguise what was going on. The thing was a rout. On a hill above the city, our lads were digging in. There were a couple of hundred of them, all that stood between the Panzers and the sea. Guderian and the boys in grey were expected any minute. To stop a tank you need the proper kit. They had bugger all, just Lee-Enfields, and you know how many bullets we'd seen fit to give each of these poor sods? Fifty, Tam. Just fifty. And even some of them were—'

The last word seemed to stick in his throat. His mouth opened and closed, a beached fish, but he couldn't get it out. Finally, his whole face contorted and the word emerged, semi-intact.

'... duds,' he said.

'So, what happened?'

'They did their best. Most of them died. The rest probably spent the next month walking to the German border. The clues had been there for years. All you had to do was listen to some of the politicians with eyes in their head, read some of the stuff coming out of Berlin, and maybe take Hitler at his word. Those poor...' He frowned. The stammer was back.

'Bastards?'

'... yes. Thank you. Those poor bastards on the hill died because of us, because of our negligence. Chamberlain was naïve enough to believe in peace and we were naïve enough to take him at his word. Denial is a capital offence, Tam. As those lads above Amiens found out.'

'And you? What happened?'

'We were lucky. The gods of war took care of us. We had access to transport and enough petrol to get us to Boulogne. You'd think getting out in one piece might warrant a glass or two and you'd be right, but no one was celebrating. We felt shame, Tam. We'd let those lads down and...' He frowned for a moment, staring hard at his empty glass, his fists balling, then looked up again, '... all we could do was drown our sorrows.'

Moncrieff was gazing at the remains of his meal. He'd heard similar stories from friends in the armed forces, an army falling apart in front of their eyes, but rarely expressed with such venom. This was a different side of Philby, hinting at an unexpected rawness, and he wondered whether it might account for the stammer. This man has belief, he thought, and a bottomless talent for disgust.

'And now?' he murmured.

'Now what?'

'You think anything's different? You think we've moved on?'

'Not at all. We're fucked, Tam. Royally screwed. We seem to have been spared an invasion but we're still flat broke. Most of Europe is busy learning German and most of America has turned its back. The Ivans are suddenly on our side, which may or may not be a blessing, but I wouldn't count on Moscow being Russian by Christmas. Plucky little England is a wonderful phrase, but it butters no parsnips. Liver OK, by the way? No chewy bits?'

Philby called for more drinks while Moncrieff excused himself and found the toilets. When he got back to the table, the envelope was still tucked into Philby's Army blouse, untouched. Philby's glass, on the other hand, was already half empty.

'The lovely Miss Menzies,' he was beaming. 'Tell me everything.'

Moncrieff parried the question with a shrug. He was getting used to Philby's abrupt conversational swerves, passion one moment, small talk the next.

'You know her well?'

'Professionally, a little. In every other respect, sadly not. You're a lucky man, Tam. She's dotty about you.'

'How would you know that?'

'Because she told me. We had a couple of drinks at Northolt the night before she left us. She couldn't stop talking about that place of yours in the mountains. It seems you walked the legs off her and did the cooking to boot. In my book that's code for besotted.'

'Me?'

'Her.'

'She's back on the books?'

'Ours, you mean?'

'Yes.'

'I've no idea. That's way above my pay grade.'

'So, what was she doing here? Back home?'

'She came over with the little sapper chap. Ilya somebody. Delivered him to Fort Halstead. I gather the boffins down there loved him. He brought vodka by the crateful and drank them under the table. Once he'd done the business, she flew back with him. She didn't tell you about Halstead?'

'No.'

'Why on earth not?'

Moncrieff let the question hang in the air. Fort Halstead was a government outpost near Sevenoaks. It specialised in explosives research.

'We were on leave,' Moncrieff murmured at last. 'Never mix business with pleasure. Isn't that what the Arabs taught your Pa?'

*

Lunch over, Philby walked Moncrieff to the Central Registry. MI6's archived and current files were stored at Prae Wood, a stately pile that also housed some of the agency's other departments. The rain had stopped now, and Moncrieff followed Philby as he stepped carefully around the puddles in front of the house.

The Registry was at the back of the building, a wilderness of shelves that seemed to go on forever. Individual files were stored in cardboard boxes. Each box was colour-coded and carried an additional line of stencilled capital letters, while the files themselves occupied manila folders, hole-punched on one corner and tied with green shoelaces. Moncrieff, ushered into the Registry's central office, found himself looking at a file with Bella's name on it. Another present, he thought.

'Is this for me?' He glanced sideways at Philby.

'Of course it is. Allow me to do the honours. Captain Woodfield is our Master Archivist, the keeper of all our secrets. He used to be in Special Branch, so watch your manners. Tam Moncrieff here used to be in the Marines, Bill. He'll know fifty ways of killing you but he's thoroughly house-trained. Be gentle with him, please. Share and share alike, eh?'

A shortish man with thinning hair rose to his feet behind the desk and offered Moncrieff a clammy handshake. His abandoned jacket hung on the back of his chair, and the food stains on his shirt looked recent. His face was purpled with a lifetime's drinking, and his eyes – post-lunch – were swimming.

'Isobel Menzies?' he nodded down at the file. 'No relation, I assume?'

'None at all. Not so far as I know.' Sir Stewart Menzies, known as 'C', was the head of MI6. 'C' stood for Controller.

'Tam here has an interest. May I?' Philby reached for the file and murmured something about finding their visitor a bit of peace and quiet, but Moncrieff hadn't finished.

'May I leave you another name?' he was still looking at Woodfield.

'Of course,' he reached for a pen. 'Fire away.'

'Krivitsky.'

'You mean Walter?'

'I do, yes.'

There was a brief exchange of glances between Woodfield and Philby, then Woodfield returned his gaze to Moncrieff.

'You have time for all this? Both files? Menzies needn't keep you long, but our Walter is probably a day's reading. At least.'

'That won't be a problem. I can always come back.'

'Absolutely, and you'll be most welcome.' It was Philby. Moncrieff felt the gentlest pressure on his arm. 'Time waits for no man, my friend. Least of all us. Cell five, Bill? The usual?'

'Four. It's got a nicer view.'

Moncrieff followed Philby out of the office. Philby was carrying the file. A line of reading cubicles lay beyond the endless shelves of file boxes, tiny cubby holes with a desk and a single chair. Cell, he thought, was a perfect description.

'View?' The cubicles had no windows.

'Bill's little joke, Tam. It's what's inside that matters.' He tapped the file and then gave it to Moncrieff. 'Page seventeen, third entry. Hope you don't mind but I had a little peek earlier. Tea in an hour or so? I'll see what I can do.' He smiled at Moncrieff and gestured towards the cubicle. '*Gute Jagd, ja?*'

Good hunting.

Moncrieff watched Philby wander back towards the office before making himself comfortable at the desk and opening the file. The corner of page seventeen had been turned over. Each of the entries was dated. On 27 August 1938, Support Officer Isobel Menzies had received a visitor at the Berlin Embassy. His name?

Moncrieff lifted his head. Me, he thought. He stared at the partition wall for a long moment, trying to remember his first sight of Bella as he'd waited beside the embassy's reception desk. He'd been sitting on a leather banquette watching comings and goings on the Wilhelmstrasse while she ghosted down the staircase, unannounced. She'd been wearing an emerald-green dress that barely covered her knees. He remembered the fall of blonde hair, how tall she was, and how tanned her bare legs had been. She'd looked down at him before he sprung to his feet, and he remembered her air of frank appraisal before she'd smiled. The smile was brimming with mischief and best of all he remembered that tiny moment of complicity between them, rich with promise.

'Knock, knock...' Moncrieff looked up. It was Philby. He was carrying two thick files. 'Our Walter,' he said. 'Compliments of Captain Bill. I'm afraid he's right, Tam, you'll need more than an afternoon. He's open for business tomorrow and you're welcome to stay the night *chez nous*. It's a bit chaotic, I'm afraid, but Aileen cooks like a dream. She's also chums with a talented poacher.' He gave Moncrieff the files and backed out of the cubicle before pausing. 'Oh yes, and one other thing. We're a man short for tomorrow afternoon's game. The weather's on the mend. Any chance?'

'Of what?'

'Of joining us. We play cricket, Tam,' that smile again. 'Though we never expect to win.'

6

SATURDAY 13 SEPTEMBER 1941

Bella awoke in pitch darkness, aware only of the presence of the kitten. It was sitting on the pillow beside her head, licking her ear, and if purring was any guide to contentment then it was settling in nicely. She began to stroke it, murmuring endearments in Russian, thinking she was alone. Then came a nearby grunt and she heard a stirring in the darkness, and when the question came, that, too, was in Russian.

'You're OK?' A woman's voice.

'I'm fine. Blame the kitten.'

'Mitya? Sweet.'

Larissa, Bella thought, Ilya's journalist friend she'd met last night. She'd been in the city less than half a day. Glivenko had taken her to the commandeered offices that served as the NKVD's local headquarters, introduced her to one face after another, told them how precious she was and how well connected. They were to keep an eye on her. They were to make sure she came to no harm.

Bella had always paid a great deal of attention to body language and everything she saw, every last clue, told her these men held Glivenko in great esteem. Hours later, he took her to a restaurant in one of the hotels on Khreshchatyk, the city's major boulevard, and when he told her that she'd be safe here, at least until the Germans arrived, she believed him. For whatever reason, the men in the Big House had rejoined the human race.

Larissa had appeared in the restaurant shortly afterwards. Thunder had been rolling towards the city for the last hour, steadily advancing – said Glivenko – like distant artillery fire, and Larissa brushed droplets of rain from her greying hair. She was a handsome woman, close to middle age, smartly dressed, strong features, hints of Jewish blood in her deep brown eyes. According to Glivenko, she worked for the city's official newspaper, *Novoe Ukrainskoe Slovo*, and was the best-connected journalist in Kyiv. If Bella was interested in what it meant to be Ukrainian, then she'd find no better guide.

By now, to Bella's enormous relief, Glivenko had concluded that his exotic English translator was in deep trouble. He'd listened hard to the few clues Bella had let slip and guessed the rest. They were friends. Kyiv, just days away from some catastrophe that Bella had yet to fully understand, was the perfect place to hide. She very definitely needed help. And The Pianist was only too happy to oblige.

The three of them shared a meal and a bottle of wine. Bella had never been in a city under siege and the very normality of everything took her by surprise. The trams were still running. There was still a little food in the shops, women bargaining for winter wear in the open-air markets, kids chasing clouds of pigeons. The restaurant was comfortably full and though men in uniform vastly outnumbered civilian diners, there was nothing unavailable on the menu, and – to Bella's unschooled eye – no obvious signs of unease.

She and Larissa bonded at once, a mysterious establishment of mutual trust that was becoming more and more rare in Stalin's Moscow. Both women attracted attention, especially from certain kinds of men at neighbouring tables. Both women were curious about the world around them. And both women, Bella suspected, enjoyed a degree of risk, even recklessness, in their professional and perhaps private lives.

Pressed by Larissa for news from Moscow, Bella talked about survival. Getting by, she said, was no longer a matter of food and drink. The madness of the *Vodzh*, of the leadership, was everywhere and if you were wise you trusted no one and kept your mouth shut. Even in high summer, with the parks a riot of flowers and the trees in full leaf, people had winter in their hearts. The national palette, she said, offered nothing but an endless variety of greys. Grey for resignation. Grey for helplessness. Grey for fear. Larissa, she'd noticed, chain-smoked one of Stalin's favourite cigarettes, Kazbekis, but her gaze never wavered behind the thin veil of smoke. She was happy to let Bella do most of the talking and, when it came to a rare question, she never wasted a word. The pitch of her voice was unforgettable, almost a man's timbre, rich and deep.

'So what are you doing in Moscow?' Larissa had just summoned the waiter after they'd decided on another bottle of Georgian champagne.

'I defected,' Bella said simply. 'I decided to join you.'

'You joined them, not us. There's a difference.' She put an apologetic hand on Glivenko's arm and told him he could be an honorary Ukrainian any time he liked.

'I'm sorry,' Bella said. 'That was my fault. Maybe I signed up for an idea, not a country at all, not a regime. Either way, I made a choice, and it took me to Moscow.'

'You work for the state?'

'Everyone works for the state.'

'I mean the NKVD, the Big House.'

'In a way, yes. Once a spy...'

'Really?' she seemed shocked. 'You *spied* for these people? In your own country?'

'In Berlin, as it happens, but it's the same sin. The small print was fascinating. You're like the tramp in the street, always looking for fag ends, little bits of information that might turn out to be useful. I had a desk in the British Embassy. I expect you can work out the rest.'

'Tell me.'

'The Soviets assign you a handler. You meet the man at agreed times and places, and hand stuff over, stuff you've either copied or stolen. It's a love affair, really. Totally illicit. Lots of trysts. Lots of moments when you think you might have blown it. Better than sex in some respects.'

'Really?' Larissa and Glivenko exchanged glances, and for the first time Bella wondered whether they were together.

The waiter arrived with the champagne and recharged the glasses. The waiter gone, Larissa lit another cigarette before proposing a toast.

'To your precious love affair,' she growled. 'Long may it last.'

*

Now, at God knows what hour, Bella heard Larissa padding across towards the window. After the restaurant, she'd offered

Bella the spare bed in her apartment and Bella had been only too pleased to say yes. The swish of the heavy drapes parting at the window made the kitten jump and the room was suddenly bathed in a thin yellowish light. Bella got up on one elbow, aware of Larissa peering down at the street. Already she'd found a cigarette and something had caught her attention. She moved slowly back, hugging the shadows, fastening the robe she'd rescued from the back of a chair, the cigarette hanging from the corner of her mouth.

'You look like a movie star. Maybe Joan Fontaine.' Bella yawned, rubbing her eyes, trying to still the beginnings of a hangover. 'Is there something wrong out there?'

Larissa shook her head. She wanted to know about Joan Fontaine.

'She's wonderful, played against Laurence Olivier in a movie called *Rebecca*. They fixed a screening for Stalin. I managed to wangle an invitation to talk him through the plot.' Bella laughed. 'Wonderful bone structure. Great presence.'

'Stalin?'

'Joan Fontaine. You should take a compliment.' She frowned, watching the glow of the cigarette in the half-darkness. 'There *is* someone down there.'

Larissa shook her head. Moments later she'd settled on the end of Bella's bed.

'What have you done to upset them?' she asked. 'Be honest.'

'Upset who?'

'Our friends from the Big House. They always drive Emkas. These people aren't subtle.'

'That's because they want to be seen. It's part of the game.'

'I know. This town will never be Moscow, thank God, but don't blame the Big House for trying. They've squeezed this place half to death, and what's left will go to the Germans.' Larissa took a long pull at the cigarette, her head back, her eyes closed. 'You haven't answered my question, by the way. Everything happens for a reason. Even here.'

Bella realised she'd made the wrong assumptions at the Big House. Glivenko, bless him, was a fantasist. There was no such thing as an NKVD man with a conscience, or even a sense of humour. They all came from the same egg: single-minded, pitiless, dead-eyed, hatched to serve no one but their current masters.

'Well?' Larissa was still waiting for an answer.

'I've upset some people in Moscow.'

'At the Big House?'

'Probably beyond, probably higher. If I sound grand, I don't mean to. The world is always more complicated than you think. My mistake was taking belief at face value. Commitment is a fine thing, and so is faith in the outcome, but never confuse it with real life. First, they grind you to dust. Then they blow you away. Does any of that sound familiar?'

Larissa smiled. Then she began to pick at a loose thread in the eiderdown.

'You like Ilya?' she asked.

'That would be my question.'

'You think he's a good man?'

'Yes.'

'You're right. And you know something else? There are good men everywhere. Here. Odessa. Even Moscow. Do they count? Does anyone ever listen to them? Yes, of course they do. At the beginning, their voices matter. Without them nothing happens. But afterwards it's different. Afterwards, the only thing that matters is power. Life is a theatre, and we all need to pay more attention to the plot. Go to sleep for half an act, maybe even a key scene, and the story's suddenly beyond you. You can't make sense of it. First you feel helpless, then you want to go home, but you know that's impossible because there are rules here, an etiquette, ways you do and don't behave, and anyway it's hopeless because they've locked all the doors. There are two men outside in their Emkas. If we're very lucky, it's just a warning. Tomorrow we'll get you out of here and find a place they'll never think of looking. And after that, you can start practising your German.'

Bella was impressed. She'd put this woman in danger and in response she'd been gracious, and eloquent, and measured, and wise. She was right about the theatre. Lenin had written the first act, to tumultuous applause, but now there was another hand at work in the script, darker, merciless, unforgiving. She remembered a picture she'd seen in Moscow, the body of Lenin en route to his funeral. There was snow on the ground in Moscow, and her eye had been drawn to the small, squat, swarthy figure in the leather boots with the felt tops, loping along behind. The path to tyranny, she thought, is paved with good intentions. You're never aware of the wolf until it's far too late.

'One question,' Bella was nursing the kitten again. 'Do you mind?'

'Not at all. With luck, we might have the rest of the night to ourselves.'

'Are you and Ilya... you know...?'

'Together?'

'Yes.'

Waiting for an answer, Bella was aware of Larissa's eyes on her. Finally, she pinched the end of the cigarette and let it fall to the floor. Then she unbelted her robe until it hung open. Bella could only guess at her age, but she had the body of a woman in her twenties, flat belly, firm breasts. She reached for Bella, cupping her face. When they kissed, Bella could taste the harshness of the tobacco Stalin loved.

'It's a big bed,' Larissa nodded down at the kitten. 'I'm sure there's room for all three of us.'

*

She left before dawn, with a whispered promise to be back within an hour or so. Bella was on no account to answer the door or show herself at any window. There had to be a phone in the apartment because Bella heard the low murmur of Larissa's voice before the tell-tale click when she put the receiver down. Then came a creak as she opened the front door and pulled it shut behind her. Bella remembered the endless flights of steps from last night. Fifth floor, she thought. At least.

She lay still for a moment, Larissa's scent still on the pillow. She'd never had sex with a woman before but she'd occasionally thought about it, tempted by sheer curiosity, and now she was warmed by how natural it had felt. There was a rough urgency about Larissa's lovemaking, which sat oddly with how calm and attentive she'd been in the restaurant, but Bella had been happy to follow her cues, and if the price of survival was having your saviour sitting on your face, then so be it.

After a while, with the faintest twinge of guilt, Bella wrapped herself in Larissa's bed robe and tried to find the kitten. Half a lifetime living with cats took her to the most unlikely hiding places – the lined insides of a pair of discarded boots, a tiny cardboard box that had once contained bath salts, a barely open bottom drawer – but Mitya had disappeared. There were four other rooms in the apartment, including a handsome lounge complete with a grand piano, and she searched them methodically one by one, calling Mitya's name, pausing only at the front door. It was made of steel. Two eye holes offered nothing but the darkness of the stairwell but there were bolts top and bottom and she slid them both across.

With the kitten still missing, she returned to the bedroom, hugging the wall, moving very slowly, one tiny step at a time. Ignoring Larissa's instructions, she risked a peep down at the street. A metal grille masked the window of a jewellery shop across the road, and a uniformed guard was smoking a cigarette outside what looked like a hotel, but, to her relief, she could see no car. A prosperous little area, she thought. Doubtless a tribute to her new lover's standing in the city.

Larissa was back within the hour. Wide awake, Bella caught the footsteps on the stairs, hoping to God the Emka hadn't returned. Then came the turn of the key in each of the two locks, and the softest knock when Larissa realised the door was bolted. Still wearing the dressing gown, Bella opened the door. Larissa stepped inside and kissed her.

'You smell of me,' she said.

'You approve?'

'I do.' The nod came with a rare smile. 'You told me that was your first time. I'm not sure I believe you. Come.'

She led the way to the bathroom and closed the door behind them before switching on the light. Two faces appeared in the brightness of the mirror over the spotless sink. There was a moment of silence as they studied each other, then Larissa propped the bag on the edge of the bath and unpacked it.

'I had to guess,' she said. 'But it won't really matter.'

'Guess what?'

'Your height. Your build.'

'You had no clues? Did I imagine all that?'

'Bitch,' the laughter was full-throated. 'Here. Take that off. Let's see what we can do for you.'

The clothes were old, unwashed, and belonged to someone a good deal fatter than Bella. A pair of heavy woollen work trousers. A stained singlet that would have looked better on a man. A rough serge jacket, olive-green, with two buttons missing and a collar that felt greasy to the touch. Larissa helped Bella put the garments on and then stood back to take a look.

'Perfect,' she said. 'All you need now is a job digging the bloody roads up.'

'Where does this stuff come from?' Bella could smell boiled cabbage and the reek of old cooking oil.

'It doesn't matter. You'll meet her soon enough. Take them off again.'

'Why?'

'Just do it, *chérie*. This is for your good, not mine.'

'*Chérie?* You speak French as well?'

'*Bien sur. Vas-y.*' Of course. Just do it.

Bella shrugged and began to undress. By the time she was naked again, Larissa had produced a comb, a pair of scissors and a cut-throat razor from the bathroom cabinet. The implications were all too clear but when Bella began to protest, insisting she could wind her hair inside a hat, Larissa put a finger to her lips.

'You're in the wild, *chérie*. You have to be careful. You have to hide.'

Bent over the edge of the bath, Bella heard the snip-snip of the scissors as long hanks of blonde hair began to fall onto the pitted enamel. The sight distressed her, and she closed her eyes. Then Larissa filled the sink and moments later Bella felt the warmth of her hands as she soaped her scalp. She was deft with the razor, long, confident strokes that carved through the remaining stubble. When she was finished, she wiped the blade clean and invited Bella to inspect her handiwork.

Larissa's blade skills weren't quite as perfect as Bella had hoped. When she moved the bareness of her head in the mirror, blood was seeping from tiny knicks in her scalp. Larissa mumbled something in Russian that might have been an apology and turned her gently round.

'Bend towards me,' she said.

Bella gazed at her, and then shrugged. For whatever reason, she seemed to have stepped into a horror film. She did Larissa's bidding and bent her head. For a moment nothing happened, then she felt the lightest pressure on her poor shaven head, first here, then there, before Larissa announced that her work was done.

Bella lifted her head again. Larissa's face was inches away, her lips bloodied.

'Kiss me,' she said.

7

SATURDAY 13 SEPTEMBER 1941

Moncrieff was back at the Registry later than he'd planned. Woodfield, the Archivist, was already at his desk, as wrecked as ever, and Moncrieff wondered whether he'd spent the night there. He gazed at Moncrieff with a slightly quizzical air.

'You survived The Spinney?'

'I did. Just.'

'Beethoven?'

'Yes.'

'That César fella?'

'Franck. Yes.'

'Enough to drink?'

'They were more than generous. I knew I'd regret the third bottle.'

Moncrieff had spent the night in the bosom of Philby's family. His wife, Aileen, had conjured a wonderful stew from the remains of a rabbit, the baby had kicked its plump little legs at the sight of the tall stranger beside her cot, and Philby himself had been the perfect host. Aileen, slight, pale and tone-deaf when it came to music, had retired early pleading the beginnings of a headache, leaving Moncrieff and Philby to open another bottle. To Moncrieff's relief, there'd been no mention of Souk, or even

Bella. Instead, they'd compared notes about pre-war Europe, Philby easing up and down from his armchair to attend to the gramophone between movements of Beethoven symphonies.

Germany, they'd both agreed, was the place to have been in the tumultuous days after Hitler's rise to the Chancellorship. Moncrieff had spent a year in Germany as part of his Edinburgh degree course, but he'd seen very little of Berlin. Philby, on the other hand, had been present on a balcony in the Potsdamer Strasse in 1933, watching a Communist from a neighbouring window unfurl a roll of toilet paper over the heads of the marching stormtroopers below.

'The Nazis murdered socialism,' Philby – glass in hand – was swaying along to Beethoven. 'Hitler wanted to make the Reich safe for all those fucking capitalists. *Für das Volk?* For the people? You can sell anything if the lie is big enough.'

Aside from Germany, Philby had also spent time in Vienna, the Balkans, and then Spain. After they'd broached the third bottle, he'd mentioned a woman called Litzi, who might have been Austrian. In any event she seemed to stand in the way of his plans to make an honest woman of Aileen upstairs, so Litzi may have been his wife, as well. Either way, Moncrieff had tucked the name away for later. Ursula Barton, he'd thought. She's bound to know.

Now, still in Woodfield's office, Moncrieff asked for the Krivitsky files. Woodfield fetched them from a safe in the corner.

'You started them yesterday afternoon?'

'I did.'

'And?'

'Fascinating.'

'Anything in particular strike you?'

'How he came to grief. I started at the back and began to work forward. Shot to death in a Washington hotel? Gun left beside his body? A message for all those other defectors? He probably thought he was home safe. How wrong can a man be?'

'Exactly,' Woodfield gazed up at him. 'Stalin never takes prisoners. Maybe we should all remember that.'

Indeed, Moncrieff thought. He picked up the files and made his way back to Cubicle Four. Here he'd spent most of yesterday afternoon reading and rereading Bella's file, disappointed at how little it told him. Born in Scotland. Daughter of Guards officer who died at Mons and whom she barely remembered. Grew up in what the file termed 'comfortable circumstances', thanks to her stepfather, a businessman called Oliver Sanderson who'd made his fortune in Malaya. Won a place at Oxford. Emerged fluent in German and Italian. Dallied for a while with a series of inconsequential jobs after graduation, and then applied for a post in the Foreign Office.

The latter sounded a rather formal process but thanks to conversations in Berlin, once they were sleeping together, Moncrieff knew different. With her fluent German, her arresting looks, and most of all her connections, she'd bluffed her way into the diplomatic service. Within weeks, the result of a quiet word in the right ear, Bella had found herself assigned to Berlin as a Support Officer, responsible for liaison with the German press. This gave her access to an endless round of diplomatic receptions, with all the associated gossip, and by every account she was a success. Neither her stepfather, nor anyone in the Embassy, and least of all Moncrieff himself, had the slightest suspicion that all the time she'd been feeding anything she could get her hands on to Moscow.

These acts of treason MI6 had belatedly traced to a passionate affair she'd conducted during her last year at university. Moncrieff knew about this, too, because Bella had mentioned it in Berlin, but he'd only realised its full significance once she'd fled. According to the file, her lover's name was Matthew Gore-Bainbridge. A committed Communist, he'd been reading Spanish at Oxford, and short stories he'd had published in one of the university magazines were excerpted in the file. Moncrieff had read them with some care, recognising talent when he saw it, and it came as no surprise to learn that Comrade Gore-Bainbridge had ambitions to become a presence in the left-wing press, and thus help change the world. Enlisting with one of the International Brigades had been part of that journey but, alas, a Nationalist mortar bomb had blown him apart on a rocky plateau on the edge of besieged Madrid.

Now, starting on the Krivitsky file anew, Moncrieff paused. After her years in Moscow, Bella had arranged for them to meet again in Lisbon. Moncrieff had been busy trying to tease out the tighter knots in the Hess affair, while Bella was on Politburo business she wasn't prepared to discuss. She'd felt different – tougher, more wary – but they'd rekindled the affair and he remembered with absolute clarity the afternoon they'd idly discussed the possibility of a life together.

In Berlin, before she'd defected, she'd been suggesting an elopement to Seville. In bed in a Lisbon hotel, three years later, the only possibility left was getting together and making a new life in the Soviet Union. They'd both known it was a fantasy, dismissed with some reluctance, but what remained in Moncrieff's memory was the way that conversation had ended. Philby was behind an MI6 desk in Madrid. Moncrieff had recently bumped into him on a flight back to England, a chance encounter that turned out to be anything but. Philby, in his benign way, had warned Moncrieff off SIS territory. Later, back in Lisbon, he'd shared the encounter with Bella. 'Be careful,' she'd told him. 'Because that man is different. He was never an amateur. Ever.'

Amateur? Different? What, precisely, had she meant? At the time, without much real interest, he'd tried to press her for more details, but she'd shaken her head and changed the subject. Now, after nearly a week together at the Glebe House, he knew he had to get to the bottom of this man. Was he some kind of threat to her? To MI6? To all of them? Or was he what he claimed to be? A somewhat dishevelled patriot, gifted in all kinds of unusual ways, a linguist, an ex-journalist, a man of many worlds, pledged to King and Country?

Moncrieff opened his notebook and bent to the Krivitsky file. As Philby had warned, it was a long and complex story, badged by the NKVD man's growing realisation that no one in the apparatus of state was immune from Stalin's raging paranoia. Trusted colleagues working undercover across Europe, sincere Communists, pledged to the cause, were suddenly recalled to Moscow and accused of being part of a giant counter-revolutionary conspiracy. Under torture, to spare themselves yet more agony, they confessed their sins and were duly shot. But in Krivitsky's view, the real counter-revolution was headed by Stalin himself. He'd doused the last embers of real Bolshevism and replaced it with the sour reek of tyranny. Word of this apostasy had somehow got back to Moscow and Krivitsky, fearing the worst, had fled to the West.

At this point, after hours of putting together the jigsaw that was Walter Krivitsky, Moncrieff knew that the essence of the man probably lay in his interviews with Jane Archer. Ursula Barton had already given him the headlines – how the Soviets spent years and years carefully nurturing bright young prospects already won over to Communism – but what she hadn't mentioned were the specific leads that Krivitsky, for an undisclosed sum of money, was only too happy to share. These were top level agents-in-place, busy being spies.

The first was 'a Scotsman of good family, educated at Eton and Oxford'. He was, according to Krivitsky, 'an idealist who works in the Foreign Office and is happy to work for us without payment'. His minders who ran him in London were Theodore Maly and Arnold Deutsch, both of whom had recently returned to Moscow.

Moncrieff sat back a moment, bewildered. These interviews had taken place barely a year ago. While he was certain that a number of diplomats owed their education to Eton and Oxford, surely a lead like this would have triggered, at the very least, a major investigation? An enquiry like that would have come at once to the ears of MI5, charged with keeping the nation safe, yet he could remember no mention of the issue. Why not? What had kept this idealistic young diplomat unmolested?

Turning the page, his eye fell on the next paragraph. Jane Archer had pressed the ex-NKVD man for more leads. One of them, unnamed, was described by Krivitsky as 'a young English aristocrat who'd worked as a journalist during the Spanish Civil War'. He, too, had been run by Theodore Maly, and had been assigned by his newspaper to the Nationalist side. Moscow, scenting the possibility of a major blow against the rebels, had ordered him to assassinate General Franco but evidently the journalist had declined. He was there to report, in detail, the workings of Franco's army. Killing the man himself was beyond him.

Moncrieff sat back a moment, staring at the slightly smudged lines of type. Philby had been in Spain. Philby had been working as a journalist. Through his father, a noted Arabist and explorer, he may or may not have had aristocratic connections, and Moncrieff didn't know which of the warring armies he'd been assigned to, but his years in counter-intelligence had taught him never to discount coincidence. Circumstantial evidence was all too easy to dismiss. And here might be the perfect example.

Did Ursula Barton know about any of this? And, if so, had she ever asked herself why Jane Archer had been sacked?

Moncrieff reached for his notepad and uncapped his pen, and as he did so he became aware of a presence behind him. The stench of alcohol told him it was Woodfield. He was right. The keeper of the files was staring down at the open Krivitsky file. Then his gaze drifted to Moncrieff's notepad. Yesterday, in this same cubicle, Moncrieff had made a note in bold capital letters of Bella's first love. Matthew Gore-Bainbridge. Underlined three times.

'Damn clever,' Woodfield was nodding in approval. 'Has to be, doesn't it?'

'Has to be what?'

'Walter's little mole. Thank God he didn't knock Franco off.'

'You think he was the one?'

'I do, yes, stands to reason. Well bred, a name like that. Clever, too. And a journalist in the making. Where better to make your name? With half the bloody world watching? Thank

72

God the chap got himself killed. Saved us all a lot of trouble.'
He leant a little closer and tapped his watch. 'Don't forget the
cricket this afternoon. I'm keeping score, by the way. We draw
stumps here in half an hour.'

*

The cricket pitch, by happy accident, was a couple of minutes'
stroll away. Moncrieff decided he'd gleaned more than enough
from the Krivitsky files and suggested a brief detour en route
to a pub of Woodfield's choice. As one colleague to another,
he wanted to say a modest thank-you.

Woodfield jumped at the invitation. The pub was called the
King Harry, and the moment Woodfield walked in, a pint of
bitter and a pink gin appeared on the bar.

'And you, sir?'

'Same, please,' Moncrieff assumed the beer had been for
him, 'without the gin.'

They settled in a corner. When Moncrieff suggested a snack,
perhaps a sandwich, Woodfield shook his head.

'Waste of alcohol,' he grunted. 'Cheers. Down the hatch.'

Half the beer had gone in seconds. Moncrieff pressed him
lightly about life in the Indian police.

'Kim says you had a grand time.'

'Kim's right about that. He was born there so he should know
the place, but God knows how he ever coped with the climate.
The heat gets you down in the end. Proper rain should cool
you off. Not there, my friend, even in the bloody monsoon.'

'And now?'

'Me, you mean?'

'Yes.'

'Now's perfect. A job that matters. Late nights when there's a flap on. Lovely people, too, and so bloody *young*. I've one or two chums in your outfit. They tell me it's too bloody *big*, too bloody *impersonal*, takes itself too bloody *seriously*. Does any of that ring a bell?'

'I'm afraid I'm the wrong person to ask,' Moncrieff took a sip of his beer. 'Most of our people work up in Blenheim Palace. They used to be in Wormwood Scrubs, so they're not making a fuss. Big? You're right. Too big? God only knows. Go back a couple of years and we were dealing with floods of refugees, Free French sailors, Polish airmen, sundry riff-raff. You need to man the parapets, sort out the wheat from the chaff, and you need staff for that, in serious numbers. Your lot? I'm guessing it's very different.'

'You're right, it is. And you know the real trick? Leadership. It's one thing recruiting a bunch of bright young kids, quite another to get the best out of them. For that, says me, you need someone special, someone who can whip them into shape without them even noticing. With my background, I'd be hopeless. The last thing you need in an operation like Five is a policeman. We coppers stick by the rules. Everyone toes the line. Last thing you need.'

'Five? You mean *Section* Five?'

'Of course. You've been up there in that office of theirs, I know you have. It's wonderful, what he's done, what he manages to get out of them. Give a man a proper education, ideas of his own, and you've got a problem. But for some reason, God knows how, that never happens. Those boys up in Five love him, absolutely adore him.'

'Him?'

'Kim,' he drained his pint and reached for the pink gin. 'MI6's favourite son.'

Minutes later, they were heading for the cricket pitch. Through a line of trees, Moncrieff could see that many of the players were already on the pitch, tossing the ball to each other. They wore an assortment of kit including, just occasionally, proper whites. Philby, deep in conversation with one of the umpires, wore grass-stained flannel trousers and an old shirt, open at the neck, that he probably saved for gardening. It was warm now, barely a cloud in the sky, perfect for the afternoon to come.

'Don't you feel out on a limb here?' Moncrieff asked Woodfield. 'With everyone else up in Broadway?'

'Not at all. Like I just said, *corps d'esprit* is everything. We're masters of our own little patch and that's the way we like it. If we really need to talk to Broadway, we can. That's what telephones are for.'

'But there must be meetings, surely? Organisations die without them.'

'Of course there are,' Woodfield was still watching Philby. 'That's why he goes up there twice a week, poor bugger.'

*

Philby, last night, had promised to sort out something to wear for Moncrieff. In the draughty hut that served as a pavilion, he found an assortment of garments that properly belonged in a jumble sale. Nothing fitted. Everything was too small. Eventually, after struggling to climb into a pair of Army-issue trousers, he re-emerged into the sunshine to find Philby consulting a page torn from a secretarial notepad.

'Nothing serious,' he said. 'This is just a pick-up game. Think opera. Enjoy the overture and the rest happens in the pub.'

Moncrieff needed to establish that cricket wasn't his game. Apologies in advance, he said. Expect nothing and you won't be disappointed.

'Absolutely no problem, Tam. We've lost the toss. The enemy have put themselves into bat.' He glanced down at his notes. 'I've got you down at long leg. Enjoy the sunshine.'

The game began. Long leg took Moncrieff down towards the boundary, marked by a privet hedge. Staring up towards the wicket, he had the sun in his eyes. The opening bowler he recognised from the Section Five office. He hurled the ball down the wicket with immense conviction, much to Philby's delight, but failed to make any impact. From time to time, one or other of the batsmen would glance a delivery towards long leg, and Moncrieff would do his best to return it, but it was obvious from the start that Section Five were hopelessly outclassed.

Then Philby, exercising the captain's prerogative, called for the ball and beckoned the fielders closer to the wicket. His pace was much slower, more artful, and as over followed over, Moncrieff began to pay more attention. The sun in his eyes was still a problem but, as Philby sauntered up, he became fascinated by his delivery. He bowled front-on, with a round arm, head and chin raised high as if he was peering over some obstacle, yet his face wore a distant air of meditation, even as – with a flick of his wrist – he released the ball.

The batsmen facing him were equally bemused. One tried to sweep him to leg and failed. The other took a step forward, determined to drive the delivery over the distant hedge, but he, too, was caught by the vicious spin on the ball. Then, in

Philby's third over, came the moment when he dropped the ball a fraction wide and the batsman seized his opportunity, half turned at the crease, and belted it high towards the boundary.

Moncrieff knew the ball was coming his way. The law of physics was incontestable. But in the blinding glare of the sun, he could see nothing. He tried to shade his eyes, aware that the rest of the team were watching him. Then the ball landed with a dull thud just inches away, and he looked up to see the batsmen completing another run.

Embarrassment, Moncrieff knew, was too small a word. He picked up the ball, returned it to the wicketkeeper, and then held his hands wide. *Mea culpa*. My fault.

*

A couple of hours later, the wicketkeeper bought him a pint. They were back in the King Harry, thoroughly beaten and dying of thirst.

'Here's to chaos,' he said. 'Grand effort.'

'You're too kind.'

'Ivor Maskelyne,' the wicketkeeper thrust out a hand. 'I'm the standing reserve. When they call on me you know times are hard.'

Moncrieff recognised the name at once. Jasper Maskelyne was a stage magician who specialised in creating illusions. His talents had been snapped up by General Wavell, fighting Rommel in North Africa, and it was whispered in certain quarters that the magician had plans to make Alexandria disappear.

'The great Jasper? Any relation?'

'Sadly not. We've always kidded ourselves that he might be a distant cousin, but I suspect that's an illusion, too.'

Moncrieff smiled. Maskelyne was a big man, as untidy as everyone else. His face had reddened in the sun and his broken glasses were secured with a grubby twist of white medical tape.

'You work here?' Moncrieff asked. 'Section Five?'

'Oxford, I'm afraid. Balliol. Our mad world still has room for a degree in Classics and I'm happy to oblige.' He lifted his glass. 'Here's to Byzantine literature. Long may it last. Christ, look who's here.'

Moncrieff glanced round to catch a figure in a striped blazer and flannels who'd just stepped into the pub. He had his arms round Philby and was whispering in his ear while he took a good look at everyone else. A bottle of champagne, cork still intact, dangled from one hand and the moment his eyes settled on Moncrieff he disengaged himself and staggered across.

'Moncrieff? Can this be true? Do my eyes deceive me? My bro pays daily tribute to your loveliness, but nothing can prepare a man for this. By God, you're handsome. Dare I touch?'

Like everyone else at St James's Street, Moncrieff knew about Guy Burgess. His brother, Nigel, worked for MI5, monitoring the activities of the UK Communist Party.

'You're drunk.' It was Maskelyne. 'Again.'

'Christ, I hope so,' Burgess was still gazing in mock-wonderment at Moncrieff. 'Dear Kim tells me you're staying the night. Me too. You'll know about the domestic arrangements. Only one spare bed, alas, but I used to be a sailor so bunking up comes naturally. Does a needy man get a goodnight kiss? Just one? I do hope so.'

Moncrieff studied him a moment. Wavy black hair. Full lips. Stained teeth. Appalling breath. Wet eyes.

'Maybe I'm spoken for,' Moncrieff said. 'We'll have to see.'

Philby had joined the group, steering the four of them towards a spare table. Burgess gave him the bottle of champagne, accompanied by an extravagant wink.

'Kim says you cut a dashing figure out there...' he nodded towards the door, '... on the field of battle. Is this true? Is there yet more to your lovely self?'

Moncrieff was no stranger to difficult situations but repartee this extravagant was something new.

'Your reputation goes before you, Guy. I'm glad to say I'm not disappointed. That brother of yours is too generous. I'll have him shot tomorrow morning. Leave it to me. I'll see it happens.'

Burgess paused for a moment, his mouth half open. Philby, still clutching the bottle, had a smile on his lips. Moncrieff hadn't finished.

'Nigel tells me you were with Kim in Spain? True?'

'False. My brother lies. Shoot him twice.' He beckoned Moncrieff closer. 'You know about Kim in Spain? The fucking Ivans blew him up and nearly killed him.' He turned to Philby. 'Teruel, Kim? Have I got that right? You and a bunch of other scribblers? Sitting in some fucking car or other, minding your own business?'

'The rest died,' Philby nodded. 'Which I imagine made me lucky.'

'There,' Burgess's hand lay on Moncrieff's arm. 'From the horse's mouth. Franco even gave him a medal, fool's gold of course but no thanks to the fucking comrades.' In the absence of a drink of his own, he seized Moncrieff's glass and proposed a toast. 'Death to the comrades. May Stalin die in hell. Poor Kim. I bet it frightened you, didn't it? A big bang like that?'

Philby, looking at Moncrieff, murmured something that sounded like an apology. Then he got to his feet and clapped his hands for quiet. Laughter and conversation died. Heads turned at the bar.

'As your captain...' he began, '... it once again falls to me to award the Victor Ludorum. We have, of course, been soundly beaten but no matter. In victory, grace. In defeat, more beer.' There was a roar of applause, stilled by Philby. 'And so it gives me the greatest pleasure to award – yes – this fine bottle of Moët, courtesy of my very good friend here. A few words, Guy? We'd be grateful.'

Burgess got unsteadily to his feet, gripping the back of the chair, half turning to the rest of the bar. Then he reached for the bottle and his gaze settled once again on Moncrieff.

'This, dearest Tam, is for services to Isaac Newton. I'm told that non-catch of yours was a sitter, but my friends here hold no grudges. Gravity, alas, always wins in the end, and in any case the taking part is the thing. So, three cheers for the sainted Isaac. Hip hip...'

The bar erupted. There were shouts of bravo. Philby was still on his feet as Burgess kissed the bottle and handed it to Moncrieff. Moncrieff raised it high and took a bow. More applause, even wilder. Then Moncrieff heard a voice in his ear.

'You're welcome any time, Tam.' It was Philby. 'Absolutely our pleasure.'

*

Maskelyne drove Moncrieff back to London. The two men shared the front of the Alvis, as the darkness stole in from the east. The party in the King Harry was still in full swing when they left but Maskelyne had a late dinner appointment in Kensington and Moncrieff was grateful for the offer of a lift.

'You've been with these people long?' he asked.

'Since the outbreak of war. I'm never quite sure what I bring to the table, but they seem to appreciate another pair of eyes from time to time.'

Moncrieff nodded. From his perch in MI5, he'd been aware of the spillage from Oxbridge high tables, of senior academics who'd made their way into the world of intelligence gathering.

'So what did you make of them?'

'Them?' Maskelyne's eyes didn't leave the road. 'Or all of you? Plural?'

'Them. MI6.'

'I was first astonished, then – to be frank – incredulous. Incredulity, believe me, is worse.'

'May I ask why?'

'It's difficult to explain. You're there in the heart of the machine, in the belly of the beast, and you look round, and you have a conversation or two, and you meet more chaps, and shake hands, and attend meetings, and do more than your share of listening, and all the time you've got the feeling that all this fatuity, this senseless blather, this posturing, this endless chasing of ghosts, is some clever camouflage for the real thing.'

'An illusion?'

'Precisely. I used to tell myself that out there somewhere, God knows where, there was a proper organisation, people of quality, folk who knew what they were doing, a *real* secret service. But then comes the moment when you have to accept that this isn't true, that what you're seeing and hearing is indeed the real thing, and at that point you're left with only one conclusion.'

'Which is?'

'That we're fucked. My only hope, and it's a slim one, is that the enemy is even more deranged. But that, I'm afraid, might be whistling in the dark.' He slowed to overtake an old man wobbling along on a bicycle, and then allowed himself a soft chuckle. 'You know what I really think?'

'Tell me.'

'The whole thing, from where I sit, is a waste of time and money. Just now, we have very little of either. If I was in the chair, I'd wrap the whole thing up. A subscription to a decent newspaper, just one, would give you all the intelligence you'd ever need.' He shot Moncrieff a look. 'Does that sound unduly treasonable?'

'Not at all. You're talking about MI6? Broadway?'

'I am. That's my bailiwick. I speak as I find.'

'No qualifications? Nothing in mitigation?'

'Good question.' Maskelyne was smiling now while he thought about it. Then he laughed. 'That catch you fluffed this afternoon. I was watching Philby like a hawk. That's what us wicketkeepers do.'

'And?'

'His bowling had been OK, more than OK, straight down the middle, very disciplined.'

'And then?'

'And then he lobbed down a loose one, plum on the leg side, an absolute gift. Whatever happened, it was coming to you in the outfield. The batsman couldn't miss.'

'You mean he set me up?'

'Of course he did. The sun was in your eyes. That's why he put you there. He *knew* you'd fuck it up. He was absolutely certain he could make a fool of you. Clever...' he nodded, '... not Broadway's style at all.'

8

SUNDAY 14 SEPTEMBER 1941

Larissa shook her gently awake before dawn. They had to leave, she said, before the city began to stir. The clothes lay beside the bed, carefully folded, a womanly touch that made Bella smile.

'Where are we going?'

'Another place. Safer. Somewhere to wait.'

'And then what?'

'Someone else will collect you there.'

'Who?'

'Put the clothes on,' Larissa nodded at the floor. 'Please.'

Bella shrugged. She knew she had no choice. Fully dressed, she did her best to avoid the full-length mirror in the bedroom. Once, at Oxford, she'd briefly dallied with a career on the stage, but she'd never auditioned to be a tramp.

'Wonderful,' Larissa was back with a camera. 'You look like a man. Put the coat on.'

'Now?'

'Yes.'

Bella did what she was told. Larissa gave her a cap, grey wool, leather-rimmed, stained and greasy to the touch.

'You want me to wear this?'

'Yes.'

Larissa took a step back, cocked her head this way and that, then stepped forward and adjusted the cap until it sat lower over Bella's eyes. Only then did she start taking more pictures, adjusting the exposure for the dimness of the light, making sure that the background was as neutral as possible.

'These are for your ID card,' she said. 'We have people who can supply them. Fakes but good fakes.'

'How long am I staying here?'

'That depends on the Germans. But they'll be issuing ID cards, too, and they'll need to see your old one.'

'I'm Ukrainian forever?'

'That might be wise.' Larissa smiled. 'Now take the cap off.'

'Why?'

'I want one last shot,' she stepped forward, and kissed Bella softly on the lips. 'For me.'

*

They left the apartment shortly afterwards. Larissa's car was parked a short walk from the apartment block, away from the street lights. At this time in the morning, the traffic was thin and Larissa drove fast, constantly checking the single wing mirror, shaking her head at a brief glimpse of soldiers throwing up barricades at key intersections. Finally, they rattled into a much poorer area of the city, no trees, yawning potholes in the bare earth. The houses were terraced, visibly neglected, drifts of rubbish everywhere. It had been raining overnight and Larissa hurried Bella around the puddles, making for a door that already appeared to be open.

'This is the place?'

'Yes.'

'Who owns it?'

'Call her Mama. She's very old. Sweet, but old.'

A spectral figure was waiting in the darkness of the narrow hall, impossibly thin, a collar of white lace faintly visible at the neck of her black dress. She reached for Bella's hand, thin fingers, no weight at all, and led her deeper into the house.

Bella recognised the smell of the place from the clothes she'd been given. The old lady paused at an open door at the end of the hall. A single candle propped in a saucer shed an uncertain light over the space that evidently served as her home. The space formed part of a bigger room and Bella could hear snoring beyond the fall of sheets that gave her a little privacy.

'You're OK?' It was Larissa.

'I'm fine.'

'Later, yes?'

'Whatever you say.'

When Larissa had gone, the old woman made Bella sit on the sagging sofa that served as a bed and insisted she eat. Bella picked at the bowl of cold *kasha* in the light of the single candle, aware of the old woman beside her: the sprout of grey whiskers from her chin, the gnarled fingers plaiting and re-plaiting, the gummy smile of contentment as the *kasha* went down. When Bella returned the bowl, the old woman inspected the smear of buckwheat porridge and disappeared into the shadows, quick bird-like movements that seemed to belie her age. She returned with a cup of water and a sprinkle of tea leaves. She began to warm the cup over the candle flame, never taking her eyes off Bella.

Bella was looking at a nest of icons on a nearby shelf. Above them, taped to the wall, was a sepia photograph of a young man in his twenties. The smile he'd tried to summon for the camera was far from convincing. He looked nervous, overwrought, and the flatness of his features told Bella he might have come from further east.

'Your son?' Bella asked in Russian.

'*Da.*' Yes.

'His name?'

'*Da.*'

'What do you call him?'

'*Da.*'

'You speak Russian?'

'*Da.*'

The old woman dipped a bony finger into the cup and scowled. Then she gave it to Bella and glanced up at the picture before linking her thin arms and rocking them like a cradle.

'*Da,*' she said again.

Bella sipped at the lukewarm water, realising that conversation was pointless. She was grateful for the safety of this anonymous slum, and she'd ceased to worry about what might happen next because events were so entirely beyond her control, but she suspected the old woman was crazy. Now she was nodding at the sofa, her hands prayerful, her head cocked against them. You must rest, she was saying. Lie down. Bella emptied the cup, slipped off her boots and did her best to get comfortable. Her head was at a strange angle, and her legs dangled over the other end of the sofa, but she could still hear snoring from beyond the blankets and within seconds she, too, was asleep.

She awoke hours later, feeling something wet between her toes. She struggled up onto one elbow. In the thin grey wash of dawn through the single window, she could see the old woman. She was on her knees at the end of the sofa, a bowl of water on the floor beside her, and she was soaping Bella's feet, shaking her head and muttering to herself in a language Bella didn't recognise. From time to time, she'd look up at the icons on the shelf, crossing herself with a dripping hand, and Bella briefly wondered whether she'd been assigned a special role in these troubled times, the stranger with no name, the mysterious saviour with the shaven scalp come to ward off the impending apocalypse, the bringer of grace and the scourge of the approaching Germans. Then she heard footsteps outside in the hall, and a grunt as someone pushed at the door, and she looked up to find herself looking at the face taped to the wall.

In the flesh, he was thinner than she'd imagined, almost spectral. His hair was long, tied into a ponytail with a scarlet bootlace, and a silver ring dangled from the lobe of one ear. In late-summer, his face was pale, and since the photo had been taken he'd grown the beginnings of a beard. The sight of the old woman on her knees brought a smile to his face.

'Mama,' he said. Then he looked at Bella. 'I'd like to say sorry,' his English was perfect, barely accented. 'On Larissa's behalf.'

'For what?'

'For what she did to you,' he touched his own head. 'She's a fine journalist. As a barber, she'd starve.'

'That bad?'

'Worse. The Russians will cross the road to avoid you. Maybe that was her plan.'

'Shit.'

'Exactly.'

Bella was gazing up at him. In the photograph he'd looked nervous, ill at ease. Now, he was anything but. 'And this lady is your mother?' she asked. The old woman was still washing Bella's feet, seemingly oblivious to the presence at the door.

'No. I call her Mama because that's what she wants. She's younger than she looks, and a little crazy.'

'She's been kind. Tell her I'm grateful. Will you do that?'

'No need. She lives in a world of her own. Here, Mama—' He had a package wrapped in stained newspaper tucked under his arm. The old woman at last looked up. She seized the package and unwrapped it. Inside were three fish, none of them longer than a finger. 'A friend of mine sleeps down by the river when it gets hot.'

'They smell bad.' Bella had turned her head away.

'Sure. He found them washed up. You get a present, too. My name's Ponomorenko, by the way. You can call me Yuri.'

'You don't like Ponomorenko?'

'I prefer Yuri.' He was wearing a heavy canvas jacket. From one of the pockets he produced a tiny bundle of fur that Bella recognised at once.

'Mitya,' she reached out.

'Mitya? Lovely. That's what his friends called Shostakovich. Larissa found her this morning. Keep her away from dogs, Mama. Maybe people, too. Otherwise she'll get eaten.'

'She's staying here?'

'Yes.'

The kitten had caught the scent of the fish. She was in the old woman's lap, eager for the decaying flesh. Yuri stepped across and hooked her out, scolding her in Russian. Beautiful hands, Bella thought. Long fingers. Clean nails.

One of the hanging sheets stirred and another cat appeared, fully grown. She, too, wanted the fish.

'Her name's Svet,' Yuri said. 'She's nursing kittens of her own. One more won't make any difference. Larissa's idea, not mine. Enough...' he gestured Bella to her feet. '... we must go. An hour on foot. Maybe longer.'

*

Much longer. Once again, Bella found herself in an endless maze of side streets, doing her best to keep up with Yuri's long stride. Within minutes they'd left the area where the old woman lived. The houses were bigger, in better condition, and there was a shop or two where one street intersected with another. Waiting for a horse and cart to pass, Bella caught sight of herself in the window of a shop selling hardware. For a moment, she didn't recognise the tall figure hunched in the Army greatcoat, a greasy cap hiding her baldness, then she felt a presence at her elbow, Yuri turning back from the kerbside.

'You want to buy a hammer? Nails? A samovar, maybe?'

'I'm trying to walk like a man,' Bella ignored the question. 'Do I look the part? Do you think anyone's fooled?'

'You look great. You speak Russian?'

'*Da.*'

'Prove it.'

'Now? Here?'

'Yes.'

Bella shrugged. She was tired. There were consequences of getting stopped that didn't bear contemplation. But Yuri's question, the aggression in his voice, stung her, and so she launched into a description of her apartment overlooking the

Moscow River, which of her neighbours were first to finish a bottle of vodka by lunchtime, how easy it was to buy anything you liked if you could lay hands on hard Western currency.

Yuri took a step back. Amused? Yes. But impressed as well.

'Larissa was right,' he said. 'Welcome to Kyiv.'

'Right, how?'

'You knocked her over. I can't remember when that happened last.'

Knocked her over? They crossed the road and plunged down a street that led towards the river. Bella was feeling better now, buoyed by her little moment of theatre, beginning to understand the risks these people were taking on her behalf. One occupation was about to end. Another set of thieves were only days away from taking over the city. At the bottom of the street, faced with a major boulevard, they paused again. Beneath a tree a chalked symbol – a circle pierced on two sides – had survived the overnight rain. Bella stared at it a moment, then asked what it meant.

'It's the work of the nationalists,' Yuri said. 'When they can, they use paint. Ukraine for the Ukrainians. We live in hope.'

The boulevard turned out to be Khreshchatyk. Yuri confirmed that Larissa lived near there.

'A big apartment? Up at the top of the building? Where I stayed?'

'Yes.'

'And now?'

'Now you come to my place. They watch Larissa, like everyone watches Larissa. She never complains so maybe she likes it that way. You'll see her again.'

'How do you know?'

'She told me. Come.'

They hurried across the wideness of the boulevard, avoiding the traffic in both directions. This part of the city might have been anywhere in Europe, Bella thought: the big plane trees, the grand hotels, the well-stocked shopfronts, the hint of haute couture and a whiff of perfume from some of the women who stalked past. A tram clattered around the corner, two soldiers hanging out of the back, trying to get a smile from these women, and Bella instinctively turned her back, earning a stern word from Yuri.

'Don't,' he said. 'Remember what these people have survived. Be afraid, try and hide, and they'll smell it.'

They crossed the road. One of the hotels was the Continental. Three army trucks were parked outside, well-guarded, and, as they mounted the pavement, soldiers were manhandling wooden crates out of the back of the biggest truck. Bella paused a moment, staring at one of the crates. She recognised the line of stencils, the loops of rope on both ends, the tell-tale clasp and padlocks. She'd flown thousands of miles with these very same crates. They'd come from Northolt.

'Something wrong?' It was Yuri.

'No. Nothing,' she nodded at the hotel, suddenly playful. 'We're stopping for coffee?'

'No.'

Another half-hour took them into the oldest part of the city. A cobbled street wound up a hill, climbing away from a park and the river beyond. The houses looked ancient, crooked, as old as the rocks in the park below, and there were churches everywhere, onion domes glinting in sudden bursts of sunshine. At the top of the hill, without warning, Yuri ducked into an alley between two houses. Stepping carefully round curls of dog shit, Bella followed him. At the end of the alley was yet another church, much smaller, more intimate. A path led between the headstones in the graveyard. At the rear of the church, surrounded by tall yew trees, was an extension, a single storey, ugly, recently added. Yuri had produced a key. A glance left and right, and he was standing to one side, inviting Bella in.

'Welcome,' he murmured. 'Larissa again. Her idea.'

About to step inside, Bella hesitated. Away to the south, she thought she caught the rumble of yet another thunderstorm, yet a glance at the sky revealed no trace of a cloud. Yuri, watching her carefully, understood at once.

'The Germans,' he gestured round. 'Maybe two days? Maybe three?'

9

SUNDAY 14 SEPTEMBER 1941

Moncrieff knew that Ursula Barton had been manning one of the weekend desks at St James's Street. He invited her to a bite of midday lunch, and the restaurant of St Ermin's Hotel seemed richly appropriate. Barton, arriving late, was amused.

'If this is your idea of being discreet, think again. Half the people in this room are politicians and the rest are just as nosy,' she was studying the menu. 'The kidneys, please. With mashed swede.'

Moncrieff described the two days he'd spent at St Albans. When it came to conversations that might interest the queen of 'B' Section, he was spoiled for choice, but the encounter that had really stuck in his mind was the drive back to town with Maskelyne.

'Dons have minds of their own,' he said. 'Thank God for higher education.'

'You really believe that? My ex-husband went to Oxford. It made absolutely no difference. He was born obdurate and stupid and he went to great lengths to stay that way.'

'Maskelyne's different. Obdurate, yes. Stupid, never. Do you know anything about cricket? There's one player who watches everything, sees everything, knows everything. He stands behind the wicket. Big pair of gloves. Sentry at the gate. Huge responsibility.'

Moncrieff described the ball Philby had floated down on the leg side, the invitation for the batsman to belt it high in the air in Moncrieff's direction.

'I'm guessing you dropped it.'

'I missed it completely.'

'A huge embarrassment.'

'I'm afraid so.'

'Much laughter all round.'

'Indeed. But that's the point. It was a sunny day, not a cloud in sight. Philby placed the field. The right ball, and he knew I'd be catching blind. That ball wasn't just meant for me. It was for all of us.'

'Is this a plea in mitigation?'

'On the contrary, it's a tribute to how clever the bloody man is.'

'Meaning what, exactly?'

'Meaning he wanted to mark our card, send a message if you like. Be careful who you offend. Be careful in your choice of enemies. The message couldn't have been plainer, but the real art is the way he chose to deliver it. Maskelyne has a very dim view of our Broadway friends. He thinks they're a liability and he doesn't mind saying so. The one exception is Philby. Another phrase I heard is "favourite son". He's twenty-nine, Ursula, and he's on manoeuvres. One day, they'll all wake up and he'll be running the place.'

'But you just told me he's clever. So maybe he deserves to.'

Moncrieff didn't answer. Instead, he wanted to know why Barton had directed him towards the Krivitsky file.

'That's a question I might ask you.' She sat back as the waiter appeared with their order, then reached for her knife and fork and waited until he'd gone. 'Well?'

'Krivitsky believed the Soviets were running an agent in Spain. He was working as a journalist. And he was reporting from the Nationalist side. That's what he told Jane Archer. Here, upstairs at this hotel. Did you know any of this?'

'I did, yes.'

'And you're aware that Philby meets all those criteria? Every single one?'

'Yes.'

'So, did anyone from our massed ranks trouble themselves to pursue the matter? Call him in? Have a chat?'

'Not to my knowledge.'

'Which must mean no.'

'Indeed. That would be a fair assumption.'

'So why not? What stayed our hand? *Prima facie*, Krivitsky was the real thing. He really did work for Moscow. He really was NKVD. In fact, he ran most of their agents across Europe.'

'I know, Tam. I was there in The Hague where he'd pitched his tent. We all knew what he was up to. His pedigree was never in question.'

'So why didn't anyone believe him?'

'They did, Tam. Jane believed him. And said so. Not just the agent in Spain but the FO plant as well. Eton, Oxford, well-bred, good family. Krivitsky's words, verbatim.'

'And no one took it any further?' Moncrieff couldn't believe it.

'Nobody. At the time, of course, we were swamped. Some weeks it felt like half of Europe was at our door. All those people to be screened, locked up, weighed in the balance, occasionally turned around and pointed at their former masters. We were puffing uphill, Tam, and the gradient was getting steeper.'

'That's an excuse.'

'I know it is. Jane knew, too, and she was brave enough to say so.'

'Which is why she was sacked?'

Barton shrugged, and speared another slice of kidney. Moncrieff had barely touched his brawn salad.

'If you knew all this already,' he said slowly, 'why did you send me up there at all?'

'Because you wanted to see Bella's file. Any joy, incidentally?'

'Not really, but you probably knew that, too.'

'Tut-tut, Tam. I thought we were friends.'

'We were. We are. But that's not the point. What I did was very visible. Unless I broke in and burgled their bloody Registry, just helped myself, it couldn't be otherwise. They knew I was coming. They knew what I was looking for. I filled in a form. I booked time in one of their cubicles. It was all there in black and white. The names on the docket. Isobel Menzies. Walter Krivitsky.'

'And Philby? He knew?'

'Of course he did. He knows everything. We sparred, as you doubtless anticipated. We sparred that first day in Prae House, we sparred that evening when I stayed the night at his place, and we were still at it the next day. I'm an ex-bootneck. I can hold my own in any company. I can read a conversation on any level. And more to the point, I can recognise a message when I see one.'

'Like the catch you missed?'

'Absolutely. And the beasting that followed afterwards in the pub. Good fun, most of it, but there's another message, isn't there? The one you sent. Through me. We're curious, Mr Philby. Mr Krivitsky has whetted our appetite. And now we'd like to find out more. That's why Philby put the sun in my eyes. That's why he made sure the ball came my way. That was his answer. He's running rings round us. And he's telling us to back off.' Moncrieff paused for a moment, then leaned forward. 'So, there it is. Message delivered. Can I go home now? Back to Scotland? Finish my leave?'

Barton wiped her plate clean with a corner of toast and patted her mouth with a napkin. Then she looked at her watch.

'Philby goes up to Broadway twice a week,' she said. 'Normally it's a Tuesday and a Friday. He always takes the train to and from St Pancras. I'd normally be talking to The Watchers about keeping an eye on the wretched man but, in this instance, I doubt that would be appropriate.' She carefully folded her napkin and laid it beside her plate. 'I'm very glad I asked you to go up there, Tam. I knew I wouldn't be disappointed.'

She got to her feet and thanked Moncrieff for lunch. Moncrieff held her gaze. The Watchers were responsible for surveillance.

'A pleasure,' he said. 'Just one question. Is this you asking me? Or Guy?'

Barton looked down at him. A ghost of a smile played at the corners of her mouth. Then she was gone.

10

SUNDAY 14 SEPTEMBER 1941

Bella felt at home with Yuri from the moment she stepped into the suite of rooms behind the church. The evidence of the life he led was everywhere: the desk beneath the curtained window where he worked; the bookshelves, all of them full, with yet more books in seemingly random piles on the woodblock floor; the framed prints hanging on wall after wall, most of them in charcoal, dense black strokes capturing figures at prayer, or public speakers in front of huge crowds, or kids swimming in the river, all of them his own work. And dominating everything, hanging on the back wall beside the door that led to the rest of the accommodation, the broken figure on the cross, his head on his chest, his flanks latticed with blood, the crudest nails driven through the beautifully grained wood of his open palms.

'No one has stayed here in years,' Yuri told her. 'I've forgotten how to be polite. I'm afraid you'll have to fend for yourself.'

He showed her the tiny alcove beyond the door that served as a kitchen, the open wicker basket where he kept his bread, the shelf in his one cupboard cluttered with salt, and gherkins, and three kinds of paprika, and the jars of pickled fish and vegetable he ate most days. She was welcome to the smallest of the bedrooms, an empty space without a single item of furniture, and if she was very lucky Larissa might soon turn up with a mattress and a couple of blankets. There was only a single standpipe in the bathroom, alas, but he'd read somewhere that the British owed their empire to cold water and Christianity, and he had plenty of both, so he hoped she'd be very happy. In the meantime, she was to make herself at home and only talk when she felt the need. He'd lived with silence most of his life and appreciated its many blessings.

Bella was enchanted. She was no stranger to silence either, but the conversational challenge of a man like Yuri was irresistible. Back in the room where he worked, she sat cross-legged on the floor, still huddled in the Army greatcoat, wanting to know more.

'You're a priest,' she said.

'My father. My father was a priest.'

'That's impossible. Priests aren't allowed to marry.'

'My mother died. I never knew my real father. Maksym looked after me. My mother and I were living in the countryside. She got tuberculosis. She coughed her life away. Maksym was the priest who buried her.'

Maksym, she thought. What a lovely name for a priest.

'You had brothers? Sisters?'

'No. Just me. I was three years old.'

'And Maksym could deal with that?'

'Maksym treated me like a book, treasured me, studied me. We learned together, which was fun. Here. I've got something to show you.'

Yuri opened a drawer in the desk. Moments later, he slipped something star-shaped from an envelope and gave it to Bella. It was made of stiff grey cardboard, carefully painted.

'You see the icon? The Mother of God?'

'Yes. What's it for?'

'You take it carol singing as a kid. It's Xmas time. You go from house to house in the village. Now turn it over.'

Bella did what she was told. Now she was looking at a five-pointed Soviet star, emblem of the Revolution.

'Clever,' she said. 'All you have to do is remember who lives where.'

'Exactly. The wrong household, the wrong side of the star, and no one gives you money. In those days we thought it was a game, everyone did, then everyone started dying and it became difficult.'

'Tell me how.'

Yuri said nothing. He wanted the cardboard star back. He weighed it in his hand and turned it over several times. Then his gaze returned to Bella. Deep-set eyes, almost black.

'Lenin wanted our bodies, our souls, and our grain,' he said. 'But Stalin was worse. When the peasants started hiding the grain, it was war. He put everyone in giant farms and sent the city kids into the countryside. They beat our bodies, ignored our souls and stole every last sack of grain. When the farmers protested, he told them to answer to the Proletariat. No one had any idea what that meant but it never seemed to matter. In their name, we were invited to starve. That was one way of dying. The others were quicker. In this country, believe me, it paid not to be either an intellectual or a peasant. Maksym was both: by training an intellectual, by nature a peasant. The Russians took him away one morning and I never saw him again. He probably died two deaths, poor man, though Stalin will have to answer one day because God will see to that,' he glanced towards the figure on the door and crossed himself.

'And you?'

'I survived. They called it the Holodomor. You speak Ukrainian? *Holod*, hunger. *Mor*, death. Work it out.'

'Death by famine?'

'Exactly. Maksym once called it the silence of the bells. The churches were all closed. The Bolsheviks had torn the heart out of the countryside. There was nothing left to eat because they'd stolen it all and so you followed your neighbours onto the road, as they followed theirs. If you still had a cow, you took her, too, but that was unlikely because the Russians had either thieved the beast or you'd already eaten it. If you were lucky, you ended up at a railway station, but you'd need a sense of humour because you had no money for tickets and in any case the trains never stopped. We walked in the end, station to station along the track. We ate weeds, dandelions, anything we could find. The best stuff grew beside the rails themselves where all the shit comes out when the trains go by, but you never cared. Stalin's feast? Did you ever hear the expression?'

'Never.'

'When things got really bad, people started eating the dead. The Russians told us to look on the bright side. At least we had plenty of choice.'

He said he ended up in Kyiv. The famine had reached deep into the city. People were dying of hunger in the street. Collection teams were paid in bread and sworn to silence. Thousands of bodies were buried, always at night. Once, at the Lukianivske Cemetery, all the staff were arrested and shot as counter-revolutionaries, in case they bore witness. If you saw ravens next morning, black angels in the sky, you knew that bodies were still unburied, some of them probably the staff from the cemeteries. At that time, he said, people were so hungry they were pouring water into burrows made by field mice to wash out the stored grain.

'Can you believe that?' he said. 'Bolshevik *field mice*? Furry little revolutionaries? Stealing our grain?'

The thought drew a wry smile, and he rocked back and forth on the chair, lost in memories. Then his eye drifted to a weighty black tome open on the corner of the desk, and his hand reached out to flick through the pages.

'This was our new Ukrainian dictionary,' he said. 'A scholar called Skrypnyk spent years compiling it, here in Kyiv. This was after the war. It was a new start for a new culture, a Ukrainian culture. It meant we could write to each other in our own language. Then the Russians got hold of it and seized as many copies as they could find. And you know why? Because it relied on too many pre-revolutionary sources. In other words, it was a threat to the regime. They were the barbarians at our gate. What worried them most was us having our own language, our own customs, our own paintings, our own music, our own culture. They even dropped the Ukrainian letter "g" by state decree because it brought the language closer to Russian. Can you imagine that? The heroes of Petrograd frightened by a single letter? By an innocent curl of ink? That was traitorous. Writing the old "g" could put you in a prison cell. Crazy people. Crazy times.'

Bella, wary of stretching Yuri's patience any further, retired to her cell of a bedroom and lay on the floor, her head pillowed on her folded arms, glad of the warmth of the greatcoat. A thin, grey light filtered through the grubby window. The wind was beginning to stir in the trees that ringed the church, bringing with it the growl of battle, less distant now.

She tried to sleep, a hopeless act of denial, drifting off into a netherworld of memories sieved from the last few weeks. By far the most comforting took her back to the Glebe House, waking up with Tam dozing beside her, creeping downstairs in the half-light of dawn, prowling around the big kitchen, the flagstones cold beneath her bare feet, while the old kettle danced on the range. The longer she stayed, the easier it was to imagine being there for ever, a permanent part of this implacable man's life. What would she like to change around the house? And how would he react?

Back in the bedroom with tea, she'd linger by the bed for a moment or two, looking down at his sleeping face. She loved touching him. She loved how hard his body was, how spare, the sheer strength of the man, his limitless appetite for the steepest paths up the surrounding mountains, and most of all his assumption that she would match him step for step. This, she'd realised early on, was key to the unspoken bond between them.

Tam Moncrieff, to her quiet delight, had no time for weakness, for hanging back, for not committing. He took life in his mighty stride and expected her to follow. Was this something they taught you in the Royal Marines? Did it come with the green beret and the gruff humour of the men around you? Matthew, the boyfriend she'd lost in Spain, had been very similar – high expectations, limited patience – and she relished the challenge that men like this threw down.

Tam, of course, was older, wiser, but still the prisoner of the pace he set for himself. Physically, and in a thousand other ways, she knew she didn't disappoint him, and the more time they spent together, the more prepared he'd been to lower his defences and take a proper look at the person she really was. Bella understood the solitary life only too well, the necessary thickness of the walls you lived behind, but as their time in the mountains came to an abrupt end, she'd detected something new in their relationship. She'd managed to surprise him, perhaps by surprising himself, and for that she was glad.

She woke up to find Larissa and Yuri at the door. Larissa had found a mattress from somewhere, and Yuri had helped her carry it in from the car. Bella struggled to her feet.

'Here?' Yuri had gone. Larissa was pointing to the very middle of the room.

'Over here, please.' Bella preferred the corner furthest from the door. Larissa smiled at her choice.

'You want a little privacy? I don't blame you. It's the least a woman deserves.'

Woman? There were no mirrors in this house, not even in the cupboard that served as a bathroom, an absence Bella welcomed as a blessing. She was helping Larissa tug the mattress into the corner. Then she left to reappear shortly afterwards with an armful of bedding, and a pillow. There was even a sheet.

The bed made, Bella asked her what she looked like.

'Who?'

'Me. You put me to shame. You look fine. You look wonderful. Am I allowed to say that?'

Both women knew it was a lie. Larissa had a face made for sculpting, full of depth and character, but just now she looked exhausted. The darkness under her eyes spoke of days under pressure and nights without sleep.

'You're very kind,' she said. 'But I look the way I feel.'

'Tired?'

'Resigned. Things are crazy just now. Nothing's safe anymore. Someone broke into my car, stole everything they could lay their hands on, found my camera, and stole that, too. It was a Leica. It was precious to me.' She shook her head, then stepped a little closer, cupping Bella's face with her big hands. 'We should take our pleasures while we can, my child. The new look suits you.'

*

Afterwards, Larissa insisted she had to go. A thousand appointments to keep while people still had the freedom to move around. A million calls to make while the telephone exchanges were still working. Three major articles for tomorrow's edition before supplies of paper ran out. Bella, still straddling her, said no.

'We need to talk.'

'About?'

'This,' Bella gestured at the space between them. 'And about Yuri.'

'This? You mean us?'

'Yes.'

'Really?'

'Really.'

Larissa was frowning. Maybe she doesn't understand the question, Bella thought. Or maybe her busy life is full of encounters like these, opportunities seized, pleasures shared, clothes retrieved, then the plunge back into real life. Whatever the truth, Bella needed to find out.

'You fuck other people a lot?' she asked.

'No.'

'I don't believe you.'

'You don't? And does it matter if I'm lying?'

'Yes, it does.'

'That's nice. Kiss me.'

Bella ducked her head and did the older woman's bidding. She loved the warmth of her hands against the bareness of her scalp, her eager tongue, how frank she was, and how inventive.

'Yuri.' Bella had sat up again. 'Why do they leave him alone? He's a priest's boy. He lives in a church. He's a writer, an intellectual. He hates the Russians and he doesn't seem to care who knows it. Why doesn't that put him in the Big House?'

'You like him?' Larissa wiped her mouth.

'I admire him. I think he's brave. Or maybe reckless. More to the point, he's my guardian, my keeper. But the NKVD know everything. Yuri should have been dealt with by now, arrested, tortured, liquidated. Just tell me why that's never happened.'

Larissa gazed up at her.

'He has protection,' she said at last. 'Someone who looks after him, keeps him safe.'

'And who might that be?'

'You'll know him.'

'I will? I do?'

'Yes,' she reached for Bella's hand. 'Who helped build the Metro? In Moscow?'

Bella frowned. Work on the showpiece Metro had started years ago, way before her arrival in Moscow.

'I've no idea.'

'A little man. Even shorter than Stalin. They call him Stalin's *Liubiimchik.*'

Liubiimchik. Pet. Bella finally got it.

'You mean Khrushchev?'

'I do. You're a clever girl.' She gave Bella's hand a squeeze. 'Khrushchev is almost a Ukrainian. He was born just kilometres from the border. Stalin sent him back here from Moscow, appointed him Party Leader, gave him a nice place to live, a huge dacha on the river, told him to sort the city out. He plays the local *Vodzh* and the Russians do his bidding because he has the ear of Stalin and everyone knows it.'

'He's here now?'

'No. His family fled in July. He was in Moscow the following week. He found Stalin at his command post. He said the man was a wreck, couldn't believe what was happening. Khrushchev's tough. It pays to be very careful with Stalin, but he told him exactly the way things were going down here. Problems with food, with weapons, with ammunition. Stalin pulled himself together and promised to do something about it and sent Khrushchev back. The little man makes a difference. He knows how to shout. What he lacks in education he makes up for in every other way. If he was a dog he'd be nipping your ankles. Yap-yap.'

'How do you know all this?'

'I've interviewed him. Five times. That way we got to know each other a little. My paper has the biggest circulation in the city. When Khrushchev wants to send a message, he always asks for me. I like him, if that matters. He can be crude, he can bully you if you let him, but for a little man, he has a huge spirit.'

'And Yuri?'

'It's complicated. After the Revolution, Khrushchev worked in the Donbas, with the miners. They loved him. He was their kind of guy. When he got married, that first wife of his died of typhus. Her parents wanted her buried, but Khrushchev was busy being an atheist because that's what the Revolution demanded. And so Khrushchev had her body passed over the fence of the cemetery, because that way it avoided the church itself but still got buried. It was a clever solution. He was a politician, even then.'

'And Yuri?'

'Yuri was a child,' Larissa smiled, and then nodded towards the door. 'He told me just now how curious you were, how many questions you had for him. So maybe you should be asking about the priest.'

'You mean Maksym?'

'Exactly. Maksym was the priest waiting for the body in the church. He was ready to give the wife a proper funeral. He was affronted, and so were the wife's parents, and that was a problem for Khrushchev, who was still very young. But it doesn't end there. Yuri became a writer. He was fascinated by the miners in the Donbas and he was determined to tell their story. I think he saw himself as Emile Zola, but he'll never admit it. His books began to appear. The writing was good, everyone said so, but the Party didn't much like them and when copies were seized from the bookshops, Yuri took his case to Khrushchev, who was in charge by now. Khrushchev still had a soft spot for the Donbas. He doesn't read books, but he likes people who put up a fight, and Yuri was one of them. And so the books became available again, but only if you knew who to bribe.' She smiled. 'Khrushchev has never stopped being the politician. He understands the arts of the possible. He knows how to square circles. Even now.'

'So what does that make Yuri? Khrushchev's *Liubiimchik*?'

'Yuri will never be anyone's pet. But at least he's still alive.'

Bella nodded. This woman appeared to know everything.

'One more question,' Bella said.

'Can't it wait? Until later?'

'No.'

'OK,' Larissa tapped her watch. 'Just one.'

Bella described the walk down Khreshchatyk, crossing the busy boulevard, then catching sight of the Army trucks parked outside the City hotel.

'There were big wooden boxes,' she said. 'And the soldiers were carrying them into a side entrance at the hotel.'

'So?'

'Those boxes came from Britain. I have no idea what was inside them because no one would tell me.' She paused. 'Not even Ilya Glivenko.'

'I'm not surprised.'

'Was he at the hotel? Ilya?'

'Very probably.'

'And you? Do you know what was inside those boxes?'

'Yes, I do, and if you want me to tell you, I'm afraid the answer's no. Not for my sake, *chérie*…' that same smile again, '… but yours.'

11

TUESDAY 16 SEPTEMBER 1941

By mid-morning, Moncrieff was beginning to realise why The Watchers found it so hard to recruit the right kind of officers to fill its ranks. To run effective surveillance, you needed endless patience and a talent for invisibility. You needed to make yourself so inconspicuous, and so unremarkable, that no one would spare you a second glance. At the same time, you needed to be alert to every passing face, every sudden eruption of passengers as the next train squealed to a halt, wreathed in steam, and then opened its doors. It was in the nature of the hunt that you only got one opportunity to spot your target, and tuck in behind him. A moment's carelessness, some silly distraction, and he was gone.

Moncrieff had spent many years stalking deer in the mountains around the Glebe House. Indeed, at the urging of his dying mother he'd even established a business offering catered weekends for City stockbrokers with an urge to shoot a stag or two. He'd done his best to school these clients in the subtle arts of staying upwind, of moving carefully from cover to cover, of closing on the prey until a gentle pressure on the trigger would bring the animal to its knees. But nothing had prepared him for the smoky chaos of St Pancras station on a busy weekday morning. He was six foot three. There were very few places to hide. Philby knew him by sight. Hopeless.

Nonetheless, it had to be done. Ursula Barton, for whom he had enormous respect, shared his doubts about Kim Philby. She'd assessed the evidence, all of it circumstantial, and made it very clear that this little operation of theirs was to remain strictly their own affair. Tradecraft, she'd murmured, was everything and in this respect they'd be wise to lift a page or two from the NKVD operational guide. Nothing on paper. Reporting only by word of mouth, preferably on neutral territory. The devilled kidneys at St Ermin's were the fondest memory but never again would they meet in a setting like that. A park bench in the September sunshine? Perfect. A stroll along the Embankment beneath a shared umbrella? Better still. She'd even used the word 'freelance', a clue to just how complicit they'd have to become in this adventure, because – to Moncrieff's best knowledge – she'd never once strayed beyond departmental guidelines. If anything had persuaded him of the importance of what they were up to, it was this. She scented treachery. But she needed to be sure.

Moncrieff checked his watch: 11.47. The next train from St Albans was already in sight behind a cloud of steam at the end of the platform. In his heart Moncrieff believed he'd probably missed Philby, a schoolboy error on his part, but he was trying to persuade himself that Broadway had scheduled no morning meetings, and that Section Five's rising star was about to arrive for lunch.

And so it proved. Moncrieff had found himself an alcove beside one of the station's cafeterias. He spotted Philby the moment he stepped off the train: brown corduroy suit, polished brogues, a slightly dented homburg worn with a hint of jauntiness, battered leather briefcase in one hand, a folded copy of a newspaper in the other. Moncrieff eased his tall frame behind a neighbouring pillar and let the tide of passengers wash past. Philby was among them, walking slowly, taking his time.

Moncrieff already knew that the queue for taxis, at this time in the morning, would be long. Barton had organised a car and a driver from a company retained by MI5. Moncrieff had met the driver first thing. He was parked outside the station with a view of the cab rank and the moment Philby joined the kerbside queue, Moncrieff skirted the forecourt, staying out of sight, watching the taxis come and go. With Philby at the head of the queue, Moncrieff waited until the next taxi arrived. The moment Philby bent to the driver's window, Moncrieff crossed the road and climbed into the waiting car.

'Perfect,' he muttered. 'The black Austin.'

The traffic was light. The driver, schooled in the arts of invisibility, stayed well back. Once, in the depths of Bloomsbury, they were nearly caught by a traffic light. In Kingsway, a mile or two further south, a bus had come to grief on the edges of a sizeable bomb crater from an overnight raid and passengers were milling around in the middle of the road. The queue of waiting cars stretched back hundreds of yards, and Moncrieff watched as Philby clambered out of his taxi, checked his watch and began to walk.

Moncrieff followed him on foot, glad of the midday swirl of office workers out to buy a sandwich and a cup of tea, ducking into the cover of a fishmonger's when Philby suddenly came to a halt at the kerbside. By now they'd passed the bomb crater and the bus and the road was clear again. Philby's arm was raised and another cab was already slowing to pick him up. Moncrieff cursed as he watched his precious target clamber into the back, leaning forward to tell the cabbie where to go. Just in case, he made a note of the registration plate but knew already that it was a hopeless gesture. He could find a phone box that worked and make a call to St James's Street but it would still take an age for Ursula Barton to coax a name and an address from the licensing authority, by which time the cabbie would have forgotten all about his fare with the homburg and the corduroy trousers.

Broadway, MI6 headquarters, was a forty-minute walk away. Either Philby was going straight there, or maybe he'd arranged to meet someone for lunch. In any event, Moncrieff had no choice but to lie in wait again, this time within sight of Broadway's main entrance, hoping that an afternoon of in-house meetings might bring Philby back into the sunshine for his return to St Pancras. In anticipation, Moncrieff had booked a table in the window of a restaurant in the same street. Iberica wasn't an ideal perch, far from it, but the maître d' who'd taken his reservation seemed happy enough. I'll be expecting a guest, Moncrieff had told him. She's on the flying boat from Lisbon and she's taking the train from Poole. We obviously won't be ordering until she arrives.

The restaurant was nearly full by the time Moncrieff walked in but the maître d' had been as good as his word and the table in the window, carefully reserved, was still free. Moncrieff slipped into the chair with a view down the street and consulted the menu. When the waiter arrived, he explained once again that he was awaiting a guest who might be a little late. In the meantime, he'd be very happy with an aperitif: a glass of sherry. The waiter said he understood.

Two hours later, after a third sherry, Moncrieff knew he had to eat. The waiter had become a friend by now, pausing to enquire about this wayward lunch companion, sympathising with the general uncertainty of more or less everything these days, and trusting – with the discreet raising of an eyebrow – that the wait would be worthwhile. Moncrieff, beginning to enjoy this little fairy tale, assured him that he lived in hope. His guest, he said, was the friend of a friend. She worked for the American Embassy in Lisbon and had yet to set foot on British soil. Moncrieff had seen a photo or two and it would very definitely be his pleasure to show her what was left of Central London. At the very least, he thought, she might report back to her masters and thus hasten the entry of our American cousins into the war. In that respect, this little *repas*, whenever it happened, might acquire truly historical significance. In the meantime, before he risked yet another glass of Tio Pepe, Moncrieff would like to order the pigeon with a lightish helping of mashed potato.

It arrived half an hour later, with an extravagant flourish from the waiter.

'Wine, sir?'

'I think not. Let's wait for the lady.'

'Of course, sir. *Bon appétit.*' He tapped his watch. '*Et bonne chance, quoi?*'

By now, apart from a portly Tory politician whose face Moncrieff recognised, the restaurant had emptied. Moncrieff began to demolish the pigeon and asked for more gravy, listening to the politician bewail his wife's many failings. It appeared they lived in the country. She was mad about riding to hounds, lived and died by the state of her strawberry patch, but was a dead loss when it came to rumpy pumpy. His companion, a woman half his age with a hawk-like face and very little appetite, covered his big hand with hers and assured him everything would be just fine. The maid would have serviced the flat by now and they had the rest of the afternoon to themselves.

The politician beamed, catching Moncrieff's eye and offering a companionable wink. Moncrieff nodded and concentrated on reorganising the pile of tiny bones on his plate, keen to avoid a conversation. As he did so, he looked down the street to check the stairs that led to Broadway's imposing front entrance. It was gone four o'clock and suited figures were beginning to emerge into the late afternoon sunshine. Among them, deep in conversation with another man, was Philby.

Moncrieff signalled to the waiter. He'd kept a running tally of the sherries and the pigeon and knew that a couple of pound notes, mercifully soiled, would be enough to include a handsome tip. The waiter pocketed the notes with the faintest smile.

'Giving up, sir?'

'I'm afraid so.'

'Disappointed?'

'A broken man.'

Moncrieff got to his feet and made for the door. Through the fall of lace curtains, he could see Philby making his way past on the pavement opposite. Moncrieff waited until he got to the end of the street. Then, with a parting nod of farewell to the waiter, he stepped out into the sunshine.

Philby, by now, had disappeared. Moncrieff hurried to the corner. Philby was already crossing the road, maybe forty yards ahead, looking at his watch, heading for the river. He had the briefcase tucked under one arm and at the next intersection he paused at the kerbside to extract what – from a distance – looked like a manila envelope. He gazed at it a moment, then tucked it into the inside pocket of his jacket before crossing the street. Two more corners, and Moncrieff – still in pursuit – could smell the river.

They were in Westminster now. Moncrieff knew from Ursula Barton that Philby had been at school here, a boarder like his father at one of the most prestigious establishments in the country, just a stone's throw from the Houses of Parliament, and the Abbey, and the great offices of state. He'd know every one of these streets, Moncrieff thought, every short cut, every cul-de-sac, every possibility to make a little mischief. Here, at the very heart of the nation, he might already – for whatever reason – have been harbouring doubts about King and Country. There was still no proof, no clinching evidence that he was serving two masters, but Moncrieff's instincts told him that Ursula Barton was probably justified in her suspicions. At the very least, there were questions to answer, conversations to be had, circumstances to be explained. The likelihood of coincidence went only so far.

Philby was at the end of Great Peter Street. Ahead lay Millbank, and, beyond the thickening traffic, Moncrieff could see the spread of green beside the river. Philby waited for a space between a coal lorry and a passing Rolls-Royce, then hurried across. Hidden by the traffic, Moncrieff watched him settle briefly on one of the many benches, checking casually left and right before opening his briefcase again. This time he produced the folded newspaper he'd been carrying at St Pancras. Then he reached in his pocket for the envelope, quickly scribbled something on the outside and slipped it inside the newspaper. Moments later, he was on his feet, striding away towards the looming gothic fretwork of the House of Lords.

Moncrieff shook his head, partly astonishment, partly relief. So open, so blatant, so reckless. Tradecraft told him that his minder would be waiting close by. This was a classic drop, and the information in the envelope – doubtless smuggled out of Broadway, doubtless important – was now ready for collection. Moncrieff had to get himself across this road, ready to intercept the pick-up. Maybe a Russian from their embassy. Maybe someone English in their pay, another spy, another traitor.

Moncrieff stepped into the road. His sheer presence seemed to slow the oncoming traffic. A tiny space presented itself in the wash of a trolleybus and he seized his chance. Seconds later, he was across the road, scanning the green space ahead of him, making for the bench. In these circumstances, he had power of arrest and it would be a pleasure to deliver the Russian to the nearest police station. Moncrieff knew what would follow. First, they'd ignore the pleas about diplomatic immunity and leave the prisoner to sweat a little. Meanwhile, he and Barton would plan their strategy for the days and weeks to come. Best to soft-pedal the incident? Swear the police to silence on grounds of national security? Wait until the prisoner had given them everything they'd need to make a second arrest? Up at Glenalmond? In the very heart of Section Five?

Moncrieff waited, puzzled by how few people seemed to be around. A couple of men in suits, probably politicians, sharing a joke. A mother, or perhaps a nanny, making the most of the sunshine, rocking a baby in a pram. A boy on a bike, risking the wrath of the park attendants, cycling along the path that overlooked the river. But however hard he looked he could see no one who seemed remotely interested in retrieving the folded newspaper on the bench.

A little later, a wind picked up, heavy with the breath of the river, and the pages of the newspaper began to lift in the sudden breeze. Moncrieff waited a minute or two longer, knowing that – at the very least – he had to lay hands on the envelope. The pick-up, almost certainly, wasn't going to happen and he could imagine countless reasons why. A mistake over the rendezvous. An accident of some sort. Any bloody thing.

Finally, giving up, Moncrieff walked across to the bench and retrieved the paper. Inside, as he expected, was the envelope. He weighed it in his hand for a moment, then slipped his fingernail under the crease and opened it. Inside, he found a single sheet of paper. He slipped it out and found himself looking at a menu for the restaurant he'd just left. He recognised Philby's handwriting at once, perfectly formed letters, obsessively neat. *Splendid eatery,* he'd written. *The pigeon can be a little unreliable. Next time I'd suggest the pheasant, especially at this time of year.*

Moncrieff read the message again. The hunter hunted, he thought. Hunted, shot, gutted and ready for the pot. Then he remembered Philby settling on the bench to scribble something down and he returned to the envelope, turning it over. On the front, in black ink, were two capital letters, 'T' for Tam and 'M' for Moncrieff.

Moncrieff gazed at the envelope. He felt a hot lick of anger, deep in his bowels. After the missed catch in the outfield, yet more humiliation. Then he looked up, first at the river, then left towards the Houses of Parliament. Philby was standing in the sunshine, watching him. For a moment, he didn't move. Then, after the merest tilt of the homburg, he was on his way.

12

WEDNESDAY 17 SEPTEMBER 1941

The next morning, events on the battlefields around Kyiv
signalled the city's end. Three days earlier, Hitler's armies
had finally linked hands nearly 200 kilometres east of Kyiv,
completing the encirclement. Savage fighting slowly tightened
the noose and Stalin's new commander, General Timoshenko,
knew the situation was hopeless. All day he sent messages to the
Stavko, Stalin's command headquarters, requesting permission
to withdraw nearly three-quarters of a million troops still
defending the city's outer perimeter. They'd inflicted far more
damage on the advancing enemy than the Germans had ever
expected but supplies of fuel and ammunition were fast running
out. In the evening, late, a signal at last arrived at Timoshenko's
field headquarters. It read 'the Supreme Commander has
authorised withdrawal from Kyiv'.

At this very moment, Ilya Glivenko was meeting Ukrainian
party boss Nikita Khrushchev at NKVD headquarters at the
very heart of the city. From here, in what the locals still called
the Big House, NKVD officials had been carrying out thousands
of arrests and executions over the past four years, cowing the
populace and destroying all opposition to the regime. Now,
though, the game was up, and everyone knew it. A copy of

the message from the *Vodzh* found its way to Khrushchev but he barely spared it a glance. Instead, he was looking up at Glivenko.

'Show me,' he said.

Khrushchev was accompanied by two bodyguards, a driver and a woman whose precise role was unclear. They stood in the dim light of the stairs that led down to the bowels of the building. Glivenko made it plain that only Khrushchev was allowed any further. Corridors left and right housed the bare unsoundproofed interrogation rooms where skilled NKVD interrogators extracted confessions and then returned their bloodied charges for sentencing. Even now, as the city braced itself for evacuation, it was obvious that the NKVD were as busy as ever.

'Come, Comrade Khrushchev. I don't need to waste your time.'

The Party boss was unused to other people giving him orders and his entourage knew it. There were issues of respect here, of deference to authority. The People's Revolution might have triumphed, but Khrushchev was very definitely in charge.

He shifted what weight he carried from foot to foot, searching Glivenko's face for signs of weakness. Then, abruptly, he reached out and patted him on the shoulder.

'Brave man,' he growled. 'I like that.'

With a dismissive wave, he followed Glivenko into the gloom. Three flights of steps took them to the basement, the temperature dropping, the crudely plastered walls glistening with moisture. At the bottom of the stairs, Glivenko cautioned him to take extreme care, and the two men trod carefully around piles of abandoned equipment, making for a pool of light where the corridor suddenly widened. Four men, stripped to the waist, had been digging a sizeable hole. One of them, looking up and recognising Khrushchev, reached for a ball of cotton waste and mopped the sweat from his face.

Khrushchev was peering into the hole. It had the size and dimensions of a grave, and the excavated earth was piled beside it.

'What am I looking at?'

Glivenko joined him, tallying each item at the bottom of the hole. The big battery. The wires leading to the detonators. Encased in a metal frame, the receiving equipment. Simple, really. But guaranteed to work.

'And that?' Khrushchev was pointing to a shallower excavation, barely half a metre wide, that extended from the hole into the darkness.

'The antenna, Comrade Khrushchev, to capture the wireless signal.'

'Range?'

'More than adequate.'

'You're not going to tell me where these people are? Who sends the message? Who presses the trigger?'

'No.'

'Far away?'

'Far enough.'

'Far enough for what?'

'Far enough to be safe. Those men will be very busy. Many targets.'

Khrushchev nodded. His gaze had returned to the hole.

'So how many?' he asked.

'More than five hundred. All over the city.'

'Five *hundred*?' Khrushchev grinned at the thought. Glivenko was making him a very happy man. 'And this stuff works? You swear to me on your children's lives?'

'Yes, Comrade. We had a problem with some of the equipment, but the English have helped us out.'

'Excellent,' he nodded. 'Good to know those bastards are of some use after all.'

Glivenko permitted himself a brief smile. Then he explained how the hole would be refilled and the antenna disguised after the installation work had been completed.

Khrushchev nodded. He wanted to know about the explosive. How much? And where would it go?'

'In the hole, Comrade. This building will need four thousand kilos to bring it down.'

'All of it?'

'Every last brick.'

Khrushchev was thoughtful for a moment or two, still gazing down at the tangle of wires between the boxes below. Glivenko knew that he'd been an engineer in the Donbas, a man who relied on his hands as well as his brain, understood the importance of bridging the gap between the drawing board and building something that would work.

'The Germans will be here in days,' he said finally, 'in this very building. It's got everything they need. Desks, phones, privacy, even a fucking reputation to make you shit in your pants. They'll take it over. They'll put flags on the outside and the fear of God into everyone who steps foot inside. How long do the batteries last?'

'Months. If we're careful with the sequencing.'

'Excellent. Wait until they've settled in. Wait until they feel at home. Choose your moment.' He drove a pudgy fist into the palm of his other hand. 'Then smash them in the snout.'

*

From the Big House, Khrushchev's party drove into the city's oldest quarter. Glivenko sat in the back of the big Emka, giving directions. Finally, after a tortuous detour off the main street that wound up the hill, they came to a halt. It was after midnight. The flicker of artillery fire danced on every horizon.

'He lives in a *church*?' Khrushchev was staring out of the window.

'He's a priest's son, Comrade Khrushchev. You know that. He likes to feel at home.'

The woman sitting beside Glivenko was tapping her watch. No more than ten minutes, she warned, if they were to leave the city intact. Khrushchev nodded. Five was all he needed. Six if the bloody man needed proper persuasion.

He bustled after Glivenko on the path that skirted the church, pushing the sapper aside when they rounded the corner, and then hammered on the door.

'NKVD,' he roared. 'Get your fucking papers out.'

The door opened after a second volley of blows. Yuri looked down at the pug nose, the splayed lips, the wildness of the light in his eyes. People said that Khrushchev had the face of a turnip, that he belonged in a field in some forlorn *kolhoz*, and they were right.

'Yuri Ponomorenko. Good news, my friend. You're coming with us.'

'You're arresting me?' Yuri was peering at other faces looming out of the darkness.

'We're saving your life. You have anything you want to bring with you? Not too much, *tovarish*. We travel light, these days.'

'Where are you going?'

'East. Out of the city. Away from this shit heap.' Khrushchev had caught sight of the Christ figure nailed to the door at the far end of the room. 'These days it's the Red Army that works the miracles. I've no idea how, but they'll get us out.'

'Maybe I don't want to come.'

'Then you're mad. Believe me, I'm the one who's kept you alive so far. The Germans won't be so understanding. Pack a bag, son. Think of your poor father. Three minutes. Anyone else in there?' Khrushchev was standing on tiptoe, peering round Yuri's tall frame.

'No.'

'You're lying. I can smell perfume. Larissa? Am I right?'

Larissa appeared, rubbing her eyes. Khrushchev said she could come, too. Even journalists had their uses. 'We're in the car outside. Seven of us if I'm counting right. Very intimate but you won't mind that.'

There was a movement behind Khrushchev. Glivenko had appeared. He had something wrapped in brown paper and he asked Khrushchev to step aside for a moment to let him in.

'You want to stay, too?'

'Of course, Comrade,' he smiled. 'Unfinished business.'

Khrushchev studied him a moment, then he frowned.

'A senior Major called Bezkrovny,' he said, 'from the Big House in Moscow. I had him on the phone a couple of days ago. You know him?'

'No.'

'He said he met you on the airfield at Kharkov. You were with an Englishwoman. He said you fled with her.'

'Fled?'

'Flew away. Here. To Kyiv.'

'An *English*woman?'

'That's what he said. He's sent a file. He needs her arrested and he thinks we've nothing better to do. They're all crazy in Moscow. Always were.' He beamed at Glivenko. 'Tell these children to move their arse. We'll be in the car. Two minutes, and we've gone.'

Glivenko was looking at Yuri and Larissa. Tiny shakes of the head.

'They won't go,' Glivenko said. 'I know them. They're Ukrainian. They belong here. Think of the good news, Comrade. It'll be their city, not ours, whatever's left of it.'

Khrushchev stared at him, saying nothing. Then, with a snort of disbelief, he turned on his heel, gathered his entourage, and hurried them towards the car, cursing as he tripped on a tree root. Moments later came the cough of the engine and then the crunch of gravel under the tyres as the driver accelerated away.

For a moment, still standing in the open doorway, Yuri could hear nothing but the hoot of a distant owl. Then the deep bass rumble of artillery swelled again, and the owl was gone.

*

Bella emerged from her bedroom. Yuri had found some glasses and Glivenko was already pouring generous measures of vodka from the bottle he'd just unwrapped. The bottle had no label.

'Home-brewed,' Bella caught the dull glint of a gold tooth in his smile. 'Compliments of the Big House.'

They toasted the departing Russians. They toasted the coming days of chaos before the Germans arrived. And then they toasted the Party boss who'd found the time and had the decency to stop by and offer them a passage out.

'He must love you,' Glivenko was looking at Yuri.

'He likes my writing, or he says he does. He also has a conscience about a wife he once buried. Strange how the past can still haunt you.' He raised his glass to Bella. 'Larissa told me the Big House had your name. I never believed her. What did you do to upset them?'

'Nothing. I've been their hero for years.'

'Then why this Bezkrovny?'

Bella had been anticipating the question for days. First Ilya, she thought. And then Larissa. And now Yuri. All of them wanting to know her real story.

'I defected,' she said. 'I'd been Communist in my head for years and then I did it.'

'In your heart,' it was Larissa. 'You'd joined them in your heart. In your head, you'd know better.'

Yuri grinned. When he said he wanted to write the phrase down, Bella thought he was joking. He wasn't.

'Go on,' Glivenko wanted to know more. 'You defect. You run away to Moscow. Then what?'

'They give me a place to live. They give me money. They make a fuss of me. They make me feel appreciated, wanted. I try and give them something in return. Most of what I told them they knew already.'

'They always say that.' Larissa's glass was empty. 'Normally it's a lie. They think they know everything. They don't.'

'So, you're a hero in the Big House,' Glivenko was circulating with the bottle, refilling the glasses. 'What happened to change all that?'

'They have other agents. I'm sure they're all over Europe. They'll have some in London.'

'You know who these people are?'

'No. I have my suspicions but no proof. In Moscow, I only get to see what they want me to see.'

'So, where's the problem?'

'There's someone in particular I've always worried about. Moscow sent me to London very recently, after the Germans attacked. They wanted me to wait for you, Ilya, and then bring you back with all those boxes. The man I've mentioned works for MI6. I think he's like me. I think he works for Moscow. He knows this. Which means that he thinks I might blow his cover any time. He's already important, this man, because he's very good. Moscow thinks the world of him and so does MI6. There's a phrase in English. It's called the batting order. It's a measure of importance, of value. And he's much more valuable than me.'

'So you think they'd get rid of you? To protect him?'

'I do.'

'But why would you ever give him away? To the English?'

Bella ducked her head. The vodka had warmed her, uncoiling deep in her belly. In the company of these people she felt brave, uninhibited, free. The city would fall within days, maybe sooner. Anything could happen.

'I'm in love,' she said simply. 'With a man who thinks exactly the way I do.'

'About the MI6 spy?'

'Yes.'

'Have you mentioned him to this lover of yours?'

'Yes.'

'And they know that? In the Big House?'

'They do. Because our friend in MI6 will have told them.'

*

Moncrieff lay in bed, trying to work out what had disturbed him. In the field, half a lifetime ago, he'd developed a sixth sense for the unexpected. He'd be under canvas, or in a bivvy, or even under the stars, and some tiny noise – a rustle, a breaking twig – would touch a nerve deep inside his brain and bring him into wakefulness. Like any young Royal Marine, he'd added this to the list of what his instructors called 'survival skills', and two decades later the habit still hadn't left him. Only weeks ago, in the draughty comforts of the Glebe House, Bella had wondered aloud whether he ever truly slept and after the briefest discussion he'd decided that she was probably right. Sleep, proper sleep, could kill you. Hence the need to post a sentry or two.

He'd been using the borrowed mews house as his London pied-à-terre for a couple of months now. Archie Gasgoigne, a fellow Marine, had inherited the property from his mother and Moncrieff had been only too happy to move in while Archie was up in the Shetlands, still running Norwegian agents over the North Sea. Chelsea was a stroll away. The pub around the corner managed to conjure fresh rabbit and occasionally lamb from God knows where. And the houses on both sides were empty. The silence, and the privacy, suited Moncrieff very well. There was even room for his bicycle in the tiny back garden. He was happy here.

The noise again, unmistakable. The bedroom window was open, and he could detect movement on the cobblestones below, the lightest footsteps, then a muttered curse. He was sitting up now, feeling for the automatic he kept on the floor beside the bed. There was a full clip of ammunition, and he eased the slider back, waiting for the click that told him the first round was in the breech. Only a couple of days ago, Ursula Barton had checked to make sure he was taking care of things. The latter was MI5-speak for sensible precautions, by which she meant ready access to a loaded gun. Now might be the moment he declares himself, she'd said. Very prescient.

Naked except for a pair of pants, Moncrieff eased his long frame towards the door. A tiny landing led to the stairs. The inky darkness of the blackout had stolen into every corner of the house, and he felt his way very slowly, one tiny step at a time, shallow breaths, pulse a little fast, waiting, listening, his right arm extended, the automatic steady in his hand. Nothing. Then came a woman's voice, calling his name.

'Tam? Are you there? Tam?'

He was at the top of the stairs now. In daylight, from here, he'd have line of sight on the front door but in the middle of the night he could see nothing. The voice again, softer, still calling his name. Bella? He didn't know, couldn't tell. Sometimes, playing the fool, she'd affect a foreign accent and now felt like one of those moments. Was she back already? Had she managed to avoid Moscow? Had she never gone in the first place? She certainly knew the mews, in fact she'd loved the house so much she'd been slightly disappointed to have to take the train to Scotland.

Moncrieff felt for the first step, then the next, then the one after. He was nearly at the bottom of the stairs when he heard the knock on the door, discreet, gentle. Bella, he thought. Definitely.

He was in the hall now, and he padded the few steps to the front door. It was bolted top and bottom, and he slid the bolts back with his spare hand, then pulled the door open. As he did so, he heard another movement, behind him this time, and he managed to half turn in the narrow hall before his head exploded, and the masked face in the street chuckled softly, and he sank to his knees as the gun clattered onto the tiled floor.

The pain was intense, flooding his entire body, then he felt the rough kiss of a canvas bag pulled tight around his head. The bag smelled damp, with an inexplicable hint of onions. Then came a sharp prick in his upper arm, and all too suddenly the pain eased, and all he could feel was an enveloping numbness, at first multicoloured, the shades of the rainbow, then fading into a darkness he knew would steal him away.

The voice again, very faint, laughing.

'Tam…?'

13

THURSDAY 18 SEPTEMBER 1941

Bella awoke in broad daylight, with a thumping head. Larissa had gone, leaving a note on the pillow. *Again? Tonight? Take care. Your friend is a lucky man. I love you, too.* Bella stared at the note, trying to still her heaving guts, only too aware of how war, and the very real possibility of dying, could make a fleeting relationship so intense, and so precious. *Take your pleasures while you can*, Larissa had said. And Bella – even prostrate – knew exactly what she meant.

A little later, Yuri returned. He'd scouted the city as far as Khreshchatyk and reported that the Russians were streaming out of the city, heading for the bridges over the Dnieper.

'Come,' he said. 'You may never see this again.'

Bella dressed and swallowed three glasses of water. Something must have happened to the distribution system because the water was brackish, and tasted slightly sweet, but she felt better already. Yuri had been with Glivenko only an hour ago and said that the NKVD had been pulling out in strength, abandoning the Big House without even locking the doors behind them, and Bella was enjoying her new freedom. She no longer needed to bother with an Army greatcoat, an upturned collar, a working man's cap, and the need to scuttle from doorway to doorway, on the very inside of the pavement, hugging the shadows. Larissa, perhaps anticipating this moment, had left her a red beret, a declaration that she was a woman again, and she wore it with pride, able to stretch her legs, aware of covert glances from the endless stream of Soviet troops heading east.

Thanks to the last three years in Moscow, she was – in part – Russian, and it was impossible not to feel sorry for these men. They'd obviously been on the road for a long time, retreating from God knows how many battles, and most of them looked exhausted. They stumbled along the broadness of the boulevard, in the footsteps of the man ahead, trying to avoid the tramlines, lifting their heads from time to time, sweat and dust caking their faces. Their shoulders sagged under the weight of their kitbags, blanket rolls and weapons. Each man carried ammunition in heavy pouches, another burden, and Bella watched one soldier tossing round after round aside to ease the weight, the way you might distribute sweets to waiting kids. When the man behind him warned that a Commissar was coming, he merely shrugged. He'd suffered enough and he didn't care anymore.

Then came an old farm cart, hauled by a pair of bullocks, heaped with yet more soldiers who may or may not have been dead. Among the prostrate bodies sat a blank-faced youth in a fur hat, playing an accordion. Catching sight of Bella at the kerbside, his face was suddenly animated, and he quickened the tune and began to whistle, stirring the nearest body with his mud-caked boot. The prone soldier stirred. His head turned and he raised a grimy hand in salute, his tongue trying to moisten the dryness of his lips. Water, Bella thought. I should have brought water.

She shook her head, ashamed, wondering whether to beg water from one of the nearby shops, and at that moment she knew she'd never watch another carnival in her life without remembering this endless river of broken bodies. Some men had walked until their feet were swollen and bleeding. Now they limped barefoot, with their boots slung over their shoulders. Others had no shoes or boots at all, and staggered past in a crazed rattle of tea cans hanging from their belts.

Yuri had one eye on the sky. Earlier, Bella had caught the whine of an air-raid siren, but no aircraft had appeared. This time there was no warning, but the soldiers, alert to the sounds of the battlefield, were following Yuri's pointing finger. Bella shaded her eyes against the glare of the morning sun, searching the depthless blue. Then she saw a neat line of planes, gull-winged, high cockpits, peeling off, one after the other, into a near vertical dive. She watched, fascinated, until it began to occur to her that their targets were these men, hundreds of them, thousands of them, and as the planes howled ever closer, releasing their black little eggs, she took Yuri's hand and began to run.

'Stukas,' he said. It was almost a whisper.

The soldiers were running, too, scattering in every direction, swarming onto the pavements on both sides of the boulevard, desperate to find shelter. Then came the first explosions, and the raw punch of the shock waves, and men falling left and right, cut to pieces by the flying shrapnel. Yuri had pushed Bella into a shop selling flowers, and Bella found herself face down in a display of roses, shaking uncontrollably as the Stukas walked the bombs ever closer. The last one exploded on the boulevard outside. Cobblestones erupted and shards of glass were everywhere from the shattered window. One of them had caught Yuri high on his thigh, and he was staring at the blood beginning to seep through his torn trousers.

'Here,' the woman who owned the flower shop was offering a towel.

Bella widened the tear in Yuri's trousers. The wound was only skin-deep. She pressed the towel against it, letting the shopkeeper extract a rose thorn from her cheek. We've been lucky, she thought. This could have been so much worse.

Then, like a passing shower of rain, the Stukas had gone and the sky was clear again. Everywhere soldiers were picking themselves up, brushing themselves down, checking for damage. Some of them were bleeding, caught in the hail of shrapnel, and one man propped against the base of a lamp post seemed to be in shock. His eyes were glassy, and he had trouble keeping his head in one place. He looked drunk, totally incapable, and when another man stooped to offer help, he tried to push him away.

Moments later, Bella turned to find Yuri staring at a body in the gutter. The soldier must have taken the full force of a bomb blast because an arm and a shoulder had gone, and the side of his face had been ripped off, exposing his jawbone and a line of yellow teeth beneath. Bella stared at him for a long moment, aware of the yells of the Commissars, and the shuffle of the men forming up again on the broken cobblestones, and the column beginning to shuffle slowly away. They'll leave him behind, she thought. There'll be no one to give him a name, no one to bury him, no one to mourn his passing.

She lingered a moment longer, then returned to the flower shop. The woman who owned it had been watching her at the kerbside. Bella had no money, but it didn't matter. The woman selected a single rose, gave it to Bella, gesturing towards the body in the gutter. Then she cut more stems, at least a dozen, until Bella's arms were full.

'The planes will be back,' she muttered. 'Hurry.'

The woman was right. Yuri and Bella returned to the church, after laying the roses on body after body along Khreshchatyk. Yuri disappeared, limping across the graveyard, but Bella hung on beside the gate, hearing the muted roar of engines in the far distance, then staring up at the formations of bombers flying low over the city. These were bigger aircraft, twin-engined, and there was nothing but a couple of hundred metres between themselves and the targets below, no anti-aircraft fire, none of the big barrage balloons she'd seen in photos from London, nothing to disturb whoever was responsible for releasing the bombs.

Watching yet more of the black eggs tumbling from the sky, Bella tried to imagine what it must be like to be up in aircraft like these, spoiled for choice when it came to targets. Would you go for buildings designated on some map or other? Army headquarters? Power stations? Water installations? Or would you be overwhelmed by the temptation of the long brown snake still heading for the river, enemy flesh and blood, dozens of men a single black egg could destroy in a heartbeat? She turned away as the first bombs found their targets and the ground beneath her feet began to tremble, sickened by what she'd seen in Khreshchatyk. The men above her are playing God, she thought. And she hoped God was watching.

Mercifully, none of the *Luftwaffe* bombers seemed interested in the old town. Bella found Yuri on his knees in the room that served as his study, his hands pressed together, gazing up at the Christ figure on the wall. His lips were moving in a silent prayer, and he appeared oblivious to her presence in the room. She took a step back, not wanting to disturb him, and her gaze strayed to a note he'd scribbled to himself, lying on his desk. 'I know there is a God and I see a storm coming. If he has a place for me, I am ready.'

She stared at it a moment. She knew she'd seen this quote before, but she couldn't remember where.

'Abraham Lincoln,' Yuri had crossed himself and struggled to his feet. 'Just before the American Civil War.'

'And you see a storm coming?'

'Of course. In fact, it's already here.' He gestured upwards. The drone of the bombers was beginning to fade.

'And you're ready? To die?'

'I'm ready for the Germans. It might be the same thing. None of us know. Which I imagine is the point Lincoln was making.'

Bella nodded. This was a new Yuri, somehow different. He'd told her enough about the last decade to suggest that nothing else could ever surprise him. He'd survived the famine, and the attentions of the NKVD. Thanks to Khrushchev he was still at his desk, still writing, still alive. Yet something had changed.

'Was it just now?' she asked. 'In Khreshchatyk? The Stukas? The bombs? The bodies?'

He shrugged. He didn't want to answer.

'Are you afraid, Yuri?'

'A little.'

'What else, then?'

'I'm resigned. I know what happens next. And I think I know what happens after that.'

'And you can do nothing about it?'

'I can pray.' He gestured towards the figure on the door.

'And that helps?'

'Always.'

'Because he has a place for you?'

'Because he has a place for all of us.'

Bella held his gaze. Then she heard footsteps outside. Moments later, after a soft knock at the door, she was looking at Glivenko. Blood was seeping through a bandage wound around his forehead. He offered her the briefest nod of acknowledgement. His business was with Yuri.

'Done?' Yuri asked.

'*Da.*'

'All of them?'

'*Da.*'

There was a moment of silence.

'You got caught in the bombing?'

'*Da.* And so did Larissa.'

'She's all right?'

'No.' He touched his own arm. 'I think it's broken. They'll need to set it.'

He hesitated a moment longer, his eyes on Yuri, then he shrugged and left. Yuri was already at his desk. From one of the drawers he produced a thick handful of manuscript, handwritten. He flicked over a page or two, nodding, then tidied the pile and searched for an envelope big enough to take it all.

'What's that?' Bella nodded at the bundle.

'A book. A novel. Beginnings. Maybe more than that. These creatures grow in the making. That's the magic.'

'Creatures?'

'The book. The characters. I'm writing about the Pechersk Monastery. You know it?' Bella shook her head. 'It's down by the river. Way back the monks used to live in caves above the water. Then they built the monastery and after that came the Cathedral. The book's about the Cathedral. Why it was built, how it was built, what it did for the men who worshipped there.'

'And the Cathedral's still standing?'

'Of course. It's survived nearly a thousand years, and maybe that's the point. Faith lives forever. In here...' he touched his bony chest, '... in the Cathedral of the Dormition, and I hope in here.' His hand closed around the manuscript.

'So what will you do with it?'

'I'll finish it. One day.'

'I meant now.'

'I have to hide it.'

'Am I allowed to know why?'

'Because everything will change. *Everything.* Here. In the city. Everywhere. We love the Russians going, but we should be careful what we wish for.'

He shot her a look and then picked up the manuscript and asked her to accompany him into the church. In a far corner, towards the altar, he knelt over a paving stone that proved to be loose. He inserted his long fingers where the mortar had crumbled and prised the stone up. Beneath was a void.

'Here—' he gestured for Bella to hold the stone upright. In the dim light through a neighbouring window, she watched him slip the thickness of the envelope into the hole and then make sure the fit was snug.

'You might be tucking in a baby,' she said.

'You're right.' He reached into the hole and gave the envelope a final pat. 'Sleep well.'

*

Ilya Glivenko took his final swim in the river in the late afternoon. He slipped into the murky brown water fully clothed and waded deeper and deeper until the muddy bottom fell away. In the distance, beyond the island, he could see the endless column of Soviet troops still crossing the faraway bridge, a brown smudge against the yellows and golds of autumn. Smoke from the air raids hid most of the city and every breath he took brought the bitter, acrid taste of dozens of fires.

He could feel the tug of the current now, and he rolled onto his back, surrendering to the river, just another piece of debris drifting south. Pillowed by the water, he gazed up through the smoke at the blueness of the sky, wondering what the city's birdlife had made of the attention the *Luftwaffe* had been paying the city.

Only weeks ago, before he'd left for England and the real work started, he'd spend his evenings fishing for carp and eels on the riverbank, and part of Kyiv's magic had been the company of storks, motionless in the shallows, sentries at the city's gates. They always caught far more than he ever did but he loved the moment when, sated, they eased the stiffness from their legs, and stretched their wings, and flapped and flapped until – improbably – they were airborne. The way they cheated the laws of gravity, climbing slowly into the golden dusk, never ceased to amaze him but today, hard as he looked, he could see no sign of them. Like the soldiers, they'd had enough of smoke and ruin. Very wise.

The island lay ahead and already he could see movement. A couple of men had emerged from the treeline. One of them, spotting him, began to wave. Vassily, he thought, a Kazakh who'd made his way to Moscow, strong as an ox and good in a crisis. As far as Glivenko could make out, he'd never bothered with formal schooling, but he had a quick intelligence and an astonishing memory. At first, the Army had wasted his talents, assigning him to a mortar section, but men Glivenko trusted spoke well of him and he'd managed to wangle a transfer to the sappers. Nearly a year later, Vassily still regarded wireless transmission as sorcery, but he understood the principles and had mastered the technical diagrams and could wire a detonator quicker than any man Glivenko knew.

Now he waded into the shallows to help the older man out. Glivenko shook the water from his hair and mopped his face with his hands.

'You look like a rat,' Vassily was laughing. 'Be careful, Ilya Ilyanovich. If times get tough, we might have to eat you.'

The three of them left the riverbank and followed a path into the trees. Vassily stopped to light two cigarettes and gave one to Glivenko. Glivenko sucked smoke deep into his lungs. He wanted to know about the test transmissions.

'They're fine. They're good.'

'All of them?' Glivenko couldn't believe it.

'All except the Big House. I'll be back there tonight. I think it's one of the valves but I'm not sure.'

'And the other lads? The ones who are staying behind? You've talked to them?'

'Of course. They'll keep an eye on everything. They're saying four days, maybe five. Give the bastards time to move in, make themselves comfortable, then...' He made a plunging movement with both hands, then grinned. 'You're shivering, Ilya Ilyanovich. It must be the excitement.'

14

FRIDAY 19 SEPTEMBER 1941

Moncrieff was desperate for water, for fluid, for lubrication. Moments of consciousness came and went, brief spasms when he surfaced from the depths of oblivion and tried to swallow, coax a little saliva into his mouth, turn his head, lick his lips. But nothing happened. He was naked under the single sheet. His wrists and ankles were manacled to the frame of the bed. His bursting head appeared to be in a clamp of some kind. Unable to move in the darkness, he could only dream of his parched mouth upturned to the rain that pattered at the window. Please God, he muttered, give me water.

Later, he'd no idea when, his eyes opened again. They felt gummy, congealed, no longer part of him, and the pain in his head had intensified. Every heartbeat, achingly slow, sent the agony to every corner of his body, jolts of intense pain that he began to dread. Most frightening of all, he had no recollection of what had happened, of how he'd arrived at this place. His memory had gone. It simply didn't work. And no matter how hard he tried, he could coax no logic from events. Someone must have attacked him. But where? And how? And why? Days ago, or maybe weeks ago, or maybe even longer, he'd probably been in perfect working order. Now, he could barely remember his name. The Tam Moncrieff he'd always taken for granted appeared to have packed his bags and left, and now he'd become a vagrant, a stranger, a man with no story, no past, no future, squatting in the remains of his own body.

He drifted off again, numbed. Nothing awaited him, no dreams, no nightmares, no visions, just an intense shade of black, formless, all-enveloping, that began to soften the pain in his head and ease the yearning for water. This must be death, he thought vaguely. How strange.

Then came a voice, male, maybe English.

'Here. Drink.'

He opened his eyes again. He could feel a straw gently inserted between his lips, and he sensed a stripe of pale light between the curtains at the window. The face hanging over him was masked by a black balaclava. The eyes were watching him. The mouth was slightly open. Death, he thought again. My guardian angel.

He sucked greedily at the straw. Expecting water, he found himself trying to swallow something more viscous, with a faint edge of bitterness. A spasm of coughing threatened to choke him. He spat the liquid out, fighting to breathe, and he felt the pressure of the head clamp ease.

'Sit up.'

He forced himself into a sitting position and began to vomit. The face above him didn't move. Then came the straw again.

'More. Drink more. Good for you.' Foreign, not English at all.

'No,' Moncrieff shook his head.

'More,' the voice insisted. 'Better this than the needle.'

'But what is it?'

'Good for you.'

Moncrieff eyed him, dimly aware that there were questions he should be asking, protests he should be making, but his mind – untethered – refused to work. Pain he could cope with, just. It was, after all, the crudest evidence that he was still alive. But the emptiness, the void where his brain had once been, was beyond explanation. Not only had he lost the ability to think, and to remember, but it didn't seem to matter anymore. Zombie, he thought, settling back again, the reek of vomit in his nostrils. Moments later, or perhaps minutes, or maybe longer, he felt a prick in his upper arm and a faint burning sensation.

Then he was gone again.

*

Kyiv. The first German units burst into the city as the sun rose through the morning mist, column after column of Panzer tanks, their engines roaring, their tracks grinding over the cobblestones, each commander erect in his open turret. The streets were empty and within hours the swastika was flying from the citadel.

Bella and Yuri had been out since dawn. Larissa had been taken to a makeshift first-aid post off the Krillovskaya, a major street in the city centre near the offices of the newspaper, and Bella found her at a table with a group of other injured, her arm in a makeshift splint, staring at a bowl of *kasha*. Yesterday, she said, she'd been out in the streets with a photographer. Forewarned about the approaching Stukas, they'd been hunting for pictures when the first bombs began to fall.

The photographer had ignored Larissa's pleas to take cover and had been trampled underfoot by Russian troops flooding off the boulevard. Larissa, with the help of a policeman, had done her best to drag him to safety but the third bomb to fall had killed him. Larissa, in her own estimation, had been lucky. A broken arm and lacerations. Nothing more. This morning, the doctor in charge at the first-aid post was sending her to the city's main hospital to have the break properly set. Thankfully, it was her left arm. She could still write with her other hand.

'You're going back to work? Afterwards?'

'Of course. What else would I do?'

Now, past noon, Bella and Yuri were watching an endless procession of *Wehrmacht* trucks and marching soldiers choke the streets around the city centre. The air was blue with exhaust fumes and the stink of cheap petrol, and houses and shops emptied as people came out on the streets to watch. Uniformed motorcyclists danced through the traffic, machine guns bolted to their handlebars, and the heavy guns that had been pounding the Red Army for months ground across the cobblestones, dragged by huge workhorses.

This was a victory parade, thought Bella, an impromptu display of German vigour, German prowess. They'd doubtless taken hundreds of thousands of Soviet prisoners, sweeping all before them, making the Ukrainian steppe safe for National Socialism, and tonight, once they'd found and liberated the city's stocks of vodka, they'd raise a celebratory glass or two before moving on to the next battle. Last night Glivenko had warned her that this would be a war like no other, unforgiving, pitiless, governed by the sheer size of a country too big even for German appetites. At the time, she'd believed him, but now – watching the open limousines packed with officers whisper by – she began to wonder. These people, with their immaculate uniforms and an occasional wave to the crowds, assume they're born to conquer, and they're probably right. Victory has become a habit, she told herself, and who on earth will ever stop them?

She shook her head, thinking suddenly of Larissa, and then she felt a tap on the arm from Yuri. The crowd on the pavement had turned its attention to an approaching group of old men. At the head of the procession was their leader, slightly taller than the rest. He had a white cloth draped across his thin shoulders and he was carrying a tray. On the tray was a large, round Ukrainian loaf with a dish of salt beside it.

Confused by the sheer numbers of incoming troops, he hesitated a moment at the kerbside, not quite sure what to do next with these traditional symbols of friendship. One of the open Mercedes limousines glided to a halt beside him. The car was white, highly polished, not a scratch, not a dent, not a trace of caked mud. The officers in the car gazed up at the old man, amused. The old man presented his gifts with a deep bow, and Bella watched the senior officer take the bread and toss it into the back seat as the crowd stood in silence before the limousine purred on.

Then, from a neighbouring truck, came another cry. The soldier was young, fair-haired, his face burned red by the sun. '*Brot,*' he shouted. '*Und Butter.*' He stooped briefly, and then threw two wooden crates onto the tramlines. One of the crates burst, spilling black loaves across the cobblestones, and the crowd surged forward, already fighting for the bread. One man, squat, powerfully built, ripped the paper from a block of butter and began to cram it into his mouth, elbowing others away. Yuri, disgusted, watched him licking his fingers one by one, his lips glistening with the grease.

Later that afternoon the city centre was gripped by an orgy of looting. People told each other that victorious armies always help themselves, and, with the Russians gone, and the Ukrainian police invisible, one shop after another was plundered. By now, most of the German troops were moving through the city street by street, requisitioning houses, reassuring residents, seizing livestock. Bella watched a *Wehrmacht* sergeant driving a pig across Khreshchatyk. The pig was on a length of rope and the way he gentled the animal along with the end of his rifle told Bella he knew what he was doing. Probably a farmer, she thought, from some backwoods Pomeranian smallholding, as delighted by this extravagant outbreak of street theatre as everyone else.

At the next corner, a sizeable crowd – mainly women – were emptying a shoe shop, darting off with armfuls of boots and galoshes. One of them paused, stopped by a youth, and began to haggle a price for one of the pairs of boots. The youth had produced a grubby roll of notes but, when the woman was distracted for a moment, he grabbed the boots and ran. She shouted at him and shook her fist but, within seconds, he'd disappeared.

Later, at Bella's request, Yuri took her to the offices of the newspaper. Larissa had an office on the first floor, with a view over the Krillovskaya through her shattered window. It was early evening, and Larissa was gazing down at the street. Her arm had been plastered and was now in a sling. Her hair had been shaved at the front and a line of tiny black stitches had closed a sizeable wound on her forehead. Her face was drawn and pale and she was obviously in pain. Yuri muttered something to her in Ukrainian. She glanced at Bella and nodded.

After Yuri had left, she beckoned Bella towards the window and drew her attention to the street below. Two German Army trucks had parked at the kerbside.

'They're going through the offices room by room,' she said. 'Soon, they'll be interviewing everybody. It's the same in every city they take. Always start with the newspapers and the radio station. These men have fought their way here. From the Polish border that's six hundred kilometres,' she nodded down at her watch. 'Yet they never stop work for a moment.'

'They'll interview you?'

'Of course. No one who works here will be allowed to leave the building.'

'And me?'

'Yuri is waiting downstairs. You must leave at once. He'll take you home.'

Bella was still staring down at the street. Another of the Mercedes staff cars had appeared. It parked behind the trucks and an officer in a black uniform got out and stood on the pavement, feet apart, belted tunic, trousers tucked into gleaming boots, hands on his hips, staring up at the façade of the building. It was a gesture of ownership, Bella realised. Not just the newspaper, but the entire city.

When Larissa asked whether he was SS, Bella nodded. She'd spent years behind an embassy desk in Berlin. She recognised this uniform only too well.

'You know about these people?' She glanced at Larissa.

'I do. Talk to the Poles about them. The people here are children. They think bread and salt will solve everything.' She shook her head, then her fingers lightly traced the shaved patch around her sutured wound. 'So we have something else in common, *chérie*. Thanks to our new friends.'

*

That night, at Yuri's insistence, Bella spent the night at Larissa's apartment. He'd appointed her to be chauffeur, cook, dresser, and – in his own words – anything else Larissa badly needed. Bella was happy to say yes.

From the moment they'd met at the hotel restaurant that first evening in Kyiv, she realised this woman had taken charge of her, the way a mother might. Bella had been flattered by her attentions, and surprised by what had followed, but the last three years had made her a great deal wiser about the trade-offs and accommodations that had come with her new life. In Moscow, you could get anything if you were prepared to barter a favour or two, and experience had taught her that sex with a powerful stranger, if it opened the right doors, could be strangely erotic. Here in Kyiv, Bella knew that her very survival might be at stake, but even so she felt a growing kinship with Larissa that had nothing to do with the striking of bargains and opening of doors. Her self-appointed protector now needed something more from her than sex, and Bella was only too happy to try and supply it.

Bella watched over her for most of the night, sharing her bed, making sure she didn't roll over and damage the plaster cast. At dawn, she inspected the kitchen cupboards, looking for something to eat. Apart from a jug of sour milk and the remains of a stale loaf, there was nothing. She must eat at work, Bella decided. Or maybe she relies on the restaurant meals that go with the many interviews she has to conduct.

Back in the bedroom, Larissa was listening to the radio. The voice, she said, belonged to the regular newscaster at this time in the morning, a native Ukrainian by the name of Mikhail. Normally, he'd be reporting on the small print of city life – mainly accidents, especially fires – but today Kyiv's new masters had written the script. Life, the newscaster announced, would be proceeding much as normal. Citizens who owned arms of any kind, especially shotguns and hunting rifles, were to hand them into designated depots by nightfall. The *Kommandatura* would soon be issuing new identity cards on surrender of the old Soviet document, and these *Ausweisen* would become obligatory by the end of the week. German currency, meanwhile, would shortly be introduced, at an exchange rate with the Ukrainian *hryvnia* to be determined.

'Surprise, surprise,' Larissa grunted. 'They've come to rob us.'

Bella helped her get dressed. She said the broken arm was more an irritation than anything else, but Bella knew that wasn't true. She could see the pain in her eyes every time her shoulder moved and when Bella offered to accompany her to the office, and maybe help out with a spot of typing, she shook her head.

'They'll never let you in,' she said. 'And neither will they let us out. From now on we stay at our desks and write what they tell us to write. They made it plain last night that everything must go through the propaganda people. They and the SS arrived on the heels of the soldiers. Even the Russians were more subtle than that.'

Bella laughed. Subtle? Russians? Larissa asked for a glass of water. When Bella returned from the kitchen, she held it up against the daylight. Tiny particles were suspended in the murky liquid, prompting a shake of the head from Larissa.

'A favour?' she put the glass to one side.

'Anything.'

'We need people out on the streets, watching, making notes, maybe taking a photo or two. The occupation will be long, but it won't last forever and there has to be a record. This is our country. Whatever happens next will be history.'

'You want me out there? On the street?'

'I do, *chérie*. Today will be chaos. That's how occupations start. Be careful. Watch. Listen. You have good ID. It will fool any German. You also speak their language but don't be too clever.'

'Clever?'

'Fluent. You're Ukrainian. It says so on your ID. Your German will be like mine. Enough to get you a loaf of bread or a night in a hotel, but no more.'

'And English?'

'You know no English. Your Russian is excellent but your Ukrainian needs attention. Make the most of that. If you sense trouble, tell them you've been in Moscow for a while and now you're so happy to be back. But nothing will happen, I guarantee it, not for a day or two. The Germans like to get their house in order. The fact that it belongs to us won't worry them for a moment but even the Master Race will still need time to settle in.'

Larissa had a spare camera but couldn't find it, and on reflection she thought that was probably a good thing. The lower Bella's profile on the street, the better.

'No news on the Leica?'

'It's gone. Bastards. Listen, you'll need money, take this—'
She dug in her bag and produced a roll of grubby notes. 'Drive
me to work. I'll show where it's safe to leave the car. I finish at
six o'clock. All you have to do is be there.'

She searched Bella's face for a long moment. The voice on
the radio had given way to classical music.

'Beethoven,' she offered her lips for a kiss, 'not Wagner. Be
grateful for small mercies.'

*

En route to the newspaper offices, their path took them down
Khreshchatyk. Shop windows the length of the city's main
boulevard had been knocked in overnight, and a few families
were still struggling home with rolls of carpet and armfuls of
crockery. According to Larissa, the new term at school had just
begun, and a shop catering to children's educational needs in a
street behind Khreshchatyk had also been emptied. Bella pulled
in at the kerbside while Larissa questioned a mother with two
young children. She was hunting for a couple of new satchels
and had just been directed to an address in an area at the end
of one of the tram lines, where a mountain of these items was
now for sale.

Mention of trams took them back to Khreshchatyk. Bella had
noticed one of them outside the Grand Hotel, abandoned after
the Russians had switched the current off before evacuating the
city. She parked again, leaving Larissa in the passenger seat. The
tram was surrounded by tiny steaming piles of horse manure,
and when she clambered up and went inside, she noticed that
someone had unscrewed all the light bulbs. They'd started
on the windows, too, and a row of wooden seats behind the

driver's position had been unbolted from the floor and carted off. Back outside on the cobblestones, Bella paused to gaze at a German poster on the side of the tram that had already been pasted over a Soviet sketch of a crazed Hitler. The new poster showcased beaming Ukrainian women in peasant dress grazing their fat cattle while adoring children looked on.

Back in the car, Larissa was shaking her head. She, too, had seen the poster.

'Fairy tales,' she muttered. 'Stalin starved you to death. With us Germans, you can prosper again. You think anyone believes that shit?'

The newspaper offices were five minutes away. Bella dropped Larissa and parked the car in a nearby side street before setting off on foot. The traffic was heavier now, and the pavements were beginning to fill with office workers. Of the Germans, there was so far no sign.

One of the city's theatres lay at the next intersection. At the kerbside, three men were wrangling over a wicker basket brimming with costumes. Bella watched them for a moment, wondering whether a uniform of the Imperial Guard was really worth what the seller was demanding, realising that the overnight looters had even been at work here. Taking advantage of the theatre's open door, she ventured inside. According to a poster in the lobby, the next production was to be Chekhov's *The Cherry Orchard*.

'You want a ticket?'

Bella spun round. The man at her elbow was old. His smell had the sweetness of camphor balls, and he badly needed a shave. He was also drunk. He said he was the caretaker, the guardian of everything, and he beckoned her towards the door that led into the theatre itself. Only last week, he said, the set designer had rebuilt one of the lavish interiors demanded by the play. Now, every stick of furniture, every stage prop, every painting on the wall, had gone.

'So what did they take?'

'Everything. Even the grand piano. Even that bust of the fucking Tsar.'

Bella was standing at the back of the theatre. A single shaft of daylight fell through what appeared to be a hole in the roof and when she asked about it, the caretaker shrugged.

'Stukas,' he said. 'Lucky for us the bomb never went off.'

Bella nodded. The effect, she thought, was appropriately dramatic. The rows of empty seats stretched away into the gloom and the stage looked bare, picked clean, ready for an audience with a rich imagination. Chekhov, she thought. With a little help from the *Luftwaffe*.

'The curtains?' she asked. 'The drapes?'

'Gone. You want a drink? Vodka? Come...'

He led her towards the stage, feeling his way by instinct, his boots echoing on the bare wooden floor of the aisle because the carpet, too, had gone. A door beside the stage led to a tiny cubby hole which evidently served as the caretaker's lair. Here, the tart smell of camphor was even stronger. The old man struck a match and lit a candle propped on a saucer. The bottle of vodka on the floor beside the single chair was nearly empty. He took a swig, wiped his mouth with the back of his hand and offered the rest to Bella. She shook her head. She wanted to know why he hadn't chased the looters away.

'Asleep,' he pillowed his head on his hands.

'And that?' Bella nodded down at a hessian sack on the floor.

'Ah...' A smile creased the thin face. He picked up the sack and emptied the contents onto the floor. Among the stage props, Bella recognised a faux-silver champagne bucket.

'Yours?'

'Theirs. They said it was a present.'

'For what?'

'Staying asleep,' he offered Bella another gummy smile, and then held out the bottle again. 'Finish it,' he said. '*Tovarish.*'

Bella hesitated and then did his bidding. The vodka, undoubtedly home-made, scorched the back of her throat. She managed to suppress a cough, her eyes already beginning to swim, and the old man put his hands together, a gesture of applause. Then he nodded at the downy fuzz of blonde hair on the bareness of her scalp.

'You're ill? Because I have more vodka.'

'No, thank you,' Bella shook her head. 'But it's a kind thought.'

With some care, she made her way back to the street. Overnight, she thought, the city has fallen into the grasp of the free market. After years of going short to fill bellies in Moscow and Leningrad, the Ukrainians are reclaiming what they regard as rightfully theirs. For years, in Yuri's phrase, they've been milked by Mother Russia, and now – thanks to the Germans – they might just become their own masters again. Bella knew this was wildly optimistic, the triumph of vodka over common sense, but she couldn't hide from herself the feeling that spring had come very late indeed this year, that Kyiv was turning its face to the sun and beginning to flower.

A café across the boulevard from the theatre had just opened. Bella took a seat in the window, her belly warmed by the vodka, and ordered a second glass. Larissa had given her a pad and a couple of pencils and Bella spent the next hour trying to tease some order into her racing brain. At first she played the apprentice journalist, writing diligently about the theatre, about the caretaker, about the finger of dusty sunlight that revealed so little, and so much, but then she began to track backwards, taking tiny sips of vodka, tracing the whole of her journey into this madness, recasting it as a letter to Moncrieff.

Dearest Tam, she wrote, this morning finds me under new ownership, a burned-out defector in a faraway city, half in love with a goddess journalist who makes me feel very good about myself. The Germans have made their usual entry, stage left, noisy, fierce, knocking over the furniture, pushing squillions of Russians onto the steppe. Imagine that. And then imagine the emptiness – all that *space* – they've left behind.

Au moment, my lovely man, one half of this crazy city is robbing the rest. No one knows what money is worth anymore and so you do the sensible thing and barter your mother-in-law for an ounce or two of home-grown tobacco and maybe quarter shares in next door's cow. It's all wildly pleasant and picturesque and the Krauts are biding their time in the wings because someone's mislaid the script and they're reduced to behaving like human beings. That won't last, of course, because everyone's having far too fine a time, but this morning finds me contemplating a third glass of God's little blessing, and probably another glass after that.

To earn my keep, dearest Tam, I've promised to play the journalist for my new mistress and her bloody newspaper but getting the right words in the right order isn't as simple as you might think. Events are already getting out of hand, but life is full of surprises, some of them – to be frank – delightful, and my handsome friend has introduced me to a couple of variations on the usual theme. She has the hands of a man, and an appetite to go with it, and a heart-stopping profile in certain lights. A couple of days ago, the *Luftwaffe* did their best to blow both of us up, but I survived and most of her did, too.

You'd like my new friend. She's noble. She has grace. And, like you, nothing seems to frighten her. I've also met a man who writes novels and wants to live in the eleventh century in caves full of monks with nice views of the river. This still strikes me as bizarre but it may – God only knows – turn out to be a wise decision because, as ever, no one has a clue what might happen next. Dearest Tam, you're utterly wonderful on mountains and in a proper bed, and I miss both. Kiss Scotland for me. All of it.

Bella sat back, toying with the remains of the vodka. Proper bed? She loved the phrase, so idiotic, so un-Moncrieff, so childlike, and she was still thinking about Tam when a woman paused beside her table, and then nodded at the spare chair.

'Please...' Bella gestured for her to sit down.

The woman looked poor. There was dirt under her nails, and her blouse was missing a button, and Bella sensed at once that she was selling something.

'You're a writer?' the woman asked.

'Yes.'

'Are you famous?'

'Very. I expect you think I'm rich, too.'

'And are you?'

'Yes,' Bella held her gaze. 'In all kinds of ways.'

Bella tried to get to her feet and end the conversation, but then changed her mind. The woman behind the counter was watching her. Drunk by mid-morning? Unforgiveable. Semi-bald? Deeply suspicious.

'You want another one?' The woman was looking at her empty glass.

'Yes, please,' Bella frowned. 'No, thank you.'

'Are you sure?'

'No.'

The woman turned towards the counter, gesturing at the glass. A bottle of vodka arrived on the table.

'And you? You're drinking, too?'

'No.'

'Just me, then?'

'Yes. And then we'll go.'

'Where?'

The woman named a street Bella had never heard of.

'You know this city?'

'I've been away for a while.'

'Where?'

'Moscow.'

'And is that why your Russian is so good?'

'*Da.*'

'But you're Ukrainian?'

'I might be. I'm a writer. Writers lie for a living. That's why I'm so good at it. Tell me what you're selling. Tell me about this street of yours.'

The woman was uneasy now, wrong-footed by the sudden twists and turns in the conversation. She sat back in the chair, slightly prim, a little offended, her hands in her lap.

'Well?' Bella asked. 'What have you got for me?'

The woman shrugged. The street she'd mentioned was where all the new apartment blocks for the *apparatchiki* had been built. These people, of course, were Russians.

'And they've gone? Packed their bags? Fled? Is that what you're saying?'

She nodded. The apartments are big, she said. Five rooms, sometimes six, fully equipped, the best of everything.

'So who owns them now?'

'We do, all of us. My husband was the manager. Also there are watchmen, and plumbers, and lift attendants.'

'Serfs.'

'Exactly. But serfs no longer. We've moved in, chosen our own apartments, and emptied the rest. We can sell you anything. You want one of those new fridges? No problem. It's yours. You want the Director's fancy car? We have the key. Money is all we need. A writer like you? So rich? So famous. Just tell me yes,' she reached for the bottle, still corked, 'then we'll go.'

Bella shook her head. She knew she needed to bring this conversation to an end. The guts of the story were there already, and she didn't need to see the place because she could imagine the rest. Larissa, she thought, would be delighted with this little exchange.

Bella seized the bottle and headed for the counter. She was drunk now but the beautiful thing was that she didn't much care. She folded the letter to Moncrieff and stored it in her bag, along with the vodka, watching the woman from the *apparatchiki* apartments leave the café to find someone else to buy her loot. At the counter she paid for the vodka and asked about the Besserabka market. Larissa had mentioned it this morning. If you want to understand Kyiv, she'd said, it's the best place to start. The woman behind the counter agreed.

'Down Khreshchatyk to the very end,' she said. 'It opened again this morning.'

*

Bella spent the rest of the day at the market, mostly asleep. It was warm in the afternoon sun, and she found a bench behind a stall selling pierogi with peas and potatoes, waking from time to time to watch the queue lengthen and contract as customers, mainly women, haggled with the beefy young cook. No one was bothering with money anymore and Bella tried to work out an exchange rate based on home-grown tobacco, bags of eggs, and – in one case – a live hedgehog.

Towards the end of the afternoon, she joined the queue herself, returning to the bench to demolish the pie, uncapping the bottle and washing it down with another mouthful of vodka. Watching the market beginning to empty, the bottle still in her hand, she realised with a little jolt of pleasure that she'd become part of the pulse of the place, an honorary resident, sun-kissed, full of vodka and hopelessly optimistic.

*

An hour and a half later, already waiting by the car, Larissa watched her weaving down the street.

'I got lost,' Bella put out a hand to steady herself. 'My fault.'

'You're drunk,' Larissa was smiling. 'It suits you.'

'You still want me to drive? You're not frightened?'

'Frightened? Never.'

Impressed by this act of faith, Bella slid behind the wheel, concentrating hard on every turn, every gear change, every stab on the brake. The streets were beginning to empty now. From time to time, Larissa warned of German patrols, soldiers in threes and fours, sauntering along like tourists, and Bella blew them kisses through the open window as the little car sped by. It seemed an altogether civilised way to start an occupation, and when they finally climbed the stairs to the apartment, she stopped Larissa on the top landing and tugged her closer.

'I meant to buy you a pie,' she said. 'But all I've got is vodka.'

They finished the bottle, and afterwards Bella slept like a baby, her arms wrapped around Larissa, oblivious of the plaster cast. Next morning, badly hung-over again, she returned from taking Larissa to work and did her best to type up what she could remember from the previous day. The results, she knew only too well, were wooden, poorly written, and did scant justice to what she'd witnessed. She read it twice, then threw it in the bin and unfolded the letter she'd handwritten to Moncrieff. If it was truth that Larissa was after, she thought, then here it was. Dearest Tam. Proper bed.

For the next couple of days, the city continued to bask in the warm autumnal sunshine. The chestnut trees along the riverbank were turning to bronze and the blue and yellow striped flag of the Ukrainian nationalists flew beside the long scarlet banners hung by the Germans. Out of sheer curiosity, freed from any other obligation, Bella wandered up and down Khreshchatyk, paying special attention to the city's new chieftains. Kyiv's main boulevard – no longer the preserve of the Party – was now theirs for the taking, and Bella watched German commanders moving purposefully from building to building, checking on whether or not it met their needs.

The enormous Continental Hotel, for example, had been quickly occupied by dozens of German staff officers, and more were appearing by the hour, accompanied by soldiers laden with boxes of paperwork. *Wehrmacht* High Command, meanwhile, had taken a fancy to the towering property on the corner of Proreznaya Street, with the popular Children's World shop on the ground floor. The Germans, to her surprise, were still behaving themselves and the instalment of a seemingly benign military regime over a store selling toys and children's winter clothing struck Bella as symbolic, richly promising for the weeks and months to come. If Kyiv's luck holds, she thought, the city's prospects might indeed be bright.

This thought was comforting but other questions remained. How long would the occupation last? Would the Germans be in Moscow by Christmas? Would Stalin sue for peace? And if this huge country ended up as a permanent part of the Reich, where would that leave a wayward defector with a taste for home-made vodka and a lingering faith in the blessings of Marxism?

Bella had no answers to any of these questions, but she knew that, if only for her own sanity, she had to find a role for herself. Becoming a journalist was a non-starter. Nor, so far, did there appear to be any kind of organised resistance to the Germans. So, for the time being, she'd become a *babushka*, a grandmotherly figure, fat and happy, devoted to Larissa's care and welfare. She'd buy a headscarf, and a pair of felt slippers, and return to the market every morning to haggle for the best vegetables and perhaps a little meat. She'd buy peasant bread and have wholesome stews bubbling on the stove night and day, and while Larissa was still out at work she'd make the time to take a stab at learning the piano.

At Christmas, she thought, she'd find a chicken or a goose from somewhere and they'd invite Yuri over. There'd be snow at the window, and lots of vodka, and once they were drunk enough, they'd gather round the piano and sing carols. She'd have to play the tunes from memory, and she'd have to teach Larissa and Yuri the words, but that would be fine. Larissa was probably concert standard already, so they might end the evening with a little Rachmaninoff. Dear Tam, she thought. Maybe you should come, too.

*

That evening, she tabled the proposition but Larissa was in no mood to listen. The piano, she said, was there to be played. Help yourself. And as for proper meals, she simply shrugged. She seemed troubled, preoccupied, fretful. Bella tried to get to the bottom of whatever had gone wrong but got nowhere.

Mid-evening brought a knock on the door. They'd been listening to the radio again. Bella unbolted the door. It was Yuri. He pushed past her, embracing Larissa. She nodded at the radio and put a finger to her lips. There were yet more announcements from the *Kommandatura*, a long list of diktats, of dos and don'ts, of forms to be collected and filled out, of items to be surrendered, and of an imminent curfew. Then came a roll of drums, and yet more classical music.

'Bruckner,' Larissa was looking up at Yuri. 'Well?'

Yuri said nothing, just nodded. Larissa turned the music down and went across to the window. She gazed out at the street, and beckoned Bella to join her. The street was deserted, as if the curfew had already begun. Larissa's eyes were closed. Bella asked her again whether everything was OK, and again she refused to answer.

'Tomorrow?' she said. 'You'll take me to work?'

'Of course.'

'And afterwards?'

'I don't know.'

'Then you must come back here.' She tried to force a smile. 'And teach yourself the piano.'

Bella stared at her. Then she realised what Larissa was really saying.

'You don't want me out on the street?'

'No, *chérie*,' she was nursing her arm. 'I don't.'

15

WEDNESDAY 24 SEPTEMBER 1941

Bella was on Khreshchatyk, walking back from the Besserabka market, when the first bomb went off.

First came a blinding flash, the colour of lightning, then the blast wave rolled down the boulevard, a giant bellow of anger, destroying everything in its path, blowing out windows, tossing cars aside, tearing off branches, uprooting smaller trees, leaving passers-by in pools of blood as panes of glass, falling from above, shattered around them. A huge dust cloud rose around the seat of the explosion, and as it slowly cleared, the scale of the damage became apparent. The entire front of a building towards the end of the street had been ripped off, exposing floor after floor of offices, and the air was still full of sheets of paper, dancing in the wind.

Bella had been thrown to the pavement by the blast wave. Now, she got to her feet and did her best to remove the fragments of glass from the light summer coat she'd borrowed from Larissa. A woman nearby was examining a cut on the back of her hand. Bella offered her a handkerchief she'd found in the pocket of her coat. The woman looked up, white-faced, gesturing down the street.

'A gas explosion,' she said. 'It happens all the time.'

Bella didn't answer. In her heart she knew this was no accident. She took a brief look at the woman's wound, told her she'd be OK, and gave her the handkerchief. Potatoes had spilled from the bag Bella had filled at the market, but she ignored them. Columns of flame were erupting at the end of Khreshchatyk and she began to run towards the inferno. The closer she got, the name of the missing shopfront and the gaunt remains of the offices above began to dawn on her. Children's World, she thought. Gone.

She was right. Badly out of breath, she had to stop. German soldiers, their uniforms grey with dust, some of them still in shock, were linking arms at the bellowed command of an officer, holding back a crowd of onlookers. Then a second squad of soldiers appeared, dragging dozens of civilians with them, heading away from the wreckage.

One of the prisoners, a tall, red-haired youth, tried to give them the slip. He managed to wriggle free but then a *Wehrmacht* sergeant caught him by the neck and threw him to his knees. The youth stared up, pleading for his life as a rifle butt from another soldier smashed into the side of his face. Inert on the cobblestones, he tried to protect himself, but they were kicking him now, heavy boots, blows to his head and chest. Finally, his face a mask of blood, he slumped unconscious. The sergeant wiped his hands on his uniform and rejoined the prisoners heading down the boulevard. They, too, had already taken a beating and the crowd parted as they stumbled onto the pavement.

Bella found herself beside an old man in a threadbare grey coat. The chaos around him appeared to come as no surprise.

'They've been arrested?' Bella was still looking at the soldiers pushing the prisoners through the open doors of a building fifty metres away. 'And what's that? Where are they going?'

'It's a cinema.'

'A *cinema*? What will they do in a cinema?'

The old man shrugged, then drew a bony finger across his throat. At that same moment came the roar of a second explosion, and the terrifying punch of the blast. People turned away, crouching, kneeling, covering their ears, and when heads lifted again the remains of the Children's World building was a pile of rubble.

Then, dizzyingly, a third explosion. Bella, already deafened, had a perfect view. By now she knew these attacks were deliberate, the work of saboteurs, and the target this time was the building across the boulevard from Children's World. The upstairs offices had been requisitioned by the Germans but the café at street level had evidently been full of gas masks and now they were scattered in a huge circle across the glass-flecked cobblestones.

Bella stared at them. With their yellow Perspex eyes and rubber snouts they looked grotesque, severed heads from some alien planet. God help us, Bella thought, turning away. For the first time, she realised she was trembling. The sheer violence of the explosions, what they could do to bricks and mortar, to flesh and blood, was something new to her. The Stukas had been bad enough, but this was something far, far worse. Everything she'd taken for granted, like the permanence of these huge buildings, had turned out to be a lie and she'd been crazy to ever think otherwise. You've been foolish enough to assume you were safe, she told herself. Wrong.

The old man was still beside her, as unmoved as ever. He was looking at the cinema. The doors were open again, and officers and soldiers were pouring out, followed by the prisoners. One of the officers had a pistol in his hand. He began to shoot upwards, attracting attention, shouting at the crowd. Bella couldn't hear a word.

She turned to the old man. She wanted to know what the officer was saying.

'He's telling us to run. He says the Khreshchatyk's going up.' For the first time, the old man smiled. 'All of it.'

*

Bella was arrested fifteen minutes later. She'd half walked, half run, back towards Larissa's car, trying to avoid the drifts of broken glass, terrified of the next explosion, half expecting the boulevard to erupt around her. Then, quite suddenly, the pavement was blocked by a line of soldiers. There were at least a dozen of them. Their rifles were trained on the oncoming pedestrians. There was no way through.

An officer appeared. He had a gun in his hand. He shouted something in German that no one understood.

'He's telling us to stop,' Bella told the woman beside her. 'He's telling us not to move.'

'But why?'

'I don't know.'

The crowd had come to a halt. Some were trying to turn back, but more troops had appeared, forming another line, and suddenly they were surrounded. The officer had put his gun away. A truck had appeared at the kerbside and the officer was shouting orders to the driver. The driver got down from the cab and lowered the tailgate at the back.

'That's for us,' Bella nodded at the truck.

She was right. The officer was moving through the crowd now, pausing to study each face. A brief nod to his sergeant was enough to bring a soldier to seize the man or woman and push them through the crowd to the waiting truck. Soon, the back of the truck was nearly full.

The officer came to Bella. This time, he paused for longer. 'Your name?'

'Alina Antoniv.'

'Ukrainian?'

'Yes.'

He gazed at her a moment longer, the faintest smile playing on his lips. Then he nodded to the sergeant and she, too, was heading for the truck.

They drove away from the city centre, swerving to avoid fire engines racing towards the towering columns of smoke. People exchanged glances, risked a shrug or two, but no one spoke. Two soldiers were sitting on the tailgate, their rifles erect between their knees. When the truck finally slowed, Bella managed to steal a look back. A huge pall of smoke was still drifting over Khreshchatyk, and as she watched there came another explosion, and a second, and then – seconds later – a third. The woman beside her was crossing herself.

'The Russians,' she whispered to herself. 'They're bombarding us.'

The truck ground to a halt. The place looked like a military barracks, abandoned by the Red Army. There were soldiers everywhere, bellowed commands, men running, engines starting. Bella watched two men struggling with a huge reel of canvas firehose, trying to hoist it onto the back of a trailer. Then the soldiers in the truck dropped the tailgate and ordered everyone out. At gunpoint, they were herded towards an open door. Then the officer in charge had second thoughts.

'*Halt!*'

Soldiers were suddenly among them, pushing them roughly into ranks, facing onto the barrack square. Another officer had appeared, younger, leaner, black uniform, knee-high boots in polished leather. He unfolded a sheet of paper, and began to read it aloud in a high, thin voice.

Bella understood every word. The *Schutzstaffel*, he said, were empowered by the Reich to take control of this chaos. The city was under threat from saboteurs. First, the fires would be put out. Then those responsible would be hunted down. And, finally, justice would be done. In the meantime, those present – here and elsewhere – would be held as hostages against further acts of terrorism. Kyiv was burning, he piped. The innocent would suffer, but – thanks to the SS – the guilty would pay.

Bella heard the roar of yet another explosion, hoping to God the newspaper offices had been spared. The SS officer flinched but then composed himself. A nod to the soldiers, and they were all heading for the open door again. Stairs led to a basement, a big empty space barely lit, pitted concrete floor, bare wires hanging from the ceiling, an overwhelming smell of damp. The steel door slammed shut and, in the half-darkness, people looked at each other, seeking reassurance, trying to make sense of what was happening, and slowly there came a low, hesitant mutter of conversation.

People were comparing notes, the women especially. Some had been on the way to the market, others had friends to meet, calls to make, children to pick up. Then had come the terrifying explosions, the city blowing itself apart in front of their eyes, and now this. What had we ever done? Why us? Bella listened. Lives so suddenly interrupted, she thought, and people rightly fearful of what might happen next.

Hours went by. People sat down, backs against the wall, seeking comfort in each other, and Bella found herself beside a big woman whose age she could only guess at. She was blonde, with an enormous chest, and she'd had a bad time with a Russian official who'd demanded her favours in exchange for a weekly supply of chicken livers. The meat had been a godsend, especially for her husband who had to dig up roads all day, but the bloody Russian had fallen in love with her, or so he claimed, and she'd ended up half dying of exhaustion. The Soviets, she said, belonged in a zoo. They made love like animals and rarely bothered with conversation. Bella, who knew a thing or two about Russian men, could only agree, and she was about to share a memory of her own when the door opened.

This time, there were three officers, and they divided the basement room between them, moving from person to person, demanding their papers, noting down names and addresses and dates of birth. Bella confirmed her false name again. According to her ID papers, she lived at the address of the old woman everyone called Mama, and Bella wondered whether these people ever bothered to check. Kyiv, she told herself, would still be a mystery to the Germans, every corner of the city a jigsaw of streets, and for the time being – with luck – she'd safely remain a native Ukrainian.

Alas, no. Everyone had been listed. The officers had gone. Bella was back in conversation with her new friend, telling her about the empty apartments in the *apparatchiki* block, when the SS officer with the squeaky voice appeared at the door and called her name. For a moment, she thought she'd misheard, but then he shouted again, louder this time, and her companion dug her in the ribs.

'That's you,' she said. 'Maybe they're letting you go.'

Bella stood and picked her way between bodies, aware of the stir she was causing. The SS officer was waiting for her beside the door.

'Alina Antoniv?' Bella nodded. 'Follow me.'

One flight of stairs led to another. Finally, the SS officer found the door he was after. The office was bare, except for a wooden desk, two chairs, and a lighter oblong on the wall where something had been removed. The windowpane was broken, most of the glass missing, and Bella could smell burning. Children's World, she thought, and God knows where else.

The officer settled in the chair behind the desk and removed his cap. Smooth cheeks, perfectly barbered. Black hair cut high around the whiteness of his scalp. Thin lips and a hint of weakness in his receding chin. From a drawer in the desk he produced a pad. The pen came from the breast pocket of his SS jacket.

'*Hinsetzen!*' Bella sat down. 'You speak German?' The question, in English, was a trap.

Bella looked blank. 'I'm Ukrainian,' she said in German. 'I speak Russian, too, and a little of your language.'

'You live here?' German again.

'I do.'

'Born here?'

'Of course. But you know that from my papers.'

'And you learned your German where, exactly?'

'In Halle. I worked as a maid.'

'For how long?'

'Two years. Enough to learn your language.'

'You have a name? An address?'

'It was near the station. Her name was Frau Schmidt.'

'And this was when, exactly?'

'1937.'

'I see.' He'd been jotting down notes. Now his head came up. The tightness of the cap had left a faint pink mark around his forehead. He's far too young for a job like this, Bella thought. The SS was normally home for older men, seasoned psychopaths with a playful taste for serious violence. This man belonged in a classroom. Pupil or teacher? She wasn't sure.

'And then you came back?' he enquired. 'Here? To Kyiv?'

'Yes.'

'Just a little fish, then? This morning? Caught in our net?'

'Yes,' Bella hugged her bag closer. 'Can I go now? Might that be in order?'

'I'm afraid not.' The officer checked his pad a final time and got to his feet. Moments later, he'd left the office. Bella heard a key turn in the lock, and then came the sound of his footsteps receding down the corridor.

In the sudden silence, Bella could hear the faraway rustle of leaves blowing in the wind, and when she got to her feet and went to the window she was surprised to find the parade ground below completely empty, except for a black Mercedes. The driver, in SS uniform, was busy polishing the long bonnet, and as she watched he moistened a fingertip to remove a tiny mark. During her years in Berlin, German attention to detail had never ceased to amaze her. Conquest was one thing, she thought, and the Germans were very good at it, but when it came to occupation they were even better, and here was why.

She sat down again, staring at the scribbled notes on the pad, wondering whether she'd told the SS officer too much. In the NKVD's Big House in Moscow, where she had a desk, experienced interrogators always counselled reticence, but his questions had been direct and any whisper of evasion on her part would have raised whatever suspicions he had still further. The question she really had to answer was why she'd been the first to be called out. Had it been unwise to choose a name beginning with 'A'? Were the SS in thrall to the alphabetical order? Or was there some darker motive at which she could only guess?

She was aware she was checking her watch far too often. She knew that good interrogators always used time to their advantage, letting the prisoner sweat a little, and she did her best to relax. Prisoner? Was that the word? Undoubtedly, yes. Be kinder on yourself, she thought. Admit your own helplessness. Because the truth is never supposed to hurt.

Moments later, she heard the sound of a car door open and close down in the parade ground, and she tried to imagine the driver back with the comforts of the leather upholstery, and perhaps a cigarette or two. Then her gaze returned to the oblong on the wall, with the tell-tale pock where a nail had once been. Only days ago, with the Soviets still in charge, she suspected that a framed photo of the *Vodzh* had been hanging here, and she marvelled at the way the winds of war could sweep countless images off countless walls the length and breadth of this immense empire. Stalin, one day. Hitler, or perhaps *Onkel Heine* the next.

Onkel Heine. The image it conjured made her shiver. Heinrich Himmler. Head of the SS. In charge of Hitler's private army. The rimless glasses. The owlish expression. The jug ears. The carefully clipped moustache, doubtless in homage to his beloved Führer, and the little pot belly he did his best to hide on state occasions. This was the man, she told herself, who'd built an entire empire on a fierce appetite for savagery and – yes – on a painstaking attention to the smallest details. A monster from one angle, a bureaucrat of genius on the other. Was Kyiv ready for *Onkel Heine* and his disciples? Was she?

*

It was nearly dark by the time she heard the footsteps returning, and by now she'd recognised that the knots in her belly had been tightened by fear, rather than hunger. When the key turned in the lock, and the door opened, she deliberately made no effort to turn around. Expecting her first inquisitor, she found herself looking at a much older man.

She was no expert when it came to SS insignia, but he had the presence and authority that comes with senior rank. He put his briefcase on the desk and settled carefully in the chair. The cast in one eye made him look slightly deranged and too many sleepless nights were beginning to show in the hollows of his face. Like his boss, he wore a thin sprout of hair on his upper lip, and the climb to the top floor had left him visibly sweating.

He opened the briefcase and peered inside. Then he sat back, gazing at the notepad, his manicured nails tapping lightly on the tabletop.

'My name is *Standartenführer* Kalb,' he looked up. 'I'm in charge here. Your name again?'

'Alina Antoniv.'

'From Kyiv? Yes?' He had a Bavarian accent.

'Yes.'

'And you understand me? You speak a little German?'

'Yes.'

'And you have good Russian?'

'Yes.'

'But no English?'

'No.'

'I see.' His good eye held her gaze. 'Do you think we're stupid? Be honest.'

'I have no opinion in the matter. All I'd like is the opportunity to go home.'

'To the old lady's house?'

'To Mama's, yes.'

He nodded, taking his time. 'But she hasn't seen you for weeks,' he murmured. 'In fact, she only met you once, Fraulein Antoniv. So how do you explain that?'

Bella stared at him. She hadn't got an answer, but worse was to come. From the briefcase, Kalb extracted a file and laid it carefully on the desktop where she could see it. All NKVD personal files were colour-coded, according to the classification of the subject. Purple was for foreign nationals, with the name typed on a white sticky label on the front. Even upside down, and even in Cyrillic, there could be no mistake. *Isobel Menzies.*

'Where did you get that?'

'NKVD headquarters,' he gestured vaguely towards the road outside that led back into the city. 'In what your Russian friends call the Big House. It was there for us to find. It was on display. Even we couldn't have missed it.'

Bella ignored the sarcasm. Bezkrovny, she thought. The NKVD officer despatched from Moscow to meet her at Kharkov and bring her back. Either he delivered it in person, or had it sent through. Taking her chances with Ilya Glivenko had been a mistake. Lesson one for any senior NKVD officer under the cosh of Moscow? Assigned a task, a prey, you never give up.

Kalb was leafing through the file. He'd obviously been through it before. Finally, he looked up.

'Do we agree you're English?'

'Yes.' She saw no point in lying.

'Yet you ran away to Moscow.' A brief frown. 'Might I ask why?'

'Because I believed in it.'

'Believed in what?'

'Marx, Engels, Lenin, the October Revolution, equality, the Proletariat, the rightness of all that.'

'And now?'

'Now's no different. The Revolution has fallen into Stalin's lap but that's no fault of the Revolution. Stalin may yet save it from Stalin. Funnier things have happened,' she shrugged. 'Who knows?'

Kalb nodded. For a brief moment, Bella sensed she'd won his full attention and wondered why.

'What happened to your hair? Do you mind me asking?'

'Not at all. I suffer from alopecia, baldness. It's hereditary. My mother has it, too.'

'Really?'

'Yes.'

'So how do you explain this?'

Kalb slipped a photograph from the back of the file and handed it across. The focus and the lighting were perfect, even the tiny scabs of blood on her newly shaven head. The room behind was in deep shadow but she recognised Larissa's grand piano.

'This is you?'

'This is me.'

'When?'

'Recently. Maybe a week ago.'

'So, who took the photograph?'

Bella shook her head, wouldn't say.

'Was it this woman?' More photographs, Larissa herself this time, shot by someone else. 'We think these photographs probably came off the same roll of film. The backgrounds are very similar. The photos were in your file. I'm assuming your NKVD friends are sending us a message.'

'About?'

'You.' His smile had no warmth. 'They wanted us to find you. And, happily, we've done just that. What remains is to find your friend. Larissa Krulak, am I right? A journalist with a reputation. A journalist with many admirers. Someone with influence. Someone with a following. We know where she works. We know she was injured, and we've found the surgeon who set her arm. We also know where she lives but here's the problem. She's gone, fled, disappeared.'

Bella nodded. Whatever she thought of the SS and *Onkel Heine*, it would be wrong to underestimate this man. Details again, lots and lots of them. Only one question remained.

'Why do you want her?'

Kalb sat back, took his time. In war, he said quietly, you never took anything for granted. At considerable expense of blood and treasure, his countrymen had taken one of the biggest cities in Europe. Victory had been complete, overwhelming, and – in its way – clean. So far, both officers and men had been gentle with Kyiv, taken care of it, restored the power, started to mend the water supply, reopened the market and the shops, even made the trams run on time.

'We've done our best to behave like human beings,' he gestured towards the window again, 'but look how the Soviets repay us. Those *Untermenschen*, your *Untermenschen*, have laid explosives everywhere. This we know already. You want a list? The State Bank, Children's World, the Grand Hotel. We dig in the ruins and we find many dead and injured, some of them ours. This is no way to fight a war. It's cowardly and it has to stop. Are we surprised? In a way, we shouldn't be. Russians are animals. But it still has to stop and for that to happen, we have to *make* it stop. We believe there will be more mines, more explosions, more deaths. Someone knows where to find all these mines. There may be dozens of them, perhaps more. But someone, somewhere, *knows*. We have investigators flying in from Berlin. Let's call them specialists. But in the meantime, we need to prepare a wider response. Killings like these can't go unpunished. In Paris, for the death of a single German, we shoot a hundred Frenchmen. In Kyiv, for what happened today, we may need a different calculus, more blood.' He paused. 'Which brings us back to your friend.'

'Larissa?'

'Indeed. There are two points of interest here, and it's only fair to share both of them. In the first place, we think she probably knows about these mines. For that reason alone, it might pay us to have a conversation.'

'And the other reason?'

'Far simpler.' The smile again. 'She's a Jew.'

16

WEDNESDAY 24 SEPTEMBER 1941

The Mercedes was still waiting when Bella emerged from the barracks. Kalb had assigned her to the care of his bodyguard. Valentin, at first glance, looked like a retired wrestler Bella knew in Moscow. Leaning against the car, he wore a black leather coat that nearly reached his ankles. One of his huge hands cupped the remains of a cigarette, and his eyes never left Bella as she crossed the parade ground. His shaven head and the pastiness of his face was out of scale with the rest of him and under different circumstances, thought Bella, he might have featured in a child's cartoon, but just now this caricature of a man felt intensely dangerous.

The certainty of sudden death was prowling the city centre. More explosions were expected by the hour and time was the enemy. Kalb, it seemed, had taken this chaos personally. He wanted names, leads, and he wanted them now, before his masters in Berlin started to lose patience with the *Schutzstaffel*'s man in unruly Kyiv.

Valentin ground the cigarette beneath his boot and opened the rear door.

'In,' he said.

'Where are we going?'

'You don't know? He hasn't told you?' The prospect seemed to amuse him. 'In,' he said again.

Bella sat in the back, watching Kalb hurrying towards them. Valentin had produced a pair of handcuffs. He was examining her with a frankness she found disturbing. A dog, she thought, ungovernable, off the leash.

'Give me your hand.'

'Why?'

'Just do it.'

She felt the jaws of one of the cuffs close around her wrist. Valentin attached the other cuff to his own wrist. Bella stared down at the two hands, interlinked against the black leather of the seat. Another caricature, even more gross.

'You think I'm going to jump out?' she was trying to make light of it.

Valentin didn't answer. He was looking, this time, at the thin silver chain she wore around her neck. His breath was sour and rank, and she hated his physical closeness. Huge hands. Spade nails. Whorls of black hair.

The moment Kalb got into the passenger seat at the front, they were off. The driver barely slowed for the turn onto the main road that led back to the city centre. Oncoming traffic swerved to avoid them as the driver hit the throttle and accelerated away.

Dense smoke still shrouded the city centre, and there were soldiers everywhere. At the foot of the hill, troops had thrown a barricade across the road with heavily guarded access to only a handful of vehicles. A queue had formed. Papers were being inspected. A soldier stepped forward, his hand extended, ordering them to stop.

Kalb told the driver to ignore him. The soldier was unshouldering his rifle when he caught sight of the SS emblem on the fender. He stepped back, offering the Nazi salute, his face a mask as the Mercedes swept past.

'In the park, your people are cutting the hoses from the river,' Kalb gestured at a line of fire engines parked on Khreshchatyk. 'They don't make it easy for us.'

Your people? Bella shivered, knowing that this wasn't the moment to protest her innocence. The script, she knew, had already been written, her part assigned. They believed she was complicit in this murderous conspiracy and the NKVD file was all the proof the men in black would ever need. Thanks to Bezkrovny, and the hasty evacuation of the Big House, they were looking at a gift from God. Kalb had already used that very phrase. Moscow had sent her here. She'd come from the biggest of the Big Houses. She'd linked up with the bombers. She knew exactly what they were up to, maybe not every detail but certainly the sheer *scale* of the operation. She'd doubtless know names, where to get hold of these people, and now – with a little encouragement – she was going to share that knowledge.

They'd come to a brief halt while a couple of water tankers lumbered past. Wherever Bella looked, there were sudden eruptions of flame, jets of the brightest yellow against the thickening dusk, and she watched half a dozen men hauling a length of hose across the boulevard towards a burning hotel, their bodies bent low against the scalding breath of the firestorm.

'These places are full of combustibles,' Kalb was shaking his head. 'Ammunition, kerosene, grenades, even mortar shells. First you blow the bottom up, then it sets fire to itself. It's not a hotel at all. It's a warehouse full of explosives. Clever.'

The driver was nodding in agreement. The water tankers had gone now and he was urging the big limousine across the cobbles when Bella heard the roar of yet another explosion in one of the adjoining streets, and she saw smoke-blackened faces turning and looking upwards with a kind of awe as yet more smoke billowed into the darkening sky.

My people again, she thought. Russians. God help me.

Minutes later, they were outside Larissa's apartment block. A line of vehicles was already parked at the kerbside. Manacled to Valentin, Bella struggled out of the back of the Mercedes, trying to slow her racing pulse. Dignity, she kept telling herself. Show no fear. For her own sake, and for Larissa's, she would never grant these bullies an easy victory.

Valentin hurried her up the endless flights of steps, the tightness of the handcuff biting into her flesh. On the landing at the top, an SS guard was standing watch over a pile of possessions. All of them belonged to Larissa. Bella recognised items from the kitchen – a samovar that had belonged to a favourite aunt, two enamel cooking pots, a lovely cut-glass decanter – and on top of the heap of clothes was a fur coat Larissa had fetched out for the coming winter. Bella wanted to pause a moment, take a proper look, but Valentin dragged her on. This is already the house of the dead, she thought, and now they're attending to the estate.

The door to the apartment was open. Breathless from the climb, Bella knew she was stepping into a nightmare. Even the bulk of Valentin, so close, couldn't hide the savagery of the violence. Everywhere she looked, Larissa's life had been torn apart: drawers ripped out and emptied, furniture dismembered, drapes and curtains torn from their fixings, pictures smashed, hand-embroidered cushions disembowelled. A pickaxe was lying beside the remains of the parquet floor and someone had taken a sledgehammer to the grand piano.

She stared at the piano. The gleaming top she'd watched Larissa polish had been stoved in, splintered beyond repair, and the keyboard had ceased to exist. Black and white notes were scattered everywhere, a mad sonata that would never reappear on any score. There had to be a logic in all this, but the violence felt wanton, deliberate, vengeful. Kalb and his men were sending a message. On a larger scale, she thought, this was what the departed Soviets were doing to the city centre.

In the next room, which Larissa used as a study, an SS soldier was still at work with a bayonet, hacking and thrusting at the sofa. Stuffing spilled out of the plumpness of the upholstery and he paused for a moment, digging a hand deep into a corner of the sofa, looking for anything that might have been hidden. He'd taken off his jacket and his shirt was dark with sweat and Bella wondered about the secret pleasures of a night like this.

Kalb dismissed the soldier with a grunt, then led the way to Larissa's bedroom. Valentin paused at the door and removed the handcuffs. Bella, rubbing sensation back into her wrist, was staring through the open door. Unlike the rest of the apartment, nothing had been touched. On the contrary, someone had gone to some trouble to turn down the counterpane, to adjust the lighting, even to find a modest stand of flowers for the vase on the table beside the bed. The flowers were roses, the deepest red, and Bella, for the first time, had the taste of real fear in her throat. This is theatre, she told herself. And bad things are going to happen.

'Sit,' Kalb patted the bed. 'Please.'

'Please' came as a surprise, a sudden twist in the script, far from welcome. Bella sat down. She'd always admired Larissa's taste in furniture, and one of her favourite pieces was a replica Louis XV giltwood armchair, cleverly made, legs beautifully turned, exquisite proportions. Larissa normally kept it in one corner of the room, away from the morning sunshine. Only days ago, they'd made love in that very chair, Bella sitting, Larissa on her knees, as deft and attentive as ever, but now Kalb had moved the chair much closer to the bed. He sank into it and loosened his collar. Then he produced a single sheet of paper and muttered something to Valentin that Bella didn't catch.

'We found this under one of the pillows,' Kalb had turned back to Bella. 'We think it might be for you.'

Bella took it. The handwriting was Larissa's. It was a love letter, penned in Russian, and it began with the phrase *Prelest moya Svecha*.

'We have difficulty reading this note. What does it say?'

'Are you looking for secrets? Is that what you're after?'

'Just translate it,' a thin smile.

Bella shrugged, and bent to the letter. 'My precious Svecha...' she began.

'*Svecha?*'

'It's Russian for candle.'

'She called you that?'

'She did.'

'Why?'

'Because she was religious. Not always, but sometimes, when she felt the need. She was fascinated by labyrinths. A labyrinth is a puzzle. You walk and walk, very slowly, finding your way, thinking hard, praying hard, looking for the light. The light is the candle.'

'You, in other words.'

'Me,' Bella agreed

'And you? You do this, too? Walk the labyrinth? Pray hard?'

'I'm afraid not.'

'Then maybe you should,' he nodded at the letter. 'What else does it say?'

Bella didn't answer. She was looking at Valentin. He was standing in the shadows in the corner of the room, slowly removing his clothes, letting each item drop to the floor. For the first time, Bella realised he hadn't been wearing a uniform. Naked, he was huge.

This, she quickly realised, was meant to intimidate her. She returned to the letter. Larissa, she realised, was saying goodbye. Her job was becoming impossible. She had no desire to work for the city's new masters. And now that the partisans were declaring their hand, there would be other difficulties. But she wanted Bella to know that she'd never forget her, that their brief coming together had been one of the labyrinth's unexpected delights, and that life, God willing, would one day smile upon them both.

'Sweet. She was in love with you? This woman?'

'I think she was.' Kalb's use of the past tense was disturbing.

'And you?'

'She's taught me a lot. I admire her. She's brave, and wise, and wherever she is, I hope she's safe.'

'You're telling me you don't know where she is?'

Bella shook her head, said nothing. Valentin was bending over an apparatus in the corner, making an adjustment on a dial. Whatever it was had never been in this room before.

'It's a recording device,' Kalb said. 'Every word we say, every noise you make, everything will be recorded. A photograph in sound. Something, perhaps, to treasure. Our friend over there has many children. He even knows the name of some of them. Am I right, Valentin?'

Valentin grunted assent. He was carefully positioning a microphone in the direction of the bed, small, delicate movements for so big a man.

'Take off your clothes, please.' Kalb's hand was extended. He was asking for the letter back.

Bella shook her head. It was hers. She wanted to keep it.

'What do you need from me?' she said.

'We need to find your friend. And we think you know where she is.'

'You're wrong. I don't.'

'You're lying. Escape is something you will have discussed. Pillow talk? Am I right? What to do when the Reds start blowing us up? Don't shake your head. Tell us now, and everything will be so much simpler.'

'I can't tell you. Because I don't know. Larissa never mentioned leaving this apartment. Neither did we ever discuss what's happening now.'

Kalb studied her for a long moment and Bella sensed that he and patience had never been best friends. The clock was ticking. Someone, somewhere, was expecting a phone call, names, an address, the place of safety to where Larissa had fled. Then would come a volley of knocks on a door, the thunder of boots on a staircase, and the moment when the Reich began to unpick the plot that was blowing Kyiv apart.

'You flew to London on 29 August. That's what your file tells us. Is it right?'

'Yes.'

'You accompanied an engineer from the Soviet 37th Army, Ilya Glivenko. Correct?'

'Correct.'

'And you planned to spend a little time with a friend while he talked explosives at Fort Halstead. Yes?'

'Yes.'

'On 11 September, you and Glivenko flew back. He was always coming here. He was rejoining his unit. Instead of returning to Moscow, you came with him. Doesn't that suggest you were part of all this?'

'All what?'

'The explosions? The chaos? How carefully you chose the targets? How successful you've been? The top, please. Your top garment.' Kalb gestured at the thin woollen cardigan Bella was wearing, another loan from Larissa's wardrobe.

Bella didn't move. Kalb shook his head, a gesture of regret. Valentin needed no further prompting. He abandoned the recording device and stood over Bella, behind her, invisible. When he reached down to pull off her cardigan, she shook her head, pushed his hands away, did it herself. Kalb wanted the blouse underneath off, too. Again, Bella complied.

'Your brassiere?' Another gesture from Kalb, impatient this time.

Bella shook her head. She'd had enough of this pantomime. Kalb was playing with her, visibly extracting pleasure from every tiny moment of anticipation.

'Your brassiere,' he said again. 'Take it off.'

'No. You want this man to rape me, tell him to go ahead.'

Kalb held her gaze. He looked briefly sulky, the way a child might when he doesn't get his way. Then the merest suggestion of a nod brought Valentin's big hands to her brassiere strap. She felt the closure bend and then snap. Naked above the waist she was still staring at Kalb.

'You want to rape me, too?' she asked. 'Or might a girl be disappointed after your donkey has his way?'

In retrospect, it was a foolish thing to say, needlessly provocative, but here and now Bella wanted this man to know that she wasn't afraid and insulting him gave her just a moment's pleasure.

'Hurt her,' Kalb said quietly. It had the force of an order.

Valentin pulled her backwards until she was lying on the bed. His sheer bulk loomed above her. Then she felt his knees pinioning her arms as he straddled her face, tearing off her skirt, and then ripping the lacy undergarments she'd also borrowed from Larissa.

'Here—' Valentin looked briefly up, tossing the torn silk to Kalb, a trophy for his boss. The knickers landed in Kalb's lap, and he glanced down at them, his mad face contorted with pleasure, and for the first time Bella caught the glint of a silver tooth in his leer. Then Kalb got to his feet, telling Valentin to stop, to take his time, and left the room.

Moments later, he was back with the shopping bag Bella had brought from the market. In the bottom was a stone pot full of goose fat. He dipped his fingers in the pot and then slipped them between Bella's thighs, working the goose fat deeper and deeper. Bella could see nothing but the heavy bag of Valentin's testicles. Her world had suddenly shrunk. It smelled of bad drains, of caked shit, of folds and crevices unwashed for weeks, and she closed her eyes, knowing that she had to concentrate on one single image, one single thought, remembering a tip from Moncrieff weeks after he'd survived the attentions of the Gestapo. Think about someone or something you love, he'd told her. It might be a landscape, a favourite view. It might be a glass of malt. God knows, it might even be me. But hold that thought. Close the door and double-bolt it. Nothing else matters. Except the smile on your face.

Heroic, she thought. Heroic and probably wrong. Her eyes still closed, breathing as lightly as she could, tiny sips of the foulest air, she struggled to settle on that one image that might keep the very middle of her intact. Her times with Larissa? No. In bed with Tam? Yes. Kalb had given up with the goose fat. She felt remarkably warm, even readied, which she guessed might be the point. So far, she'd had no control of anything, and as Valentin eased his weight off her face, she knew that this sense of helplessness was about to get a whole lot worse. Except. Except.

Tam, she thought. Tam in Berlin, those first nights they'd slept together in her apartment. Tam in the Glebe House, her chieftain, her laird. Tam and his simple glee at some of the pleasures she'd teased from their times together.

'Stop!'

It was Kalb. In his excitement, he'd forgotten to start the machine. She heard his footsteps as he edged around the bed, the click as his finger depressed the switch, the tiny whirr as the spools of tape began to revolve. Then he was back in the carefully angled chair, watching, taking advantage of a perfect view. Had his greasy fingers found the buttons of his trousers, she wondered. Might he wake up tomorrow with finger marks on the fly of the carefully pressed black serge? Was he enjoying himself?

She didn't know, couldn't possibly tell, but it didn't matter because Valentin was inside her now, thrusting and thrusting, and as he went deeper the pain made her forget Tam, forget the Glebe House, and reach for something else. Black and white, she thought. Hot nights in the cinema beside the Moscow River. The fug of cheap cigarettes. Newsreels ahead of the main feature. Images flickering on the screen, stilling the chatter of a Moscow audience. Tanks, Stukas, truckloads of grim-faced infantry, bombs tumbling earthwards, women running for cover, hugging their children, falling to their knees, begging for mercy. Valentin, so aptly named, was doing to her what the Reich had done to Poland, to Belgium, to France, and now to Russia. No more laughter in Moscow cinemas, she thought. Because the Germans had arrived here, too, doing what they did best. Fuck them, she thought. Fuck them all.

She heard herself screaming, arching her back, reaching up, trying to somehow wriggle free, raking her nails across the sagging planes of her rapist's face. She was drawing blood, but it didn't matter. He was beyond reach, implacable, impervious to anything but unfinished business and the brimming pleasure to come. Then, as she watched through her tears, his jaw dropped, and his rhythm slowed, and she was left with nothing but a spreading hotness inside her and the faintest whimper of glee from the armchair as Kalb, too, was done.

The weight of Valentin's body had collapsed on her. She was fighting for breath, knowing that – for a moment or two – the pain was over. They'd finished with her, she told herself. She was finished. And now, with luck, they'd dispose of whatever remained.

*

Dawn. Birdsong. Life was a cliff face, Moncrieff had decided. Below, surf boiled among the rocks. Above, its outline still dim as the sky began to lighten, was the limitless promise of survival, of getting there, of feeling the springy dampness of turf underfoot, of leaving the cliff edge, and the torrent of rising air, behind.

He tried to open his eyes, to blink, to take a look around. Impossible. But the parching dryness in his mouth, his throat, his lungs, had gone and for that he was deeply grateful.

Birdsong again, rising and falling, like a programme on the wireless with a stranger's hand on the volume control. A nightingale? A thrush? Something equally tuneful? He couldn't be sure but at last his eyes opened. Pain? Very little. Discomfort? Plenty. But no seagulls. And therefore, no cliff face.

He sniffed. He thought he could smell cigarettes, something foreign. He frowned, trying to make sense of the pattern of pleats and wrinkles above his head. Then he tried to move, to ease the ache in his shoulders, and as he did so he realised he was on the rear seat of a car, not a big car, his long body carefully jigsawed to fit the space, his knees pressed hard against the back of the seat in front. Where had he come from? Who had engineered him into a position like this? And, even more important, where were they now?

He struggled slowly upright, trying to remember the last time he'd been conscious. Then, he had a memory of nakedness. Now, his fingers confirmed a shirt, buttons, trousers, probably serge, and when his vision had cleared enough to penetrate the gloom, a pair of shoes, brogues, maybe even his own.

Very softly, he called out.

'Hello?' he whispered.

Nothing. Just the birdsong.

Bolder now, he struggled upright and peered out of the window. The car was parked in some sort of clearing. He could see a stretch of rising ground through the trees, and a bristly pelt of heather. Brown, he thought. Autumn. He massaged the feeling back into his legs and then tried to find a door handle. After several minutes, feeling foolish, he realised the search was hopeless. No door.

He bent forward on the rear seat, gazing at the dashboard. The steering wheel was on the left and he recognised the emblem on the boss. This was a Peugeot, a French car. He'd driven something similar before the war, in Germany. It had belonged to a French friend from Alsace Lorraine, attached to the Humboldt University in Berlin. He permitted himself a smile, not because he'd even got the name right – Alain – but because his memory worked at all. More recently, everything was still a blank, an impenetrable wall of fog, a thick grey blanket tossed over lost days, maybe weeks, maybe longer.

Out, he thought. I have to get out.

That memory again. The little spring-loaded catch you had to depress to push the seat forward. His fingers found it. The back of the passenger seat hinged towards the dashboard. He reached for the door handle. To his relief, it worked. Moments later, limb by limb, he'd negotiated his way out of the car. It was a Peugeot 302, in deep maroon. He gazed down at it for a moment, perplexed by the French registration plates.

It was daylight now. He looked around. A rough track led towards the promise of a metalled road. Overnight rain had pooled in the ruts and he watched a sparrow washing itself in a frenzy of wingbeats before he took an exploratory stride towards the treeline. Everything seemed to work. He gazed at the frieze of trees, looking for signs of life, but there was no one to be seen. His bladder was uncomfortably full, but habit and modesty drove him to the shelter of the trees before he unbuttoned and sought relief. Somewhere in France, he thought. Somewhere out in the sticks beyond the reach of the Germans. Normandy? Brittany? One of the many forests further south? He shook his head and buttoned up. Impossible to be sure.

Back at the car, he opened the door on the driver's side, gladdened by the sight of the keys dangling from the ignition. When he bent in to turn the key, and bring the instruments to life, even better news: a nearly full tank of petrol. Simple, he thought. Drive down to the road, find the nearest village, and make enquiries. The thought of a conversation, the presence of other human beings, brought a smile to his face. This was France. He was deep in the country. These people had access to fresh food, eggs, bread, maybe even bacon. For the first time, he realised how hungry he was.

Then he saw the envelope. It was lying on the driver's seat, impossible to miss. He picked it up, weighed it in his hand. Light as a feather, he thought. Was it empty? Was this some kind of joke? Another mystery to taunt his feeble brain? He studied it a moment longer, then slipped a thumbnail under the gummed flap. Inside was a single photograph. He shook it out and stepped back into the golden slant of the rising sun for a proper look. Then, as he recognised the face, his blood froze. Bella, he thought. Bella against the darkness of some room or other. Bella, bald as a coot, her bare scalp bloodied.

He stared at the face, shaking his head, wondering if the darkness had taken him again, his mind collapsing inward. Was any of this real? A real car? A real Peugeot? And, if so, then what on earth was he doing in France? And why should someone leave an image like this where he couldn't fail to find it?

He looked in the envelope again and saw the folded sheet of paper. On it, in a Cyrillic typeface, was a message that meant nothing. У каждой жизни есть цена. He stared at it, deeply frustrated. It was Bella, definitely. But what had happened to her glorious hair? Where was she? And how would he ever find out?

Now, more than ever, he knew he had to stir the car into life. He slipped behind the wheel, laying the photo on the passenger seat beside him, easing the car into gear, and bumping slowly down the track towards the road. The car was light and responsive. He swung left onto the road, remembering to keep on the right-hand side. Almost immediately, the road plunged into yet more trees, the spill of the rising sun suddenly gone.

At first he drove carefully, 30 kph on the speedo, but in the absence of traffic he became bolder, hugging the right hand of every bend, sparing longer and longer moments to glance down at the face on the passenger seat, the face he remembered from Berlin, from the Glebe House, from the depths of his wrecked memory.

Russia, he thought. She'd gone back to Moscow. That's where she lived. That's where she'd made her new life. That's where, God willing, he might one day find her.

The thought warmed him, and he stole another glance, and then another, failing even to register the presence of the oncoming lorry, on his side of the road, until the huge radiator filled his windscreen and it was far, far too late. The moment of collision took him briefly back to his training days with the Royal Marines on an unforgiving stretch of Dartmoor. Thunderflashes, he thought. Live mortar rounds. Even the bark of field artillery.

Moncrieff did his best to brace his arms against the steering wheel. Then his head hit the windscreen and quite suddenly there was nothing. Not even birdsong.

17

THURSDAY 25 SEPTEMBER 1941

Ilya Glivenko had saved the last of his cigars for the first of this
morning's explosions. A small circle of sappers were enjoying the
first rays of the rising sun through the canopy of trees. They'd
now been on Trukhaniv Island for a full week, stretching their
meagre rations to the very limit, saving their last bottle of vodka
to toast the first full day of operations. That had come to an
end last night with the spectacular demolition of Kyiv's tallest
building, the fifteen-storey Ginzburg Skyscraper.

While daylight lasted, Glivenko and fellow sappers in other
platoons had outwitted the Germans. They relied on constant
reports from Soviet agents still in place in the city. While rescue
and fire crews rushed to the scene of the first explosion, Glivenko
would order radio transmissions to trigger a second, and then
a third, trying to lure the city's new masters into blast traps as
they tried to fight fire after fire.

This lethal game of chess, with German killed and wounded
now in three figures, had delighted Glivenko's men. In the
frenzied chaos before the evacuation, they'd worked day and
night, laying huge quantities of high explosives in location
after location, and the lazy days that followed on the safety
of the thickly wooded island had been more than welcome.

Glivenko had always insisted on waiting for the occupation to bed itself in. The Germans needed to make themselves at home, he said. They needed to feel secure, organised, even relaxed. Only when they'd lowered their guard would the moment come to hammer them.

And so it had proved. Yesterday's operation had opened with the attack on the Khreshchatyk, but a moment of pure delight had arrived with a neighbouring platoon's designs on a viewing platform in the grounds of the Pechersk Monastery, built on a bluff above the river. The platform was in clear view from Mikhail Tatarsky's men, hidden on the island. Through binoculars, they'd watched groups of German soldiers gathering to gaze down at the long bend of the Dnieper. They arrived every half-hour or so, dozens of them, and Tatarsky had managed to bag at least twenty, blowing them to pieces as they enjoyed the autumn sunshine and a last cigarette. Then had come a second attack, this time on the Kyiv's old Arsenal building, also under observation, and low growls of applause had greeted the news from the agents across the water that the death toll included the Artillery Commander of the 29th *Wehrmacht* Corps.

Glivenko knew that trophy scalps like these would really hurt the Germans, but best of all, in his view, had been the Ginzburg Skyscraper. By eleven in the evening, the exhausted Germans were beginning to assume that the worst was over, precisely why Glivenko had kept the biggest bang until last. A nod in the darkness to Vassily, crouched over the transmitter, and the flash of the huge explosion through the trees had briefly illuminated the entire city centre. Then, as the darkness returned, thunder rolled across the water, engulfing the island, masking the cheers from the watching sappers. Glivenko had broached the vodka shortly afterwards, passing round the bottle, toasting a day's work that had exceeded his wildest expectations.

'The Ginzburg wasn't to everyone's taste,' he murmured. 'So maybe we've done them a favour.'

Now, with the smell of charred timber still hanging in the trees, he was thinking about the NKVD headquarters. He knew the building well, partly because he'd shared a secured office on the third floor during the long weeks of target selection and detailed planning, and latterly because he'd supervised the installation of four tons of high explosive in the sub-basement. As he knew only too well, the building was now under new management, a gift to SS officers eager to put NKVD interrogation suites to work again, and the only issue he had to resolve in his own mind was when, precisely, to trigger the explosion.

The vodka bottle now empty, the discussion had raged until the small hours. The building would already be full of prisoners. Inevitably, most of them would be killed. Was it kinder, more humane, to blow them up in their sleep, before they faced interrogation and torture, or would it make better sense to wait for the working day to begin properly, with dozens of SS officers at their desks? In the end, Vassily had consulted the agent in the city who seemed best informed about the working habits of the *Schutzstaffel*.

'The bastards sleep in their offices,' he radioed back. 'Give them an early wake-up call.'

Good advice. Once again, Vassily was crouched over the transmitter, waiting for Glivenko's signal. The Big House had been their last installation job before leaving for the island and it felt good to be gifting the Germans yet another little present.

Glivenko checked his watch. Five past seven. His last cigar was a Montecristo, a souvenir from his brief stay at Fort Halstead. His bosses in the Big House had forbidden him to share any details of the Kyiv operation but most of them, on the basis of his shopping list, had worked out the operational task for themselves. The little man who enlivened mess evenings at the piano was undoubtedly in the business of blowing stuff up. Where this might take place was anyone's guess but on his final day, the president of the mess had given him a box of cigars.

'Share these with your men,' he'd said, 'but save the last for the target that really matters.'

Glivenko smiled at the memory. There were still lots of targets awaiting their attention – the State Bank, the Opera House, the Museum of Lenin – but the one that really mattered was the Big House. The Germans had grabbed it, put their smell on it, assumed it was theirs for eternity, and now they would pay the price. Never take anything for granted, he thought. Especially in a war like this.

'Ready?' He glanced down at Vassily. The Kazakh nodded, his finger reaching for the transmission switch.

Glivenko waited a moment, rolling the fatness of the cigar between his fingers.

'You want a match for that?' It was Vassily.

'I do,' Glivenko nodded at the transmitter. 'But do your business first.'

*

Bella felt the first of the morning's explosions before she heard it. For a moment, she thought the apartment building might collapse. She was still lying on the bed, dazed, hurting, defiled.

Then came the thunder of the explosion, a noise impossibly loud, the building first shivering, then swaying as the blast wave swept across the city centre. She'd never been in an earthquake but this, she thought, must come close: one of Larissa's pictures at a crazy angle on the wall, a bottle of perfume sliding off the dressing table, a distant tinkle as the remaining glass in the window shattered on the street below. Close, she thought. But not quite close enough.

She waited for the aftershocks to subside. She could hear the howl of a siren in a neighbouring street, then came the urgent clanging of a bell and distant shouts, first of warning, then of distress. Finally, unmistakably, a woman screaming. This was very close, disturbingly close, so close it could have been the room next door.

She lay back, shutting her eyes, trying very hard to block her mind to the flood of images that threatened once again to engulf her. At Kalb's invitation, or perhaps insistence, Valentin had raped her a second time. Kalb himself had departed, too busy or too bored to watch, and for this small act of deliverance she'd been thankful. On this occasion, Valentin had lasted and lasted, still urgent, still making the bile rise in her throat, but she'd lost the energy, or even the will, to fight back. When he'd finally finished, the pain had left her semi-paralysed, barely able to move, but the knowledge that this had been a private act, unwitnessed, unaccompanied, had been a kind of solace.

While the man was getting dressed, she'd managed to ask him what might happen next. Had the SS finished with her? Did Kalb accept that she knew nothing? Or was she to be dragged off somewhere else for more humiliation? To these questions, Valentin had no answer. Instead, he'd just shrugged. Maybe they'd take her to the Big House. Maybe not. Then he'd left the bedroom without a backward glance, a satisfied client in the brothel of his dreams, and from the wreckage of the room next door Bella had caught a brief murmur of conversation and a sudden cackle of laughter before the key turned in the lock. She'd become a prisoner in Larissa's bed, she thought, left to stew in Valentin's juices, a parting gesture from Kalb to bring the evening's revels to a close. Even the NKVD would have drawn the line at that.

Now, lying motionless with a hint of sunshine through the billowing clouds of smoke over the neighbouring rooftops, she wondered what might happen next. The last explosion had been undeniably close. Another hotel? One of the business blocks commandeered by the Germans? More rubble? More casualties? Just a dribble of water from hosepipes half severed by partisans down by the river?

She moved slowly, with great caution, knowing it would be a while before she was able to walk properly. Moscow had taught her the meaning of helplessness, of having to surrender to the iron grip of the *Vodzh* and his million acolytes, but last night, mercilessly intimate, had been far worse. She could still smell Valentin, taste him, feel the bulk and bristle of the man against her face. Sex, she knew, would never be the same again. Maybe the next bomb, she thought. Or the one after that. One day, she told herself, Kalb would meet his maker and if there was just an ounce of justice in the afterworld, he'd burn in hell.

Moments later, she heard the scrape of a key turning in the lock of the bedroom door. She struggled half-upright, the counterpane clutched against her chest, praying that Valentin hadn't come back for more. Instead, she found herself looking at a face she knew only too well, perhaps a year or two older, a decade or two more exhausted, but definitely the same man.

'Schultz,' she said.

'Me,' he agreed.

She looked him up and down. In Berlin she'd never seen Wilhelm Schultz wear anything but a battered leather jacket, and now was no different. The last time she'd met him, barely weeks before the outbreak of war, he'd had more hair but the eyes were the same – watchful, pouched in the wreckage of his face – and she remembered, too, the way he held himself. Valentin had been a wrestler, imprisoned in his own bulk, but looking at Schultz, Bella remembered a phrase of Moncrieff's. Willi Schultz, he said, had the wit and the guile of a decent boxer. Valentin would crush you to death but Schultz – in Tam's phrase – would keep you at arm's length, jabbing and jabbing until the hook you never saw coming would put you on the floor.

'You OK?' Schultz hadn't moved.

'No. There's a man called Kalb.'

'I know Kalb.'

'And?'

'The man's an animal. He belongs in a zoo.' He paused, sniffing. 'What's that smell?'

'His bodyguard. He raped me last night. Twice.'

Schultz gazed at her, seemingly impassive, but Bella thought she caught a flicker of disgust in the brief frown.

'And Kalb?'

'He watched. And if you want the truth, watching is probably worse.'

'For who?'

'For me.'

Schultz nodded. Then he motioned for her to move and made himself comfortable on the end of the bed.

'I've read that file of yours,' he said. 'Quite a journey.'

Bella stared at him. In the numbness that had engulfed her, a proper conversation was out of the question. Yet this man might represent just a flicker of hope. That Tam thought the world of Schultz was all that mattered. Whatever happened, she had to force herself to reach out, to connect, to try and make a friend.

'Journey?' she whispered.

'Defecting to the Ivans. Be honest with me. Do you like it in Moscow?'

'Moscow's awful and the rest of the country's probably worse,' she briefly closed her eyes and swallowed hard. 'Was I expecting that? No. Does it matter? Not in the least. It's the idea that counts, or that's what Stalin tells me.'

'You *know* him?' Schultz looked briefly impressed.

'We've met. On days when they can't find anyone else, I translate for him. I'm good with movie plots, too, and he appreciates that.' She tried to summon a smile. 'Strange, isn't it? This is a man who sees conspiracies everywhere, yet movies baffle him. How come people betray each other? Is there no fairness in the world?' She shook her head, engulfed by a sudden, irrational anger. 'You're here to beat me up? Rape me? I'm afraid I'm soiled goods, Herr Schultz. Blame Valentin. Blame Kalb.'

'I need to know what you're doing in Kyiv.'

'You do?'

'Yes. For your own sake, and probably mine, too.'

Bella nodded, then lay back, grimacing at a sudden stab of pain. She knew from Tam that Schultz worked for the *Abwehr*, the Army's intelligence organisation. The *Abwehr* had been fighting a savage turf war with Himmler's SS since Bella could remember but thanks to people like Schultz, solid and doubtless streetwise, they'd so far held their own.

'I came here to avoid going back to Moscow,' Bella said. 'I had the opportunity, and I took it.'

'They didn't assign you here?'

'Far from it. I think they want to kill me. Here's safer, if you can believe that.'

She began to laugh, lying on her back, naked, stinking of Valentin and goose fat, staring up at the ceiling. Safe? She shook her head, then wiped the tears from her eyes, hysterical now, totally out of control. Finally, the storm passed.

Schultz hadn't moved. Then he put his hand in his pocket and produced a reel of thin brown tape.

'What's that?'

'It's you. Last night. They played it to me next door when I arrived. They think you were the evening's entertainment. Their phrase, not mine. Here,' he tossed the reel onto the bed, 'it's yours.'

'I don't want it. Get rid of it. Burn it. Send it to Kalb for Christmas. That man gives sadism a bad name. But I'm guessing you'd know that already.'

The ghost of a smile briefly warmed Schultz's face. Then he wanted to know about a Red Army engineer called Ilya Glivenko.

'I flew to London with him. Brought him back. I expect all the details are in the file.'

'You're right. So, where is he?'

'I have no idea, and that's the truth. He played for the masses on Leningrad street corners during the October Revolution. That's why they call him The Pianist. The piano was looted but I expect it was the music that mattered. Is all that in the file, too?'

'He's probably responsible for this,' Schultz nodded towards the chaos beyond the window. He wasn't interested in Leningrad street corners.

'You're probably right. He's a clever man. He's a believer, too. Which I expect makes him very dangerous.'

'When did you last see him?'

'A week ago. Before they all pulled out.'

'Where?'

Bella held his gaze, then shook her head.

'No,' she said softly.

'No, what?'

'No, I won't tell you.'

Schultz nodded. If he was surprised, it didn't show.

'And Larissa Krulak? The woman who owns this place?'

'I last saw her a couple of days ago.'

'Where?'

'Here.'

'In the apartment?'

'In bed. We fucked a lot. We girls take our pleasures where we can. We girls take our pleasures where we can.'

'Close, then?'

'Nose to nose. And that was just the first course. The woman's a journalist, a writer. When she still had a piano, she played it beautifully. She also has the gift of tongues and believe me that can make a girl very happy.'

'You know she's a Jew?'

'Yes. Should that have made a difference?'

Schultz stirred, and then glanced at his watch.

'Kalb is organising an *Aktion*,' he said. 'Which is one of the reasons you may never see her again. Do you know what *Aktion* means?'

'Tell me.'

'It's the word the SS uses for revenge. It makes extreme violence respectable. Berlin have assigned us two tasks. My job is to bring these fucking explosions to an end. That's why they've sent me here. The Military Governor and the SS are responsible for making sure it never happens again. They'll call it punishment.'

'For the guilty?'

'For being a Jew. Though in their eyes it's probably the same thing.'

'How many Jews?'

'All of them. Tens of thousands of them,' he nodded at the bed, 'including your journalist friend. Think about it. And in the meantime, for God's sake have a wash.' He turned to leave, then paused beside the door. 'That man of yours, Moncrieff. The file says you paid him a visit. True?'

'Yes.'

'So how is he?' The smile was warm this time. 'Still trying to give us a hard time?'

*

First on the scene of the accident was an Irish American called Pearse Lenahan. At the wheel of a Jeep in US Army camouflage, he rounded the corner and braked hard to avoid the wreckage.

A car with foreign plates was entangled with a coal lorry, a head-to-head collision. Lenahan parked, leapt from the Jeep and ran to help. The lorry driver, a man in his fifties, was sitting behind the wheel, rubbing his face, dazed by what had happened. When Lenahan approached, he gestured down at the driver of the car. He was slumped behind the wheel, blood trickling down his forehead.

Lenahan found a pulse in the side of his neck. It was stronger than he'd expected and the touch of Lenahan's fingers stirred a tremor of movement. As gently as he could, Lenahan raised the driver's head. His breathing was regular, and his eyes flickered briefly open.

'You're French?' he seemed to be saying. '*Français?*'

'American,' Lenahan grunted. 'I'm a Yank.'

The driver was frowning. Then his eyes closed.

'Christ,' he whispered. 'This is *America?*'

*

Schultz had a car outside the apartment block. He helped Bella down the endless flights of stairs and across the pavement. The sky was still black with smoke and ash and Bella could smell the heavy sweetness of a ruptured sewer.

Their route took them through the maze of streets around Khreshchatyk. The NKVD Big House, to Bella's quiet satisfaction, no longer existed. Schultz ordered the driver to stop while he got out to have a brief conversation with the officer in charge. Soldiers were tearing at the rubble with their bare hands, and Bella watched the upper half of a man emerge as a huge sergeant tossed shattered baulks of timber aside. The survivor's shirt was torn and his face was a mask of blood and dirt but it was the eyes that drew Bella's attention. They were glazed, unseeing. Something terrible had happened, something utterly beyond his comprehension, and as the sergeant hauled him bodily from the wreckage, he could only shake his head.

'He's a prisoner,' Schultz, back in the car, had noticed her interest. 'They'll shoot him.'

'Lucky man. I know exactly how he feels.'

'You mean that?'

'I do, yes.' She nodded at the smoking ruins. 'Was Kalb in there, too? Just say yes. Tell me he was.'

They drove on, the driver weaving to avoid yet more water tankers. Building after building along the street had been blown up and two of them were still on fire, the roaring flames fed by broken gas mains. At the end of the street, engineers were running lengths of cable across the cobblestones to a waiting generator. Heaped against the foot of the adjacent building were dead bodies, roughly parcelled in sackcloth. There was a boot on one protruding foot. The other was missing below the ankle.

'They're forecasting high winds today,' Schultz nodded towards the generator. 'We need to create firebreaks.'

'How?'

'By blowing up more buildings.'

'But what if they catch fire, too?'

'Then we have another problem.'

Bella nodded, trying to take it in. So much destruction, she thought, so many bodies.

'You should have sent the *Luftwaffe* home,' she said. 'All you needed was Ilya.'

The thought made Schultz laugh. Bella knew his loyalties lay with the *Abwehr*, and, like his boss, Admiral Canaris, he had little time for the regime. Moncrieff had got to know him in Berlin, and later at secret meetings in Stockholm, and she sensed the two men had become allies. He thinks they're all gangsters, Tam had told her. Hitler included.

They'd come to a halt outside one of the few buildings that appeared still to be intact.

'The Museum of Lenin,' Schultz grunted. 'We're thinking they wouldn't dare.'

'You're working here?'

'We are now.'

Bella nodded. Ilya had told her that plans were afoot in Moscow to ship Lenin's body east, out of the grasp of the *Wehrmacht*, but she'd no idea if the mausoleum beside the Kremlin Wall in Red Square was empty yet.

Schultz was out of the car, one hand extended to help her onto the pavement.

'Ground floor,' he said. 'We'll spare you the stairs.'

Bella limped as far as the main entrance on the street. A worker had just finished pasting a notice on the wall. Bella stopped. It was in both Ukrainian and German. She wanted to read it. *All Yids in the city of Kyiv,* it went, *must appear on Monday September 29th by eight o'clock in the morning on the corner of Menikova and Dokterivskaya streets. Bring documents, money and valuables, and also warm clothing, linen etc. Yids who do not follow this order and are found elsewhere will be shot.*

'This is from the Military Governor?' Bella caught Schultz's eye.

'Yes,' Schultz nodded, 'and Kalb's lot will make it happen. You can't miss the meeting point. It's right across from the big cemetery. *Komm.*'

Bella struggled after him into the museum. More workers were sweeping up shards of glass from blast damage. Schultz tramped past them, Bella in his wake. The office was at the end of a corridor towards the rear of the building. It must have belonged to an archivist, or perhaps a librarian. The panelled walls were hung with framed sepia photographs, all of them featuring the Father of the Revolution, and there were books and magazines piled everywhere, the magazines bundled with scarlet ribbon. Bella limped towards the big desk. She felt ugly, bow-legged, one of the war's discards. In the corner of the room she'd noticed a cardboard box lined with an old blanket, and an empty saucer. The sharp tang of cat's piss hung in the stale air.

'The bloody animal's name was Leon...' Schultz was taking off his leather coat, '... so at least someone has a sense of humour.'

'Leon?'

'Trotsky. The cat was old. He'd been shut in this room for a week. We put the poor beast out of his misery this morning. Deviate from the Party line and that's what happens. Sit, please.'

Bella did what she was told while Schultz cleared a space on the desk. He was brisk now, a man with no time to waste. He produced a photograph, small, black and white. Bella recognised the face at once. Yuri.

'You know this man?'

'No.'

'Think. Very hard.'

'I've never seen him in my life.'

'His name's Yuri Ponomorenko. He's a writer, a patriot, two reasons why a man might find himself with enemies in a shithole like this.' Schultz paused. 'No?'

'No.'

'Khrushchev? His daddy? His protector? The man who looked after him? I'd love to think young Yuri was halfway up the little dwarf's arse but it seems that isn't true. A man of principle, our Yuri. Prepared to take a risk or two.' Another pause. 'You're still telling me you know nothing?'

'I am.'

'That's brave on your part. I mean it. But it's pointless, too. In life, establishing the truth may take a while. In war, you have to get there a whole lot quicker.'

'You're going to rape me?'

'No need. Your thoughts, please. Here. Tell me I'm wrong.'

Schultz had produced two scraps of paper. He passed the first one across. It was grubby, much folded. It's been in someone's pocket, she thought. And she was right.

'We found it on a prisoner,' Schultz said, 'first thing this morning. He was down in the park beside the river, trying to cut the hoses. Open it. Read it.'

Bella unfolded the note. The moment she recognised her own handwriting, her heart sank. Yuri, she thought. Trying to change history with a hacksaw.

'Read it to me.'

'*The only thing necessary for the triumph of evil,*' Bella murmured, '*is that good men do nothing.*'

'Is that your work?'

'Good Lord, no. Edmund Burke, I think. Wiser than most of us.'

'You're telling me it's not your handwriting?'

'Absolutely not.'

'And this one?'

Bella looked at the other note. She'd left it in the kitchen for Larissa only a day or so ago. *Gone to Besserabka*, it read. *Thank you for last night. Is there no end to your talents?* Same handwriting.

'Well?' Schultz was getting impatient.

'Me,' Bella agreed.

'Both of them?'

'I'm afraid so.'

Bella held Schultz's gaze. Clever, she thought. He hadn't laid a finger on her, yet he'd laid the truth bare. She wanted to know about Yuri. Was he OK? Intact? Still alive?

'He's upstairs. Waiting for you. So far, he's been lucky. Had Kalb's goons found him in the park, he'd be dead by now, or worse. We've talked to him, of course. The Russians have eyes everywhere. They're watching our every move. They're in touch with the sappers. Their transmissions are too brief to be useful but Yuri will be in touch with these people. Has he helped us so far? No. Will he talk under pressure? Probably not. So there has to be another way.'

'Me.' Statement, not question.

'You,' Schultz agreed.

Abruptly, there came a cough and a hesitant tap-tap and the door opened to reveal a soldier in *Wehrmacht* uniform. The prisoners have arrived, he told Schultz. You want them to start at once?

'Of course,' Schultz gestured vaguely towards the stairs. 'As soon as possible.'

'Prisoners?' Bella was looking at Schultz.

'Russians. We shipped them in from one of the camps. We've checked every floor and now we have to start on the basement.

That's where the trouble lies. We need them to dig around a little. Carefully, of course.'

'You're looking for explosives?'

'They. They're looking for explosives. Every site so far tells the same story. The trouble comes from below.'

Trouble, Bella thought. Quaint. The soldier at the door had disappeared. Moments later, Bella heard the shuffle of boots in the corridor outside. Someone was shouting in German. Down. Keep heading down.

'And us? Up here?' Bella enquired.

'We have our minds on other things.'

'Like Yuri?'

'Of course.'

'Can't we do this somewhere else?'

'No. Speed is everything. The quicker you complete the conversation, the safer we'll all be.'

'And you really think he'll talk to me?'

'I think he might.'

'Why?'

'Because I'm guessing he knows your journalist friend.'

'Larissa?'

'Yes. This city has become a battlefield. They're comrades-in-arms. That will matter, believe me.' He paused. 'Kalb has his eyes on your friend. She has profile. He has plans for her and if he finds her first, it will not go well. You could make life easier for her. In fact, for all of us. We can put Russian prisoners into every basement in the city. We can give them probes and spades and make sure they do their work properly. That will take weeks, maybe longer. What we need is a list. Yuri may have one, but I doubt it. What he might give us is one of the

Russian spotters. Young Yuri is a patriot, a Ukrainian, he has no love for Mother Russia.' His thick fingers had begun to drum on the desktop. 'Are you following me here?'

Bella nodded. She sensed the deal on offer, but she had to be sure.

'And afterwards?' he said.

'Yuri will be safe.'

'That's a guarantee?'

'It is. Your friend, too.' He got to his feet and yawned. 'If we can find her.'

18

THURSDAY 25 SEPTEMBER 1941

It took a while for Moncrieff to risk opening his eyes. The thunder in his head was intense, overwhelming, jolts of searing pain that kept time with his pulse. Light of any kind, he told himself, would simply make things worse.

'Can you hear me, buddy?'

A male voice, American, full of concern. Moncrieff was in a bed. He could feel the light press of a sheet against his chin. He lifted a hand and explored the long curve of his forehead. His fingertips paused. Something crusty. Blood, he thought.

'You've got a name, buddy? Care to share it with me?'

Moncrieff risked a nod, regretting it at once. Vomit rose in his throat. He turned his head and threw up on the pillow.

'Oh dear,' a woman's voice this time, much closer.

Then came something cool enveloping his face, a wetness, a flannel perhaps, and a pressure around his mouth and chin as the woman attended to the mess.

'Try not to be sick again,' she said. 'I know it must be difficult.'

'My pleasure,' Moncrieff murmured.

He must have drifted off again because the next time he asked after the woman, she'd gone.

'Back soon, buddy,' the American again. 'She's fetching the doctor though she thinks you've been lucky. The outside's not too bad, nothing permanent. Only you can tell us about the rest.'

'Rest?'

'Inside. Open your eyes. Look at me. How many fingers?'

Moncrieff opened his eyes. Even looking hurt.

'Three,' he said. 'Three fingers. No rings.'

'Detail? We love it, buddy. You sound English. Give me a name.'

'Moncrieff,' he said slowly. 'Tam Moncrieff.' He was looking around now. The bedroom was big. Everything was big. The giant armoire. The pattern on the wallpaper. The embroidered explosion of flowers on the limed oak chair. The carafe of what looked like claret on the huge chest of drawers. Even the framed cityscape, a bold study in thick oils, hanging on the opposite wall. He peered at it, shading his eyes against the throw of sunshine through the nearby window. The Seine. The twin towers of Notre-Dame. Mansard roofs. Pedestrians browsing the riverside book stalls. Paris, he thought.

'You're American,' he said. 'Am I right?'

'Sure.'

'So what are you doing in France?'

'*France?* You think we're in France? We have a problem, my friend. Three fingers is on the money. Three fingers tells me you can count, no brain damage in there, everything working the way it should. Three fingers is very good news. But France? Hey, Mr Moncrieff, where have you been in that head of yours? Welcome to England.'

England? Moncrieff lay back, totally confused. There was something very likeable about this man, and the comfort in the woman's voice had warmed him, but everything he looked at, every last detail, still told him he was in France. Not, perhaps, Paris. Not even some other city. But definitely France. Maybe somewhere deep in the country. Birdsong. Clouds. Wind in the trees. A distant meadow. Even a cow or two.

'France,' he repeated.

'England,' Moncrieff was looking at an outstretched hand. 'Pearse Lenahan. Glad to be of service, Mr Moncrieff. Just trust me. It was England yesterday, and God willing it will be England tomorrow.'

'So how come...?' Moncrieff's weary gesture took in the entire room.

Lenahan laughed, and briefly disappeared from view. Then came the scrape of a chair and he was back beside the bed, eager, friendly, happy to help. A long summer in the open air had given him a deep tan. The explosion of blond curls made him look impossibly young.

'Where are we? I'd love to give you a clue, buddy, but I can't.'

'Why on earth not?'

'Top secret. If I told you, I'd have to kill you. No kidding. King and Country, right? Tonight, we'll get you out of here, or maybe tomorrow night, or maybe even the night after. Depends how you're feeling. We'll keep it discreet, trust me. No questions, no answers. All we need is an address to mail you to. That's a joke, by the way.' He paused. 'London, maybe? A fella deserves a clue. Just one.'

'That could be difficult.'

'Why?'

Moncrieff gazed up at him. His memory, at last, was beginning to clear, little splinters coming together, beginning to make sense, recomposing a recent past that had inexplicably vanished.

'I work for the Security Service,' he muttered.

'You're kidding me?' Lenahan was staring at him. 'MI5?'

'You know it?'

'Sure,' he rocked back in the chair. 'You're not snowing me? You can prove that?'

'Not unless...' Moncrieff frowned, concentrating very hard. The pain in his head was definitely easing.

'Unless what, buddy?'

'Unless you found any ID.'

'Nothing. I found nothing. A situation like that, you take a good look. Nothing. Except this.'

He got up and fetched an envelope from the top of the dresser. Moncrieff recognised it at once. The photograph, he thought. Bella. Totally shorn.

'You mind if I open it, buddy? Take a look? It was in that car of yours. On the passenger seat.'

'Help yourself.'

Lenahan opened the envelope and shook out the photo inside. Then he found the message that went with it.

'Russian, right?'

'Yes.'

'What does it say? You mind me asking?'

'Not at all. And the answer is I don't know.'

'Hey. Right. OK.' Lenahan was on his feet again. 'Our doc's a Pole. Speaks perfect Russian. I'll stick a cracker up his arse. Give him a hurry-up. You OK in there?' He tapped his own head, grinned, and then left the room without a backward glance.

Moncrieff lay back and closed his eyes. A part of him was still convinced he was in France but in truth it didn't seem to matter. He knew he should get out of bed, make it across to the window, take a look at his surroundings, but the effort was beyond him. He may have dozed, even slept properly, he didn't know, but the next thing he heard was conversation below the window, and then the heavy boots on the stairs, and Lenahan's face at the open door.

'Dr Paczynski, buddy. Believe me, in these parts, there's none better.'

Moncrieff looked up at the figure stepping towards the bed. He was tall. He was wearing a parachutist's smock with a sprig of heather pinned on one breast, and a pair of baggy camouflage trousers tucked into leather boots. The boots, unlaced, badly needed a clean.

He bent low over the bed, peering at Moncrieff's forehead. When he asked about the accident, how it had happened, what kind of speed he'd been doing, Moncrieff could only shake his head.

'I can't remember,' he muttered.

'The other driver said you were on the wrong side of the road. Do you remember that?' Paczynski's accent was thick but he took care to pronounce every word.

'No. But I expect it was my fault.'

'Your head hurts?'

'Yes.'

'Any other pain?'

'A little,' Moncrieff gestured at his rib cage. Paczynski drew back the sheet and unbuttoned Moncrieff's shirt for a closer look. His fingers on a particular rib drew a wince of pain.

'There?'

'Yes.'

Paczynski explored further, gently probing his lower abdomen.

'There?'

'Nothing.'

'And here?'

'Fine.'

'Good. Button your shirt, please.' He turned to Lenahan. 'One cracked rib, definitely, and maybe a hairline fracture of the skull. Otherwise our friend here is a lucky man. He should stay for a couple of days at least. Make him eat properly. He needs to put on weight.' He glanced down at Moncrieff. 'No dancing for a while, my friend, you hear me?'

He turned to go but Lenahan was blocking the path to the door. He had the note from Moncrieff's envelope in his hand and he wanted a translation. The doctor studied the line of text for a moment, then nodded.

'*Every life has a price,*' he said.

'That's it?'

'That's it. Every life has a price. Very philosophical. Very wise. And probably true, too. Good luck, Mr Moncrieff.'

He left the room. Lenahan turned back to the bed and sank into the chair.

'Make any sense?' He still had the message.

'Alas, yes,' Moncrieff nodded. 'It does.'

Moncrieff lay back again. The clouds, thank Christ, had finally parted. He was thinking of Bella, that last morning he'd been with her at the Glebe House, the phone message to meet a friend in Aberdeen, the rendezvous that had left her alone in the house. Philby, he thought. He'd stolen her away, taken her down to London, despatched her back to Moscow.

Everything, very suddenly, was clear. He was able to focus at last, to draw a bead on what must have happened. Bella, he thought. The NKVD, Philby's masters, were holding her hostage, probably deep in Siberia in some godforsaken camp or other. Hence the haircut and the rough serge collar. They were sending a message, spelling it out. Your precious girlfriend is half a world away. Whether she lives or dies is our decision, or perhaps yours. Leave Mr Philby well alone. Or live with the consequences. *Every life*, in other words, *has a price.*

Moncrieff pondered the implications for a moment or two longer, aware that Lenahan was studying the photo again.

'You know this woman?'

'I do, yes.'

'Lovely mouth. Great eyes. You know her well?'

'I thought so, once. And then I didn't. And now...' He shrugged, '... we live in hope.'

Lenahan stared down at him for a moment, then his gaze returned to the face in the photo.

'Sure...' he said, suddenly uncertain. 'Anything I can do to help?'

Moncrieff thought hard about the question. Then he nodded.

'I've got a name for you,' he murmured. 'Ursula Barton. You'll find her through the main switchboard at MI5. You can do that for me? Make the call? Tell her I'm in rude health?' He did his best to force a smile. 'Can you lie a little? Are you good at that?'

*

Yuri was waiting in a room upstairs. There was a guard on the door, and as he and Schultz exchanged salutes, Bella wondered how much difference an extra storey of protection would make if the place blew up. Then she dismissed the possibility. Would the Russians really lay waste to the Museum of Lenin, of the building dedicated to the hero/prophet who'd ridden the sealed railway coach from Zurich, of the liberator of all those bourgeois Leningrad pianos? Impossible.

Yuri had his nose in a book. As the door opened, he didn't seem to hear it. Then his head came up and he caught sight of Bella.

'What happened?' She was staring at him. His face was swollen and bruised. There was a deep cut over one eye and the other one had closed. When he put the book to one side, Bella saw more lacerations on his hands.

'They caught me,' he said simply.

'And?'

'Two of them had been fighting the fires. They took me to the site of the nearest explosion, beat me up, then made me work.'

'Doing what?'

'Wrapping up the dead. I blessed one of them, went down on my knees. That's when they beat me again.' He was speaking with difficulty, every word accompanied by a thin trickle of pinked saliva.

Schultz told Bella to sit down. Yuri watched her shuffle slowly across the room, and then took a good look at her face.

'You're walking like an old woman,' he said. 'And you've been crying. What happened?'

'I was raped.'

Yuri stared at her. He was shocked and it showed.

'I'm sorry,' he said at last.

Bella had noticed a woman sitting in the shadows in one corner of the room. She was thin and her hair was grey. She was wearing glasses and there was a large pad on her lap.

Bella wanted to know who she was.

'She works here,' Schultz grunted. 'We wanted to record everything but the machine's broken, so she'll do it for us. Her Russian is perfect. Use any other language and there will be consequences. Speak your minds. Be frank. Half an hour. No longer.'

Schultz left the room. Bella was still looking at the woman in the corner.

'I know her,' Yuri said. 'There won't be a problem. Her name's Kataryna. She's an archivist. I've met her here many times. We talk and talk. She's Ukrainian. She understands.'

'Does Schultz know that?' Bella nodded towards the door.

'I think he does, yes. He plays games, that man. Kataryna will keep the bosses off his back. Everyone needs insurance these days, even spy catchers.'

Spy catchers. The description put a brief smile on Bella's face. Would Schultz be pleased with a cartoon phrase like that? Would Tam Moncrieff?

'Schultz wants a list of targets,' Bella said.

'I know. He's tried to find a pattern so far, and he can't. We blew up that house on Pushkin where the Central Committee meet last night. It's full of party records. You know the Communists. They're born with pens in their hands. They live for paperwork. That place was like a shrine, and now it's gone, and the Germans can't understand it.'

'You said "we". You said "we blew up".'

227

'Yes. I meant they. I meant the Russians.'

'But you *do* have the list?'

'No. Not all of it.'

'But part of it?'

'Yes. A tiny part.'

'How? How did you get it?'

'Ilya told me. In return for information.'

'So how many targets are there?'

'Hundreds.'

'*Hundreds?* Does Schultz know that?'

'No. Though it wouldn't do any harm to tell him. They want to make life tough for the Germans. They don't want them to sleep at night. Ever.'

'They think they might abandon the place if life becomes impossible? Is that the plan?'

'No,' he shook his head. 'They know that will never happen until the Red Army come back.'

'So what's the point?'

'They want to provoke them,' he said slowly. 'They want to get under their skins. They want them to start behaving like proper Germans.' He gestured at his face. 'You were here when they arrived. You saw the bread, the salt, all the women making fools of themselves. This is war. The Germans are thieves. They've stolen our country from under our noses.'

'But so did the Russians. They did exactly the same thing. So what's the difference?'

'Wait,' he said. 'And you'll see.'

Bella nodded. Then came a dry cough from the woman in the corner. She had a question for Yuri. She hoped he didn't mind. Yuri nodded. Go ahead.

'What about here?' she said. 'Have they mined this place as well?'

'Yes,' Yuri nodded. 'I'm afraid they have.'

'For when?'

'I don't know. It could be now, in the next minute or so. It could be this afternoon, tonight, tomorrow. But the answer is yes.'

'And us? Here? Now?'

'We'll be gone. If it happens.'

'Gone?'

'Dead. Killed. Over. Finished. Done with.'

Bella shook her head, studied the hands knotted in her lap, faintly aware of movement in the corner of the room. The woman is crossing herself, she thought. She's making preparations for the moment when the floor erupts, and our ears explode, and everything goes black inside what's left of our heads. Is she worried about the journey to come? Does she think it will be long? Fraught with numberless difficulties? Or does she think her faith, her God, will be on hand to offer a little comfort, a little protection? These questions are pointless, she told herself, especially now. Bella had a good friend in Moscow, an oldish man who'd fought in the civil war and survived the madness that followed. *Life is dangerous*, he'd once told her. *No one survives it.*

'A bomb here answers nothing,' she said softly. 'There are Russian prisoners in the basement. They may find the bomb. They may set it off. Or someone might turn up and make it safe. Whatever happens, we need to talk about Larissa. Do you know where she is?'

'Yes.'

'Is she safe?'

'Yes. As safe as anyone can be.'

'There's a man called Kalb,' Bella said. 'He's SS. I've met him. He has plans for the Jews.'

'Kalb is part of the *Einsatzgruppen*,' Yuri was staring at his ruined hands. 'They tidy up behind the Army. I've talked to people in Poland. It doesn't pay to be a Jew once the *Einsatzgruppen* arrives.'

'Kalb will do the same here. Especially now, after the bombings. And Larissa is Jewish, as you know.'

'They'll never find her.'

'They might. Do you want to take that risk?'

For the first time, Yuri didn't have an answer. Bella glanced at the woman in the corner. Her pad appeared to be blank.

'Schultz says there are Russian spotters in the city,' Bella had turned back to Yuri. 'Red Army people talking to the sappers. Is that true?'

'Yes.'

'Do you know any of these people?'

'A couple, yes.'

'And you know where to find them?'

'Yes.'

'They're Russians, Yuri. Kalb will kill as many Jews as he can. Stalin let millions of peasants die in the Famine. It was you who told me that. The Holodomor? Am I right?'

'Yes.'

'So what's the difference? Just tell me. Just keep it simple. Hitler. Kalb. Stalin. And now Larissa. Schultz will guarantee her life in return for one of those Russians. That's what he says. That's what he's offering.'

'And you believe him?'

'Yes. I knew the man in Berlin. There's history between us. I'd trust him with my life.'

Yuri nodded. The silence stretched and stretched. Then came the sound of footsteps, louder and louder, until they paused outside. It was Schultz. He stepped into the library, holding the door open.

'*Komm.*'

Bella got to her feet, Yuri, too. They followed Schultz down to the ground floor. Another flight of steps disappeared into the basement. Bella could hear a faint murmur of conversation.

Schultz led the way to a door and a final flight of narrow wooden stairs that led to the sub-basement. At the bottom, Bella could feel bare earth beneath her shoes. Light from a single stand threw long shadows over the vaulted brick ceiling but Bella's attention was rivetted on a group of men bent over a long, shallow trench, maybe a metre wide. Two of them were on their knees, still scraping soil away with hand trowels. Running the length of the trench was a long, flat metal structure, still flecked with soil, gleaming in the light.

'You know what this is?' Schultz was looking at Yuri.

'An antenna. It picks up a radio signal.'

'And then what?'

Yuri gazed at him for a long moment, and then beckoned him to the far end of the trench. Attached to the antenna was a small metal box. Two wires disappeared into the soil.

'At the end of those wires is a detonator,' he said, 'and three boxes of explosive. When the signal arrives,' he shrugged, 'we all die.'

'You know how these things work?'

'Not really.'

'But you think you could stop it?'

'I could try.'

'What would you need?'

'A pair of cutters. Maybe even a knife.'

Schultz was looking at the wires again, digging in his trouser pocket. Bella could hear the Russians muttering to each other. Moscow accents, she thought. She might have been back on the Metro, eavesdropping on some chance conversation. How strange.

Schultz had found his knife. It was standard *Wehrmacht* issue, single blade. He gave it to Yuri.

Yuri studied it for a moment, then ran his finger along the blade. This man's a writer, Bella told herself. He works with his brain, not his hands. He hasn't a clue what to do next.

She put the question to him in Russian, hoping Schultz wouldn't understand. Yuri glanced up. Something had kindled in the eye that was still open. It was alive, ablaze. This is martyrdom, she thought. The priest's adopted son has put his faith in the Lord, and the Lord will decide. Schultz had sensed it, too.

'You're good with knives?' he said uncertainly. 'You'll really make this happen?'

Yuri nodded, said nothing. He was on his knees now, testing the wires, pulling them gently upwards. One was red, one black, both coated in thin rubber. Bella was thinking about booby traps, about hidden devices, about the fiendish lengths that lovely men like The Pianist, Ilya Glivenko, were prepared to go to kill as many people as possible. *Nothing works*, she was thinking of another Russian expression. *Until it does.*

Here, then? In this damp, gloomy space? With a war raging above? A private death? Unimaginably violent? In the company of strangers?

Yuri asked for everyone to pray and sank to his knees beside the exposed wires. Bella lowered her head. Schultz didn't move. The Russian prisoners, meanwhile, had spotted the knife in Yuri's hand. They exchanged glances. They looked terrified. When one of them began to curse, and made for the stairs, Schultz caught him and hauled him back. When he tried to struggle free, Schultz clubbed him to the ground, and then kicked him hard in the groin. The man screamed with pain, curled in a foetal position, cursing Schultz, cursing the war, cursing everything.

Yuri was still on his knees, his lips moving in a silent prayer, and watching him Bella wondered what kind of God had kept his fingers off the last decade. Did he have an accounting book up there in heaven? Did he make daily entries of lives lost, families shattered, cities razed to the ground, entire countries overwhelmed by violence of someone else's making? And would a word in his divine ear really make any difference to what was about to happen?

Yuri was back on his feet. He made a loop with one of the wires. He inserted the blade, adjusted the angle and then pulled hard. Bella shut her eyes. When she opened them again, she saw that the cut was clean. Two ends of bare wire sprouting from the rubber sheath.

One wire remained. Bella glanced at Schultz. He was rubbing his bloodied knuckles, seemingly untroubled by the next cut. Absurd, thought Bella. Blacks and whites. Yes or no. Life or death. Heads or tails. So simple.

Yuri was repeating the trick with the second wire. The loop looked a little tighter. He laid the blade against the rubber coating, and then he, too, shut his eyes. The Russians had turned their backs. They didn't want to watch. One had his hands over his ears, an image Bella knew she would take to the grave. Then, moments later, it was over, both wires cut.

Yuri rocked back on his haunches and wiped his ruined face with the back of his hand.

'Done,' he muttered.

19

THURSDAY 25 SEPTEMBER 1941

Pearse Lenahan made the call to MI5 that same afternoon. He'd spent all morning supervising a demolition course on a corner of the estate protected by blast walls. Now, picking up the phone and dialling the number one of the secretaries had scribbled down for him, he could still smell the sweet almond scent of the explosives he'd been shaping.

The MI5 number rang and rang. Finally, he heard a woman's voice. He offered the day's codeword and asked to speak to a Miss Ursula Barton.

'It's Mrs Barton, sir. You're already acquainted?'

'Not yet.'

'Then I'd stick to her surname. I'll see if she's available.'

Within seconds, another voice on the phone, older, sterner. Lenahan introduced himself.

'SOE, you say? Beaulieu or Brickendonbury Manor?'

'Beaulieu. STS 31.'

'It must be lovely down there at this time of year.'

'I beg your pardon, ma'am?'

'Autumn, Mr Lenahan. Fall. The New Forest. All those glorious trees. How can I help you?'

Lenahan began to explain about Moncrieff, the accident, the doctor's prognosis, but Barton cut him short.

'When?' she asked. 'When did this happen?'

'Yesterday, ma'am. It's true? The guy works for you?'

'Indeed, he does. Keep an eye on him. Put a guard on his door.'

'You're telling me he's an escape risk?'

'Far from it, quite the contrary. Expect me this evening. I'm coming down.'

*

She arrived in a taxi from Brockenhurst station. The Special Operations Executive was a new delinquent in the intelligence playground, one of Winston Churchill's more startling initiatives. Barton knew that it would be years before a proper invasion of the Continent could be organised but in the meantime, in his own words, the Prime Minister wanted 'to set Europe ablaze', and the agents charged with doing exactly that were under training at a requisitioned estate on the edge of the New Forest.

It was dark by the time the driver dropped Barton at the Beaulieu gatehouse, and she spent half an hour establishing her credentials with the fussy lieutenant who was manning the desk. Heavily armed guards lurked in the gloom outside. From the taxi, she'd counted five of them.

'If you people had this kind of problem getting into Europe,' she told the lieutenant at the desk, 'I dare say you'd never bother.'

It was Lenahan who drove down to pick her up. It had begun to rain by now, which did nothing for Barton's temper.

'So, how is he?' She wanted to know about Moncrieff.

'He's fine, ma'am. A little bruised, maybe, but I guess he knows he was lucky.'

'An accident, you say?'

'Yes, ma'am.'

'And he was driving?'

'Sure.'

'So where's the car?'

'I guess it was towed away. Honest to God, I've no idea.'

She shot him a look and tried to shield her face from the driving rain. After the fug of the taxi, it was freezing in the open Jeep.

'Present from Uncle Sam, ma'am.' Lenahan, sensing her discomfort, gave the steering wheel a little tap. 'Call it a down payment. Look on the bright side. The next bunch might even have roofs.'

The road wound uphill, into the darkness. Barton could make out a line of trees but little else. Finally, they came to a halt. Lenahan killed the engine and gestured at what looked like a cottage. There was a faintest hint of candlelight at an upstairs window and wet thatch was dripping water into the gravel path below.

'We call this the French house, ma'am,' Lenahan seemed impervious to the rain. 'We have a German house, too, and a little place that's meant to be Italian, but I guess you know that already. Agent training is fun, believe me. You can be French before you even set foot in the damn place.'

'Moncrieff?' Barton nodded up at the window. 'Would that be his room?'

It was. Lenahan opened the door and let Barton pass. Candlelight danced on the crudely plastered walls.

'You want me to stay, ma'am?'

'No, thank you.' She didn't look round.

'You're sure?'

'Perfectly.'

She waited for the door to close. Lenahan had been right about the decor, she thought. Very definitely French.

Moncrieff was doing his best to struggle upright but Barton told him not to bother. She pulled up a chair, and then opened the door to check that Lenahan had really gone.

'He's fine,' Moncrieff murmured. 'He's American. One day soon we'll need a lot more of them.'

'I gather he saved your life.'

'Is that what he told you?'

'In terms, yes. Is it true?'

'I've no idea. He certainly scooped me up and brought me here. It might be the same thing.'

Barton unbuttoned her raincoat and hung it carefully on the hook on the door. Somebody had left a pile of clothing on the chest of drawers. She sorted quickly through and selected a thick ribbed sweater, big even for someone of Moncrieff's height.

'Do you mind, Tam? These people must be in training for the bloody Arctic.' She pulled the sweater over her head. The hem came down to her knees.

'You approve?' She did a little twirl.

Soft applause from Moncrieff. She obviously had reservations about Lenahan, but otherwise he'd never seen her so playful. He couldn't remember when she'd last called him Tam.

'Well?' she settled on the chair. Lenahan had told her Moncrieff had lost his wits. She wanted a full explanation.

'Witless? He said that?'

'As good as. Short-term, of course, but it seems you're having difficulties remembering anything.'

Moncrieff did his best. He'd spent most of the last twenty-four hours anticipating a moment like this, and he'd managed to piece together a fragment or two of what might have happened over the last week or so, but his last real memory had been waking up in Archie's mews cottage with something happening outside, down in the street.

'Something?'

'Footsteps. Maybe voices. I'd have investigated, gone downstairs, I know I would.'

'You had a weapon?'

'Yes. I remember you insisting earlier on. I'm a bootneck, remember. Orders are orders.'

'Strange. We never found it.'

'You looked?'

'Of course we looked. You were due in next morning. There were meetings in the diary, one of them with Guy. Your reputation goes before you, Tam. You've always been a stickler for being on time. When you didn't show up, I began to make enquiries. We sent a chap to knock on your door. Nobody at home. By lunchtime we were phoning the hospitals. That wretched bike of yours. Anything might have happened.'

Moncrieff nodded. Guy Liddell headed Section 'B'. Missing the sub-committee he chaired would have been a capital offence. Already, they were heading deep into the yawning void, time Moncrieff simply couldn't account for.

'And then what?' he said.

'We had to break in. You lodged Archie Gasgoigne's details with us. We managed to make contact with him yesterday. I'm afraid the colour of his new front door won't please him, but war is war.'

'The colour?'

'Pink.'

Moncrieff laughed. In the Marines, Archie Gasgoigne had always found it hard to laugh at himself. A pink front door? Delicious.

'But no gun?'

'Nothing. Someone had been through the place before we got there. To be frank, they could have been gentler. It was a pickle. Here's where you might help, Tam. What were they after? What were they looking for?'

'I've no idea.' His long fingers briefly touched his head. 'I used to keep my secrets up here but that's a pickle, too.'

Barton winced, an expression – Moncrieff sensed – of sympathy. She wanted him to go back in time. She needed him to think very hard.

'You went up to St Albans,' she said. 'At my invitation.'

'I did. MI6. Glenalmond House. The man Philby. But you and I met after that.'

'We did, Tam. You bought me lunch. Can you remember where?'

'St Ermin's. You had the kidneys with mashed swede.'

'Excellent. And you remember the next favour I begged?'

'You asked me to run surveillance on Philby.'

'I did, Tam. I did. And...?'

'I went to St Pancras to meet his train...' He frowned. Remembering was suddenly a struggle. It was like prising open the pantry door as a child and reaching for a jar of something delicious on the top shelf. Tantalising. Just out of reach. He tried and tried, and then – quite suddenly – he had it. 'The bloody man was late. It was nearly lunchtime. He took a taxi. You'd arranged a follow vehicle.' The frown again. 'Bugger. Lost him.'

'Then or now?'

'Both, probably. He's a slippery bastard.'

'Can you remember *anything*?'

'No. I'm really sorry. This is hopeless. No... wait... he'd have gone to Broadway. Am I right?'

'Yes.'

'Then I'd have found cover, pretended I was out in the hills, waited. That could have been tricky, though. I could have been there all afternoon.'

'You were.'

'You *know* that?'

'I do. I had a look at the street myself. There's a restaurant called Iberica with line of sight to the Broadway buildings, and I commissioned some discreet enquiries. The maître d' denied all knowledge, but I managed to trace a couple of guests who stayed as late as you did. One of them was an MP, the other was his girlfriend.' She paused. 'Portly chap? Fond of a drink? He got the impression you were waiting for a friend from Lisbon. The lady, of course, was fictitious and it seems you didn't fool the maître d'. He knew you were a watcher. You stayed far too long, Tam. And you told him far too much. Philby uses the restaurant regularly. He and the maître d' are pals of a sort. The maître d' probably phoned him while you were still there, marked his card. We also believe that Philby was aware you were following him that day, and that he probably knew from the start. The Broadway crowd put great store on tradecraft. In this instance, it served him well.'

'You said "we".'

'Myself and Guy.'

'Liddell knows about St Albans? And about me cocking up the tail?'

'He does, Tam. And your disappearance concerned him as much as it did me. So...' she extended a cold hand, and put it on his arm, '... have a think. Pretend you're in the restaurant. It's late afternoon. The MP said gone half past four. You spot Philby. My guess is that he's emerged from Broadway. He'd need to get back to St Pancras. It's quite a hike from Victoria. Did he take a cab? No. Impossible. Because you left the restaurant and followed him. So where did he go? We need to know, Tam. We really do.'

Once again, Moncrieff was in the pantry. And, once again, the delights on the top shelf eluded him. Following Philby. Staying out of sight. Seeking cover where he could. Shop doorways, maybe. Or burying his head behind a newspaper.

'Newspaper...' he murmured.

'What?' Barton was straining to catch the word.

'Newspaper. Philby was carrying a newspaper. He had it at St Pancras. And he had it later.'

'You're sure?'

'Yes. Certain.'

'And the significance?'

'It was *The Times*. He was going towards the river. Traffic on Millbank. Bicycles. Lots of bicycles. That time. Late afternoon. Early evening. Half of London was on the move.'

'And Philby?'

'He crossed the road. I can see him now. And then he sat down.'

'Where?'

'On a bench. Overlooking the river. I thought I had him. I was sure I had him.'

'Had him how?'

'It was obvious. He was waiting for someone. He had something to hand over. He folded it into the newspaper. I can see him doing it now. I had him. I truly did.'

'Relax, Tam,' Barton was looking concerned. 'Is this an effort? Be frank. Tell me the truth.'

'Of course it's an effort. Everything's a bloody effort. But that's hardly the point. The point is, it's working. I'm back there, on the other side of the road, hidden by the traffic, waiting for the handover.'

'And?' Barton was excited now, Moncrieff could feel it.

'Nothing.'

'Nothing?'

'No one. His handler never turned up. In the end, Philby left the newspaper on the bench, in plain view, and walked away.'

'And you, Tam? What did you do?'

'I waited, of course. I'm sure I did. But still nothing happened. I can't remember how long but after a while I crossed the road and picked up the paper. There was an envelope inside.'

'An envelope? You're sure? Absolutely certain? What kind of envelope?'

'Manila, it was manila. And sealed. I remember that.'

'For the handler?'

'That's what I thought.'

'And you opened it?'

'I did.'

'And?'

Moncrieff lay back, exhausted. All he could think about was the photo of Bella, and the line of Russian that came with it, so blunt, so explicit, so chilling. *Every life has a price.*

'There was a restaurant menu inside,' Moncrieff's eyes were closed. 'It came from the place I'd been all afternoon. The bloody man had sent me a message, clear as daylight. Something about which dishes to avoid, I can't remember exactly, but he was marking my card. He knew everything, *everything*. He'd made a fool of me yet again. He'd led me by the nose all day. You're probably right about the maître d'. Philby may even have phoned him while I was still there. Just to check. Can you guess what was on the envelope?'

'Tell me.'

'My initials. T.'

There was a long moment of silence. Moncrieff could hear the soft patter of rain against the window. Then Barton stirred.

'Did you keep that menu, by any chance?'

'Yes. I took it home. It was on the table by my bed. Iberica. Definitely. That was the name of the restaurant. Didn't you find it? The menu?'

'No,' Barton withdrew her hand. 'Regretfully not.' She gazed briefly round the room. She was obviously cold, but when Moncrieff suggested the dressing gown on the back of the door she shook her head. 'We have to talk about here, Tam. About now. You were in a collision. You were driving a French car. Were you on the wrong side of the road? I understand the other driver thinks you were.'

'I was,' Moncrieff agreed.

'You remember that?'

'Very clearly. I thought I was in France. Everything told me I was in France. It was just a road. No signs. Nothing to say England.'

'But where had you been? Beforehand?'

Moncrieff explained about coming to in the back of the car. He'd seen trees. He'd managed to get out. There was a road nearby. There were keys in the ignition.

'And the accident happened when?'

'Very soon afterwards. Within a mile or so, once I was on the road.'

'And before that?'

'Nothing. Darkness. I badly needed a drink. Water. I remember that.'

'Other people?'

'There must have been.'

'When was this?'

'I've no idea. I may have been in bed. I simply don't know.'

'Did you see these people?'

'No, not properly.'

'Did they talk?'

'I suppose so.'

'Accents? Do you remember *how* they talked?'

'Not really. Foreign maybe. But I'm guessing.'

'Anything else? Traffic outside? Might you have been in a city? London, perhaps?'

'I don't know,' Moncrieff was rubbing his upper arm. 'How long was I gone?'

'You've been away from us for nearly a week, Tam.'

'A *week*?'

'Yes. At the start, we went house-to-house down the mews, we talked to everyone we possibly could. We commissioned other enquiries. We even checked up in Scotland in case you'd gone home for some reason. What worried me then was the state of Archie's place, the fact that people had been through it. And what worries me now is where these people chose to leave you.'

'Outside SOE?'

'Exactly.' She bent a little closer, as if someone might be listening. 'You're aware of who was instructing here? Just months ago? Of who knows the place inside out?'

'Tell me,' Moncrieff winced at a sudden stab of pain.

'Kim Philby.'

20

FRIDAY 26 SEPTEMBER 1941

Schultz turned the Museum of Lenin into *Sicherheitsdienst –* SD – headquarters. German engineers clattered down to the sub-basement, examined the antenna and agreed that the buried cache of high explosive was probably safe. Orders went out for more digging equipment, and by noon the Russian prisoners had exhumed three wooden boxes, all of them packed with blocks of TNT, and all of them rigged with detonators. This was the first of the Kyiv mines to be retrieved intact. The German engineers made the explosives safe and removed the bulky receiver for further examination.

The officer in charge reported to Schultz, who was organising the installation of field telephones. The wireless receiver attached to the explosives, he said, was powered by a sizeable battery.

'Meaning what?' Schultz was no engineer.

'Meaning it would have remained active for months. All it needed was a command signal. There are obviously others. We have to find them all.'

Schultz nodded. Smaller explosions were still rocking the city, he said, like an old man snorting and farting in his sleep. The Germans, he knew, had a fight on their hands and he intended to make the most of this first, if modest, victory. The museum was now safe.

Over the hours to come, he moved his small staff into offices on the first floor. He wanted the boxes of explosives and the excavations in the basement photographed, and he told a trusted aide to find him a journalist from the city's biggest newspaper who might have Kyiv's best interests at heart.

The journalist, an oldish man who'd worked on *Novoe Ukrainskoe Slovo* for most of his life, was brought to the museum in the early afternoon. Waiting for Schultz, he spent the time browsing the exhibits on the ground floor. He was examining a photograph of Lenin in temporary exile at Vyborg when an aide appeared at his elbow and took him up to the first floor.

Schultz was sitting behind a desk that had belonged to the museum's director. Two field telephones linked him to *Wehrmacht* headquarters, and to the Colonel in charge of the engineers. Beside the untidy tangle of wires stood a bottle of vodka Schultz had found in one of the desk drawers. To his surprise, the journalist refused the offer of a drink.

'We need to be friends,' Schultz growled. 'You and I.'

The journalist didn't reply. Instead, he produced a pad and enquired what Schultz wanted him to write.

'As simple as that?'

'Of course. You are the masters now. We do your bidding. We don't make a newspaper, not anymore, we just pass messages. Yesterday's was a phone number. Were you aware of that? No? A phone number for the SS. Private. Confidential. Ring this number if anything bothers you. Give us a name, and address, and the Reich will make you a little richer. Do it for your families. Do it for your children. Who could possibly say no?'

'Rats,' Schultz said. 'An appeal for rats. It worked in Paris so maybe it will work here, too.'

'Exactly. And us? How do you think we feel? Helping turn this city into a sewer? Believe me, Herr Schultz, it's not an easy life.' He gestured wearily towards the window and the clouds of thick, black smoke, laced with streaks of yellow and crimson, still boiling over the rooftops. 'They blew up an oil depot this morning. You'll know that already. Our hospitals can't cope any more. You're probably aware of that, too.'

Schultz nodded. The Russian mines killed indiscriminately. Hundreds of Germans had died but the city had lost many more.

'We need this to be over,' his bulk loomed over the desk. 'You agree?'

'Of course.'

'Then tell your readers we have the measure of these animals. We know exactly what they're up to. We understand the way these devices work. And we're taking steps to make your city safe again.'

Another explosion, distant but not small. Neither man even bothered to glance across at the window, but the timing was perfect.

'You may need to hurry,' the journalist murmured, 'or there won't be a city left.'

*

Yuri told Bella she had to trust him. It was early evening. With Schultz's blessing, and a commandeered car, Yuri was driving her across the city to meet Larissa. Their route took them past the high walls of the complex they called the Lavra inside the Pechersk Monastery, overlooking the river. There were Germans everywhere, guarding the monastery gates, untangling the traffic, requisitioning the odd horse from weary peasants, conducting random checks on passers-by. Bella noticed how tired they were beginning to look, and how every set of papers seemed to demand minute inspection. The days of bread and salt, she thought, are well and truly over.

'They're using the priests as translators,' Yuri nodded at a tall, bearded figure in a black cassock, deep in conversation with a group of German soldiers, all of them absurdly young. 'Religion has its uses, even for the Germans.'

At the top of the hill beyond the monastery, Yuri checked the mirror and swung the big car off the main road, and into a muddle of streets that were suddenly empty. It was nearly dark by now, no street lights, and Yuri slowed to walking pace, peering at door after door, looking for a particular address.

'Larissa lives here?'

'No.'

'So where is she?'

'Trust me,' he said again.

She knew she had no option. She'd seen Yuri disappear into one of the upstairs rooms at the museum with Schultz and emerge barely minutes later. She'd no idea what kind of deal they'd struck, and, when she asked, Yuri wouldn't tell her. All that mattered, he'd said, was Larissa. Bella was right. Kalb was going to slaughter the Jews. And Larissa was a trophy target.

The car had finally come to a halt. Yuri checked his watch and glanced at the house.

'You're OK?' Bella was looking at the wreckage of his face.

'Eating's hard. I need a dentist.'

'Is that all?'

He forced a smile. He was nervous, Bella could tell. She'd always assumed that faith was something you could rely on in situations like these but in the company of Yuri she was beginning to wonder.

They sat in silence, Yuri's fingers drumming on the steering wheel. A black cat stalked across the street, impossibly thin, all but invisible in the gathering darkness, and Bella was still thinking about the kitten she'd left with the old lady, when a figure materialised from nowhere, and bent urgently to the driver's window. Bella had a perfect view of his face: young, white, hints of Slavic blood, the beginnings of a beard.

'Russian,' she murmured. 'Am I right?'

Yuri was already out of the car. A brief embrace, a whisper of conversation, an exchange of nods, then the other man was clambering into the back seat. He was carrying a canvas bag. It looked heavy.

Bella didn't turn around. In any other circumstance, she'd extend a hand, offer a name, introduce herself, but she sensed that this moment belonged to her two companions. Comrades-in-arms, she thought grimly. More surprises in store.

They were under way again, plenty of acceleration in the big engine. Yuri was heading back into the city, enjoying the power at his fingertips. Then came the sound of movement from the back seat, and a cough as their passenger cleared his throat.

'*Vodzh*,' he whispered.

This time, Bella glanced back. The young man was hunched into one corner of the back seat. He was wearing a pair of headphones, and he had something black in his hand. Wires trailed into the canvas bag. *Vodzh*, she thought. A call sign of some kind, or maybe a code. Short. Terse. Wholly appropriate. *Vodzh*. This boy was one of the spotters. The radio was on his lap. He was doing his best to raise the men with their hands around the city's scrawny neck.

'*Vodzh*,' he tried again.

'Everything OK?' Yuri's eyes were on the rear-view mirror.

'Nothing.'

'Shit.'

They were back in the city centre now, hugging the side streets that ran parallel to Khreshchatyk. Yuri slowed to avoid a body in the street, then another. Vodka? High explosive? Despair? Bella had no idea.

Yuri was accelerating again, heading into the suburbs beyond the old town, taking a road that ran north, out towards the marshes beside the river. Hard winters had wreaked havoc among the cobblestones and the car bounced and juddered from pothole to pothole. Houses were becoming sparser. Bella glimpsed a black space that might have been a field. Then Yuri spotted something he seemed to recognise, a landmark of some kind, and he braked sharply, pulling the car to a halt.

'Try again,' he said in Russian.

The boy pulled on the headphones. '*Vodzh*,' he said. Then again, louder this time.

Bella had turned around in the seat. Like it or not, she'd become a player in this drama. For a second or two, still hunched, still tense, the boy didn't move. Then Bella caught a crackle of static from the headphones, and a thin voice acknowledging the codeword, and the boy – elated – responding.

'Stand by,' he said. 'Maybe an hour. Maybe sooner.'

The radio went dead. Yuri was peering into the darkness.

'And the other call?' he said.

'They're waiting.'

'They've got the number?'

'Everyone's got the number. This is fucking Kyiv, or had you forgotten, *tovarish*?'

Other call? Bella had no idea what this meant. She was still thinking about the *Vodzh* message. Might Ilya have been on the other end? Was it his finger on the button? Was he playing God with building after building? Life after life? She was tempted to ask, but they were on the move again, slowly this time, Yuri searching – once again – for an address.

It was a cottage. It stood at the roadside, nothing more than a shape in the darkness. No sign of life, not a flicker of light. Bella got out of the car. She could smell the slightly rank sweetness of the river. Yuri, she sensed, had been here before. He took her by the hand and led her round the side of the property. She felt the coldness of the dew as unseen plants brushed against her bare legs. At the back of the cottage was a door. Already, it was easing open.

'Bella,' Yuri whispered. Then he was gone.

Bella could smell Larissa before they were within touching distance. It was the scent of the perfume she wore, of days and nights before Children's World erupted and everything went crazy.

'*Chérie?*'

Bella stepped in from the darkness, felt Larissa's fingers on her cheek, the sudden warmth of her lips on her mouth, then a one-armed hug that was all the sweeter for its awkwardness.

'Yuri said they raped you.'

'He's right. They did.'

'But you're here. You're here. Stop. Don't move. I want to look at you.'

Bella heard the scrape of a match in the darkness. Then Larissa was holding the stub of a candle, bending over it. The flame guttered in the draught.

'Shut the door, *chérie*.' Larissa was laughing now. 'I've run out of hands.'

Bella closed the door. In the candlelight, Larissa looked thin, drawn. She was wearing a thick sweater against the autumn chill, and her hair tumbled over her shoulders the way she wore it at night, but her eyes were alive in the gauntness of her face.

'Kiss me,' she said.

Bella was happy to oblige. She knew they had business to transact and she knew how hard it was going to be. Larissa probably had no faith in anyone, least of all a German spy catcher. Would she really believe that Schultz would protect her from the coming bloodbath? Had she any notion about the blackness of Kalb's soul?

'I missed you, *chérie*. I missed us both. Living in the country may suit other people. I hate it.' Her face was very close. 'Did he hurt you, Kalb?'

'It wasn't Kalb. He left it to his bodyguard. The man was a dog.'

'All men are dogs. I think I told you before. But Kalb. He was the one. He was responsible. No Kalb, no rape. Am I wrong?'

Bella shook her head. It was Yuri who'd pressed her for a full account. He must have passed it on, she thought, every single detail.

'Kalb,' she agreed.

Larissa had taken her hand now, giving her the candle. Bella began to protest that Yuri was waiting outside to take them back to the city, back to the sanctuary that was the Museum of Lenin, but Larissa wouldn't hear of it. She'd known Bella was coming. They had a little time and before the war once again had its way with them, she wanted Bella to herself.

'All of me?' Bella shuddered at the thought.

'Everything. I know about rape, believe me. You have to be strong. You have to take a spade and bury those memories. Your body will be kind to you, and you know why? Because I'll be kind to your body.'

They were in a bedroom. The blankets were already turned down, and Larissa had managed to find a pillow slip from somewhere. Larissa settled on the edge of the bed.

'There's a saucer for the candle, *chérie*.' She nodded at a wooden stool beside the bed. 'Just hold me. And tell me you love me. That's all I want. Just that.'

Bella set the candle down and put her arms round Larissa. She sensed the older woman knew already that this was where the evening would stop.

'Thank you,' Bella murmured. 'Thank you for understanding. You've been here a long time?'

'Days. Far too long.'

'Alone?'

'Of course. Yuri brought me here. I have lots of food. There's more in the garden. Maybe I was always a country girl. Maybe that's when I learned to hate it.'

'Is it the silence?'

'Partly.'

'What else?'

'I miss people. Conversation. Work.' She cupped Bella's face with her good hand. 'And you, *chérie*.'

'That can't be true. You barely know me.'

'Really?' Her face was very close. 'You don't think our lives turn on a glance? A smile? That single moment that tells you who you really are?'

'That's a lovely phrase. I wish it was true.'

'It's belief, *chérie*. You have to *believe*. Ask Yuri. With him, it happens to be God. That's fine but God can be unforgiving.'

'And you?'

'God never forgave me. I found my own path, and so did you.'

'When I went to the restaurant, that night? With Ilya?'

'When you went to Moscow. With your little bag packed. *Das Kapital*? Lenin's scribblings from Zurich? Am I wrong?'

'No.' Bella felt a sudden warmth flooding her whole body. This woman, she thought, had listened, watched. Now she was moistening a finger and tracing the outline of Bella's lips.

'You make me happy, very happy,' she whispered. 'Do you mind me saying that?'

'Not at all. I'm glad. Does that mean you trust me?'

'It does.'

'With anything? Any decision I make?'

'Of course, *chérie*. You have something in mind?'

'I do.'

'In both our interests?'

'Yes.'

'Then do it, *chérie*. Take charge.' Larissa smiled and closed her eyes.

They lay together, under the blankets, a rare moment of peace. After a while, it began to rain, and Bella could hear the steady drip-drip of water through holes in the roof. Larissa seemed oblivious, her breath warm on Bella's face. Then the candlelight shivered and died, and the darkness returned. Yuri will be waiting, Bella thought. Time to go.

A moment or so later, Bella caught the distant growl of an engine. It grew louder and louder, then came the squeal of brakes, and the crunch-crunch of heavy boots on gravel, and the splintering of wood as the door was kicked in. Larissa, still half asleep, was struggling to sit up while Bella lay still, her eyes on where she guessed the door might be. Another kick, the door bursting open, then the beam of a torch sweeping the room. It paused briefly on a typewriter, and then settled on the two figures in bed.

'*Raus. Komm.*'

The voice and the smell were the only clues Bella needed. She closed her eyes, turned her face to the wall, her arms reaching for Larissa again.

Valentin, she thought.

*

There were two of them. With Valentin was another man Bella had never seen before. Unlike Kalb's bodyguard, he was wearing an SS uniform. At gunpoint, Valentin pushed the two women out of the cottage and into the road. The gravel and the cobblestones were wet underfoot, and Bella did her best to avoid the puddles as they headed for the car parked on the road. In the sweep of the torch, Bella recognised Kalb's Mercedes. Of Yuri and the Russian she could see no trace.

The SS man took the wheel. Valentin folded Larissa into the passenger seat beside him, and then locked the door. Bella had already climbed into the back. At all costs, she didn't want this man to touch her. She looked up through the window, aware of his huge face and the hint of a smile as he stared at her through the dirty glass. Then he was settling beside her, and the car was rocking under his sudden weight, and he was shouting something at the driver.

They were on the move now, bucketing over the broken cobbles, heading for the main road that would return them to the city. As the junction approached, the driver barely slowed, pulling the Mercedes into a savage turn. Bella heard the squeal of rubber as they hit the main road, and for a split second she glimpsed another car, Yuri's, parked beneath a stand of trees. There were figures inside and it was beginning to move. Valentin, Bella realised, hadn't seen it. So far, she'd pushed his hand away, but now she let him touch her. Anything, she told herself, anything to keep his attention.

They were moving fast now, Bella resisting the temptation to check for the car behind, the long throw of the headlights tugging them towards the city centre. More houses. Kerbside spaces cleared for tomorrow's market stalls. Then the metallic gleam of the first tram tracks. At this time of night there was very little traffic, and while Valentin's thick fingers were mercifully still, she tried to understand just what had brought him to Larissa's door. Had they been betrayed? Had some enemy of Larissa's, someone from the newspaper offices perhaps, someone she'd offended or upset, had this person known about the cottage, and lifted the phone, and made a call? Whatever the explanation, she knew it didn't matter. The next face they'd see would be Kalb's. And at that point, Larissa's fate would be sealed.

Suddenly, at the next intersection, she recognised the ghostly remains of the Ginzburg Skyscraper. They were on Khreshchatyk now, still moving at speed, the wideness of the boulevard flanked by one bomb site after another. Then came a sudden turn to the left, and she had time to recognise the remains of the Continental Hotel before the big car began to lurch to the left and they rolled to a halt. The driver was cursing.

'Fucking tyre,' he swore in German.

'How far?'

'Five hundred metres.'

'Just drive.'

The driver got back behind the wheel and stirred the engine into life. Slowly, they bumped over the cobblestones, and Bella could hear the metallic grinding of the tyre rim destroying itself.

'Where are we going?'

'The State Bank,' Valentin laughed. 'It's a shit heap. You'd have been much better off in the Big House. Blame the fucking Russians, not us.'

She'd heard Yuri mention the State Bank, but she couldn't remember why.

'You're working there? All of you?'

'Sure. That's where we do our business now.'

It wasn't hard to spot the bank. Bella saw it coming a couple of intersections away, a tall, grey building, handsome windows, unusually intact for this area of the city. The driver nursed the Mercedes a little closer. Then, sixty metres away, he shook his head and came to a halt again.

'Enough,' he nodded at the street ahead. 'We walk from here.'

Valentin grunted something Bella didn't catch. The driver half turned and tossed him the keys before getting out to inspect the damaged wheel. Valentin manoeuvred his bulk out of the car and circled the boot, bending to unlock Bella's door. As he did so, there came a blinding flash and the roar of an explosion, and, as the blast wave lifted the big car bodily and then slammed it down, Bella had the briefest glimpse of the pillars of the bank beginning to collapse. Valentin's face at the window had gone.

Moments later, she became aware of another figure, young, pale, emerging from the clouds of dust. The gun in his hand was pointing down. Three bullets. She counted them. Bang-bang-bang. Then he wrenched the door open, and she found herself staring at the Russian. He pulled her out and gestured at the body at her feet. Valentin was sprawled on the cobblestones, three neat holes in his temple beneath the hair line, blood pooling around his head.

Bella stared down at him. The explosion had robbed her of everything. When she tried to speak, nothing came out.

The Russian had just put more bullets into the driver. Already, the street was alive with soldiers running towards what remained of the State Bank. None of them spared the Mercedes a second glance.

'Larissa?' Bella mumbled.

The Russian was already helping her out of the car. She'd had to struggle over the driver's seat, protecting her plastered arm. Now she stared down at the two bodies, numbed by this torrent of unceasing violence.

'*Toropit'sya*.' The Russian was getting nervous. Come, he was saying. We need to go.

The three of them made their way against the tide of soldiers pouring down the street. One of them stopped and asked if they needed help. Bella shook her head. She was thinking straight, at last.

'We were lucky,' she muttered in German, gesturing back towards the bank. 'We managed to get out.'

'You're SS?'

'*Ja*. Clerical. Just a secretary.'

'Fucking Ivans.' The soldier ran on.

The car was parked on the side of the road. Bella recognised it at once. The Russian bent to the window, peering inside. Bella joined him.

'Yuri?'

The Russian shook his head. 'Gone,' he said. 'And the equipment, too.'

21

SATURDAY 27 SEPTEMBER 1941

With a little help from Lenahan, Moncrieff made it to lunch. Meals at Beaulieu were served in a big tent filled with long trestle tables covered in sheets. Food was cooked at a field kitchen behind the tent and the clatter of the generator made for shouted conversations. According to Lenahan, this was strictly a temporary arrangement, but Moncrieff waved his apology away. He rather liked the set-up. It reminded him of his early days in the Marines.

The tent was full, and while Lenahan fetched helpings of the day's stew Moncrieff gazed around. There had been a number of occasions in his life when he'd been in danger of slipping his moorings but nothing to compare to this. At one moment, France. The next, rural England, with Ursula Barton suddenly at his bedside. And now here he was, surrounded by strangers, mainly men, mainly young, and most of them foreign. He had a good ear for languages, even with competition from the generator, and by the time Lenahan returned with the food he'd identified at least half a dozen.

'French? German? Polish? Czech? Spanish? Dutch? Am I right?'

'And more, buddy,' Lenahan was juggling the plates of stew. 'Try teaching these guys. My field is explosives. You have to get this stuff right. On a good day I'm looking at a bunch of crazy bums from all over Europe. Most of them speak a little English. Some of them don't. And it's those mothers you have to be very, very patient with. Maybe that's why God invented sign language. You wire the detonator *this* way. Watch me. Do it. Then do it again, and again, and again. By the end of all that, the chances of blowing yourself up are down to fifty per cent. Some of them can live with odds like that.' He shrugged. 'Some don't.'

Moncrieff smiled. The young American, with his manic energy and his cheerful despair, was making him feel better.

A stranger approached, accompanied by one of the sentries from the gate. Lenahan jumped to his feet.

'Frank! Great to see you, buddy. They gave you a pass? Are they blind or is this your lucky day? This is Tam. He won't get up but don't take it personally. He's also Scottish but that's not his fault, either.'

Moncrieff was trying to struggle to his feet but Lenahan pushed him gently back down to his seat before setting off for more food.

'The name's Jennings.' Moncrieff shook the proffered hand. 'I don't think surnames ever occur to our American friends. You are...?'

'Moncrieff. Tam for short.'

Jennings sat down. He was small and poorly shaved. He wore the uniform of a Major in the Royal Engineers. He had a pair of glasses on a lanyard around his neck and a nervous habit of running his fingers through what remained of his greying hair. He said he'd been on the road for the best part of seven hours.

'From? Am I allowed to ask?'

'Sevenoaks. Lovely part of the country but never try to get anywhere in a hurry. The roads are atrocious, which must be one of the reasons our German friends haven't invaded. The bloody traffic jams would bring them to their knees. One wretched village after another. Happy days. Do they serve alcohol here?'

Lenahan had just returned with another plate of stew but Jennings despatched him at once in search of beer.

'Make that three,' he called. 'One each. Halstead's paying.'

'Fort Halstead?' Moncrieff was warming to this little man.

'The very same. You know it?'

'Of it. Your reputation goes before you. When all else fails, blow the enemy up.'

'Exactly. My thoughts entirely, Moncrieff. Some of us argue that chemistry is a calling, a vocation. That's a bit fancy for me. I'm still the kid in his raincoat on bonfire night. I just love all those bangs.'

Jennings, it turned out, had come to Beaulieu to deliver a series of guest lectures at Lenahan's invitation. He'd done it before, with some success, and appeared to be entranced by the place.

'It's deeply refreshing, if I may say so. The quality's a bit uneven and I'm sure some of these people are duds, or worse, but you can't fault the thinking. Set Europe ablaze? Doesn't that prospect fill you with joy?'

Lenahan was back with the beer. Jennings seized the nearest tankard. With apologies to Moncrieff, he needed to share some good news with his young host.

'Kyiv, dear boy. I got word from our chaps in Moscow last night. The city's in flames. It bloody *worked*.'

Lenahan wanted to know more. Jennings was more than happy to oblige. Dozens of targets, all of them carefully chosen, all of them full of Germans, and all of them blown to kingdom come with nothing more complicated than a wireless signal.

'How many killed?' Lenahan was eager for numbers.

'Hundreds, thousands, zillions. The advance has ground to a halt. Hitler has had second thoughts and ordered a retreat. The Krauts will be back in Berlin by next weekend.' Jennings broke off. 'I jest, Moncrieff, but, believe me, it's excellent news. A Ruski flew in and popped down to Halstead for a spot of technical advice and extra kit. Lovely little chap, name of Ilya. Ilya Glivenko. We had him round for supper and I think my wife fell in love with him. We did our best to help the Ruski, of course, but it turned out they'd got most of it right already. Impressive people. Think things through. Plucky, too. Not that they have much choice in the matter.'

'This was when?' Moncrieff wanted to know more.

'Blowing up Kyiv?'

'Meeting your Russian.'

'Couple of weeks ago. I drove him up to Northolt and saw the little chap off, handed him over to a delightful woman who'd be taking over as Ilya's escort.'

'From whom?'

'Me. They were heading off on the long route south. Gib. Cairo. I'm sure you know the score. This Russian thing has been a bit sudden for some of our chaps down the line. Ilya needed someone to smooth the way, take care of any problems en route, at least that's what she told me.'

'You talked to her?'

'Briefly. She had fluent Russian. That's what stuck in my mind. Bloody clever, says me. Amazing the talents this little country can lay its hands on.'

'She had a name?'

'Of course,' he frowned. 'Menzies? Know her, by any chance.'

'Yes, I do,' Moncrieff allowed himself a smile. 'Her first name's Isobel.'

'You're right. I dare say that makes you a lucky chap. She told me she was off to Moscow. Not looking forward to it at all.'

'The city?'

'Winter,' he pulled a face. 'And all those bloody Germans at her door.'

*

Bella was sitting in Schultz's new office at the Museum of Lenin. There were armed guards outside on the street, and *Wehrmacht* – at Schultz's insistence – were sending extra security. Earlier this morning, roused from nightmares she was still trying to forget, Bella had asked whether these precautions were really necessary. Neither she nor Larissa were planning to escape.

'This is for your benefit, as well as ours.' Schultz had sounded weary. 'The SS have no sense of humour. The moment they decide that you blew up their headquarters is the moment they'll come looking. We have to keep these bastards at arm's length. No one needs complications. Least of all me.'

Schultz said he'd been on the phone for most of the morning. Word from the Military Governor's office suggested that the bomb beneath the State Bank had killed most of the handful of staff who had just moved in.

'I got the whole story from our Russian friend, the one we picked up. You want to know how they did it? Yuri knew where to find Krulak. He also knew one of the Russian agents in contact with the sappers. The sappers had just blown up the Big House. The SS needed to find somewhere else to nest but neither Yuri nor the Russian knew where. Yuri took what happened to you personally. He wanted to make Kalb pay.'

'And Larissa?'

'She's another one on Kalb's list. He wants to lay hands on her. Badly. She's his trophy Yid. So, all Yuri needed to do was set Kalb's dogs on her.'

'How did he do that?'

'There's a phone number for the SS. It's for snitches. Anyone can call and so Yuri picked up the phone. Larissa Krulak? An *address*? The SS couldn't wait. And neither could Yuri. She was out in the country, as you know. Yuri knew which route they had to take on their way back, and after he dropped you he parked up and waited. He had the Russian with him to make contact with the sappers. All the sappers needed was the target.'

'The State Bank.'

'Exactly. There were three more tons of high explosive in the cellars. Last night, we understand the SS were in the process of checking. Too fucking late. Bam—' Schultz drove his big fist into the palm of his other hand.

'And Kalb?'

'He wasn't there.'

'You're sure?'

'As sure as I can be,' he nodded at one of the phones. 'I had him on this morning. The man's frothing at the mouth. You want a direct quote? He's trying to get thirty-three thousand people in a line and he's telling me none of them will stand still. These are Jews. Yids. Kalb's got a day and a half to decide what to do with them all. I think he was trying to pick my brains but I'm here to win a war, not settle some private fucking debts. Thankfully, our tame Russian has given us a head start.'

'He gave you the list of targets?'

'We found it when we searched him. They're all in code but we know which order these buildings went up in and from that we can work the rest out.'

'How many?'

'Hundreds. And that's just his list. There may be others, but in the meantime we know where to start looking.'

'And Yuri?'

'They caught him last night. That was the real reason for Kalb's phone call.'

*

Bella took the news back to Larissa. They'd been sleeping in the same room, Bella on the floor, Larissa on a sagging leather couch. Last night's explosion, so close, coupled with the killings beside the car, had left their mark. Since the Russian had delivered them back to Schultz's safe-keeping, she'd barely said a word.

Now, she was huddled in a corner of the couch, still wrapped in a single thin blanket. The force of the explosion had shattered part of the Mercedes' windscreen and, with the aid of a pair of tweezers, Bella had spent half the night extracting tiny splinters of glass from her cheeks and forehead. She thought she'd got them all out. She'd been wrong.

'Well?' Larissa's fingers were still mapping the damage on her face. Now and again, they stopped, probed, scratched, drew blood.

Bella explained how the SS had found the address.

'*Yuri* told them?'

'Yes. He wanted to kill Kalb.'

'And did he?'

'No.'

'Was he injured?'

'He was somewhere else. I don't know where.'

'And Yuri?'

'They caught him.'

'This is the SS? Kalb?'

'The Germans. I don't know precisely who. But Kalb's got him now.'

Larissa nodded, said nothing, turned her face away. When Bella tried to comfort her, the older woman pushed her aside. She was still in shock. That was obvious.

Bella told her about the Russian who'd killed Valentin and the driver. Schultz was holding him somewhere, but the important work was already done.

'Meaning?'

'Schultz has a list of targets. He's already organising the engineers to start defusing the bombs. The Russians did their best but now it's just a question of time. I'm afraid it's over, but thank God you're still in one piece.'

'Here, you mean?' Larissa gestured bitterly at the pictures on the wall. Lenin arriving at the Finland Station. Lenin hoisted shoulder-high by a huge crowd. Lenin looking thoughtful beside a window. 'These people helped themselves to our country, mine and Yuri's.' Larissa shook her head. 'And now we have to deal with your German friends.'

*

The rest of the day crawled by. There were no more explosions. The two women remained in the museum. Twice, Larissa got up to try the door and on both occasions it was locked. Then, in mid-afternoon, Schultz appeared. He'd acquired a link of cold sausage and some bread from somewhere. With it came a china jug full of steaming black tea. So far, he said, Russian prisoners had been put to work at a dozen of the suspected sites and were unearthing antennae and receiving equipment. At three of the sites, he said, the antennae appeared to have been manufactured in England and he'd made a note of the markings. Coventry, Bella confirmed. Lots of factories. Lots of expertise.

'This is the equipment you escorted from England?'

'It must be. We're allies now, remember. Friends for life.'

Schultz held her gaze. He wasn't smiling.

'You're lucky I'm not Kalb,' he growled.

'Of course I am. I'm lucky you're not Valentin, too, but happily your Russian has seen to him. What will you do about him now? The Russian boy?'

'Protective custody,' Schultz said stiffly. 'Just like you.'

Larissa was still on the couch. She wondered aloud whether protective custody extended to a favour. She needed to use the toilet.

Schultz nodded. 'One of my guys is outside the door. Ask him to show you where to go.'

Larissa got up, briefly checked her face again and then left. Bella heard a murmur of conversation outside the door. She turned back to Schultz. She remembered very clearly an evening they'd once shared in a bar in Berlin. 1938, she thought. With Hitler still digesting the Sudetenland.

'You remember *Der Teufel*? Just around the corner from *Abwehr* headquarters?'

'Of course I do.'

'You took me there once, had a driver pick me up from the embassy. It was just before Christmas. You promised to drink me under the table and that never quite happened.'

'Impressive,' Schultz conceded the point. 'You were English, and you were a woman. Two reasons why you should have been unconscious by midnight. I admit it. I failed. But don't blame me for trying.'

'I blame you for nothing. What interests me is that phrase of yours. Protective custody. You used it that evening, too.'

'With respect to?'

'The Czechs. I said the rest of that poor bloody country was next on Hitler's list and you half admitted it. Protective custody, you said. Which somehow meant protecting the Czechs from themselves. Grabbing their country in their own best interests. Is that fair?'

'The phrase was theirs, not mine.'

'Theirs?'

'Hitler's. Goebbels's. That fool Ribbentrop's.'

'So you didn't believe it?'

'Not for a moment. If we'd still had a legal system, it wouldn't have stood up in a court of law. Not for a moment.'

'Yet you went along with it.'

'I did, yes. While the going was good, you went along with all kinds of nonsense.'

'And now?'

'Now's different,' Schultz rubbed a big hand over his face and half stifled a yawn. 'We're in the shit, and most people with a brain in their head know it. No dog bites off more than he can chew. Not if he's wise. Russia, the Soviet Union, is a very big bone. Our sainted Leader might have borne that in mind. Belgium was a titbit. France was a proper meal. I've served in both countries and that, believe me, was a pleasure. This place? Kyiv? And all the other Kyivs to come? Kharkov? Rostov-on-Don? Stalingrad? You have to be kidding. This winter will freeze the balls off us. The winter after that might be our last. Hang on here for a couple of years and you'll all be speaking Russian again. Is that a message that anyone in Berlin wants to hear? Not in a million years. Drive the Ivans east of the Urals, grab the oil, grab the grain, do a deal with Stalin, it's just a matter of time. Time and all that Aryan will. It's crazy, but these are crazy times. Just ask your Yuri. Unless he's lucky enough to be dead by now.'

My Yuri? If he belongs to anyone, Bella thought, he belongs to Larissa.

'Do you have a son, Schultz?'

Schultz frowned. Questions this intimate had never been part of their relationship, not even in Berlin, but the speech he'd just delivered had come straight from the heart and they both knew it.

'No,' he said. 'We thought about it once, but it never happened.'

'We?'

272

'Me and my ex-wife. She has three boys now, so I guess that makes them both very happy. He's a good man, Klaus. She did well. And so did he.'

'And you?'

'I take my pleasures when I can. I doubt there will ever be children.'

'Does that make you sad?'

'Not at all. Sadness is a luxury these days. No one has the time for a long face. Enough' – he checked his watch – 'Where's your friend? How much time does a woman need to empty her fucking bladder?'

He clumped across to the door. The sight of the guard outside put a frown on his face.

'Where is she?' he demanded.

'Still in the toilet. She said she knew the way.'

'Check, my friend. Run along there. *Schnell*, eh?'

The guard disappeared. Schultz stood in the open doorway, tapping one foot, waiting for him to reappear. The guard was back within the minute.

'Gone?' This from Schultz.

'*Ja.*'

'*Scheisse.*' The door slammed shut and Bella heard the key turn in the lock. Then came a roar from Schultz and the heavy thunder of boots.

Bella sat back, suddenly exhausted. Protective custody, she thought. If only.

22

The car arrived for Tam Moncrieff early on Sunday morning. He said his goodbyes to Lenahan and wished him well. He'd quietly acquired a box of matches from one of the cooks in the field kitchen and pressed it into the young American's hand as a farewell present.

'Set Europe ablaze,' he said, giving his shoulder a squeeze.

'Sure,' Lenahan grinned. 'It's been a pleasure, buddy.'

The car, a dark green Rover, appeared to have come from London but when Moncrieff enquired where they were going, the driver wouldn't say.

'Talk to the lady, sir,' he muttered. 'I expect she'll tell you.'

They picked up Ursula Barton from a big hotel on the outskirts of Brockenhurst. She and Moncrieff made themselves comfortable in the back of the car. It turned out that Barton had been in residence for a couple of days, since the night of her arrival. She'd managed to track down the remains of the Peugeot to a garage in Southampton and taken full details. The car still had French registration plates but according to the mechanic there was evidence that UK plates had been recently removed. He'd given Barton the number stamped on the engine block and confirmed that the colour – maroon – was very probably original.

Armed with this information, Barton had initiated further enquiries through the government department responsible for importing foreign cars but knew that progress would be slow. In the meantime, she'd had another chat to Lenahan on the phone.

'About?'

'You, Tam.'

She reached forward and closed the sliding glass panel that masked the conversation from the driver.

'Me?'

'Yes. You won't mind me saying this, but you're different, you're not the man you were. That's a judgement, of course, that only I can make. Lenahan didn't know you before. But we both agreed that you're nervous, unsure of yourself, unsure of anything, not at all the Tam Moncrieff I used to know.'

Moncrieff nodded. He supposed it might be true, but he couldn't really tell. Which was – of course – the measure of the problem.

'You're sacking me?' he enquired. 'That would sound logical.'

'*Au contraire*. We're going to nurse you back to health. We will, of course, have ulterior motives and you won't be surprised to know that one of them is that memory of yours. I'm the layman here but I refuse to believe that a man in your condition, in the prime of his life, can simply lose six whole days. There has to be an explanation, and we intend to find it.'

'We?'

'Guy and myself.'

'Anyone else? Or is this a private party? Invitation only?'

'That's better, that almost qualifies as wit,' she offered a thin smile. 'Maybe there's more of the old you in there than meets

275

the eye.' Her gaze wandered to the ancient bag Moncrieff had acquired from Lenahan. 'Would that be yours?'

'It belonged to Lenahan. He gave it to me.' Moncrieff had turned to gaze out of the window. They were crossing an old bridge. On the one side, a river. On the other, a gleaming stretch of water edged by docks.

'Southampton, Tam. The River Test.'

'Trout,' Moncrieff murmured. 'Fine fly fishing. My father would have loved it in his prime. You haven't answered my question, by the way.'

'About?'

'Who else will be bothering themselves with me.'

'Nobody, Tam. You have my word.'

'Not even Philby?'

'Absolutely not. Would that possibility disturb you?'

'It might.'

'May I ask why?'

Moncrieff was in two minds. Barton might be right, he told himself. I used to be decisive. In the Corps, and latterly in the Security Service, that came with the territory. You made the call fast. You acted on your instincts. And most of the time it worked out. Now, he didn't know what to do, where to even start, and that bothered him.

'This is difficult,' he said.

'I'm sure it is, Tam. I'm here to help. Believe me.'

'Help who?'

'You, of course.'

'And?'

'Us.'

'Us?'

'The Service.'

'And King? And Country?'

'You're wincing, Tam. Why is that? Are we having doubts?'

'About?'

'The job? The people we're here to defend? Everything – our terms of service, our education, our upbringing, our families, all that, are you starting to wonder? Just a little bit? Or perhaps a lot?'

Moncrieff closed his eyes. He wanted to bring this conversation to an end, but even that was a puzzle he couldn't solve.

'You're German,' he said quietly. 'What would you know about any of that?'

'Quite a lot as it happens. Yes, I'm German, but you can't be married to my fool of an English husband for all those years and not pick up a clue or two.'

Moncrieff opened his eyes and apologised for what he'd just said. He assumed he'd insulted her, or at least upset her, but once again he'd got it wrong.

'Absolutely no offence, Tam. If this thing is going to work, we have to be totally honest with each other. It's also a question of appetite. Do you *want* to go through with this thing? Do you want to lay hands on the old Tam Moncrieff and drag him back? If the answer's no, just say so.' She smiled. 'Is that fair?'

'Of course it is.'

'So, what's your answer?'

'My answer is that I simply don't know.' He winced again. 'Hopeless, isn't it?'

Barton sat back. They were in Southampton now, the inner city disfigured by bomb damage. Kyiv, thought Moncrieff, must look a little like this.

'I suspect there might be a photograph in that bag of yours, Tam.'

'You're right. Did Lenahan mention it?'

'He did. He also said it obviously meant a great deal to you. Might I take a look?'

Moncrieff shrugged. He could hardly say no, but he knew he didn't want to share it with anyone else, least of all Ursula Barton. Yet another dilemma.

After a while, he bent to the bag and pulled out the envelope.

'Help yourself,' he muttered.

Barton slipped the photo onto her lap, face down. When she turned it over, she took a long look.

'Isobel Menzies,' she said. 'With no hair. I take it this isn't charades?'

'Anything but.'

'Lenahan mentioned a little message as well.' She peered into the envelope. 'May I?'

'Of course.'

She found the message. Moncrieff knew she spoke little Russian.

'Every life has a price,' he muttered. 'That's what it says.'

'Meaning?'

'Meaning that she's gone back to Moscow, as we all know, and that they've taken her hostage. Shaving the head is standard practice in Siberia. It goes with the serge shirt and hard labour and all the rest of it. Look at her face, her eyes. She was never easy to frighten but they've done it.'

'And that's really where you think she is? In the depths of Siberia? Doing her penance? For what, Tam? Why would they send her there? She's a hero. She saw through all our little foibles, like democracy, and constant hot water, and Elgar walking the Malvern Hills. Marx matters to her. She's a believer. Why on earth would they ship her to Siberia?'

'Because that way, they'll buy my silence.'

'About?'

'Philby. Who else? They think she knows. And they're assuming she's told me.'

'Told you what?'

'That he's a traitor. That he's working for both sides. That his heart lies where hers does. In Moscow.'

'And has she told you that? Be honest, Tam. We need to know.'

'She's hinted.'

'Evidence?'

'Nothing she's shared.'

'So why say it at all?'

'Because she loves me...' he was frowning. '... I think.'

'And you? You, Tam?'

'The same.'

'You love her?'

'I want to, yes.'

'But you're not sure?'

'I'm not sure about anything,' Moncrieff turned his head away again. His eyes were filling, and he knew there was nothing in the world he could do about it.

'Camp dust,' he swallowed hard. 'That was the last thing she said to me.'

*

Schultz commissioned an immediate search for Larissa. He gave Bella a driver, plus an armed escort, and told the driver to cruise the local streets, one by one, looking for a woman who didn't want to be seen. The driver nodded and when he asked in which direction the search should progress, it was Bella who was first to answer. In her heart she knew why Larissa had fled.

'Make for wherever the SS have gone,' she said. 'Kalb in particular.'

Schultz gave the driver the name of a building up towards the Pechersk Monastery. While the driver consulted a map, Schultz leaned into the car. Bella could smell alcohol on his breath.

'You're sure?' Schultz asked.

'Absolutely.'

'But why?'

'She'll offer Kalb a deal. One life for another.'

'Hers for the boy's?'

'Exactly.' Bella withdrew as the car began to move. Schnapps, she thought. The man deserves the whole bottle.

They searched until nightfall, street after street. On Schultz's orders, news that the bombings would soon come to an end had been announced on the radio and through the pages of the city's newspapers, and the city centre had come alive again. Bella sat beside the driver, scanning face after face as they crawled slowly past, wondering whether Larissa would have laid hands on a disguise of some kind, a different coat, a headscarf that might hide most of her face. Look for an arm in plaster, she kept telling herself, but even this wasn't really a help. The *Luftwaffe*'s visits, and now the bombings, seemed to have touched everyone's lives, and the pavements were full of the walking wounded.

In the darkness, they made their way back to the museum. Schultz, alone in his office, was studying a pile of documents. The only illumination came from his desk light. The bulb was dim, and his thick finger moved slowly from line to line as he battled with the text. He heard the door opening and his head lifted as Bella came in.

He told her to sit down. He didn't ask about the search because he didn't need to.

'She's with Kalb,' he said. 'He phoned and told me. Don't waste the fuel, he said. She came here because she can't resist us. Take a leaf from our book. Keep an eye on your prisoners. Heil fucking Hitler.'

He threw his pen onto the desk and sat back in the chair.

'And Yuri?' Bella enquired.

'He wouldn't say.'

'You asked?'

'Of course I fucking asked.'

'So, what do you think?'

'What do I think? I'll tell you what I think. What I think is what I know. The SS has them both. As long as it suits their purposes, they'll keep them alive. If you want the truth about your girlfriend, she hasn't got a prayer. She's high-profile. Half the city knows who she is. If the SS want to send a message, and they do, she's the perfect opportunity. The way we are now, nothing protects you if you happen to be a Jew. Not fame, not money, not connections, nothing. Sending her to her death will raise one or two glasses of whatever those bastards drink.'

The way we are now.

Bella shook her head. 'That's exactly what Yuri said,' she muttered.

'Surprise me.'

'But she'd have insisted on a deal. I know her. She's strong. She gets what she wants.'

'Insists? Are you serious? Negotiation stops the moment she sets foot on their turf.'

'Then he's lying,' Bella said hotly. 'She'd never be that naïve. She'll have found a phone somewhere. She'll be talking to him at arm's length, insisting on Yuri's release first. I *know* her, Schultz. That's the way she works.'

'Very Jewish.'

'Of course. And maybe that's why she's so good at what she does. I'm not sure the Kalbs of this world have realised it but Jews are an asset. Liquidate? Is that the verb?'

'It is.'

'Then it's madness.'

'I agree. The Jewish thing is a distraction and a waste of everyone's time, but that won't get your girlfriend back. You saw her this morning. You saw the state she was in. People like me know a thing or two about pressure. We know how to apply it and we know what it will do. The pressure on her is immense. She's been blown up twice. Ask any soldier what that does to you.'

Bella nodded. In her heart, she knew he was right. The *idea*, she thought. Another victim, overwhelmed by their own certainty, totally unaware of what might follow.

'One suggestion,' Schultz had opened a desk drawer and produced a bottle of schnapps. 'Or maybe two. Drink?'

'No, thank you. And your other idea?'

'It's more than possible they'll interrogate Yuri. That process will have started already. With Jews, it tends to be easy, they just shoot them, but with non-Jews, especially educated white males, they like to build a case and kid the world they have some regard for justice.'

'So?' Bella had no idea where this was heading.

'Do you know where Yuri lived?'

'Yes.'

'Is there anything there they'd like to get their hands on? Anything incriminating?'

Bella frowned, thinking back to the suite of tiny rooms behind the church. The very bareness of the place argued against Schultz's suggestion, then she remembered the thick sheaf of manuscript Yuri had hidden in the church itself. That, at the very least, deserved to be somewhere a little safer, out of the reach of Kalb's men.

'You've read it?'

'I know about it.'

'And?'

'It's a fable, really. It's about faith. And about the Old Ukraine.'

'Really?' Schultz drew a finger across his throat, and then reached for the bottle. 'You're sure you won't take a drink?'

*

Schultz ordered the same driver to accompany Bella to the church that Yuri called home. By now, thanks to their efforts to find Larissa, the two of them were getting to know each other. Berndt Fischer was an older man, late forties at least, and had been with Schultz since the outbreak of war and the campaign in Poland. At first, he'd been wary of Bella but her perfect German and the tales she told from her posting to

Berlin had impressed him and when she'd lightly enquired about what the war was doing to his boss, he'd been surprisingly frank.

'Schultz copes,' he'd said, 'because he's that kind of man. Give him a task and he'll get on with it, but there are some days when you know he's really angry, and he's definitely drinking too much.'

'Because he wants to forget? Blot it all out?'

'Because it helps. We love the man. He's big on the outside and big on the inside. Most of the people he has to deal with are dwarfs.'

They were skirting the city centre, heading for the old town. Most of the fires were out now but curls of smoke still hung in the cold night air. Berndt stopped to let a long file of Russian prisoners under guard cross the road. Most of them were carrying picks or shovels, hunched against the rain, and Berndt said they were probably heading for what remained of the Ginzburg Skyscraper.

'They're tidying up,' he said. 'Very German, but I'm guessing you'd know that.'

'And the rebuilding? When will that start?'

Berndt laughed, and then shot Bella a look.

'Is that some kind of joke? The Russians did this in the first place, and they'll be the ones to put it all right.'

'You mean those men?' Bella nodded at the soldiers.

'No. I mean proper Russians. Your lot. When they're back in charge again.'

Bella nodded. Schultz had said exactly the same thing. Turn your back on Berlin, she thought, and you'll find yourself looking at thousands of kilometres of steppe every morning.

The music from the homeland will be as martial as ever but, out east, this war is suddenly a very different proposition.

'You told me you're a Rhinelander this afternoon,' Bella said idly.

'That's right. I grew up in Rheydt. At school I was in the same class as Goebbels.'

'Really?' He suddenly had Bella's full attention. 'What was he like?'

'He was a little fellow. He always had trouble with his foot, couldn't walk properly, not his fault. He was crazy about acting and we laughed at him at first because he tried so hard to play all these parts. He wrote some of the plays himself. I can see him now, flinging his arms around, beating his chest, going down on his knees, trying to kid us he was someone else. Another thing: he was mad about the pastor. His name was Mollen, Johannes Mollen, and when you couldn't find Goebbels you knew he was at confession. I was pals with his family. His mother wanted him to study theology because that way the Church would pay for him to go to university.'

'And now? You ever see him? Make contact? Take tea at the Promi?'

'Never.'

'Then maybe you should,' she laughed. 'Before my friends in Moscow turn up and ruin the party.'

They were bumping slowly up the hill in the Old Town towards the dome of St Sophia.

'Just here,' Bella indicated an alleyway on the left. 'We have to walk. You've got a torch?'

Berndt led the way, the light from the torch pooling on the wet cobblestones. The black shape of the church loomed ahead. Berndt pushed through the gate. In the beam of the torch, Bella could see two wooden trestles abandoned in the graveyard.

'Someone's been sawing wood,' Berndt peered around. 'You can smell it.'

He was right. Bella could smell it, too, the sweetness of the resin. Berndt unholstered the pistol he was carrying and stepped towards the door of the church. The door was a centimetre or so open. There was mud on the flagstones inside.

'Someone's been here. Recently.'

The body of the church was suddenly cold and standing in the darkness Bella could hear a steady dripping from a leak. There was a new smell, too, a different sweetness. Incense, she told herself.

'Where is this thing?' Berndt was sweeping the torch left and right across the plain wooden pews. 'Can you remember?'

'Yes.' Berndt's torch had settled on the altar. Everything valuable – pictures, icons, the cross on the altar – had gone. 'Over there,' Bella told him. 'There's a loose flagstone in the corner.'

Berndt led the way again. When a sudden noise erupted from the corner, he spun round, levelling his gun, but it was only a bird.

'Shit,' he said. 'These places give me the creeps.'

'There—' Bella was pointing down at the flagstone. 'Yuri managed to get his fingers beneath one corner. There's a knack.'

Berndt grunted and handed Bella the torch. On his knees, he succeeded in wriggling his fingers under the flagstone. Then he leaned back, pulling hard, and the flagstone began to hinge upwards. Bella stepped sideways, letting the light fall on the cavity inside. Instead of a thick wad of manuscript, she found herself staring at a book.

'Was that there, too?'

'No.'

'Fetch it out.'

Bella knelt beside him and lifted the book out. Berndt let the flagstone fall, and the dull thud disturbed another bird in the darkness.

'What is it?' Still on his knees, Berndt nodded up at the book.

Bella shook her head. She'd seen hundreds of these books in her years in Berlin, probably thousands. It was the Reich's new bible. How fitting, she thought, to find it in a Ukrainian church.

'Well?' Berndt was getting impatient. 'Does it have a title?'

'Yes. *Mein Kampf*,' Bella had opened it. 'With Hitler's personal signature.'

Berndt struggled to his feet.

'We need to take a look outside,' he growled.

'Why?'

'This is the SS. They always leave a message. There may be others. *Komm*.'

Bella followed him out of the church, glad to be in the open air once more. At Berndt's suggestion, she'd left the book on a pew. Outside, the rain was heavier, and Bella could hear the tolling of a distant bell, carried on the wind. Berndt was moving cautiously around the side of the church, following the path that led to Yuri's quarters. Then, abruptly, he stopped, and Bella watched as the beam of the torch tracked slowly upwards.

At first, she couldn't believe it, not here, not beside a church. They were looking at a crude wooden cross, two stout timbers, freshly sawn, nailed together and erected against the biggest of the trees. Hanging on the cross, totally naked, was a thin figure she recognised only too well. The beam of Berndt's torch had steadied on Yuri's head. The wreckage of his face lolled against his bony shoulder. His mouth was half open and rain, pinked with blood, was running down the whiteness of his cheeks. His one good eye had been gouged out while the other, still swollen, was closed.

Bella remained quite still, staring up, barely aware of the rain and the darkness. Was he still alive? Breathing? Just? Was it her duty to somehow get him down, ease the pain of the nails they'd used to crucify him, show a little tenderness, a little mercy, try – at the very least – to be with him at the hour of his passing? She shook her head, knowing that it was already too late, that they'd probably killed him elsewhere before plotting this grotesque piece of theatre. Then the beam of the torch wavered and she felt the lightest touch on her arm.

'*Komm...*' It was Berndt. Enough, he was saying. We go.

23

MONDAY 29 SEPTEMBER 1941

The house, Edwardian as far as Moncrieff could judge, was built into a wooded slope, facing south. In the sunshine, from the flagstoned patio, he could almost touch the stands of beech, ash and yew. The locals, according to his host, called this area 'Little Switzerland', and he could understand why. The soft green swell of the hills had a genteel charm quite at odds with the mighty Cairngorm landscapes of his youth, but it touched him nonetheless. Barton had promised him peace of mind, and here it was. Rural Hampshire at its best.

Ursula Barton had delivered him yesterday afternoon. Matheus Groenbaum, she'd told him, was German, a Jewish doctor from Lindau who'd fled Bavaria after the murderous chaos of *Kristallnacht* and settled in England. He'd met and married an Englishwoman after she'd lost her husband, and he now occupied their family house in the hills north of Petersfield.

Groenbaum, she said, had abandoned conventional medicine for something she called Gestalt therapy. Barton had used him for MI5 casualties on a number of occasions and had been impressed by the results. Groenbaum took people in difficulties, people who'd tied themselves in all kinds of knots, and made them well again. Still trying to account for the missing week in Moncrieff's life, Barton had previously consulted a senior physician in Harley Street, a man whom she trusted, and he'd told her that it was probably too late to find some rogue substance or other in Moncrieff's bloodstream. By now, he'd told her, all traces would have gone. Best, therefore, to concentrate on the mind rather than the body. Hence Moncrieff's presence in the deckchair, face lifted to the autumn sun, his eyes closed as the soft footsteps approached.

'Tea, Mr Moncrieff? It's dandelion and burdock. I picked the dandelions myself.'

'It's Tam. I thought we agreed last night.'

Geraldine was tall and slim, blonde hair carefully curled, the blush of an early ride still visible in her smile. She kept a horse stabled just down the road. It was a big bay gelding, she'd told him last night, and it knew every inch of the surrounding hills. Once, when her first husband was alive, they'd persuaded it into a horse box and driven to Dorset for a day's hunting. She'd never hunted in her life and she'd loathed the experience. The horse was called Thatch. And she suspected they were both pacifists.

'My husband will be joining you shortly,' she said. 'Call me if you'd like more tea.'

Gestalt therapy? In German, the word meant 'shape', as in 'shape in the darkness', and if the latter phrase was any clue, then Moncrieff was only too happy to volunteer. Ursula Barton, with her usual bluntness, had made him uncomfortably aware of just how fragile he'd become. That, somehow, had to stop and if Matheus Groenbaum could glue him back together, then so be it.

He arrived moments later, a tall man, darkly handsome, tanned face, still in tennis whites after an early game on court at a neighbouring house. Watching him and his new wife together at supper last night, they might have been married forever. The same physical ease. The same effortless charm. These people are comfortable in their skins, Moncrieff had thought, and they were tuned into exactly the same wavelength. A subtle glance, a nod, a wink, the ghost of a passing smile. This was a language so subtle that itself spoke volumes. That's all it took, he told himself, if you were lucky enough to find the right partner.

Groenbaum fetched a stool and perched himself beside Moncrieff. He was nursing a glass of apple juice, cloudy and probably home-made, and the warmth of the sun raised a light film of sweat on the broadness of his face.

'You won?'

'I did, Tam. I blame my partner. She's better than me in every department. If I'm lucky, I get to hand her a towel at the end. She's brutal at the net. I admire that. Golf is your vice, Ursula tells me. Is she right?'

'I played a bit in Scotland. Up there it's difficult not to.'

Groenbaum nodded and studied his glass for a moment or two. Watching him, Moncrieff wondered what else Barton had shared. Ex-Marine? Owner of a falling-down house in the mountains? Hopelessly in love with a serial traitor? A man so careless, so confused, that he'd somehow misplaced an entire *week*?

'We address the whole person, Tam. You need to know that.'

'We?'

'Myself and Gerri. We're a team. We share everything. We find that makes a difference. You can be part of that team. We'd like that very much.'

Moncrieff could only nod. Team? He hadn't a clue what this invitation could possibly mean.

'Ursula gave me the impression that fitness really matters,' he said.

'Ursula's right. We have a weights room. I'll show you later. We also have a number of local circuits in the hills, various distances, different gradients, but, given your accident, it might be wiser to start with the weights. Your mobility will return but we ought to err on the side of caution. In the meantime, we need to get to know each other. In Lindau, I spent nearly ten years dispensing various medicines, and you know what it taught me? That most of our troubles happen up here.' He tapped his head. 'Gestalt, Tam. Getting you back together again, whole, complete...' – the lightest touch on Moncrieff's arm – '... ready for anything.'

Moncrieff nodded. Groenbaum's English was faultless, barely accented, and he spoke with an easy grace that still managed to preserve a certain authority. No wonder Gerri had dispensed with widowhood so quickly, he thought. To most women, this man would be irresistible.

'You liked the tea?' Groenbaum nodded at Moncrieff's half-empty cup.

'It was a little bitter for me.'

'That's good.'

'Good? How so?'

'We find that most people can't cope with being honest. You're an exception already, Tam. Come with me.'

Moncrieff struggled to his feet and paused to let a moment of dizziness pass. He had the feeling that he'd passed a test. Had the tea been deliberately undrinkable? Was this all it took to put a man on the road to recovery?

He was following Groenbaum around the corner of the house. At the end of a gravelled path lay what looked like a driving-off platform on a golf course. From here, the garden dropped steeply away to a stream below, climbing again to the other side of the valley. The flanks of the valley were thickly wooded, magnificent stands of beech, autumn-gold in the sunshine.

'There's a choice of drivers,' Groenbaum nodded at the bag of clubs waiting in a wheeled cart. 'You choose.'

'You want me to tee off?'

'Yes.'

'Where to?'

'It doesn't matter. I want you to put the ball in the trees. You've played the game before. We're talking no more than seventy yards. I just want you to concentrate on the swing, the impact, the sweetness of that little ball flying off into nowhere. What happens to it afterwards is not your concern. You'll never see it again, never spend a moment worrying about where it might be. And that, Tam, is the whole point.'

'It is?'

'Yes.' From the pocket of his tennis shorts he produced a golf ball and a wooden tee.

'Just the one?' Moncrieff was staring at his hand.

'Just the one.'

'You're sure?'

'Of course.'

Moncrieff took the ball and weighed it in his hand. Then he planted the tee, giving himself plenty of room to swing. He hadn't done this for a while, more years than he cared to remember, but he told himself that you never lose the balance, the grip, that feeling of transferring all the power you can muster into that single, brief, explosive moment of contact.

He stepped back from the tee, gazing across the narrowness of the valley to the trees. How many other golf balls had flown across this gap, and where were they now? Did Groenbaum, or his wife, or some flunkey, scour the woods once a week, reclaiming precious golf balls? Or had the woods become a giant nest for these little white eggs?

'Remember it's you, Tam. Part of you. You don't need to choose which part, which memory, which relationship. Not yet. All that matters is that sense of departure, of getting *rid* of it, and of not giving a damn about where it's gone. You're ready to give it your best? Just nod.'

Moncrieff nodded. Then he took a tiny step forward, letting the face of the club kiss the ball, letting his long legs settle, getting the space between his feet just right, flexing his wrists, drawing back the club. No practice swing, he told himself. Be brave, be confident, let the club descend at the very edge of this mighty arc, maximum power, maximum impact.

He was ready now, the club raised, his head down, his eyes focused on the waiting ball. Then came a flashback to a course and a moment he didn't recognise, a younger Tam Moncrieff, same stance, same intense concentration, and he unleashed the elastic in his shoulders and his back, and brought the club face smoothly down, a sweet blur of effort that sent the ball high across the valley. His head lifted to watch it disappear over the trees and there came a moment of the purest release when he realised that Groenbaum was right, that something deep inside himself had shifted, that he was a little lighter, a little more free.

Groenbaum's soft applause was music to his ears. He was about to nod again, a nod of thanks this time for Groenbaum letting him into this little secret of his, but then his attention was caught by a brief glint of sunlight beneath the trees. Binoculars, he thought. I'm being watched.

*

Schultz was reading the morning edition of *Novoe Ukrainskoe Slovo* when Bella knocked on the door of his office in the museum. They'd talked last night after Berndt had brought her back from the church in the old town. She'd cleaned him out of schnapps, but he didn't begrudge her a drop. There wasn't enough alcohol in the entire city to salve the wound she needed dressing.

'You slept?' He looked up, one finger still anchored in the paper.

'No.'

'You need to translate this for me. That's your friend, am I right?'

He showed her the photo beside the article. One glance told Bella it was Larissa. The article was in Ukrainian but Bella's Russian coped well enough. The article was a plea for the city's Jews to do the bidding of the Military Governor. It repeated the demand to gather at the corner of Menikova and Dokterivskaya streets and suggested the possibility of a train journey. The marshalling yards were ten minutes away. The little ones and the older folk would easily cope. With the weather set fair, and each family making sensible provision – something to eat, plenty to drink – the days to come carried the promise of an extended picnic, with every Jew's just rewards at journey's end. Larissa had ended the article by looking forward to joining this expedition. The word she used was exodus.

'It's nonsense,' Schultz grunted. 'Kalb probably wrote it himself and put her photo at the top. He's playing with her, just like he played with Yuri last night.'

'So where is she?'

'With Kalb. At the SS place. My guess is he'll feed her into whatever he has planned at a time of his choosing. The SS put a lot of store on timing. Pain, for those bastards, is a science.'

'What do we do?'

'We?'

'You, me... us. Larissa went there to save Yuri's life. Instead, they killed him. You know what he once said to me? Yuri? He said that religion always had its uses, even for the Germans. They didn't just kill him, remember. They crucified him.'

Schultz nodded and rubbed his big face. Bella suspected that he, too, hadn't slept.

'I talked to the Military Governor's people this morning,' he grunted. 'They're aware of Krulak.'

'Meaning?'

'They know she's being held.'

'By the SS? Protective custody?'

'Both. I made a case for sparing her.'

'How?'

'I pointed out how useful she could be. She's a journalist. She's well connected. She cares about the welfare of the city, as we should. We're on top of the mines, at last. A peaceful occupation would suit us all.'

'And they listened?'

'Of course. They always listen. But listening's easy. The SS are a law unto themselves. When it comes to the Jews they insist there'll be no exceptions. The word they use is purity. Can you believe that? Purity of the mission. Purity of the blood. All those bastards have to do is lift the phone and talk to Berlin. Himmler's halfway up Hitler's arse. He has the ear of the right people. At the Military Governor's, they're shitting their pants.'

'So what happens?'

'They may give us an official release demand. In which case, we have to argue with Kalb.'

'And if there's no release demand?'

'You tell me.'

*

In the late morning, with no word from the Military Governor, Schultz assigned another SD escort to accompany Berndt and Bella to the Viskove Cemetery. He wanted to find out what was happening to the Jews, and whether or not there'd be enough rolling stock on the railway to take them out of the city.

The new escort was a younger man, a favourite of Schultz's called Andreas. Bella knew from Berndt that he'd been recruited from the Berlin police after a glittering career as a young detective. Now, he slipped into the front seat alongside Berndt. He was nursing a sub-machine gun.

The Viskove Cemetery lay at the heart of one of the city's biggest parks, and the roads around it were already impassable. After days and nights in a city that had felt abandoned, Bella had never seen such a crush of people. They were of all ages and they were mostly poor. According to Andreas, who'd taken a look for himself earlier, they'd flooded out of the Jewish sections of the city at first light, desperate to get the best places in the queue for the trains, but now – hours later – all sense of order had gone. They were still half a kilometre from the cemetery, on the main road that ran beside the railway lines, their way forward blocked by the sheer mass of people. Thousands, she thought. Probably tens of thousands.

She sat in the back of the big Mercedes, aware of the gauntness of the faces peering in. Many of these families were pulling trolleys and carts piled high with possessions, grey bundles tied with string, worn-out cases made from plywood, boxes of carpenters' tools. Mothers carried children in their arms. Older children wore strings of onions around their necks. One father had an old man folded over his shoulder, like a roll of carpet, and kept patting his thin leg, trying to reassure him. Andreas wound down the window and shouted at two men who were quarrelling over a basket of turnips. Over the stir of the crowd, Bella could hear the clank-clank of a nearby train and every whistle of a steam locomotive turned more heads in the crowd. The sunshine promised in Larissa's newspaper article had failed to happen. Instead, it was starting to rain again.

Berndt was using the horn now to clear a passage through the teeming crowd, and Bella glimpsed the faces of German soldiers watching the Jews shuffling slowly past. Some of the prettier young girls sparked a wave, or a shouted comment, and the girls waved back. Anything, thought Bella, anything to regain a little dignity, a little hope.

The cemetery was in sight now, grey mausoleums semi-masked by dripping trees. The Germans had flung rolls of barbed wire across the street, leaving a narrow passage between two big obstacles fashioned from iron girders.

'Anti-tank,' Andreas shook his head. 'Are they frightened of these people?'

Not at all. Berndt spotted the logic at once. There were rows of Germans wearing badges on their chests, and Ukrainian police with their black uniforms and grey cuffs, and between them they were funnelling the Jews through the gap between the anti-tank obstacles. The Jews were reluctant to go further. Many of them kept looking back, towards the promise of the railway line, shaking their heads, but the sheer pressure of the crowd forced them on. Bella watched them, already fearing what might lie down the road. Some mistake, they must be thinking. We came here for a picnic. And now look what's happening.

Berndt was out of the car. A tall Ukrainian in an embroidered shirt appeared to be in charge. Berndt showed him his SD pass and gestured back at the Mercedes. The Ukrainian shook his head, but Berndt kept talking. Finally, with a volley of oaths, the Ukrainian ordered the gap to be widened.

Berndt drove on. Progress was quicker now, the crowd thinner. Some families had stopped by the side of the road to eat, or simply to stare into the distance. Their breath clouded in the cold air and some of them were looking skyward at a tiny circling aircraft, their kids pointing and dancing, and then the Ukrainian police arrived with dogs and whips and beat them until they got up and began to move again. Berndt had stopped. His head was out of the window. He seemed to be listening.

'It's the plane,' Andreas said.

'No. Listen. It's shooting. Small arms. Just listen.'

Berndt was right. The Jews had heard it, too, but there was no turning back. Kids, sensing that something had gone wrong, were crying. Mothers and fathers stared at each other, then stumbled on, helpless, bewildered, lost. Bella turned round in the back seat. The road behind them was black with people. How would she ever find Larissa in a crowd like this? And what difference would a piece of paper make? She had no answer but as they got closer to the gunshots, the sheer scale of the nightmare began to overwhelm her. Finding Yuri last night had been bad enough. This was beyond her comprehension. Surely they couldn't kill them all? Surely there weren't enough bullets in the world for all these people?

Ahead was a square of flattened grass, covered with what looked like scraps of paper, but as they got closer Bella realised that they were articles of clothing: underwear, men's boots, jackets, work trousers, even a fur coat. Ukrainian police were everywhere, forcing people to strip naked, women, men, children. Those who protested were clubbed to the ground by SS troopers. They ripped their clothes off and then set dogs on them. The Jews struggled to their feet, blood pouring from their wounds, trying to fight the dogs off while the soldiers looked on, jeering and laughing.

A little further on, partly hidden by the press of naked people, more soldiers and dogs had formed a narrow corridor. At one end, a huge sergeant with a whip was calling for the Jews to run. They obeyed blindly, their heads down, babies in their naked arms, mothers reaching for their children, fathers trying to ward off the dogs and the rifle butts, crazed by fear. The Jews stumbled on, some running fast, ducking and weaving, others starting to falter, while the torrent of violence rained down.

Andreas was shocked. Bella could see it in his face. A grassy knoll beyond the scatter of garments afforded a view beyond the corridor of soldiers and the hapless Jews.

'Up there,' Bella pointed.

'Why?'

She didn't answer. Instead, she got out of the car and began to run. Andreas followed, his gun cradled in his arms. From the top of the rise, the harsh patter of gunfire was suddenly louder. Bella paused, gasping for breath. She was looking into a huge hole in the earth, a quarry of some kind. The sandy banks were steep and a narrow path had been cut on both sides. On the left, as Bella watched, a line of naked Jews, men, women, children, were making their way along the path. Rain had plastered their hair and made the going slippery. They moved slowly, with great caution, some of them reaching out to steady themselves as they teetered over the drop. Already, the quarry was full of bodies. One mother paused and bent to comfort her wailing son. The boy was pointing down at the bodies, then he turned his face away, unable to look any more.

Soldiers were on the other side of the quarry. They had a path of their own and every ten metres or so they'd set up machine guns on tripods. Figures in black sat behind the machine guns and there was also a fire of some sort. Bella could see steam curling from a pot, and one of the soldiers was passing mugs down the line. Halfway along the quarry, the Jews were ordered to stop and face the soldiers. Motionless, they awaited their fate. Then, on a command from an officer, the soldiers drained the last of their tea, and the machine guns began to chatter and the Jews, in twos and threes, tumbled onto the mattress of bodies below. Dazed, Bella attempted to put a number on this slaughter but before she'd got to double figures she knew it was pointless. Already there were hundreds of bodies down there, bleeding, rained on, dead, and there were many thousands more to come.

'Enough.' It was Andreas. 'We go.'

Driving back against the press of the Jews was a nightmare of its own. By now, Bella knew exactly what awaited them. Some, especially the younger ones, still had hope in their eyes. Older men, veterans of the Kyiv shtetls, knew better. For reasons they'd never understand, their time had come. All that remained was the hope that it wouldn't take long. One man, a rabbi of uncertain age, was intoning a prayer. He had a baby cradled in the crook of his arm. The tiny face was gazing up at him and, as the crowd suddenly surged forward again, the baby kicked its legs in excitement. That was the moment, Bella later realised, when her faith in God – what little remained – guttered and died.

*

Back in the city centre, the museum was surrounded by *Wehrmacht* trucks. Heavily armed troops were milling around on the pavement and Bella glimpsed Schultz in conversation with an officer. The officer had a map he was trying to protect from the rain and Schultz was pointing something out with his finger. It was the first time Bella had seen Schultz wearing glasses, and they made him look suddenly old.

Still in the car, Bella wanted to know what was going on. Andreas was also watching Schultz.

'It's a big operation,' he said. 'Schultz has wanted to do it for days and now he's been given the troops to make it happen.'

Bella wanted to know more but Andreas was already out of the car. He crossed the pavement and picked his way through the mill of soldiers until he was at Schultz's elbow. Schultz spared him the briefest glance and he must have asked him a question because Andreas nodded, and then drew his forefinger across his throat.

Bella sat back and closed her eyes, oblivious to everything but the patter of the rain on the car roof. She could see the rabbi again, and the gurgling infant. Then, abruptly, they were gone.

24

TUESDAY 30 SEPTEMBER 1941

Moncrieff spent exactly an hour in the weights room, which occupied a corner of the house on the first floor. It was another glorious day, the merest hint of cloud over the rising ground to the south, but the wooden parquet flooring was cold underfoot and it took Moncrieff a minute or two of calisthenics in the throw of the sunshine to warm up. Overnight, he'd devoted far too much time to brooding about the presence he'd sensed in the trees across the valley. By dawn, he was convinced the watcher didn't exist. A figment of his fevered imagination, he told himself. An aftershock on the heels of last week's earthquake.

Last night, before turning in, Groenbaum had talked him through a programme of leg exercises. Moncrieff was still in pain from the broken rib, but his legs were undamaged apart from livid bruising and Groenbaum was keen to get him out in the hills as soon as possible. Moncrieff started with a series of thigh thrusts, glad to be left alone, and then spent the rest of the hour on the stationary bicycle. The bike was Groenbaum's own design, based on an idea stolen from an engineer he'd known in Augsburg, and it pedalled beautifully.

Moncrieff imagined himself back in the Glebe House, setting out on a favourite circuit that took him down to the river, away from the mountains. Fifteen miles later, sweating now, he paused to swallow a mouthful of water before stripping to the waist, tightening the friction nut and tackling the long uphill slog back to the village. By the time the door opened, he was pleasantly exhausted.

It was Geraldine. Mercifully, she was offering apple juice.

'Matheus says you loathe my tea.'

'Loathe is a bit strong.'

'Dislike? Might we settle for that?' She gave him the juice and perched herself on the nearby weights bench.

'You've been riding again?' He took a long pull at the apple juice.

'Yes.'

'Glorious morning.'

'Perfect. Thatch loves this time of year. Just a hint of winter first thing. Dew on the grass. We ride west as the sun comes up. I think she's in love with her own shadow, that mare of mine. Typical woman.' The way she watched him while she laughed touched a nerve in Moncrieff. Bella, he thought. The same playfulness. The same easy wit.

'You remind me a little of my late husband,' she said. 'Do you mind me saying that?'

'Not in the least.' Moncrieff reached for the singlet Groenbaum had provided. 'This wasn't his, by any chance?'

'You're right. Same build as you. Tall. Fit as a butcher's dog. You need to put on a little weight, Tam. We'll see what we can do.' She smiled. 'His name was Giles, by the way. Farming stock. Welsh Borders. A lovely man. I was lucky to have him.'

'I'm sure. You must miss him.'

'Every day. Mornings are the worst, oddly enough. He was always so *buoyant* first thing. Quite wore me out but in a nice way. I expect that's why I go riding. Poor Thatch. She deserves someone more gentle.'

She got up and stretched, hands held high, arching her back. She was wearing a cashmere sweater that smelled of fresh air, and Moncrieff glimpsed a tiny silver fish on the thin chain around her neck.

'You like it?' She'd sensed his interest.

'Very much.'

'It was a present from Giles. Our fifth wedding anniversary.'

'You have children?'

'Sadly not,' she smiled again, holding his gaze. 'Though we tried hard enough.' She collected Moncrieff's empty glass and made for the door. Then she paused. 'Matheus is in the Lindau Room, by the way. Once you've had a douse, I think he'd like a word.'

'The Lindau Room?'

'His study, Tam. Nothing in Matheus's world is simple.' She fingered the glass for a moment, and then looked up. 'How was the juice, by the way? Do I hear the word delicious?'

The Lindau Room turned out to be a replica of Groenbaum's office when he was still practising in Bavaria. Glass medicine jars sat on a shelf behind the big leather-topped desk. An anatomical chart was unrolled on a wooden stand for handy reference. Rows of medical books filled an antique bookcase. Moncrieff was especially drawn to a framed sketch of a soaring church spire, wildly Gothic, meticulously rendered in black ink.

'The Minster,' he said. 'In Ulm.'

'You know it?' Groenbaum, behind the desk, seemed surprised. He was wearing a dark blue blazer, hemmed in pink.

'Very well,' Moncrieff pulled a face. 'Seven hundred and sixty-eight steps. I counted them. From the top, on a clear day, they promise you the Alps.'

'And?'

'It was misty. I could barely see the bloody river.'

'Didn't you take that into account? Before you started climbing?'

'Of course I did. The point was getting to the top. The view was always secondary.'

'And is that something you still believe? The effort? The lack of reward?'

Moncrieff laughed. The hour on Groenbaum's bicycle had made him feel lighter, even cheerful.

'You did the sketch yourself?' he asked.

'I did, yes.'

'And this?' Moncrieff's gesture took in the entire office. 'Another work of art?'

'Far from it. I used to sit at this desk in Lindau, dispensing potions. It took me years to realise I was wasting my time.'

'And you still need reminding?'

'On the contrary, every time I open that door is a moment of celebration. It might sound perverse, but I enjoy remembering how misguided I was. Sit down, Tam. Every Jew carries his own curse. I never lived in the past, though professionally I nearly died in it. Thank God for patients like you, Tam. But you'll still need to sit down.'

'Where?' There was a choice of chairs.

'Over there.'

Moncrieff took the seat in the window. The view south over the golden woodlands was sensational. He heard the scrape of another chair as Groenbaum joined him. Moncrieff took a closer look at the blazer.

'Leander?' Moncrieff asked. 'You row?'

'I do, when time permits. That's where I met Gerri. Her husband was a member when I joined. I did most of my rowing on the Bodensee. You know it at all?'

'A little. I rowed too, first at university, then in Berlin, but never – alas – on the Bodensee. I was there in high summer. The place was overrun with tourists.'

'Including you?'

'Of course,' Moncrieff was gazing at the blazer again. 'His name was Giles, am I right? Your wife was telling me about him this morning. Tall chap.'

'Very. She was besotted. I'm afraid I'm a pale copy of the real thing. Did she tell you that, as well?'

Groenbaum didn't wait for an answer but dug in his pocket and produced something in his clenched fist.

'You're a magician, now?' Moncrieff couldn't suppress another smile.

'In a way, yes. I want you to look very hard at this object. I don't want you to talk. I don't want your attention to wander. The whole point is to concentrate. I may bring it closer, I may take it further away, but whatever happens it should overwhelm you.'

Moncrieff nodded. Overwhelm carried implications he understood only too well.

'Fine,' he said. 'Whenever you're ready.'

Groenbaum unclenched his fist. Inside was a golf ball. Groenbaum took it in his other hand, holding it between his forefinger and his thumb at eye level.

'Is that yesterday's ball? The same one?' Moncrieff asked.

'I asked you not to talk.'

'I'm sorry.'

'Just look at it, Tam. Let it in.'

Let it in? Moncrieff stared at the ball, trying to do Groenbaum's bidding, understanding what was at stake. His only other brush with hypnosis had been years ago at a mess night at the Royal Marine barracks in Portsmouth. A visiting magician had asked for after-dinner volunteers, and Archie had pushed him forward. On that occasion, drunk, it had been easy to slip his moorings and drift away but now was very different. Concentrate, he told himself. Forget your surroundings. Forget the last couple of weeks, Pearse Lenahan, Frank Jennings, French motor cars, Kim bloody Philby. Think golf. Think ball.

It didn't work, even when Groenbaum eased the ball away, and then back again. At last, he gave up.

'You know what I'm trying to do here, Tam.'

'I think so.'

'Then that's why. Hypnosis is surrender. It has to take you by *surprise*. You're a canny man, Tam Moncrieff, and you're far too honest.' He frowned, pocketing the ball. 'So how might we cure that?'

The answer, as Moncrieff later realised, was Groenbaum's wife. The three of them lunched together around a table on the patio, a light salad from the garden with a glass of white wine. The conversation drifted back to Germany, idled for a while over the delights of the Bodensee and then settled gently on the difficulties of finding decent coffee when the bloody U-boats were sinking so many freighters. Groenbaum was recorking the bottle when his wife sprang to her feet, her hand extended to Moncrieff.

'A walk,' she said. 'Weather like this? We absolutely must.'

They set off on a path that ran obliquely across the face of the hill towards the trees. The dog came too, a handsome red setter that had belonged to Gerri's first husband. Before they ducked into the shadow of the huge elms, Moncrieff glanced back at the house. Sunlight glinted off the windows at the front of the property, but he thought he saw movement behind the window on the corner. The Lindau Room, he thought, with Groenbaum plotting yet another route into Moncrieff's subconscious.

Under the trees, it was much cooler. Gerri took Moncrieff's hand again. They were climbing now, on the other side of the valley from the house, and Moncrieff was looking for golf balls.

'It didn't work, did it? My husband sets a great deal of store by it. If you want the truth, that's how he first got me into bed.'

'Hypnosis? Is that ethical?'

'Certainly not. But it worked.'

'Bed?'

'Hypnosis. I know it's a cliché, but Matheus is deeply neurotic. He loves the chase. What happens afterwards isn't so important.'

'You were disappointed?'

'Not at all. Women are used to being let down. If anyone was disappointed I think it was Matheus. He'd been eyeing me from the moment we met. I was too easy, Tam. Unlike you.'

'Was your husband still alive?'

'God, no. Disappointment? He didn't know the meaning of the word. Giles was utterly reliable, and not just *à deux*.'

À deux. Moncrieff smiled. He'd spotted a golf ball, then another, then a third. He bent to all three and slipped them into his pocket. Then he looked round. Here, he told himself. Had the watcher existed, then he might have been standing here.

'How many patients does your husband treat?' Moncrieff was looking back at the house, high on the opposite slope.

'Regular patients? Maybe a dozen. Maybe more.'

'And are they all in my line of business?'

'Most of them, yes.'

'MI5?'

'Some of them.'

'MI6?'

'Why do you ask?'

'Because I need to know.'

She smiled and studied him for a long moment. Then she gave his hand a squeeze.

'Need is an interesting proposition, Tam. At the end of this path is a caravan. It belongs to us. I have a key.' She nodded up the hill. 'And afterwards you can ask me any question you like.'

Moncrieff gazed at her. She knew she attracted him, and he sensed the attraction was mutual, but the offer couldn't have been blunter. Absurd, he thought.

'Is this part of the therapy?' he asked. 'Do all us spies get the same treatment?'

'Not at all, Mr Moncrieff. Under the circumstances, it might help to take a compliment.'

25

TUESDAY 30 SEPTEMBER 1941

Ilya Glivenko, the sapper they called The Pianist, waited until early hours before giving the signal to move. The officer in overall command of the Kyiv operation had ordered them to stand down. The Germans, it seemed, had somehow accessed the list of targets and were dismantling them dozens at a time, using relays of Russian diggers to find the receiving equipment and then disconnect them. More troubling still, they'd worked out exactly which wavelengths the teams on the island were using and had taken steps to block their transmissions. In short, the operation was over.

At the end of the command message, there was applause for every engineer involved with the promise of awards to follow. The Germans had paid dearly for their arrogance and their treachery. Soviet determination and Soviet know-how had reduced key parts of the city to rubble and soon the world would know that the Hitlerites could be stopped. But now was the time to beat a careful retreat.

Glivenko's men, all four of them, were eager to move. No one had eaten for more than twenty-four hours and there were rumours of a cache of supplies hidden beside the boat. Glivenko's torch moved briefly from face to face. He anticipated getting to the end of the island within the hour. Heavy rain had swollen the river and by daybreak, with four paddles, they should be at least thirty kilometres downstream. Command had sent an extraction team to meet them. In a couple of days, with luck, they'd be back behind Soviet lines.

The beam of Glivenko's torch settled on a nearby tree trunk. The Kazakh, Vassily, had removed his cap badge and nailed it to the ancient pine, and the sight of the Red Star sparked a ripple of laughter. These men, Glivenko knew, had revelled in delivering the task assigned to them: first to spend all those back-breaking days mining target after target, and then to linger among the trees and watch the fruits of their labours boiling over the city. This was a story, Vassily had insisted, that would pass from generation to generation. Not a story, said another. A legend.

The men set off, Glivenko in the lead. They were used to the busyness of the forest at night, the scampering of unseen creatures, the sigh of the wind, the creak of the forest overhead, and just occasionally the call of a nightingale. Glivenko had insisted on bringing their equipment with them, and the men took turns to carry the heavy batteries. They tramped on, using paths down the spine of the island, as invisible as ever to watching eyes on either bank. The fact that the Germans had neglected to put search teams on the island had first astonished, and then gladdened Glivenko, and once they had their hands full trying to contain explosion after explosion he knew his sappers were probably safe. German efficiency, he thought. Another fantasy.

The tree cover grew steadily more sparse towards the southern end of the island, where the mossy soil surrendered to the river. Glivenko motioned his team to a halt. Ahead, he thought he recognised the outline of the steel assault boat they'd been allotted but low cloud had blown in from the east and in the darkness he had to be sure.

Leaving his men behind, he moved ahead, staying low, one step at a time. Within minutes, he'd confirmed the boat. It was lying in the reeds at the water's edge. There was plenty of room for all of them and four men could lift it with ease. There were five wooden paddles carefully stowed in the bottom of the boat, and, better still, his fingers found a canvas bag that had to contain food. He was about to head back to the treeline when his gaze was drawn to the bow of the boat. Something was wrong. He knew it.

He crouched on the soggy eel grass, using his fingers again to explore the thin metal skin. There were holes, lots of them, below the water line. Someone had been here, he thought, probably recently. Five minutes with a hammer and an iron spike, and the boat was useless. He lifted his head, scenting danger, and, as he did so, the darkness erupted in a blizzard of muzzle flashes. An ambush, he thought. Shit.

Bullets were pocking the surface of the river. Some tore clean through the boat. His own men, all armed, were doing their best to return fire but he knew the odds were against them. Someone had planned this. Someone had taken great care to lure them into the trap. Then came a voice, impossibly close, a German voice, telling him not to move, and he instinctively shielded his face from the sudden brightness of the torch.

'You're The Pianist?' the voice grunted in German. 'Am I right?'

*

It was late morning by the time Schultz arrived at the airstrip. After the chaos of the last week, the operation on the island had been flawless. Three of the Russian sappers had been killed, their bodies left for the wild dogs, and the other two captured. One of them, Ilya Glivenko, was even now under armed guard in the museum's Leningrad Gallery. Later, the little man would be facing a barrage of questions. In the meantime, Schultz had other business to attend to.

The offer of an hour aloft in the little Fieseler Storch had come from *Wehrmacht* headquarters. The military were no friends of the SS and it had required little effort on Schultz's part to secure the aircraft. The pilot, it seemed, had been flying over the city yesterday afternoon and had reported troubling developments in a quarry to the north of the city centre. Streams of people choking the approach roads. Evidence of widespread violence. He'd spoken to the pilot himself. Bodies, he'd said. Lots of bodies.

Now, Andreas pulled the big Mercedes to a halt beside the tiny plane. The pilot was already at the controls. Schultz got out of the car and stifled a yawn. Andreas handed him the camera and two extra rolls of film.

'Over a hundred exposures,' Andreas muttered. 'Let's hope you don't need more.'

Schultz pocketed the camera and looked round. The retreating Soviets had done their best to wreck the runways, cratering the concrete with high explosives, but the little Storch was nimble and could be airborne within a hundred metres.

Schultz opened the passenger door and introduced himself. The pilot extended a hand. No Hitler salute.

'You got the bastards,' he said.

'Which ones?'

'The fucking Ivans on the island, of course. Good work, sir.' He patted the spare seat. 'Help yourself.'

The pilot had been studying a map of the city which he now shared with Schultz. His leather-gloved finger traced the roads leading to the sand quarry.

'They call it Babi Yar,' he said. 'Or sometimes just the Yar. None of this stuff is pretty but I dare say that won't surprise you.'

Schultz nodded down at the Mercedes. His driver, he said, had taken a look for himself only yesterday and the poor man wouldn't be sleeping for at least a week.

'He was there? In the Yar?'

'As good as.'

'And?'

'He'll tell you himself, when we get back.'

Schultz had produced the little Leica. The pilot watched him checking the exposure and advancing the film.

'You want pictures?'

'I do. Our friends in black do our reputation no favours.'

The pilot nodded, said nothing. He stabbed at the control panel and the propeller began to turn. A cough from the engine, and then another before it caught, and then he was easing the throttle, allowing the revs to settle. Moments later, after a glance left and right, they were picking their way through the debris, heading for a stretch of sodden turf. Then came a roar from the engine and Schultz felt the punch of acceleration before the little plane lifted into the air, shook its feathers, and headed back towards the sprawl of the city.

The slaughter at Babi Yar was by no means over. From five hundred metres, Schultz looked down at the endless columns of tiny dots flooding out of the city's shtetls and converging on the yellow scar of the quarry. The scene, from up here, he thought, had an almost biblical dimension, telling a story that young Andreas had found so hard to grasp. Thousands of people, maybe tens of thousands, ordered to their deaths.

'Lower,' Schultz had spotted what he assumed was the quarry. 'That's it? Down there?'

The pilot dropped a wing, hauling the aircraft into a near-vertical turn, and Schultz felt his snatched breakfast rising in his gullet as he gazed down. A black corridor of soldiers, just as Andreas had described. Piles of abandoned clothing, possessions, lives. A white worm, wriggling between the soldiers, naked flesh and bone, scurrying towards the quarry. And then the giant pit itself, plaited with bodies, arms, legs, a hideous stretch of embroidery on the dampness of the sand, and the soldiers perched on the ledge above, attending to their business, crouched behind their guns, ridding the city of its Jews.

Schultz took picture after picture, ordering the pilot lower and lower until he could see individual soldiers looking up, waving their arms, telling him to fuck off. One even raised his rifle and tried to draw a bead on the little plane, the way you might swot a troublesome insect, and Schultz got a picture of him, too, perfectly framed, the wind-tanned face contorted with anger.

'I wonder if they feed them raw flesh in the morning,' he was looking at the pilot. 'Or maybe those bastards down there are just bred that way.'

*

Schultz was back at the museum by early afternoon. He gave Andreas two rolls of exposed film and told him he wanted the prints by nightfall. He also ordered recording equipment to be installed in the museum's Poster Archive.

'Top floor,' he said. 'The little room at the end.'

Back at his desk, a series of messages awaited him. One was from the office of the Military Governor, congratulating him on cleaning out the island in the Dnieper. Another asked him to contact an aide at *Wehrmacht* headquarters. Schultz called for tea and something to eat before lifting the phone and dialling the number. The *Wehrmacht* aide at the other end, a Berliner he'd known from pre-war days, said that the General was delighted with his efforts.

'These people have no faith,' he chuckled. 'I told them you were the best and they never believed me. They were resigned to these bloody explosions going on forever. As a matter of interest, how did you play the Russian you took when they blew the bank up?'

'I made a friend of him,' Schultz grunted. 'Before I had him shot.'

*

Moncrieff was uneasy. He didn't want to make an enemy of this woman, neither did he want to insult her, but somehow he sensed he'd managed to do both. They'd made it up the hill to the caravan. She'd unlocked the door and invited him in. A faint tang of cigarette smoke hung in the stale air, and he'd glimpsed breadcrumbs on the mat beneath the folding table. She'd wanted him at once. There was a mattress on the floor, with a couple of blankets and three cushions.

'You're very welcome to fuck me,' she'd murmured. 'Isn't that a reasonable proposition?'

In most other situations, Moncrieff could only agree. She was witty, she was excellent company, and the moment she peeled off the cashmere sweater and asked him to remove her bra he knew Groenbaum was a lucky man. She had Bella's body, the same tight stomach, the same tilt to her breasts, the same appetite for sex spiced with laughter and a surprising trick or two.

'This?' she'd murmured, sinking to her knees before him. 'Or perhaps this?'

He'd muttered his apologies and reached down to ease her to her feet but she shook her head.

'Tell me what a girl needs to do.' She unzipped him and slipped her hand into his trousers. 'No complications. I promise you.'

Complications? At the time, Moncrieff had laughed. 'You don't want to fall in love with me? Is that what you're saying?'

'No need, Tam. A fuck will do nicely. Can you handle that?'

He couldn't. Wouldn't. And now he knew there was a price to pay.

'You think I'm ugly?' she asked. 'Be honest.'

'I think you're beautiful.'

'You think I'm fast? Is that it?'

'Yes, very.'

'Fast or beautiful?'

'Both. I'm also wondering why.'

'Why what?'

'Why you've really brought me up here. This has your husband's blessing. Am I right?'

For the first time she paused before answering. 'I'm serious,' she said at last. 'This will be great. I promise.'

'This?'

'You and me.'

'I don't doubt it.'

'Then kiss me. Have your way with me. Or if that's too much to ask just lie back and enjoy it. Pretend I'm Bella. Might that help?'

Bella. The name killed any prospect of a rapprochement, and she knew it.

'I'm sorry,' she said. 'I shouldn't have said that.'

'Who told you?'

'It doesn't matter.'

'I'm afraid it does. Blaming your husband isn't good enough. Mine is a much simpler question. Who told him?'

Silence. She reached for her sweater and tugged it on. Her bra was still on the floor beside the mattress. She looked up at him, and lightly touched the newness of the scar tissue on his forehead.

'I'm told you had a nasty accident,' she said. 'But I'm wondering what did the real damage.' She paused for a moment, frowning at the bra at her feet, then she looked up again. 'If you really want to know about my husband, then the answer's yes. Of course he knows I've brought you here. In fact, it was his idea. Two heads are better than one, he's always telling me. And he says you're welcome in our bed anytime.'

'Are you serious?'

'Always. He likes you. He's normally choosy when it comes to men, but he thinks you've got something special. And that matters, Mr Moncrieff, because that's exactly what I think, too.'

26

TUESDAY 30 SEPTEMBER 1941

It was Andreas who escorted Bella up to the Poster Archive. She left the emptiness of the Leningrad Gallery without regrets, huddled in a *Wehrmacht* greatcoat that Schultz had liberated from somewhere, grateful for its warmth as darkness stole across the city and the temperature in the gallery plunged.

The Poster Archive occupied a bare room at the top of the building, five storeys above the street. Bella followed Andreas along the corridor, past framed sepia photographs of Lenin and his wife, pictured in various domestic settings. The door at the end was guarded by two SD men, both in civilian clothes. An exchange of nods produced a key, and the guards stood back to allow Bella into the room. The figure in the corner had his back turned and for a moment she hadn't a clue who he might be. Then he turned round, faintly curious. Someone must have removed his boots because he was barefoot on the wooden floorboards. There was mud crusted on his uniform and he'd obviously taken a recent beating because his nose was bloodied and one eye was beginning to close but his smile was as warm as ever.

'Ilya.' Bella crossed the room and held him at arm's length. 'What's that smell?'

'Me,' he turned to Andreas. 'Can't they do something about that?' He gestured up at the single window. It had been shattered by a blast, and the room was even colder than the Gallery. From the street below, Bella could hear the rumble of a passing tram. 'A hammer, maybe? Nails? A sheet of wood?' Bella knew what the answer would be.

She was right. Andreas shook his head and backed out of the room, closing the door behind him. Then came the turn of a key and a shuffle of boots as the guards settled down again.

Bella wanted to know what had happened. What was Glivenko doing here? And why did he smell so bad?

'I've been in the woods,' he said, 'across the river. No bathrooms, I'm afraid, but plenty to keep us busy.'

Busy? It dawned on Bella that Kyiv had him and his sappers to thank for the chaos of the last week or so.

'It really was your doing?' Bella nodded up at the window. 'It's your fault that nothing works anymore? That we're always so bloody cold?'

'Yes,' Glivenko nodded. 'Me.'

'So how did it work? How did you manage it?'

Glivenko shot her a look and shook his head. He didn't want to talk about it. Instead, he directed Bella's attention to the posters.

'I've been up here a while,' he said. 'It's like looking at family photographs.'

The posters, like everything else in the building, had been carefully framed and were now stacked against the wall in neat rows.

'I remember this one from those early days in Leningrad. It kept my little brother awake at night, scared him half to death.'

Bella was looking at a wild-eyed hero of the Proletariat. Dressed like a caveman, he was taking on the giant serpent of Tsarist Russia with nothing but a cudgel. Bella had seen the poster before, a relic of the October Days in Leningrad. Crude, she thought. But effective.

'And this one?'

Glivenko stepped back to reveal the tribune of the Revolution exhorting the faithful against the billow of smoke from a thousand factory chimneys. Like everyone else in Russia, Bella had lived with this image for years: Lenin's body bent against the winds of history, daring the future to prove him wrong.

'Strange, isn't it?' Glivenko was shaking his head. 'We were nothing but kids at the time and this is the way they spoke to us. I loved this artist. He made me laugh.' This time, Bella was confronted with a series of cartoon capitalists: fat bellies, waistcoats, evil leers, and just a hint of a Jewish nose. 'We used to call them the jelly-men. They were spineless, flabby, just the way capitalists should be. They told us each drawing was based on soldiers' telegrams from the front during the civil war but I'm not sure that's true. I remember seeing them plastered on walls and shop windows in the rougher areas of the city. Stuff like this was everywhere. They were telling us what to think, of course, but we never minded.'

'Exciting times?'

'The best. Wonderful days, truly.'

Bella nodded. Glivenko would doubtless have to pay for his sins against the Greater Reich but looking at him now, awash on a tide of memories, it was hard not to remember the moment her own convictions began to harden. She was looking at another poster Glivenko had cherished from his days in Leningrad. It was dominated by a group of workers in red overalls. They were stern, fiercely socialist, unyielding. To their right, another fat capitalist and his nest of lackey bankers. And holding the ring? A soldier from the front line, feet solidly planted, cap askew, rifle in hand. The question across the foot of this image couldn't have been blunter: *Who Are You With?*

Who was I with? Bella shook her head, drew the greatcoat a little tighter, tried to ignore the icy draught through the broken window. Her boyfriend at university had voiced questions like these, never personal, never bothering with the messiness of trying to find someone to love, but always addressing the bigger issues. Poverty. Exploitation. How wealth, and power, and corruption always went hand in hand.

To be on the right side of history, he'd always told her, was a duty as well as a challenge, and the days they'd collected small change for the Jarrow marchers had made her feel very good about herself. The army of sturdy derelicts had walked the length of the country, through pretty villages, past shops and country markets brimming with goodies. These men were desperate for work. She and Matthew had spent three days with them on the road, and those conversations had made her feel ashamed, as well as angry. Then Matthew had disappeared to Spain, taking the best of her with him, and the day she got the news that he'd died in some battle outside Madrid was the day she knew she had to honour his memory.

'We never had posters like this,' she told Glivenko. 'Which is a shame.'

Glivenko didn't seem to be listening. His feet, she noticed, were filthy and he had a deep cut on his right hand that was still oozing blood. He sucked at it from time to time, and then wiped his mouth on the sleeve of his uniform. When she asked whether he, too, was cold he nodded.

'The window,' he murmured. 'We have to do something about the bloody window.'

*

In the late afternoon, Andreas drove Schultz to settle things with Kalb. The meeting had been brokered by the Military Governor, who was keen to keep the peace between his warring tribes. At Schultz's insistence, the two men would talk in private at the Governor's headquarters. Schultz had no taste for conducting business on SS turf, and neither did he accept the Governor's offer to chair the meeting. The Babi Yar operation had been put together with some care over a period of days. The site had been prepared, troops assigned, announcements broadcast, proclamations posted. Tens of thousands of Jews weren't dying by accident, and Kalb, in Schultz's view, was at the heart of the killing machine.

They met in the Governor's personal quarters. There were nests of family photographs, a half-finished letter to his wife, even a piano. The Governor, Schultz noticed, was trying to master a Schubert sonata. A blizzard of pencil marks on the first page suggested that so far it hadn't been easy.

Schultz had no interest in sharing the sofa with Kalb. Instead, he took the other chair, harder, more upright. Kalb studied him a moment. Schultz had met him on a number of occasions, never a pleasure, and each time he'd looked a little madder. Now, the cast in his eye seemed to have developed a life of its own. A child might have drawn a face like this, he thought, if only to amuse his mates.

'You were in the Storch this morning?' Kalb had no time to waste. 'Over the Yar?'

'I was.'

'Why?'

Schultz didn't give him the satisfaction of an answer. When he'd slipped the photographs into his briefcase, the prints had still been wet and even now they smelled of the fluids in the developing bath.

He arranged them carefully on the low table.

'From two hundred metres, this was what we saw. Your men must have left their souls for God to mind. Are we here to fight the Russians? Or is there another plan no one's bothering to share?'

'We have our orders,' Kalb said stiffly. 'As a soldier, I imagine you'll understand that.'

'Orders from whom?'

'From Berlin. Come back here in five years, maybe ten, and every field, every meadow, every hectare will be farmed by our people. German farmers. German *Hausfrauen*. German *Kinder*. The grain will go back to the *Heimat*, oil, too, from the Caucuses. We're here to make things better, Schultz. As you well know.'

'But no Jews.'

'No Jews.'

'May I ask why?'

'You know why. Jews infest us. Jews are parasites. Ask any doctor how you fight disease. First you identify what's wrong. Then, for the greater good, you eliminate it. We're here to make a better world, Schultz, and if the logic of that mission escapes you, then I suggest a conversation with people wiser than me might be in order. Courage in this respect starts at the top. Never underestimate the power of will.' He nodded at the photographs. 'The men down in the Yar have occasionally had difficulties with the task at hand, I won't deny it. But they're good Germans, steadfast, determined. They have belief in the mission and they know they're in the brotherhood of the Chosen Ones.'

'The Chosen Ones? That's what the Jews think, too.'

'So I'm told. Unfortunately for the Yids, we do the choosing. Is the work tough? Of course it is. Should we be kinder? Gentler? Should we take account of their feelings, Schultz, before we put a bullet through their empty heads? This, I doubt. Why? Because it would be grossly dishonest. These days, my friend, the best outcomes require the harshest measures. Few are given to lifting a burden like that, but the *Schutzstaffel* are proud to offer their services, and I – likewise – am honoured to be one of those tasked to lead them. Does that answer your question? Or do you have more time to waste? The rest of the photographs, please, from that briefcase of yours.'

Kalb reached for the prints on the table, but Schultz got there first. Kalb looked up. He seemed genuinely surprised.

'These are the property of the Reich,' he said. 'Ours to keep safe. Ours to file away. What possible use could you have for them?'

'This war won't go on forever,' Schultz said softly. 'Has that occurred to you?'

'Of course. Like it or not, every war has consequences, and we in the SS have known that from the start. In victory, forgiveness. In defeat, oblivion. After the Ivans have surrendered, we may take a broader view, show a little mercy, help them to

328

their feet, brush them down. In the meantime, alas, the killing must go on.'

'But the Jews don't fight back.'

'Of course they don't. But that's because we're stronger, fiercer, more committed. Belief, Schultz, is worth a hundred divisions in the field. Belief and attention to the smallest details. The Jews don't fight back because they can't. And by the time they realise where all this is heading, there won't be any left.'

'No Jews at all?'

'None. All gone. Every last Yid. The stain on God's earth eradicated. In our line of work, Schultz, we have to think the unthinkable. Until we've made it happen, no one will credit us with the miracle of deliverance.'

The miracle of deliverance.

A tiny pulse deep in Schultz's head was beginning to quicken. The last time this had happened, he'd beaten a man to death. He was up in the air again, crouched in the tiny Storch, the Leica raised to his eye, the viewfinder full of bodies. Even from two hundred and fifty metres, you could still hear the murderous soundtrack as this man's machine guns sent thousands more toppling to their deaths. Rat-tat-tat, he thought. *Accelerando.* More and more bullets. More and more bodies. Some twitching. Some not quite dead. The devil's concerto. Scored for tens of thousands of Yids.

'We may lose this war,' Schultz was returning the prints to his briefcase. 'What then?'

Kalb had no answer. For a long moment, Schultz wondered whether this possibility had ever occurred to him, that victory was taken for granted, immutable, part of the New Order, but then his mood abruptly changed.

'You have a prisoner, Schultz. That man belongs to us.'

'Name?'

'Glivenko. First name Ilya. He's a sapper with the Soviet 37th Army. You captured him last night. That operation is already the talk of the Wilhelmstrasse. You've earned yourself a great deal of credit, Schultz. Berlin will be generous. With your medal, I hope, will come a little common sense, but that man nearly brought us to our knees and the Ivans need to understand the consequences. So, tell me Schultz. When can we expect to see him?'

Schultz took his time. The thunder in his head was receding.

'You have another prisoner. Her name's Krulak. Larissa Krulak. She's a journalist.'

'Correct.'

'The Governor is demanding an account of last night's operation. She's a fine journalist. She has many followers. People in this city trust her. We believe she is the one to do justice to last night's little outing.'

'Then send Glivenko along. You know where we are.'

'It needs to happen at SD headquarters. Our place. The Governor insists. He's also adamant that the SS should share the credit. You should talk to him more often. He has this quaint belief that we should all be marching forward as one body,' Schultz offered the ghost of a smile, 'in lockstep.'

Kalb pondered the proposition for a moment or two and then looked up.

'We get her back?'

'Of course.'

'With Glivenko?'

'Yes.'

Kalb frowned, staring at the briefcase, and then he nodded. 'Done,' he said. 'We just hope you're a man of your word, Schultz.'

He got to his feet and offered the Hitler salute before turning on his heel and making for the door. Schultz, his big hand on the briefcase, hadn't moved.

*

Andreas was waiting in the Mercedes. Kalb's car, badged with SS markings, was already accelerating out of the courtyard.

'Follow him.' Schultz pulled the passenger door shut.

'You want me to hang back? Tail him?'

'On the contrary, get up his arse. He needs to know we're serious.'

'About what?'

Schultz didn't answer. He was starting to boil again. Andreas, carving a path through the late afternoon traffic, sensed his mood. Alone, he always called him *capo*.

'You got what you wanted, *capo*?'

'We'll see. Just drive.'

Andreas knew when to shut up. The SS car was fifty metres ahead, held up in a queue of traffic behind a horse and cart. He could hear the driver hammering the klaxon and waving a uniformed arm out of the window. When the peasant on the cart finally edged closer to the kerb, Kalb's driver nosed out to overtake.

'You go, too,' Schultz grunted. 'Put your foot down.'

'But there's a truck coming.'

'Ignore it. He'll get out of the way.'

Andreas did Schultz's bidding. The oncoming truck swerved to avoid them, mounting the pavement and scattering a group of soldiers. As they passed the horse and cart, the peasant was laughing.

'Bravo...' Schultz muttered.

'Is that for the peasant, *capo*?'

'No, it's for you. You know where that bastard's going? The new SS headquarters? We need to be there first.'

'You want me to overtake him as well? Are you serious?'

'Yes.'

Andreas shrugged. The SS car, another Mercedes, was a newer model, more powerful. The driver knew his business on the wet cobblestones, and chose a perfect line through bend after bend. As the city centre approached, he eased back behind a tram and Andreas spotted his chance. He knew the oncoming intersection was always busy but he was beginning to enjoy himself. After yesterday at the Yar, he'd no faith left in God but he dropped a gear, floored the accelerator and muttered a silent prayer.

The traffic, as expected, was thick, cars, bicycles, lorries untangling themselves in every direction. As they passed the other Mercedes, Andreas caught a brief glimpse of Kalb's face in the back. He was leaning forward, urging his driver to hold this impostor off, but there was fear in his eyes as well as madness and, as they hit the intersection, the two cars were nearly abreast.

The world had erupted, a chorus of horns, and klaxons, and shouted oaths. Arms waved. Drivers braked. An oncoming tram screeched to a halt. A *Wehrmacht* fuel bowser stopped dead in the middle of the road. Then, suddenly, they were through. A glance in the rear-view mirror confirmed that Kalb's car had slotted itself neatly in behind.

'OK, *capo*?' Andreas felt sweat cooling on his brow.
Schultz didn't answer, not at once. Then Andreas felt the
lightest pressure on his thigh.

'Never better.' He was smiling.

*

At the new SS HQ, Andreas pulled the Mercedes to a halt in
the courtyard. Only days ago, this building had been part of the
city's university. It belonged to the Department of Medicine, and
when they hurried up the approach steps and pushed in through
the doors, Schultz caught the heavy sweetness of formaldehyde.
Short of occupying an abattoir, he could think of no better
place for Kalb and his team of butchers.

They were still waiting by the table that served as a reception
desk when the *Standartenführer* strode in. Kalb pretended to
be unaware of his visitors but when he headed for the staircase
that led to the upper floors, Schultz intercepted him.

'Krulak,' he said. 'Larissa.'

'At a time of our choosing, Schultz.'

'Now.'

He stopped, favouring Schultz with his good eye.

'So why the hurry?'

'We have the newspaper standing by. The radio people, too.
The Governor wants us to make a big push. We have a success
on our hands. Best to celebrate it.'

Kalb hesitated a moment.

'And us?' he gestured round. 'You'll be pointing out how
resilient we are? How we take all this nonsense in our stride?
Our second headquarters move within a week? Not a stitch
dropped?'

'Of course,' Schultz glanced at Andreas. 'Make a note. Stitch dropped. Krulak will love that. Off you go, Herr Kalb. Time and reputation wait for no man.'

Kalb nodded and began to mount the stairs. He was doing his best to mask his weariness, and perhaps a little confusion, but it showed nonetheless. When he'd gone, Schultz turned to Andreas again.

'You told Glivenko we were handing him over to the SS?'

'I did, *capo*.'

'And he believed you?'

'Yes.'

'Excellent,' Schultz checked his watch. 'God rest his soul, eh?'

*

Bella had been back in the Leningrad Gallery for most of the afternoon. Schultz had asked her to try and tease a full account of the bombing campaign from Glivenko, but The Pianist had showed no interest in talking about what had really happened. They'd been through a handful of other posters together, Glivenko reminiscing again about his student days in Leningrad, and when one of the guards had unlocked the door to enquire whether their conversation was over, Bella had said yes.

Glivenko, though, had caught the guard's eye.

'A couple of minutes, *tovarish*. Do you mind?'

The guard had tapped his watch and told them to be quick. As soon as the door was closed again, Glivenko had beckoned her closer.

'They're going to hand me over to the SS,' he said. 'If I thought you'd ever see me again, I'd find a kinder way of saying this.'

'Saying what?'

'You were right about not going back to Moscow. Stay here if you can. Stay anywhere. The NKVD have orders to kill you. You hear me? You understand what I'm saying? Anywhere but Moscow.' He forced a smile and put his arms around her. 'You promise me?'

*

Now, an hour or so later, with darkness beyond the windows in the Leningrad Gallery, Bella heard voices at the door. First to appear was Schultz. He'd plainly been drinking. Normally, a glass or two of schnapps would make little impression. Now, his eyes were bright, swimming with good cheer. He stepped into the room and closed the door behind him with a playful little flourish. It was a theatrical gesture, not Schultz at all, and Bella got to her feet, abandoning a hand of patience.

'Good news, and bad news,' he was looking round, making sure they were alone. 'The bad news first. Do you mind?'

Bella shook her head. You're in charge. Go ahead.

'It's Glivenko. You became close. Am I right?'

'Yes. *Became?* What's happened?'

'He's dead. That window? You remember that fucking window?'

'Upstairs? In the Poster room?'

'Yes.'

She looked at him. She didn't need the rest of the story.

'He threw himself out? Is that what you're going to tell me?'

'Yes.'

'And that's why you never mended it?'

Schultz said nothing. Not even sorry. Then he stamped hard on the floor, his heavy boots shaking the wooden boards, and the door opened and there was another figure outlined against the dim lights in the corridor outside. Her arm was still in a sling. She took a tiny step forward, then shook her head. Disbelief? Caution? Delight? Bella didn't know.

'The good news?' Schultz was swaying a little as he nodded towards Larissa. 'Your night is young.'

27

Tam Moncrieff sat in the big drawing room, gazing out at the darkness. Except for the dog curled at his feet, he was alone. Supper had come and gone, himself and Groenbaum picking at plates of cold venison supplied by a local poacher. Gerri was out for the evening, playing bridge with friends, and Groenbaum, with an apology for the weight of his current caseload, had retired to the Lindau Room to confront, he said, nearly a week of accumulated paperwork.

He and Moncrieff had spent a long hour together on the teeing-off platform. Hitting balls across the valley had by now become a ritual, a coda to the intimacies Groenbaum was still trying to extract during long face-to-face sessions seated in the window of the Lindau Room. These always followed the morning's workout in the weights room, and Moncrieff – buoyed by the exercise – did his best to part the curtains on episodes in his life that, in Groenbaum's phrase, deserved a little attention.

In Berlin, three years ago, he'd killed an American businessman. The circumstances, to Moncrieff, fully justified the steps he'd had to take but within weeks he was under interrogation in one of the basement rooms the Gestapo reserved for difficult clients. Those hours in the basement of their Prinz-Albrecht-

337

Strasse headquarters would stay with Moncrieff forever. They'd strapped him to a board, and covered his face with a towel, and poured a steady trickle of water on the towel until it filled his nose and throat. After that, he began to drown and when Groenbaum insisted on details he did his best to describe the coldness of the water in his lungs, and his determination to hold his breath, and then – within seconds – the realisation that some primitive instinct had taken over, that he was sucking in more and more water as he fought to breathe, and that death, or perhaps dying, was a far simpler proposition than he'd ever imagined. First you feel bubbles in your lungs, he'd said quietly. And then darkness and resignation take care of the rest.

Groenbaum had listened intently to this account, making notes on a pad, returning again and again to the word 'darkness'. What exactly did Moncrieff mean? How did he *feel*? Was there an element of guilt involved? That he wasn't stronger? More resilient? That he'd let himself and, by extension, the Service down?

Moncrieff had dismissed all of these questions. As a Royal Marine, he was no stranger to the possibility of interrogation. There were tricks you could play on yourself, resistance techniques they taught you, but once you were in the hands of experts, you surrendered all control. They took you to places they'd been exploring for most of their working lives. They'd mapped pain and they understood panic and they knew every one of those little pathways that led to your deepest fears. In short, they could do whatever they wanted with your helplessness. That realisation, said Moncrieff, was deeply, deeply troubling but there was no room left for guilt. These people were about to kill you. All you wanted them to do was stop.

But afterwards, Groenbaum had insisted. How did you feel *afterwards*? Moncrieff knew exactly how he'd felt once they'd decided to set him free before expelling him from their precious Reich. Bella, bless her, had collected him from Prinz-Albrecht-Strasse. It was the middle of the night. He had twelve hours to leave Berlin. That left time for a proper farewell but the Hungarians in the basement, the specialists the Gestapo so prized, had done their work well. He didn't want to set foot in Bella's apartment. He didn't even want her to touch him. Instead, he wanted to walk the empty streets, all the way to Tempelhof Airport, alone, utterly lost, every breath of the cold Berlin air a fresh reminder that death would never be a friend.

'She forgave you? Bella?'

'There was nothing to forgive. The Gestapo had taken it all.'

'All of what?'

'Me.'

'That's really how you felt?'

'Yes.'

'And did she understand?'

'Probably not. She defected to Moscow within weeks, but that's another story.'

To date, he and Groenbaum had yet to touch on Bella. His wife obviously knew about her, and so Moncrieff assumed that Groenbaum was also *au fait*, but Moncrieff was in no hurry to go any further. In Groenbaum's view, she'd doubtless be an issue but in the meantime the episode in Berlin had given him plenty to work on. Hence, this afternoon, yet another session on the teeing-off platform.

'Let it *go*, Tam. Another one. Hit another one. Ready? You feel the tension? You're the coiled spring. Go. Release it.

Get rid of it. Beautiful shot, truly wonderful. Just watch it, Tam, just watch it fly. Imagine it's a little bird. And now it's gone.'

Ball after ball soared over the valley and into the trees, and Moncrieff began to wonder exactly what kind of psychological burden he was supposed to be getting rid of. Having someone pour water into your lungs wasn't the kind of episode you'd ever forget so what, precisely, would bag after bag of lost golf balls really achieve? By the time they returned to the house, this feeling had hardened into something close to an impatience salted with resentment. He felt they were both marking time, getting nowhere. The real issue was his lost week, the void that no one seemed able to explain, but when he'd broached the subject just now, over supper, Groenbaum had shaken his head.

'Too soon, Tam. Too early. Trust me, please. I know that's hard for people in your line of work, but we all have your best interests at heart.'

Now, looking for something to read, Moncrieff spotted what looked like a photograph album. It was lying on the low table beside the sofa on top of a pile of magazines. He fetched it and returned to the armchair. Groenbaum was in the habit of playing classical music on his gramophone when he was working, and this evening he'd chosen Brahms. The German Requiem, Moncrieff thought. Richly appropriate.

He opened the photograph album, realising at once that this had to be Gerri's work. A family tree on the inside cover celebrated the coming together of Geraldine Plover and Giles Tice. There were four shots per page, black and white prints with serrated edges, years and years of a marriage tidied neatly away, each print carefully dated. The opening pages were a tribute to the social reach of rowing. 'Henley Royal Regatta, July 1932' read an entry on the first page, 'Giles in his Pa's blazer!'

Moncrieff studied the photograph. Giles, he knew, was Gerri's first husband, and he saw the physical likeness at once: tall, lean, just the hint of a stoop. Turn the clock back a decade, Moncrieff thought, and I might have been this man's brother. The camera had caught Giles in conversation with an older couple, and the expression on the woman's face – rapt, smitten – told Moncrieff everything he needed to know. Giles Tice would have been a catch for any young gal. No wonder Gerri missed him.

Their wedding occupied several of the pages to come. Gerri at a wicket gate outside the church, posing with her two bridesmaids. The happy couple hours later at the reception, both standing behind an enormous cake, knife raised, doubtless acknowledging the applause of friends and family. Giles running the gauntlet through a blizzard of confetti, one protective arm around his new bride, making for the open door of what looked like an Alvis. And on the next page, the camera lent briefly to someone else, the honeymooners on the balcony of a hotel, palm trees and the long curve of a bay behind them. 'Torquay', read the caption. 'Bliss.'

Moncrieff sat back a moment, putting the album to one side, wondering whether Gerri realised how lucky they'd both been to find each other. Even now, nearly ten years later, she was still – in his eyes – immensely attractive, but the presence of Giles had given her beauty a luminance that the camera never failed to pick up. Bella, he thought wistfully, reaching for the book again. If only.

Pages later, they were abroad. Photos of a city, first: a long corniche, more palm trees, handsome waterside hotels, horse-drawn carriages, elderly women on park benches eyeing the beginnings of the evening *paseo*. According to the captions, this was Barranquilla, August 1935. In one shot, especially striking, Giles had captured his wife in a moment of total candour, her face half turned to the camera. She was wearing a straw hat against the sun and it must have been windy because one hand was reaching for the brim. In the background, Moncrieff could see fishing boats, and what looked like the bow of a liner, but what drew his attention was the light in Gerri's eyes. By now they'd been married for nearly three years. Yet she was still besotted.

He turned the page again. They'd evidently left the seaboard for the mountains. An explosion of banana leaves filled the foreground while ridgeline after ridgeline receded towards the far horizon. The slopes of the mountains were thickly wooded, and mist coiled up from the valleys. 'Above Medellín', ran the caption. 'Bloody hot!'

Moncrieff checked the next few pages. As well as mountains, there was a plantation of some sort: peasants squatting in the long grass, their brown arms on their knees, taking advantage of the shade; Gerri with a white bandana around her head and a native child in her arms; Giles on a horse, amused and imperious. Then they were back among the bushes, and Moncrieff was looking at a wicker basket brimming with beans, an Inca face turned towards the camera, another smile captured for the album.

'You naughty man.'

Moncrieff glanced up. Gerri had ghosted into the room. Not a sound, he thought. Not a single clue.

'I'm sorry,' he said. 'I couldn't resist it.'

'You were bored?'

'Curious,' he nodded at the album. 'Colombia? Am I right?'

'Clever boy. Giles's family had a business over there. They grew coffee up in the mountains behind Medellín. After his father died, we took it over.'

'You liked it?'

'I loved it. We both did. The climate's perfect for coffee beans. They only grow arabica but that happens to be everyone's favourite. Sweeter, lighter, yet still rich. Yum-yum,' she smiled, nodding down at the album. 'My father-in-law had done all the hard work. The market was already there. All we had to do was keep growing the stuff.'

Moncrieff started turning the pages again. Then he paused. Giles was standing beside a biplane, one gloved hand on the propeller.

'He was a pilot?'

'He was learning. It was always something he'd wanted to do. The coffee estates gave him the perfect excuse. He said he could monitor our efforts from a distance. Never have to be a bother to anyone.'

'And he passed? Went solo? Flew himself?'

'Yes. But only briefly, I'm afraid. Next page, I think.'

The photo, this time, was part of a report scissored from a newspaper. The image was grainy, but there was no doubt what had happened. Giles Tice, apprentice aviator, had come to grief. Of the biplane, very little was left intact.

'Was he hurt?'

'Yes. Both legs broken, damage to his knees, fractured pelvis.'

'Christ. Poor man.'

'Quite.'

'Hospital?'

'Four months. It was run by the Catholic church in Medellín. They did everything they could for him, but my poor lamb was suffering. It was horrible to watch.'

'But he recovered?'

'More or less. They set the breaks and his pelvis healed itself. The real problem was up here.' Her hand settled lightly on Moncrieff's head.

'Really?' Moncrieff had turned the page again. Now he was looking at Tice in a hospital bed, his face gaunt against the whiteness of the pillow. Even his wife's presence, perched on the bed, one arm draped across his thin shoulders, could barely raise a smile. 'So what happened?'

'We got a so-called expert in. On reflection, I think he may have been a witch doctor. He prescribed a drug. Or maybe we should call it a potion. Does scopolamine mean anything to you? It comes from the deadly nightshade plant. The Indians use it a lot. They call it "the Devil's Breath". It's meant to be the world's best painkiller. In Giles's state you'd take anything.'

'And did it work?'

'It knocked him for six. I was there at the hospital day and night. The nuns were very kind. They didn't much like the stuff but Giles had insisted and they respected that.'

'And it took the pain away?'

'It took everything away. My poor man could remember nothing. Not the accident. Not me. Barely his own name. Everything came back in the end, but it took weeks and weeks. When I told him we were married, that I was his wife, he had to take it on trust.'

'Did he object?' Moncrieff tapped the photo of Gerri trying to cheer her husband up. 'I find that hard to believe.'

'That's sweet,' she bent quickly and kissed him on the cheek. 'But I think you're missing the point.'

'Which is?'

'It changed him. Totally. He became another man.'

'No more flying?'

'No more anything. When the war came there was a moment when he told me he wanted to join the Air Force, fly a Spitfire, but I told him they'd never have him, and I was right. It was the same with the Army. I'm afraid he drew the line at the Navy, though they'd have turned him down as well.'

'Why?'

'Because he couldn't cope, couldn't function. He did his best to disguise it, pretend nothing had happened, but he was a bag of nerves. Spend any time with him, and it was obvious. Towards the end he wouldn't even look at me.'

'The end?'

'He took his life, Tam. There's an orchard at the back of the house. Trees? A rope? He'd been gone all night. I found him in the morning.' Her eyes were moist, and she turned her head away. 'You understand now?' she muttered. 'My missing man? My paradise lost?'

Moncrieff didn't know what to say. He shook his head and started turning the pages again. Then he stopped. He guessed Giles was dead by now. These images were far more recent. There was no second marriage, no church wedding, no honeymoon, but he recognised the wooded hills beyond the patio, and the hint of a smile on Groenbaum's face as he posed for the camera.

'Who are these people?' He showed her the album. 'Who is he with?'

Moncrieff turned the pages, going from photo to photo, while Gerri supplied the names. Most of them were foreign: Pieter, Alonso, Manuel, Frederico.

'Clients?'

'Potential double agents. Most of them came through your lot, MI5. These were people you wanted to turn but you thought we might take a look at them first. In many cases that was wise. Some of them were crazy. Others were crooks. We passed them through the sieve, as Matheus likes to put it.'

'We?'

'We. Myself and Matheus.'

Moncrieff nodded. He'd never heard the faintest whisper of any screening programme. Then he turned another page and stopped. He was looking at a face he recognised at last, and the rumpled jacket, too, and the hint of shyness in the smile. He gazed at it.

'You know who that is?'

'Of course I do. It's our Kim. Kim Philby.'

'*Our* Kim? You're telling me he was a patient here?'

'Not at all. He popped down from that place at St Albans. He'd heard the kind of results we were getting for your lot and he wanted to look at the set-up for himself.'

'He approved?'

'He did.'

'And has he sent anyone down?'

'Not so far, but I'm sure it's just a question of time.'

Moncrieff nodded. Then he turned the pages again, backwards this time, until he was looking at Giles Tice in hospital.

'That drug again,' he said softly. 'That potion. What was the name?'

'Scopolamine. The Devil's Breath.'

'You told me it turned your husband into a zombie. You said it wiped him out.'

'It did.'

'Were there other symptoms? When he was taking the stuff?'

'Yes. He said it made his mouth dry, his throat, everything. He was perpetually thirsty.'

'And later?'

'The symptoms went away. Along with the rest of him.'

Moncrieff nodded, said nothing. Then Gerri was kneeling beside him.

'What's the matter, Tam?'

'Nothing.'

'Be honest. We're here to help. I mean it. You can sleep with me, or both of us. Your choice.'

Moncrieff stared at her. Then his eyes returned to the album. 'Did Philby see this?'

'Yes, he did. He was fascinated.'

'And you told him everything? Going out to Colombia? The coffee plantation? The accident? The potion?'

'Yes.'

Moncrieff nodded, then – for the first time – he realised that Groenbaum was standing at the open door. It seemed he'd been there for a while.

'Leave him alone, *Liebling*.' He smiled at Moncrieff. 'It'll happen when the time is right.'

28

WEDNESDAY 1 OCTOBER 1941

Early next morning, Bella was roused by Andreas. She and Larissa had spent the night under a couple of blankets in the Leningrad Gallery. Andreas looked down at them. Schultz, it seemed, had ordered him to find them somewhere else in the museum a little more comfortable to live. In the meantime, her presence was required in the basement.

'Why?' Bella was struggling to her feet, trying not to wake Larissa. Four hours of fitful sleep on the hard floor had left her exhausted. Everything ached. 'Where are we going?'

'Just follow me.'

They were out in the corridor, heading for the stairs. Bella wanted to know what was happening in the city. Andreas shot her a look. The city, they both knew, meant the Yar.

'The shooting stopped last night. We think it may be over.'

Bella nodded. They were still heading down the stairs. At the bottom, Andreas indicated the door that led down to the sub-basement. Andreas had a torch. At the foot of the wooden steps, Bella sensed movement in the darkness. The beam of Andreas' torch swept across the trenches the Russians had dug to find the cache of explosives. Beyond it, lit by two candles, stood Schultz. A naked body lay on two planks. Bella recognised the wooden trestles from Yuri's church.

'*Komm*,' Schultz beckoned her closer. His breath still stank of schnapps but he seemed sober enough. 'You need to be kind to this man. He's filthy. We have to clean him up.'

It was Glivenko. Andreas and a couple of other SD aides had recovered his body from the pavement below the top-floor window. The impact of the fall had killed him outright, but a low hedge had spared him serious disfigurement. A pinkish liquid was still oozing from a wound at the back of his head and the lower half of his torso was beginning to darken as the blood settled.

'His hands and feet, mainly,' Schultz grunted. 'But you might wash the rest of him, too. He was a friend, I think. Am I right?'

'Yes.' Bella couldn't take her eyes off Glivenko's face. Despite a week's growth of beard, he seemed to have shed years in the fall. The button nose. The gleam of gold in his open mouth. A younger man, she thought, but no less beguiling.

'Andreas will find you soap and water and maybe a towel. He will also be laying hands on someone who knows about embalming. It's cold down here but your friend won't last forever.'

'Embalming?' Bella thought she'd misheard. 'Are you serious?'

'Yes. This little man has earned his place in history. It's the least we owe him.' He peered at Andreas. '*Alles gut?*'

The two men left together. Bella, sensing she wouldn't be alone for very long, took advantage of their absence. She looked down at Glivenko's body, and raised his cold hand to her lips. She'd always had a fear of heights and she knew from conversations on the Halifax that he did, too. High explosives, he'd told her, I can cope with. Vertigo starts at twice my height. She gazed at his face. Someone – possibly Schultz – had had the decency to close the dead man's eyes, and in the candlelight it was easy to believe he was asleep.

'You jumped, you brave man,' she murmured. 'Thank you for bringing me here. Thank you for saving my life.'

Andreas was back within minutes. He had a bucketful of tepid water and a pebble of soap. Now he was off to hunt for an embalmer.

Bella waited for the thump-thump of his footsteps on the wooden steps to fade, and then began to wash Glivenko's body. She thought she could still smell the explosives, a sweetness that lingered in the dancing shadows thrown by the candles, but she wasn't sure. What mattered more was that Schultz had been right. Ilya Glivenko, The Pianist, had briefly raised the Red Flag against the marauding Germans and for that he deserved full credit.

She and Larissa had discussed the mining operation for most of the night. Larissa knew already that she owed her freedom to the article she was about to pen, and when Bella admitted that she'd got nothing in the way of detail from Glivenko, she said it wouldn't matter. She'd write the piece on the basis of what little she knew, and then invent the rest. Journalists, she said, were good at filling in holes, especially when no one else would be in a position to contest the fiction. What mattered were the piles of rubble that had once been the city's centre, some of them still warm to the touch. Glivenko and his men had dared and won. No one could argue with that.

Bella finished washing Glivenko's body before the first of the candles guttered and died. The other one had barely minutes left, and she had no taste for remaining beside a dead body in the dark. Ilya Glivenko had gone. Gravity, and fear of the SS, had taken his life and what remained was nothing but a shell. A brave and noble end, she thought, reaching for him one last time and giving his cold hand a squeeze.

*

Moncrieff rose early. Before going to bed, he'd lodged a chair beneath the door handle. Now, fully dressed, he nudged it free and then returned to the bed for one last look at the photo. He shook it out of the envelope. Even with her head so crudely shaved, even in the numbing chill of some remote Siberian labour camp, Bella Menzies was no less beguiling. This was the woman who had managed to extricate him from the hands of the Gestapo, the face that had taken him closer to happiness than he'd ever dreamed possible. He dwelt on it a moment longer, then left the photo on the pillow. Someone would find it later. It was both an explanation and an excuse. I let them take me for the sake of the one person who ever really mattered. No greater love. Literally.

Moncrieff stepped out into the hall. Groenbaum and his wife slept in the big bedroom at the front of the house. The door was open, and Moncrieff could hear one of them snoring. He paused a moment, motionless in the half-darkness, then tiptoed down the stairs.

Outside, away to the east, the first grey light of dawn. It was still cold, the grass wet beneath Moncrieff's feet, and once he was clear of the house he broke into a lazy trot. He was glad of the tracksuit Groenbaum had lent him for the weights room, and the tennis plimsolls that had once belonged to Gerri's late husband were a perfect fit. Another piece of the jigsaw, he thought. No wonder she's been so keen to bed me.

At the foot of the hill, he picked up the pace a little. This was the first time for months that he'd run in the open air, and after the accident he was surprised at how easy it felt. Deep breaths did nothing for his fractured rib but the moment he reined himself in, the sharpness of the pain went away. He felt good. Not least because – at last – he could sense just a hint of light in the darkness of the last ten days. Be big, he told himself. Be obvious. Look for twigs to step on, drifts of fallen leaves to run through. Make yourself known. *Offer* yourself. Would he welcome an end like this? The answer, he knew, was yes.

Moncrieff now understood where his missing week had gone. Like Tice, he'd been the victim of a chemical that had wrecked his head. Life was a cliff. You depended on handholds, tiny creases on the rock face, a route to the top you knew you could trust. Scopolamine had stolen all that, robbed him blind, left him exposed to the wind and weather, hanging on for dear life. They must have injected him again and again, he thought. He must have floated on a tide of deadly nightshade, barely conscious of the Devil's Breath, no pain, no memory, no bearings, not the slightest clue of who or where he might be, while all the time they checked on him, paid regular visits, made sure the Satan inside him was still alive and breathing.

They?

He didn't know. Couldn't be sure. Except that he'd been right, after all, about the Watchers. They were here, now, among the trees, in the woods, maybe camping out, maybe occupying a rented room down in the village, but always lying low, keeping him under observation, ready, prepared, waiting for their moment. He strode on, limping a little now, pausing to jump the little stream in the bed of the valley, glad of the first rays of the rising sun. At the top of the rise, still hidden by the elms, he'd find the caravan, and there he'd rest for a while. Until the moment came.

*

In Kyiv, it was raining yet again. Schultz had the grace to knock on the door of the Leningrad Gallery before barging in. Larissa was seated at the long table that dominated the middle of the display space. She'd handwritten the article and now she needed a typewriter.

'*Bitte.*' Schultz extended a hand.

'You don't trust me?'

'I trust you completely. Give it to me.'

'But you don't speak Ukrainian. You can't read it.'

'Hand it over.' He was impatient now. 'Just do it.'

He took the two sheets of paper to Bella. She was asleep in the far corner of the gallery, curled up beneath a blanket. He stirred her with his boot.

'*Komm,*' he grunted.

She followed him to his office. An empty bottle of schnapps lay, neck-down, in the ammunition box that served as a wastepaper bin. The desk was empty apart from a big typewriter and a pile of yellowing paper.

'Sit,' Schultz pointed at the chair behind the desk. 'Read me what she's done.'

By now Bella was used to Larissa's hand. In Cyrillic, she wrote at speed, foot to the floor, ignoring the speed limits, caring nothing about oncoming traffic. She pointed herself at a subject and let her imagination off the leash, and when the individual characters on the page began to blur into each other, Bella knew it was a sign that she was closing on her prey.

In this case, she'd started her account in the long shadow of the Ginzburg Skyscraper, a moment to which all of her readers could relate. This was the first of many body blows the city was to suffer over the coming days, and she painted a richly detailed picture of the scene that awaited the survivors of the blast. None of this was new to Schultz. Khreshchatyk suddenly full of flying glass? An eruption of smoke and dust? Secondary explosions from stored explosives? Passers-by, felled by the blast wave, picking themselves up, numbed by the seeming return of the Russians? Still impatient, he wanted Bella to get a move on.

She did her best. Cleverly, working on supposition rather than evidence, Larissa had wound the clock back to the last days of the Soviet occupation, with NKVD teams on the move under cover of darkness, hauling wooden boxes of explosive and all the ancillary gear down to the bowels of target after target. In this account, leadership of the sappers fell to Ilya Glivenko. He selected the transmission wavelengths and fine-tuned all the other communications protocols. He decided how long it would take for the Germans to make themselves comfortable in the new quarters they'd requisitioned. And once they'd lowered their guard, wrote Larissa, it was that same Glivenko who'd so artfully plotted patterns of multiple explosions to send the Germans scurrying from one pile of smoking rubble to the next, only to find themselves ambushed en route by a third blast. The little genius they called The Pianist, she'd concluded, had scored an anthem to chaos which had become the soundtrack of a city in flames.

Schultz was warming to this version of events. In Berlin, he muttered, they might even understand just what class of enemy he and his SD team had been fighting. The popular view of all Slavs, Russians in particular, was wildly misconceived. These people not only believed in their fucking revolution, but they had the guts and the know-how to make life near impossible for their enemies. Nothing works, he muttered, until it does.

'What next?' he grunted.

Bella bent to Larissa's account again. She'd followed The Pianist and his teams of sappers to the island on the Dnieper. She'd described the twilight lives of the stay-behind agents who were in constant touch. She'd revealed how they'd spent their days on the city's streets, invisible nobodies, carefully noting which buildings had been requisitioned, where the limousines of the High Command gathered at the kerbside, which of the juiciest plums should fall first from Glivenko's tree.

Schultz was laughing now. He loved the thought of plums and trees. 'The little bastard gave us a real shake,' he said gleefully. 'Until we put him out of business.'

The SD operation to end the bombings occupied the rest of the article. Larissa had embroidered what little Schultz had told her with a pacy account of two agencies – the SD and the SS – joining forces to understand the demolition mechanism, block the transmission frequencies and finally locate Glivenko's team of sappers on Trukhaniv Island. The final raid had been led by Schultz, but – in a wildly improbable quote – he'd been very happy to acknowledge the key contribution of his comrades in the *Schutzstaffel*. 'Without our friends in the SS,' he'd said, 'it would have taken far longer to smash the Russian operation. The cost in yet more lost lives would have been unimaginable. We thank *Standartenführer* Kalb and his men for their invaluable assistance.'

'That's the purest shit,' he shook his head in admiration. 'These people kill Jews by the tens of thousands. What do they care about more blood on the streets?'

'She's being ironical. You asked her to put a smile on Kalb's face and that's what she's done. Think of it as a thank-you.'

'For what?'

'Getting her out of their hands.'

'But she's taking the piss. He'll see that.'

'He won't, Willi. I know the man, remember. I've been very close to him. He's an accountant when it comes to killing, and a spectator when it comes to rape. But he has absolutely no sense of humour.'

*

Andreas returned to the museum less than an hour later. He'd located a lecturer at the university's Medical School who'd once been a pathologist and was only too happy to embalm Ilya Glivenko. After the SS seizure of his faculty buildings, his normal schedule of lectures and seminars had been badly disrupted. He had access to an electric pump and the required chemicals, and he could start immediately. The process, he said, would take between two and three hours.

Schultz checked his watch. Half past nine. Bella was still translating Larissa's article into German, adding one or two flourishes when Schultz felt the need.

'How long before you've typed it all up.'

'An hour, at least.'

Schultz nodded. Andreas was still at the door.

'Fetch the embalmer,' Schultz told him. 'Take him down to Glivenko and make sure he's got anything else he needs. Then deliver the article to Kalb. Tell him from me that we need to know he's happy with it. Only then can he come for Glivenko.'

'He wants the body, *capo*? He wants him dead?' Andreas didn't bother to hide his confusion.

'On the contrary,' the briefest smile. 'He's expecting to start work on him this evening.'

*

It was early afternoon by the time Moncrieff at last heard a stir of movement outside the caravan. Every hour or so, he'd shown himself at the open door, stretched, taken a look round, made himself visible. To his slight surprise, nothing had happened. The Watchers are elsewhere, he told himself. Either that, or they're waiting for the cover of darkness before making their move. The latter, strictly in terms of tradecraft, would make perfect sense. Even with a silencer, a handgun in broad daylight might attract attention. The calm of the woods disturbed. A sudden eruption of birds from the trees. Movement around the caravan. Tell-tale clues that all was far from well.

Now, though, they appeared to be having second thoughts. Brave, he thought, and perhaps a tad reckless. He'd made a nest for himself on the floor of the caravan, an arrangement of blankets, a coverlet, and three cushions that enabled him to stretch out his legs with a degree of comfort. From here, he had a perfect view of the door and, as the footsteps came closer, he tried to imagine what these final few moments of his life would really be like. A bullet in the head, he thought, would be infinitely preferable to lungfuls of cold water and the urgent press of the ropes the Gestapo at the Prinz-Albert-Strasse had used to strap him to the tilting board. He half closed his eyes for a moment, imagining the figure framed against the afternoon light, the raised arm, the black nozzle of the handgun. What were the NKVD using these days? Tulas? Tokarevs? In any event, it barely mattered. At this range, they couldn't miss.

Bella, he thought again. Did she ever spare a thought for where he might be? What he might be thinking? Might she somehow survive the camps, and the endless hours of forced labour, and the unimaginable cold of a Siberian winter? And if she did, what would be left of her precious Revolution, once the Germans had laid hands on Moscow? Darkness, he thought. Better soon, better now, than later.

The footsteps had come to a halt. He caught the scrape of a key in the door, metal against metal, and a murmur of surprise to find the caravan unlocked. Then the body of the caravan rocked as someone mounted the stairs and pushed the door open.

Moncrieff was up on one elbow now, already confused. Did the Watchers have a key?

'Tam? Are you all right?'

Not one figure at the door but two. Gerri was one of them, but the question had come from the other woman. Ursula Barton had never had much of a dress sense and today was no exception.

She looked down at him, unpegging the front of her duffel coat.

'Tam?' she said again. 'What on earth's going on?'

*

The embalmer's name was Dmytro. It was Schultz's suggestion that he might need an assistant, and Bella said she was happy to volunteer. Contrary to Schultz's orders, he'd arrived at the museum at the wheel of his own car, a rusting Gaz, the survivor, he said proudly, of countless Kyiv winters. Bella helped him carry a box of chemicals and a pump down to the sub-basement. Schultz had organised an electrical supply from the ground floor but the socket at the end could only take a single plug which meant relying, once again, on candles. Bella was glad. She'd never seen an embalmer at work before and it was hard to imagine the procedure being anything but brutal. Better the softness of candlelight, she thought. Glivenko wouldn't feel a thing but she most certainly would.

In the event, she was wrong. Schultz had laid hands on an entire box of candles and she used four to circle his prone body while Dmytro made his preparations. His years teaching at the university had obviously accustomed him to an audience and he was only too happy to talk Bella through the procedure.

'He's very clean,' he was examining Glivenko with some care.

'I washed him earlier.'

'You did a good job. He had a fall of some sort?' He'd found the gash on the back of Glivenko's head.

'From the fifth floor.'

'Someone got rid of him?'

'No.'

Dmytro shot Bella a look, then his fingers were exploring the top of Glivenko's spinal cord.

'He was lucky,' he murmured. 'There's a high break, second vertebra down. It would have snapped his neck just like that,' he clicked his fingers. 'Gravity can be kind, believe me.'

'Meaning what?'

'Meaning his lights went out. Bang. Gone. I helped out in the hospital last week. High explosives can be unforgiving.'

Bella nodded. The news that Glivenko would have known nothing about his own death was an undeniable comfort.

Dmytro had positioned the pump beside Glivenko's thigh.

'Here it is, the femoral vein.' Dmytro was making a tiny incision. 'The mixture goes in here. The pump does the rest.'

'Mixture?'

'Five chemicals. You're sitting an exam tomorrow? You want their names?' he laughed. 'Now we need to drain the dead blood.'

He was standing beside Glivenko's head. Bella fetched him a stool that Schultz had provided. Comfortable, he took Bella's hand and placed it gently against the side of the little Russian's neck.

'Here—' he said. 'This is an artery and we're in luck because it's in excellent condition. All we need is a drain tube and a bucket.' He sat back. 'Bucket?'

This time Bella had to go back upstairs. Dead blood? Technically, she imagined this ex-pathologist was probably right. The moment Ilya's life had come to an end was the moment everything began to decay, but the phrase lay unhappily beside everything else she knew about The Pianist. His physical vigour. The sharpness of his wit. His irrepressible good humour. The sheer generosity of his spirit. That single gold tooth in his smile. None of these things belonged in the same sentence as 'dead blood'.

By the time she returned with the bucket, Dmytro had connected the pump to the thin tube that now snaked into Glivenko's thigh. With an adjustment to the drain tube, and the bucket perfectly aligned, he told Bella to start the pump.

'It's the little red switch,' he said. 'I always tell my students it's the closest we've come to making a human heart and it's always the girls who laugh.'

'Not me, I'm afraid,' Bella had started the pump and was looking hard at Glivenko. For a moment or two, neither of them said a word. Then Bella felt the lightest pressure on her arm, a gesture – she thought later – of comfort.

'It won't bring the poor chap back, I'm afraid. If that's what you're hoping.'

By late afternoon, Dmytro was done. He fashioned a line of stitches to keep Glivenko's jaw in place and inserted tiny caps beneath his eyelids to keep them closed, before stepping back to admire his handiwork.

'Not bad,' he said. 'I've never done this by candlelight before. Quite Egyptian, don't you think?'

Bella had been washing Glivenko's body for a second time. The smears of blood around the two carefully sutured entry wounds had now gone. She wiped her hands on a towel, aware of Dmytro watching her.

'You knew him well?'

'We spent a couple of weeks together. Difficult weeks. He was a great help. I liked him very much.'

'And now?' Dmytro nodded down at the body.

'He looks peaceful,' she hesitated. 'How long will he last?'

'A couple of years, maybe. It all depends on the humidity. Bacteria have no manners. They eat every last gram of us, even when we take steps like these.'

Bella nodded. The last couple of hours had been richly educational. Life is dangerous, she thought. No one survives it.

*

Schultz telephoned SS headquarters in the early evening. Kalb's delight at the contents of the article appeared to be unfeigned. He'd telephoned the editor of the *Novoe Ukrainskoe Slovo* personally and despatched the article with instructions to give it maximum prominence in tomorrow's paper. He was grateful for Schultz's gesture in sharing the limelight and added that his superiors in Berlin would be suitably impressed. As a small gesture in return, he had a gift for Larissa in recognition of the fine job she'd done.

'Bring it along,' Schultz was playing with a pencil.

'One other thing, *Kamerad*. It's Berlin again, Herr Himmler himself. The *Reichsminister-SS* wants a look at the situation in the Yar. I mentioned your photographs. Might you be able to spare a couple?'

'And this is for?'

'*Reichsminister-SS* Himmler. As I have just told you.'

'That's not what I meant. Why does he need a bloody photograph?'

'I see.' The noise Schultz heard on the line might have been a chuckle. 'He's looked at the numbers, Schultz. And he thinks we've done an exemplary job.'

Schultz gazed at the phone a moment, speechless. Then he heard the snap of the pencil breaking between his own fingers. Kalb hadn't finished.

'And Glivenko?' he queried.

Schultz leaned back in his chair, staring up at the ceiling. Then he bent to the phone again.

'He's ready for collection,' he grunted. 'Any time.'

*

Kalb arrived at the museum after dark. Andreas met him in the lobby and gave him an envelope Schultz had prepared containing a selection of aerial photographs. In return, Kalb's aide handed over what looked like a bulky manuscript.

'And Glivenko?'

'I'm afraid it might take four of you.' Andreas looked briefly apologetic.

'He's being difficult?'

'A little, yes.'

Kalb barked an order to his aide who disappeared into the darkness. Moments later, he was back with two uniformed SS men.

'Follow me, please, Herr *Standartenführer.*'

Andreas led the way to the stairs that descended to the basement. En route, he was aware of Kalb's interest in the pictures on the wall. He paused briefly by a photograph of a huge demonstration in Leningrad.

'They were going to blow all this history up,' Kalb said. 'It's their history, their doing. Doesn't that tell you everything about the bloody Communists?'

In the basement, Kalb paused, expecting to find Glivenko.

'So where is he?'

'Down below, Herr *Standartenführer.* You know the SD. We take no chances.'

Kalb nodded. He said he understood. Andreas opened the door to the final flight of wooden steps that led to the sub-basement. Schultz was waiting at the bottom, blocking his view.

'Heil Hitler!' Schultz acknowledged the salute with a cursory nod, and then stood aside.

About to gesture his men forward to seize the prisoner and carry him upstairs, Kalb found himself looking at a body in a coffin. Schultz was happy to make the introductions.

'Captain Ilya Glivenko,' he said. 'Soviet 37th Army. The uniform, I'm afraid, doesn't reflect his rank but it was the best we could do. The coffin, on the other hand, is an exact replica of Lenin's. It was featured in a gallery upstairs.' He smiled at Kalb. 'Wholly appropriate, don't you think?'

29

WEDNESDAY 1 OCTOBER 1941

Ursula Barton drove Moncrieff back to London. It wasn't until they were turning into the road where she lived that the silence of the last two hours was broken.

'I'm staying here the night?'

'You are, Tam.'

'There's no need, you know.'

'I'm afraid there is. For both our sakes.'

She parked outside a double-bay semi, studied him for a moment, and then led the way to the house. The wooden gate badly needed attention. Paint was flaking from the front door. In the three years he'd worked in 'B' Section, Moncrieff had never been here and at first sight it didn't seem to marry with the slightly forbidding neatness of her office.

She settled him in the living room at the front.

'Malt? I've made a small investment. A Talisker single malt. I thought it might cheer you up.'

She disappeared without waiting for an answer and returned with a brand new bottle and two glasses. Moncrieff had been looking round: shelf after shelf of books, and an untidy stack of records beside the gramophone. A worn carpet, cratered with burn marks around the open fire. A photograph on the mantlepiece off a little girl standing on a bridge, holding the hand of a plumpish woman who already looked middle-aged.

'Is that you?'

Barton was uncapping the bottle. 'Yes. Hausach. It's a little village on the edge of the Black Forest. I don't think my mother ever quite got over having a child. Most days I ended up thinking I'd probably arrived in the post.'

'Your father?'

'Killed on the Somme. His name was Franck. We had a strange life, my mother and I. Even when I try hard, I can remember nothing but silence.'

Moncrieff nodded. He was grateful for the malt. He took a sip, and then another.

'So what were you doing down in Hampshire?' he asked.

'I was worried. I'd been checking by phone every day and I knew things weren't going well. Groenbaum said you were being stubborn, wouldn't really co-operate, wouldn't *relax*. He said he was doing his best, but he suspected he was fighting the tide. I got the feeling you were falling apart in some way. The word he used was disintegration. Then he phoned up this morning and said you'd gone completely, just walked out, disappeared. That left me no choice. I *had* to come down.'

Moncrieff nodded, staring down at his glass. Disintegration, he thought. Perfect.

'He also said you were becoming tetchy, even aggressive. Is that fair?'

'I've no idea. If you want the truth, I think the man's a fake.'

'Really?' The ghost of a smile came and went.

'Yes.' Moncrieff described the hours he'd spent lofting golf balls across the valley after Groenbaum's attempts to hypnotise him. 'It's nonsense,' he said. 'You'd have been better off spending your money on a crate of this.' He tipped the glass to his lips and swallowed what remained.

'He also said you were mumbling about the Watchers,' Barton hadn't moved.

'That's a lie,' Moncrieff said hotly. 'I never breathed a word about any bloody Watchers.'

'Not face-to-face, that's true. The bedroom you slept in is rigged with microphones. Groenbaum claims it's all part of the protocol.' A thin smile. 'Eavesdropping on your darkest thoughts? Does that sound credible?'

'It does,' Moncrieff reached for the bottle. 'Bastard.'

Barton watched him pour himself two fingers. She hadn't touched her own drink.

'So, do they exist?' she said at length. 'These Watchers?'

'I thought so, yes.'

'Thought? Past tense?'

Moncrieff shrugged. Said he didn't know, didn't care.

'But who are they, Tam? I need an answer. It's the least you owe me. Groenbaum thinks you've changed, even over the brief time he's known you, and to be honest I have to agree. You used to be so calm, so measured. Now, to be frank, you're a mess. None of this is pleasant, Tam, least of all – I suspect – for you. Tell me what's really been happening in that head of yours.'

'Scopolamine,' Moncrieff held her gaze.

'What on earth's that?'

Moncrieff repeated the word, spelled it out, told her to write it down. The Mayans or the Incas, or some bloody tribe had used it. It came from a jungle plant, he said. First it robbed you of your memory, then it turned you into someone else. Hence its nickname, the Devil's Breath. Moncrieff was tempted to apologise, to say sorry for his rudeness, to blame it on the drug, but it simply wasn't in him.

'And the Watchers?' Barton queried.

'They were the ones who gave me the stuff in the first place.'

Barton nodded. The Russians, she said, had always been in love with poisons. When a bullet in the back of the neck felt too crude, poison was the way they settled quarrels, paid off debts, got rid of enemies of the People. Mostly, they confected various brews of their own but in this case they'd obviously lifted a page or two from someone else's script. Either way, the results were the same. A whole week gone missing, and a man she greatly admired waking up a stranger to himself.

'And the Watchers came down to get you? Finish the job? That's the impression I got from Groenbaum.'

'That's what I thought, yes.'

'But why would they do that?'

Moncrieff lay back in the armchair, staring up at patches on the ceiling where the distemper hadn't quite covered. He felt exhausted, wiped out, lost again.

'You know why,' he said at last.

'I do?'

'Of course. You came down to Beaulieu. You played the psychiatrist. You dug that lost bloody day out of me. Following the man. Keeping him under surveillance. Tracking him halfway across bloody London. And then his neat little trap at the end.'

'Philby,' she murmured.

'Of course.'

'You think he's behind the Watchers? You're telling me he'd sent them down to kill you? Was that what you were doing in that caravan? Waiting for them to finish the job?'

'Yes,' Moncrieff knew it sounded absurd, but it was true. 'And there's something else, too. They needn't have bothered.'

'Because?'

'Because I'd got their message.'

'The photo you left on the pillow?'

'Yes.'

'Bella Menzies?'

'Yes.'

Barton nodded. At last she reached for her glass. 'That's what you told me in the car when we took you to Groenbaum,' she said. 'You were alarmingly honest. You said you had to think about Bella. Every life has a price, you told me, and it wasn't going to be hers. That's why you were refusing to help me. And that's why this thing can't go any further.'

'Thing?'

'Philby. Is he playing us? Very probably yes. Is he clever? Again, yes. In God's good time, might he go to the very top? Director-General? "C"? Yes. And can we prove any of this? Little you and little me? Alas, no.'

'You've tried?' Moncrieff was doing his best to follow the logic.

'Of course I have.'

'How?'

'You know how. I've told you already. I commissioned enquiries at Archie's place. I widened the net as far as I could. I'm still doing my best to trace the owner of that French car you woke up in. But these people are good, Tam. They know

369

their job. They've made life very hard for us. As you, more than anyone else, should know.'

'People?'

'I have to assume Russians. From the embassy.'

'NKVD?'

'Indeed. Our precious allies.'

Moncrieff allowed himself another tug at the malt. At last it was beginning to silence the demons in his head.

'And the Director?' he murmured. 'Our boss? Liddell?'

'I was with him yesterday. He knows exactly what's been happening. I've kept him briefed on a daily basis.'

'Confidentially?'

'Yes. And that was at his insistence, not mine.'

'And?'

'He wants the whole thing dropped. He thinks it's a waste of time and resources. He thinks our real focus should lie elsewhere. The word he's using is distraction. He thinks we're shooting ourselves in both feet when our fire should be turned on the enemy.'

'Maybe Philby *is* the enemy. Has he thought about that?'

'My impression is that he hasn't.'

'Won't.'

'Exactly. He thinks we're looking for ghosts, phantoms.'

'And is he wrong?'

'Yes,' she nodded. 'I think he is.'

Over a sandwich supper, late now, they became friends again. Barton poured another malt for Moncrieff and made a pot of tea. Moncrieff was slow to accept that the nightmare of the last few weeks might at last be over but, once Barton had been through it all again, he realised that she was right. Their attempt to pin Philby down had always been extra-curricular, just the pair of them, and beyond a certain point, without someone with real weight behind them, they were helpless.

Barton agreed. She pointed out that something very similar had happened with Jane Archer and the defector Walter Krivitsky. Archer, she said, had worked very hard to make at least a circumstantial case against Philby, but the fruits of all her labours had simply been buried.

'I was talking to Ivor Maskelyne the other day. He dropped in for a chat.' She paused. 'The Oxford don? That cricket match of yours at Glenalmond? The Good Samaritan who drove you up to town afterwards? He has a very low opinion of us, especially Broadway. On a good day, I get the impression he thinks we're all a waste of resources. On a bad day, we're a liability. If that's true, then the likes of Philby could put us on our knees. An alarming thought, Tam.'

Moncrieff nodded. His memories of that day were beginning to slip back into focus.

'Maskelyne said something else, too, when we were in the car coming back from Glenalmond,' he was toying with his glass. 'At the time I thought it was a bit rich. Now I'm not so sure.'

'What was it? Care to tell me?'

'Of course. You know the man. Irony is his second language. In theory he accepts we might have cuckoos in the nest, but he thinks that won't be a problem because the Russians will never believe a word they say. You're telling us to trust a man because of his accent? Because of his education, his connections, his old school tie? Even the English can't be that stupid. In the car, that made me laugh. Now?' he shrugged. 'Maybe he's right. And maybe Liddell's right, too. Our game is one huge distraction, and maybe the point about war is far simpler. Find the enemy and shoot him down,' he shot Barton a look. 'Von Richthofen. Sound advice.'

*

In Kyiv, three days later, Wilhelm Schultz took an evening off to celebrate a modest victory. Andreas used his ever-growing network of connections across the city to lay hands on a suckling pig and a bag of potatoes and five jars of pickled cucumbers. Schultz himself paid a small fortune in Reichmarks for bottles of schnapps, local beer and Georgian champagne, and the SD's entire strength in Kyiv – just nineteen agents – gathered at the Lenin Museum for the barbecue.

Andreas had also found a gipsy violinist, a saturnine man with a serpent tattoo and garlic breath, to add a little pep to the evening, and after all the food had gone Schultz and Bella led the revels with a spirited dance that began as a tango and ended up with a heap of bodies, helpless with laughter, on the wooden parquet floor. Getting up and brushing himself down, Schultz proposed a series of toasts. The first was to Larissa, for achieving the impossible by putting a smile on the face of *Standartenführer* Kalb. The second was to Dmytro, the one-time pathologist, for so nearly restoring Glivenko to his former glory. And the last was to Glivenko himself, for throwing down the gauntlet and letting the SD show how fucking good they were.

'To The Pianist,' he roared. 'May the angels be kind to him.'

Bella's was the first glass in the air. Tomorrow, she knew that Schultz was flying to Berlin. There, a grateful Führer would pin the *Ritterkreuz* on his broad chest for services to the ever-expanding Reich, and afterwards she guessed there'd be more carousing in the upper reaches of the *Abwehr*. No one in Berlin with any real knowledge of events in Kyiv had been fooled for a moment by Kalb's claims to glory in what the *Völkischer Beobachter* was calling the Battle of the Bombs. The real credit belonged to the SD, and everyone knew it.

With Schultz briefly gone, Larissa and Bella would be moving out of the museum and taking up residence in the Pechersk Monastery. Andreas, whose negotiating talents appeared to be endless, had obtained rooms for each of them at the heart of the sprawling Lavra complex. The bundle of typed pages presented by Kalb had turned out to be the manuscript of Yuri's latest novel, retrieved from the church. Larissa knew about Yuri's fascination with the monastery's early days and after a long talk with the priest in charge of the Pechersk library, she'd be only too glad to pick up the pen, immerse herself in a wealth of records, and spend the coming weeks and months trying to complete the book. Bella, in the meantime, would be helping in one of the monastery's many vegetable gardens, a prospect that filled her with a quiet delight.

The barbecue was coming to an end, and Schultz stood at the door, pumping hand after hand as his team stumbled towards the darkness outside. Dmytro, who'd done such a fine job on the little Russian sapper, told Schultz he was welcome to call on his services any time. Schultz thought about the offer, then he turned to Bella.

'Who else would you like through that bloody window?' he asked. 'I'm sure Andreas could get Kalb back again.'

*

The following morning, after two nights in his own bed in Archie's Kensington Mews cottage, Moncrieff made an appearance at MI5 headquarters in St James's Street. The invitation had come from Guy Liddell via Ursula Barton. Moncrieff mounted the stairs and accepted the proffered chair beside Liddell's desk. Barton was there, too, a notepad on her lap.

Liddell, even quieter than usual, apologised for an early autumn cold. His voice was barely a whisper and his eyes looked rheumy. He perched behind the desk, his long fingers softly drumming some secret rhythm as he expressed the Section's admiration and gratitude for Moncrieff's contribution over the years. His performance in the Sudetenland before the ruinous Munich Agreement had, he murmured, been a tribute to both his courage and his fortitude. While the leadership he'd shown over the Hess debacle, sticking to his guns when everyone else in Whitehall insisted he was wrong, had won 'B' Section nothing but credit.

Moncrieff did his best to smile. This, he knew, was the end of his days at St James's Street, the Director's parting farewell, a flutter of the eyelids and the warmest possible handshake before he dismissed Moncrieff to clear his desk and head back to the mountains. His years in MI5 were over. He'd bagged a trophy or two, won a mention in despatches, but now the time had come to call a halt. Oddly enough, instead of regret or even disappointment, he felt nothing.

He glanced at Barton, seeking some kind of confirmation, but instead – with a tiny shake of the head – she cleared her throat and took over. Moncrieff, she said, had been through a great deal over the past few weeks. Now was the time for what she called 'gardening leave'. A ticket for the night sleeper north had already been booked. Archie Gasgoigne, happily, was also on leave for a week or two and after a conversation on the phone he'd be very happy to field Moncrieff off the train at Laurencekirk and drive him back to the Glebe House.

'Archie?' Moncrieff looked totally blank. 'Laurencekirk station?'

'Indeed, Tam,' the Director produced a handkerchief and blew his nose. 'Six months at least, we think. On full pay, of course.'

*

Moncrieff sped north that night. He savoured two glasses of malt in the privacy of his sleeping compartment and was tucked up in his bunk before the train had passed Peterborough. For the first time since he could remember, he slept like a baby, cradled by the lazy rhythms of the wheels.' And by the time he awoke it was broad daylight. A single glance through the window told him they were crossing the long bridge over the river at Dundee, and an hour and a half later he stepped out of the train at Laurencekirk.

Archie, as promised, was on hand to greet him. Life on the Shetland Isles was obviously treating him well. His hair was wilder than ever and with the remains of his deep summer tan he looked piratical. On the way to the car, Moncrieff brought them both to a halt.

'How much have they told you?' he asked.

'Who?'

'My people in London.'

'Nothing. A week in the mountains? No bloody Norwegians to organise? Good company? Who'd ever say no?'

Moncrieff knew he was lying but it didn't matter.

'Fine,' he said, heading for the car again. 'Let's keep it that way, eh?'

*

October brought the first real taste of winter. As fellow bootnecks, both Archie and Moncrieff had done their time in the hills and Moncrieff relished the chance to stride away from the house, ankle-deep in leaves and fir cones, and then head for the bareness of the mountains. Exercise, conversation and the freshness of the air did wonders for his broken rib and as the days spooled by, he began to feel the cautious return of someone he recognised.

In the evenings, he'd cook in the kitchen while Archie entertained him with stories of the Norwegian agents he was running into the fjords across the North Sea. All of them appeared to be called Knut, all of them were related, and all of them consumed vast quantities of alcohol. Archie had begun this adventure with barely a word of Norwegian but one morning Moncrieff paused on the stairs to hear him deep in conversation on the telephone with the exile from Bergen who served as his quartermaster.

'Impressive,' Moncrieff said when the call was over. 'I thought Norwegian was hard to get your tongue round.'

'It is,' Archie grinned. 'I make most of it up but somehow Knut always gets the drift.'

The following day, another phone call. Moncrieff thought he recognised the voice but couldn't be sure.

'Frank Jennings. We met at Beaulieu. Young Lenahan's lecturer from deepest Kent.'

'Fort Halstead?'

'The same. You'll pardon the intrusion. I'm after a scoundrel called Archie Gasgoigne. Any joy?'

Jennings, it turned out, was en route to Archie's base up in the Shetlands with a collection of what he called 'amusements'. He wanted to call by and pick Archie up en route to the ferry.

'Tell him to come up tomorrow,' Moncrieff said. 'He can stay the night.'

Archie bent to the phone, then shot Moncrieff a look.

'He's got a lorry, a driver, and two guards.'

'Full house, then. They can all bed down *chez nous*.'

Jennings arrived late the following afternoon. Archie disappeared into the back of the truck for half an hour while the Major from Fort Halstead talked him through the contents of each of the boxes. Only then did he set foot in the Glebe House.

Moncrieff was in the kitchen with the rest of the party. They had tents in the back of the truck and were more than happy to camp in a corner of the Glebe House garden. Moncrieff cooked a supper of mutton stew and after the driver and the guards had departed for the night, he arranged three armchairs around the open fire in the kitchen and broached a bottle of malt.

Jennings wanted to talk about Kyiv. There were rumours, he said, that Ilya Glivenko, the little sapper they'd hosted at Fort Halstead, had been captured and killed. If true, of course, that was the saddest news, but it was incontestable that he'd left a rich legacy in the shape of countless buildings destroyed by the caches of high explosive he'd so carefully hidden. Archie, who knew nothing about Kyiv, demanded more details. As did Moncrieff.

Jennings was in his element. The explosives, he said, were actuated by tone-modulated carrier waves in burst transmissions from a covert source. Moncrieff was lost already but Archie appeared to be familiar with the complex physics of making things go bang from a distance and wanted to know how the Germans would respond in a situation like this. This must matter, Moncrieff told himself, if your agents are running kit like this into occupied Norway. He needed to know, if only to brief his wayward Vikings.

'This is supposition on my part,' Jennings warned, 'but the first thing you'd need to identify are the transmission frequencies. Once you've done that, you can set up special intercept operations, but you'd have to have access to lots of specialists and lots of kit. The Germans had only been in Kyiv a matter of days. All occupations have to bed down and my guess is that resources like that were thin on the ground. Under those circumstances, you'd go back to square one.'

'Which is?'

'Arrest and interrogation. The Russians would have left spotters on the ground in the city.'

'Watchers?' This from Moncrieff.

'Indeed. Find these people, sweat them, and everything starts to unravel. Maybe that's how Ilya came to grief. I hope to God I'm wrong.'

Archie was deep in thought. Finally, he emptied his glass and reached for the bottle.

'So the weak spot's the wireless transmissions. Am I right?'

'Yes and no. Wireless plus the spotters gives you an instant result. The people on the ground tell you where next and you press the burst transmission button. It's a bit like artillery except you're bound to hit the target. In this respect, I have to say that the Russians have taught us a lot. But in return, I like to think we also brought something to the party.'

'Like what?'

'Delayed action,' Jennings nodded towards the window. The truck was parked outside in the darkness, carefully guarded.

'You mean the kit you showed me earlier?' This from Archie.

'Indeed. The key is battery life. Every battery is in the process of dying. There's a trickle of discharge you can do nothing about. But it turns out there are steps you can take to slow the rate of discharge even further, and that's exactly what we've done.'

'For us? In Norway?'

'Yes. And in Kyiv, as well. We sent Ilya back with lots of time-delay kit.'

'How long?'

'Under exceptional circumstances, three months. Six weeks?' he smiled. 'And we can guarantee you a very big bang.'

30

MONDAY 3 NOVEMBER 1941

The moment Larissa appeared at her door, Bella knew that something special had happened. After weeks in the monastery's library, poring over illuminated manuscripts, letters, housekeeping records, and other fragments from the settlement's earliest days, Larissa had picked up her pen in earnest and set fire to all this kindling. Bella knew it was a moment she'd been putting off for weeks, wary of trespassing onto Yuri's turf. Yes, she understood about storytelling, and about language. Yes, she could hold the readership of the city's biggest newspaper for the time it took to digest a single article. But was she really qualified to write at the length of an entire novel? Especially when the first footsteps had been taken by someone as accomplished, and as quietly famous, as Yuri Ponomorenko?

'So?' Bella was still getting dressed.

'I think it worked.' Larissa was looking radiant. 'Early days, I know, but it felt comfortable.'

'Can I read it? Aren't you going to show me?'

'Of course not. One day, maybe, but not now.' She stepped a little closer. 'I saw the doctor this morning,' she touched the plaster on her broken arm. 'He wants to take it off next week. He thinks the bone's healed. Good news, *chérie?* For us?'

Bella smiled, tightening the leather belt around her waist, and looking round for the wooden clogs she'd started to wear. Since their arrival at Pechersk she and Larissa had slept separately, in the bare stone-walled rooms the monks had assigned them. Larissa, wholly absorbed by her long hours in the library, had been distant, preoccupied, remote, and in a way Bella had been grateful. The wounds inflicted by Kalb and his bodyguard were still raw, and in any event she was in no hurry to upset the monks. She had no idea how long she'd have to rely on their protection, just as nobody had any idea whether Russia itself would be able to weather the Nazi storm. For the time being, therefore, she was content to broker a peace between winter and her more tender vegetables. Her rows of cabbages, thankfully, were in rude health. As were her beetroot and leeks.

'Excellent news,' Bella gave her a brief hug. 'Fingers crossed, eh?'

'Is that the best you can do?'

'I'm afraid it is, yes. For the time being.'

'But later. Once I'm mended?'

'Later may be different. There's no hurry. We've got lots of time. Let's see.'

'You don't get lonely?' Larissa couldn't hide her disappointment. 'Sleeping alone?'

'Never. I didn't in Moscow and I don't here. You're taking it personally. I know you are. You need to get back to that book of yours. Before it's time to pray again.' Larissa gazed at her, uncertain. Bella cupped her face and kissed her on the lips. 'Say a prayer for me, too. You promise?'

Larissa gazed at her a moment longer, and then her fingers explored Bella's new growth of hair.

'Blonde again,' she said. 'I miss you. Is that such a hard thing for you to hear?'

*

An hour or so later, from her precious rectangle of garden, Bella lifted her head to gaze across at the Cathedral of the Dormition. It dominated the area the monks called the Lavra, a glorious confection in icy white, topped with golden onion-shaped domes. The interior, in the style of the Eastern Orthodox Church, was heavy with gilt and frescos. In her youth, Bella had worshipped in bare nonconformist chapels, largely in Scotland, and had no taste for the sheer weight of ornamentation that went with the God of the steppes. The sweetness of incense, and the mournful infinity of icons, had always failed to touch the parts of her where faith still lurked, but Valentin and Kalb and the Yar had now extinguished even that faint flicker of belief. Not that she ever wanted to deny Larissa her daily visits to the cathedral. If an hour on her knees in front of the glittering altar offered any kind of solace for what they'd all been through, then so be it.

One of the cathedral bells began to toll. She knew this was Larissa's call to prayer and she laid down her hoe and stepped across to the wall to watch the scatter of black-clad priests converging on the cathedral's main door. Over the past weeks, she'd started to make friends with some of these men. She knew the presence of women, especially foreign women, was unusual in the Lavra, but she admired their tolerance and their natural grace.

She'd always half suspected that male communities were instinctively hostile to women, that they viewed the opposite sex as a distraction, a nuisance, a source of spiritual defilement, but she knew now that this simply wasn't true. Only yesterday, in the big refectory, she'd had a conversation over the soup at lunchtime with a young monk who'd spent six months in Moscow before the Germans had invaded. No Communist himself, he was struck by her fluent Russian and the fact that she'd surrendered to the teaching of Marx and Engels, and when they'd parted he'd asked whether he might offer her a blessing.

'Of course,' she'd said, 'if it makes you feel better.'

She hadn't meant it as an insult but, more importantly, he seemed to have understood. Outside in the sunshine, he'd made the sign of the cross and murmured the prayer of St Anthony, and when she'd thanked him for his comfort, he'd asked her about Kyiv.

'How have you found our city?' he'd said.

It was a genuine question, and she'd given it some thought.

'Terrifying,' she'd told him. And she'd meant it.

*

Now she spotted Larissa heading for the cathedral door. She paused to adjust her headscarf and as she did so, she caught sight of Bella watching her. She finished with the scarf and gave her a playful little wave, exactly the way she might have done when they'd first met, first made love, and for just a second or two Bella was tempted to duck out of the garden, kick the loose soil from her clogs and join her. Then she shook her head, waving back, knowing that it was the act of writing, of inventing, of stirring her imagination back into life that had made such a

383

sudden difference to Larissa. Maybe when the plaster comes off, she thought. Maybe.

Larissa disappeared into the cathedral. Bella picked up her hoe and returned to her row of cabbages. Her war against the slugs, intensely personal, was nearly won but she knew she should share the credit with the onset of winter, and the temperatures that were beginning to plunge at night. If I was a snail, she thought idly, I'd be hibernating by now, finding somewhere snug and dry, surrendering to dreams of spring.

The roar of the explosion came seconds later. Bella found herself face down on the newly turned earth, her mouth full of soil. Part of the wall between her and the cathedral had collapsed, a victim of the blast wave, and part of her was back on Khreshchatyk, only six weeks ago, ruin after ruin on fire as the smoke and dust boiled into the blueness of the sky.

She got to her feet, checking herself for wounds. Mercifully, she was intact, untouched by flying debris. She made her way to the remains of the wall, waiting for the curtains of smoke to part. Priests were already running towards the netherworld of what had once been the Lavra's pride and joy, and as a sudden wind parted the oily murk, she could only gape at what little remained. The heart of the cathedral had simply disappeared, huge pediments and pillars lying on drifts of stone and rubble, age-old trees felled by the storm that had swept over this sacred place. Revealed by the blast was a fresco of saints beneath an interior arch, each sacred head etched in golden light.

Bella shook her head, a gesture of helplessness. She knew she ought to help, ought somehow to play a part in whatever followed, but she hadn't a clue what to do. There were people, worshippers, men of God, under that huge weight of masonry and one of them, she knew with total certainty, was Larissa. No one could have survived a blast like that. No one.

A tall priest, an old man, swept past. His eyes were glittering in his parchment face and tiny particles of dust had flecked the blackness of his beard with shades of grey. One hand pressed the cross around his neck to his breast. The other hand, balled in a fist, was raised high. Bella hoped he was raging at that God of his who permitted atrocities like this but, moments later, he proved her wrong. He was on his hands and knees now, his hands pressed together, praying for the forgiveness of the victims' sins. Bella watched him, shaking her head, sensing that all hope had finally gone.

'I miss you,' Larissa had told her barely hours ago. 'Is that such a hard thing for you to hear?'

No, she thought. Christ, no.

She was back in the room where she slept. She'd closed the door and turned her back on the raging chaos outside. Now, prone on the bed, staring up at the ceiling, she could smell the foul breath of the explosion, the sour reek of smoke and ashes, and an occasional passing sweetness that could have come from anywhere.

No, she thought again. Please God, no. Would another building on the Lavra be next? Would the carnage in this city that God had somehow overlooked never end? Had the Russians returned to the island in the Dnieper? Had the embalming fluids resurrected poor Ilya and sent him back into battle? The thought tormented her, not just for her own sake, and for the sake of anyone with the misfortune to live here, but for the sake of Ilya.

That man had been so brave, she told herself, and so generous, and so full of grace. And yet he'd still taken hundreds of lives, inflicted grief and loss on thousands more. How can that possibly be? What kind of God can square a circle that perfect and yet preside over such suffering? Hours later, still no closer to an answer, she finally fell asleep.

A priest roused her shortly after dawn. She stared up at the whiteness of the face framed by his beard. His cassock smelled of incense. He must have been praying, she thought. He must have been on his knees in one of the Lavra's other churches that his God had so far spared.

'Come,' he said. 'The soldiers are waiting.'

It was Kalb. He was standing impatiently inside the main gate, his greatcoat buttoned to his neck, as the priest hurried her past the still-smoking ruins of the cathedral. There were three SS soldiers with him, all uniformed. Dead-eyed, she thought, totally impassive, figures and faces from deepest, coldest space. Didn't these people ever sleep? Did they conduct all their business in the smallest hours? When everyone else's defences were down? Were they truly creatures of the night?

Kalb didn't even bother telling her what she'd done. His gesture towards what was left of the cathedral was enough. Your fault, he seemed to be telling her. Your doing. And now you must pay.

The Mercedes again. They put her in the back and drove her across the city. At this hour, the streets were empty apart from the newly homeless, ghosts of entire families, huddled together beneath the spread of leafless branches, seeking shelter from the bitter wind. All it needed, she thought, was the stinking bulk of Valentin beside her but she knew that this time there'd be no way out, no Russian gunman emerging from the darkness, no saviour to pluck her from the car and ghost her away. This moment belonged to Kalb, and he was going to make the most of it.

They were north of the city centre now. Bella caught the single word 'Syrets' in the muttered conversation, and her heart sank. Syrets was the camp they'd built within touching distance of the Yar. Syrets was where they wrung the last particle of useful work from you before your strength failed and they put a bullet in your head. Syrets would be the last place she'd ever see.

The camp was surrounded by three fences. The Mercedes rolled to a halt while the guards at the gate saluted Kalb and gestured for the driver to roll on.

'Wait,' Kalb got out of the car and then bent to lock eyes with Bella. Mad, she thought. And evil. '*Komm.*'

Bella got out. It was freezing. She was wearing nothing but a gown she'd thrown on back in her cell of a bedroom in the Lavra. She followed Kalb to an area beside the guardhouse. He was pointing up at the fences. Two of them were made of barbed wire. The one in the middle, he said, was electrified.

'Three metres high,' his good eye never left her face. 'Ten thousand volts. If you ever make it to the middle one, we'll turn you into toast and let the dogs have their way.'

The word 'dogs' brought a grunt of approval. Bella spun round. He was bigger than Kalb, broad across the chest and shoulders, and the front of his uniform was covered in medals. He had a drinker's face, swollen, purpled, and his tiny eyes were looking Bella up and down. The big Alsatian at his side caught her scent and began to stir.

'The Commandant,' Kalb said. 'Make a friend of him and he might save your life.'

They returned to the Mercedes and drove into the camp. There were rows of huts on either side, and gaunt, shaven figures were beginning to appear. They wore grey and white prison fatigues and stared at the Mercedes as it rolled slowly past. Some of them were barefoot. Bella had seen people like these in an institution on the outskirts of Moscow and they, too, had been mad.

The Mercedes came to a halt again. This was a bigger hut, older, semi-derelict. One of Kalb's soldiers pushed Bella towards the open door. Inside, a single bulb dangling from the ceiling revealed a rusting showerhead dripping icy water. Beside it was a basket full of discarded clothing. The guard gestured for Bella to strip. Her clothes were to go into the basket.

'What for?' she asked in German.

'We disinfect them.'

'And then I get them back?'

The guard didn't answer but simply nodded at the showerhead. By now, Bella had noticed the dull glint of ice on the inside of the nearest window.

Naked, she stepped under the shower. The guard studied her for a moment. Then came a nod of approval and a gasp from Bella as the trickle of cold water caught her by surprise. Icy needles, she thought, boring into her head. She moved left, then right, then tried to abandon the puddle of water at her feet but the guard pushed her back under the shower.

'Wash,' he muttered.

'You have soap?'

'Wash,' he repeated.

At the sight of the raised whip, Bella did his bidding. The water fell on her shoulders, over the bareness of her breasts, trickling down her belly and onto her thighs. Soon she could feel nothing but a gathering numbness. Then the door opened and another figure, smaller, was briefly silhouetted against the still-grey light of dawn. He was carrying a stool in one hand and a razor in the other.

'Enough,' the guard nodded at the stool. 'Sit.'

Bella was shivering now, violent convulsions that felt like she'd been possessed by devils. She'd never been so cold in her life. She squatted on the stool, her hands pressed between her thighs, staring up at the newcomer's face. He was wearing the prison fatigues with the white and grey stripe, and his head was shaved. One of us, she thought.

'Ready?' He spoke Ukrainian with a Kyiv accent. Bella thought she caught a hint of kindness in his eyes.

'You're going to shave me, too?' She couldn't take her eyes off the razor.

'Yes.' He was gazing down at the crop of downy blonde hair. 'A shame, *ja*?'

*

Wilhelm Schultz returned two days later, earlier than expected. In the light of the latest news from Kyiv, the award of his *Ritterkreuz* had been hastily rescinded, his invitation to the Chancellery withdrawn. The near-destruction of the Cathedral of the Dormition in the Lavra was a terrible warning. The same fate probably awaited countless other landmark buildings across the city, and teams of engineers – swollen, as ever, by Russian prisoners – were working twenty-hour days to check and recheck every corner of hundreds of properties. The hunt now was for delayed-action mines, a tactic the SD should have anticipated.

Kalb waited until Schultz was back at his desk in the museum. Earlier, he'd conferenced with the Military Governor and urged the need for Kyiv's new masters to make public their disgust at what had happened. The Military Governor had agreed that a demonstration of some kind was in order and had left the details to the *Schutzstaffel*. Only now, though, did Kalb despatch a team of SS troops to empty the museum of every item relating to Lenin, and his Revolution, that they could lay their hands on.

Schultz knew he was helpless to stop them. The SS vastly outnumbered his own presence in the city. And so he sat at his desk through a very long day, listening to the tramp of boots as Kalb's men scoured gallery after gallery. Photographs, documents, uniforms and countless other revolutionary bric-a-brac was hauled out of the museum and tossed into waiting trucks. The trucks motored through the city with an SS motorcycle escort, death's head pennants flying, and deposited their trophies on the sandy banks of the Dnieper beneath the ancient walls of the Pechersk Monastery. The bonfire grew all day, as yet unfired, and mid-afternoon Kalb called for Ilya Glivenko's embalmed remains to be laid on top. The Military Governor happily consented to attend in person and set light to the bonfire. Kalb had arranged for both radio and print reporters to be present, and after a brief speech from the Governor, deploring the Soviet's latest act of vandalism, the gathering dusk was punctuated by photographers' flashbulbs as he accepted a flaming torch from Kalb and tossed it onto the bonfire, already soaked in gasoline.

The pile of looted artefacts erupted. The blaze was fierce, and hours later some of the city's homeless, alerted by word of mouth, were still warming their hands on what remained of Lenin's precious Revolution. Even the Ukrainian journalists present admitted that Kalb's gesture was a masterstroke.

Schultz, meanwhile, had remained at his desk in the now-empty museum. He was no stranger to the vicious turf wars on which Hitler had built his Reich, and he knew that – for now – he'd been bested. The loss of one of Eastern Europe's oldest cathedrals was neither here nor there. Neither was he especially concerned by the death toll, growing hour by hour. Midday worshippers, Andreas reported, had been crushed under falling masonry and barely a handful had survived. At this news, Schultz had got to his feet, checked his watch and shrugged. In a war like this, he pointed out, you took your life in your hands every minute of every day, and if you were already on your knees in conversation with your maker when death came calling, then perhaps you were blessed.

Andreas, slightly shocked, had retreated to the cubby hole he occupied down the corridor. He was still getting used to the blankness of the walls, and was wondering whether he might be able to find substitute pictures to brighten Schultz's days, when he looked up to find Kalb standing at his open door. His face, for some reason, was smoke-blackened and he smelled faintly of gasoline, but he appeared to be in the best of spirits.

'I can't find Schultz.' He let an envelope fall on Andreas' desk. 'Please see he gets this as soon as possible.'

*

By now, Schultz had driven himself to the Lavra. He parked beside the main entrance and made his way past the carcass of the ancient cathedral. Three of the towers had toppled into the mountain of rubble below, and he bent briefly to place a hand against a chunk of fallen masonry. The veined marble was still warm to his touch, and when he stepped backwards and peered up, he could see exactly how the belly of the cathedral had been ripped open. Tendrils of blue-grey smoke were still curling up into the night sky and he could smell incense on the wind from the nearby river. Schultz had never set much store on reflection. You made your decisions in life, piled your chips on a certain square, and hoped to God everything worked, but here and now, hearing the distant bass chant of what had to be a choir of monks, he knew that he was looking at the ruins of his own career. He should have been harsher with Glivenko. He should have squeezed the rest of the story out of the little Russian. But he hadn't. He shrugged again. What was done, he thought, was done. *Que sera.*

Back at the looted museum, he settled wearily behind his desk. Andreas, ever thoughtful, had found yet another bottle of schnapps and laid it carefully beside a single glass. Schultz uncapped the bottle and was about to pour himself the long evening's first drink when his gaze settled on the envelope. On the top left-hand corner was the familiar SS stamp. In the middle, in Kalb's cramped hand, Schultz's name.

Schultz picked the envelope up, weighed it briefly in his hand, tried to guess what he might find. Then he laid it briefly aside before he filled the glass with schnapps. He hung onto the glass a moment, then reached for the envelope. The glue on the flap had already come unstuck. Inside the envelope was a single black and white photo. He upended the envelope and let the image fall onto the desk. He stared at it for a long moment, then reached for the glass.

A Russian toast, he thought bitterly, tossing back the schnapps in a single gulp.

AFTERWARDS

WEDNESDAY 18 AUGUST 1943

In the early morning, just after dawn, a contingent of German soldiers arrived at Syrets concentration camp. They had dogs, and they selected exactly one hundred of the surviving prisoners before marching them to the nearby ravine at Babi Yar. The ravine was full of bodies. The officer in charge asked if there were any blacksmiths among the prisoners. A handful of arms were raised in reply.

These men were taken to an area beyond an earth escarpment. There they found a collection of long metal rails. While the blacksmiths were put to work making a huge barbecue pit, criss-crossed with a lattice of iron rails, the rest of the men were fitted with fetters and chains and handed a shovel each. Their job, that day and over the days and weeks that followed, was to dig through the layers of decaying flesh and bone, preparing the bodies for incineration.

At night, the men slept in a prepared dugout, their hands over their faces to try and mask the stench of the bodies. Fires were prepared in the barbecue pits, and tombstones were brought from a Kyiv graveyard to strengthen the structure. At the bottom of the pits, the prisoners stacked firewood. Then came a layer of bodies, topped with more firewood, then more bodies, and yet more firewood and more bodies until the stack – topped with the barbecue grill – was as high as the fences around the Syrets camp. There were many pits and many stacks. Each of them, according to designers' careful calculations, contained at least two thousand bodies. When each stack was complete, it was drenched in oil and set alight.

The smell of burning flesh drifted across Kyiv for many weeks. The Yar was eight kilometres away from the piles of rubble that had once been Khreshchatyk and people in the street tried to ignore the clouds of oily smoke, slowly shredding in the wind, but the smell made it impossible. Yids, they told each other.

At the start of the second week of excavations in the Yar, a prisoner called Davydov had started on a corner of the ravine that had yet to be touched. By now, he was paying little attention to individual corpses. Men, women, grandfathers, babies, it made no difference. After days and days with the shovel and a crude facemask, every face looked the same. He was a Jew himself, and he knew that he, too, would end up on one of the stacks. Partly because of his faith, but mainly because he knew the secret that the Germans were trying so hard to hide.

Then, on this sunny morning in late August, his attention was caught by a youngish looking woman sprawled on her back. She was in better condition than most of the bodies he'd seen, and – most unusually – she wasn't naked. He paused, leaning on his shovel, aware that the nearest SS man was busy lighting a cigarette. The woman had been beautiful. He knew she had. Long legs. Lovely shape to her face. A wisp of blonde hair where the camp barber hadn't quite finished the job. Even the grey

and white fatigues couldn't hide the way she must have been
in real life, he thought, reaching for the shovel again.

*

Russian spearhead troops reached the banks of the Dnieper
shortly after midnight on Saturday 6 November. They crossed
the river, swept through the western suburbs, and had occupied
the city centre by dawn. It had been raining for most of the
night, but a watery sun shed a thin yellow light over the columns
of weary Soviet troops crossing the foot of Khreshchatyk.
The handful of veterans who had defended Kyiv against the
Germans, barely two years earlier, stared at the grey ruins that
lined the city's biggest boulevard. They remembered shops here,
hotels, theatres, trams, people, the beating heart of an enormous
city. Kyiv, to their knowledge, had been neither bombarded nor
bombed. So what can have happened?

Slowly, over the days to come, some of them talked to local
people. They explained about the surprises lying in wait for
the Germans, the lull before the storm, and then the week of
savage violence that had ripped out the city's heart and led to
so much slaughter. The Yar, they said. Hold your nose and
take a look at the ravine.

Some had the opportunity and took it. What they found,
at first sight, was a disappointment but an hour or so in the
ravine itself told a different story. Fragments of bone. Tiny
gobbets of human flesh. Scorch marks on the bare earth. And
no birds.

Another troop of soldiers were tasked to investigate the
banks of the Dnieper beneath the towering walls of the Pechersk
Monastery. One of them, wary of hidden mines, spotted the dull

gleam of something that might conceivably have been valuable. He stopped and bent to retrieve it, brushing away the sand. It was a tooth, capped in gold. A religious man, he gazed at it for a moment, before slipping it into a pocket, looking up at the monastery and crossing himself.

*

Tam Moncrieff had been back at his desk in St James's Street for nearly a year and a half. Everyone who had reason to work with him agreed that he'd changed. A lot of his confidence seemed to have gone. He was less sure of himself, less prepared to take a risk or two, somehow *smaller*. Maybe it was something that would pass, said some. Maybe not.

Only Ursula Barton knew the truth. That Moncrieff had taken on a challenge and lost. That his innate sense of fairness, and his nose for life's fakes, had – in the end – brought him nothing but grief. He was still efficient, still reliable, still prepared to work impossible hours to see an operation to its end. He still had the knack of motivating newcomers, of sharing the spoils of his own rich experience, of gently – and sometimes not so gently – mocking the wilder delusions of the intelligence world. But his colleagues, people who still admired him, were right: that he no longer had the appetite for either risk or danger, that under his newly bluff exterior he was fragile inside and still needed very careful handling.

By Christmas, there was at last a hint that the war might come to an end. Bomber Command was bringing cities across the Third Reich to their knees. *Wehrmacht* troops were pulling back on the Italian front. And the Russian steamroller, heading west, appeared to be unstoppable.

Moncrieff, as usual, was planning to celebrate Christmas alone at the Glebe House. His preference for his own company had become the subject of quiet gossip in the corridors of MI5. Some said he was a born recluse. Others weren't so sure. Once again, only Barton knew the real story.

Before his departure to Scotland, she took him to lunch at St Ermin's Hotel. She'd knitted him a scarf with wool she'd been hoarding for years. The wool, a shade of the richest crimson, had been a long-ago present from her mother. Barton didn't much like knitting, neither was she very good at it, but she knew that red suited Moncrieff and she hoped that he'd wear it.

She'd also been waiting for the moment to broach another subject, infinitely more personal, and she sensed that this might be it.

She'd been careful to book a table in the corner of the restaurant. She was on good terms with the maître d' and in exchange for a modest *pourboire*, he agreed not to seat the neighbouring table. A degree of privacy, they both agreed, could be the essence of a frank conversation.

Moncrieff was waiting in the bar when she arrived. He bought her a large schooner of Tio Pepe and proposed a toast to the coming year. They both knew an invasion was in the offing, and Moncrieff was very happy to have been given a role in the many deceptions that would precede the first Allied boots on French soil. Working from the solitude of his own office suited him very nicely. As did the prospect of a Christmas week alone in the Glebe House.

They finished their aperitifs and went through to the restaurant. Barton had pre-ordered a bottle of Chablis, and it was waiting for them on the table. The moment they sat down, the maître d' appeared to fill their glasses.

'More than agreeable.' Moncrieff had taken a sip of the wine. Now he was looking at the label. 'Are we celebrating?'

'In a way, yes. I'm sorry, Tam. Our line of work...' she frowned. '... it's all deception, isn't it?'

'Is it? I'm not with you.'

'Maybe not deception. Maybe something kinder. Timing, Tam. It's all about timing. I'm afraid I need to be frank with you. There's something I should have shared but I haven't. Is that deliberate? I'm afraid it is. And am I going to put things right? Here's hoping.' She reached for her glass. 'To truth and beauty,' she was smiling. 'Keats, I think.'

Moncrieff sat back, mystified, watching her bend and retrieve her handbag. She put it on her lap a moment, studying him the way a doctor might assess a patient, then she made a tiny gesture of resignation and handed him the envelope.

'It came from Schultz,' she said. 'He sent it via Dahlerus in Sweden. I'm afraid I've hung onto it for quite a while.'

'How long?'

'In all?' She was counting backwards. 'More than two years.'

'Two *years*?' Moncrieff was staring at her. Birger Dahlerus was a favoured go-between, a Swedish businessman who had the ear of both the *Abwehr* and MI5. Both Moncrieff and Schultz had used him in the past.

'Open it, Tam,' she smiled. 'Please.'

'Must I?'

'Yes.'

'Will it hurt?'

'It might. But in the end, I promise, it will be for the good.'

'Sounds like some ghastly medicine.'

'You're right. That's exactly what it is.'

Moncrieff was gazing at the envelope. She'd hooked him, and she knew it. Just a hint of the old Tam, she thought: playful, bold, the prisoner of his own curiosity.

He opened the envelope. Inside was a photograph, black and white, head and shoulders. He picked it up and stared at it for a long moment. Barton caught a tiny tremor of movement as his hand began to shake.

'It's Bella,' he looked up. 'Where did Schultz get this?'

'An SS *Standartenführer* gave it to him. You were right about the camp, Tam. Wrong about the location.'

'Where was it?'

'Kyiv.'

'Babi Yar?'

'Yes, I'm afraid so.'

'Syrets?'

'Syrets.'

'There was no one left. I've read the NKVD reports. The SS murdered them all.'

'Not quite all, Tam. A handful escaped but Bella wasn't among them.'

'And Schultz?'

'We don't know. We can only hope he's still alive.' Her hand briefly covered his as her gaze returned to the photograph. 'I'm very sorry, Tam.'

He stared at her. Then he turned the photo over and left it face down on the tablecloth.

'For the best,' he said woodenly. 'I expect.'

'For the best,' Barton agreed. She held the silence for a moment. 'On a lighter note, there's also this.' From the bag she produced the scarf. 'I'm sorry I haven't wrapped it up, Tam. All my own work, I'm afraid.'

'You *knitted* this?' Moncrieff was unfolding it.

'I did.'

'But you can't knit. You told me once. You said you hadn't the fingers for it. Or the patience.'

'Both true, Tam. I'd tell you how long it took me, but that would be shaming. It's yours, Tam. Wear it for me in those hills of yours, promise?'

Moncrieff nodded. He was holding the scarf against his cheek, feeling its softness, sniffing it, smelling it. Then he wound it round his neck.

'How does it look?'

'Festive.'

'Seriously?'

'It looks perfect. It suits you. It won't let you down.'

Moncrieff smiled, and then took the scarf off.

'It was Bella's favourite colour, did you know that?'

'I guessed, Tam.' She reached for her glass again. 'There had to be some reason she ended up in bloody Moscow.'

The maître d' returned. He admired the scarf and took their order. Dover sole was back on the menu, a sure sign – thought Moncrieff – that soon the bloody war might at last be over. They talked office politics for a while and Barton shared a story about Guy Liddell. Recently, she said, he'd written Broadway a stiff note about Kim Philby's rumoured elevation to a new post but nobody in the swim understood the reason why.

Moncrieff tidied the remains of his fish and then sat back in his chair, gazing out across the restaurant. Finally, he turned Bella's photograph over again.

'Imagine I was right,' he murmured. 'Imagine she knew the truth about that man but took the secret to the grave. Does anyone deserve that kind of faith?'

About the author

GRAHAM HURLEY is the author of the
acclaimed Faraday and Winter crime
novels and an award-winning TV
documentary maker. Two of the critically
lauded series have been shortlisted for the
Theakston's Old Peculier Award for Best
Crime Novel. His French TV series, based
on the Faraday and Winter novels, has
won huge audiences. The first Spoils of
War novel, *Finisterre*, was shortlisted for
the Wilbur Smith Adventure Writing Prize.
Graham now writes full-time and lives
with his wife, Lin, in Exmouth.

WWW.GRAHAMHURLEY.CO.UK